Max, by Sonny

A cartoonist
and the lives he draws

A novel by

Simon Moffett

First published in Great Britain in 2019 by Cambria Publishing.

Print ISBN 978-1-9161619-0-0

Author's comment

There are a number of people who have made the path to writing this easier, to whom I am very grateful. Judith Barrow and what I call the 'Bloomfield Writers' contributed vast amounts of encouragement. They argued over plot details and from those discussions the format evolved. My daughter, Lowri, acted as a sounding board, gave me lots of encouragement and made many suggestions. Elidir Jones and M Pickthorne have worked through the text for me and guided my punctuation. For technical detail I have to thank Simon Morris, Bobbie Sheldrake, Colin Dewar, John Daniels and some members of Dyfed Powys Police. Others too have unwittingly given me ideas as they passed by. Thanks also to the professionals who have polished my work and provided the artwork, Ceri Daugherty and Carolyn Michel. I am very grateful to Chris Jones and Cambria Publishing for their guidance and advice and without which this project would never have happened. Finally, I have to thank Mererid, my wife, who has allowed me to spend hours fighting with my computer. However, this is my work and I will take all the blame.

Simon Moffett

The poem 'Anfonaf Angel' is quoted with the kind permission of Hywel Gwynfryn. It has been set to music by Robert Arwyn.

'Y Tangnefeddwyr' is a poem by Waldo Williams, set to music by Eric Jones.

Chapter 1: October 2011

Sonny

I am a cartoonist. My income is derived from Max's strip in a national paper, but Max isn't going to last for ever, whatever he may think.

The first frame of the strip shows Elsa, Max's friend. 'Why don't we age, Max?' she asks.

In the second frame, Max replies, 'Because we're timeless, classic, elegant, immortal ...'

And in the third frame, Max says, '... and Sonny can't draw wrinkles.'

Max has surprised me. He's never had a dig at me before. If this was a usual day my pencil would be drawing strips of Max and his humour, but I have a stock of them. So, I have decided that I have to do something different. I want to start creating a graphic novel, a whole new storyline.

My pencil draws a large crowd one side of an open grave in the pouring rain. Facing them a minister reads from a book wrapped in plastic. Behind him – off to one side – three undertakers stand in a line facing the mourners. They appear respectful, but their body language portrays boredom and their wish to be somewhere else. I'm trying something new, and I am appalled as the pencil hurries on. Now the picture has what little colour the miserable scene affords while the rain covers it with white noise.

My pencil draws Tony staring at a coffin, now in the bottom of the hole.

Tony 4th October 2011

'Karen Jones' it said on a little brass plate. Tony read the plate from where he stood. How could this be?

The voice of the minister was almost lost as the heavy rain drummed on the umbrellas at the graveside. Jessica, Tony's daughter, gripped at his arm, but she was no support. He needed his wife Karen to help him through this, as she had helped him in many other crises, but she had left him. In three short weeks in hospital she had gone from apparently fit and well to dying of a silent cancer that had eaten him up before anyone knew.

Now she was in this box in the ground, surrounded by those who had loved her in life and who were shocked by how quickly she had gone.

Behind the crowd traffic is passing and sometimes splashing, and engine noises from bigger vehicles climbing the slight slope swamp the prayers altogether.

The minister struggled on against the weather as, in his mind, Tony watched the coffins of his mother and father going into the hole. His body was wracked by a sob as the coffins of his grandparents went in as well. Jessica clutched him again and, fleetingly, he thought of his brother who he hadn't seen since his grandmother was alive. At that moment his whole life was being sucked into this evil hole in the ground. He looked up, seeking Karen among the mourners to help him with the black void building inside him, as coffins of friends, colleagues and relatives continued to vanish into the hole. His mind was trapped in this deathly parade.

Sonny

I watch the pencil shade the pictures darker and darker; reflecting the desolate nature of the scenes. I can feel pain in these colourless pictures.

I set a new sheet of A1 paper on my drawing board. I have a block I use to set the size of each frame and I mark out a sequence of rectangles with my blue pencil. This ritual sizes the cartoons to help the printer and the blue line is filtered out when the cartoon is set up for printing. I'm ready. When I pick up my pencil, it comes alive, but I've little idea what it's going to do; now more than ever.

My first frames had drawn Tony Jones as a young man receiving his PhD. The next scene showed him getting his first lectureship. Further scenes showed his early married life with Karen, and later their two children. Tony is an astrophysicist who follows an academic career. So far, his life had been black and white and unremarkable, with no colour or depth. Now the pencil takes me back to the graveside.

Tony 4th October 2011

It seemed a huge mess to Tony, all that mud and rain. Karen had been just the opposite. Neat and tidy, turned out perfectly for the occasion. When they went out together, she had said, *'Let's look at you then'*. Often, she made him change his tie or his shoes because they didn't quite match. Now it didn't matter and as he looked down at his feet, he saw his shoes were covered in mud.

'Dad, Dad,' Jessica whispered next to Tony. 'Aren't you going to give her the flower?'

'What?' He looked at her, and now understood that the minister had finished. They had talked about this, but now the time had come. It was too soon. Jessica's eyes pleaded with him and he was grateful that she had taken him out of his awful vision. He pulled himself together, stepped up to the end of the grave and looked again at the name 'Karen Jones'. He tossed the flower to hide the plate and bowed one last time. Then he tore himself away.

There was a great risk of slipping on the wet grass and mud. Matthew, his son, caught him as he started to move aimlessly away from the grave.

'You'd better thank the minister,' said Matthew, guiding him towards where the minister was both holding his umbrella and trying to save his book from the elements.

'Thank you, Mr Williams,' Tony mumbled. Karen would have told him to shake the minister's hand, but the minister didn't have one spare.

'Mr Jones, it has been my privilege. I'm afraid I can't join you for tea but call in at the Manse sometime.' Tony knew that Mr Williams was offering comfort, but he would never go to the Manse. What sort of God treated people like this? He knew Karen would have gone, as she had been the one who had attended services in the chapel.

'Thank you again. I'll see you soon.' Tony said pointlessly. He and Matthew moved on and were overwhelmed by the number of people wanting to shake Tony's hand, say how wonderful Karen had been and how shocked they were, and ask if there was anything they could do. Tony listened as the remarks washed over him and kissed and shook hands while the rain ran off his coat and onto his trousers.

Out of the queue came Alistair, Karen's younger brother. He didn't say a word but held Tony in a hug for an age, full of warmth and kinship. He stepped back and Tony could see he had been crying too.

'I'm so sorry Tony. Listen, I'll ring you. I've got Karen's papers in the office and we'll make sure the legal bit is as painless as we can make it.' Alistair was a hot-shot lawyer and although his speciality was employment law, he managed Tony and Karen's legal affairs; using other specialist lawyers in his firm where he had to.

'Thanks. Speak to you soon, and Alistair, thank you for coming in this miserable weather.'

People continued to file by and say their piece until Mrs Thoroughgood from the WI stood facing him. She shook his hand and said,

'Mr Jones, words won't ever be enough to describe how sorry I was to hear the news. I see Jessica is here. I thought she had little ones?'

'They're too young to be out in the rain and I didn't want them disturbing the service.' Tony didn't like Mrs Thoroughgood. She seemed to occupy some piece of moral high ground, so he felt compelled to justify himself to her. He wondered how Karen had managed.

'I suppose you're right; a funeral isn't a place for children,' she paused. 'Mr Jones, I'm afraid I have to ask you a favour. As you know, Karen kept the books for our branch of the WI and she kept the petty cash. Can I come and collect it sometime? It's just that over a month has gone by and we're getting into a mess.'

Tony was taken aback. This wasn't the time to talk about this. He knew Karen had done the books; she had a talent for structured record keeping. In truth he didn't know how his own banking and savings worked, as she had quietly kept it going without any fuss. He remembered her sitting at the desk in the house sorting out the post and meticulously shredding and filing. Another part of her he had forgotten until now. At least she had left everything tidy for him.

'Mr Jones? Can I call on you sometime?' Mrs Thoroughgood broke into his memory.

'Yes, yes of course. Next week sometime. I should be home.'

She thanked him and moved on, but he felt that he should have said this week, but he caught Karen's voice in his ear. *Let her wait a bit. She'll find out how much I do.'* He almost smiled before the next hand grasped his. More faces, more hugs, more handshakes, and more people worried that Karen wasn't supporting them anymore.

'Tony, I'm so sorry. Karen was so good.' Betsan Adams – who conducted the choir – put her hand on his forearm; the right balance of contact but not too familiar. Tony liked her. Betsan continued. 'She was one of the pillars of the choir for many years. We will have to find a new player to accompany us now. Do you know how much help she gave me with the music? All those events she organised for the choir. She was so generous of her time and took care of so many little details. I don't know

4

who will be able to follow her now. We will feel her loss enormously.'

He thanked her for bringing the choir to the chapel. 'The warmth of their singing was very comforting.' She started to move on, but he caught her arm.

'Call in sometime. We need to talk about the music. I'm not working this week or next.'

'Of course,' she thought for a moment and said, 'we'll call in one afternoon.'

'I'll see you then.'

He remembered that Karen had great respect for her; they had worked well together as a team. They didn't need meetings to organise anything. They would have a quick word after the choir practice and would both know what was needed and do it.

Ray Adams, Betsan's husband, had sat with him in many concerts. Ray had no singing voice, although he enjoyed listening to the performances. He just gave Tony a heartfelt squeeze of his hand and nodded. Tony took comfort from the simple act. More people followed but the line was thinning out.

Then in front of him stood Liz Stephens from the university. At last here was a face that offered more than funeral-formula conversation. She would help him face the awful grief that lay like a black hand over everything. She had been their friend for years and years.

'Hello, Tony. Are you alright?' she asked. It wasn't a stupid question.

'I think so. Thank you for coming. I'm soaking wet.'

Liz turned to Matthew and caught his arm. 'Matt, Tony's going to catch pneumonia if he stays here much longer. You should take him to the hotel to warm up.'

And so, the funeral service became the funeral tea and the empty nightmare of Tony's new life had truly begun.

Sonny

I find myself holding back a tear. The reactions of the people at the funeral show that death has snuffed out a great vitality in her prime. I set this sheet on one side to start a new scene; having no idea where the pencil will go next. I set the frames with my blue pencil, thinking that the sadness of this beginning is hardly what I should be drawing as a cartoonist.

Again, my pencil draws a grey scene where the early morning light is beginning to beat the street lamps. A man is walking his dog in a city park. He strides cheerfully and his coat is flapping open as he encourages his black spaniel to keep up. 'Come on Hector!'

There's no wind, just the distant roar of traffic. I have a bad feeling about this gloom, but the pencil hurries on.

Man 5th October 2011

Hector had been left behind and the man stopped to see why. He called again. This part of the park had many trees and shrubs, and he took a moment to see where the dog was. Hector came bounding towards him with something in his mouth. Usually he threw balls or a stick for the dog to fetch in a different part of the park, but Hector had had enough treats to bring back anything he found. He reached down to remove the rag from Hector's mouth and saw a piece of clothing; a woman's skirt. Alarmed, he walked back to where Hector had come from and in the strengthening light of the morning, he saw that someone was lying naked in the bushes. He turned away and pulled out his phone.

Sonny

I don't want to see any more of this. I'm a cartoonist and my stories should be happy and funny. For a moment I wonder if I should abandon the whole project, but – and I'll never know why – I let the pencil start again on a blank area of the sheet. It draws Max looking at me.

'You've started now. You have to carry on.' Max says.

I put the pencil down so quickly I almost throw it. Max has never spoken to me like this before. Whatever I do, I can't escape his eyes.

I'm confused too, because Max is telling me to draw a story that does not have him in it. If I retire, Max will come to an end. Why then is he encouraging me to draw this story?

I quickly remove the sheet from the drawing table and store it away. I pick up a new one and set up the frames. I take up the pencil cautiously and carry on.

Cheryl 5th October 2011

The area was now bounded by police tape and there was a little tent in the bushes. PC Cheryl Carter was standing outside the tape patiently turning walkers away. She had been here since the first call and had seen enough to know that she wouldn't sleep for days.

She was glad that at least the weather was at peace. She wasn't cold but walked back and forth, fidgeting to pass the time. Her eye caught a spot of colour on the ground that was out of place. She stooped down to get a closer look and saw a button attached to a small piece of material. She called a forensic worker over and pointed it out.

'Is that from her clothes?' she asked.

The man squatted down to look at it and then looked around. They both saw another button lying close by.

'It's the right colour,' he said. 'I wonder if she was sitting on that bench when he attacked her.'

Cheryl stared at the buttons. For her, seeing the body had been bad enough, but these buttons suggested the violence that had taken place here. She had to make an effort to pull herself together. The man broke in to her thoughts.

'Thank you for finding that. You may have saved us a bit of time. I'm afraid you'll have to move the tape further back as there could be more stuff here.'

'Haven't you got it all now?' she asked.

'Everything of hers, we think, except one earring. It's very small and distinct so it may be lost in the soil. We've still got other checks we have to make though.'

Cheryl set to work to widen the cordon. At least some activity would get her closer to the end of this awful shift.

Sonny

I stop the pencil. I've seen enough. Later the pencil shows me more, and I learn that a young woman has been sexually assaulted and murdered. This is the first time I've looked at the scene of a crime; at the newspaper things are one step removed from reality.

What a miserable story I am writing. I change the page again, hoping for more warmth. This time the scene is a wide bridleway set on a woody ridge, the colours are bright and the mid-morning sun has warmed the day. We are enjoying a proper Indian summer and a cheerful breeze is rustling the remaining green leaves.

A young woman on a proud horse is trotting through the trees. She makes a fine picture. This is more promising; there's plenty of colour in the pictures and none of the greys and darkness of the earlier bits. Maybe Max is right, I should continue. This story is more fun. So I carry on, listening to the hoofbeats and the wind in the trees.

Lisa 8th October 2011

Lisa's hobby was riding. Every Saturday she went to a stables a few miles out of City, sometimes just to ride but often to give them a hand. She had started riding as a teenager when away on holiday and after three days in the saddle she was hooked. With the practice she had gained over the years, she had become an accomplished rider and the yard now allowed her to ride some of their most challenging horses.

Lisa was riding a big bay – a thoroughbred called Blister – who was far too demanding for most of the recreational riders who came to these stables. For Lisa he was a great escape from her work. She marvelled at the power in him, and the work she had to put in to control him. He had come to know and listen to her.

She was a picture of health – which underlined her natural beauty. Her complexion glowed in the autumn sun and her blonde hair frolicked behind her where it had escaped from her helmet. Her jodhpurs accentuated her figure.

Today she was leading other riders and couldn't do what she enjoyed best, which was to have a good gallop through the scrub area beyond the woods. She looked at her watch and saw it was time to head back.

She stopped where the track widened and the other riders came up. 'Time to turn back I'm afraid. Please check your girth straps.' She rode around the group and checked that their girths and saddles were okay.

'Can't we go on some more?' said a voice. Someone always grumbled and today she wanted to agree; they seemed to have only just started.

Back along the track they rode and into the stable yard. As Lisa slipped down off Blister the stable girl, Beth, came over and held him.

'How is he today?' Beth asked. Lisa took off his saddle.

'Needs a good run, but I was with the group and didn't want to create a problem. What do you want to do with him?' Lisa asked.

'He's going to the top paddock since it's a bit drier than lower down. I'll do it if you want.'

'No, that's okay. I'm not in a rush.'

'Oh, thanks,' said Beth. Lisa enjoyed being friends with Beth, for whom nothing was too much trouble.

Lisa took the horse from Beth and started leading him across the yard. A small group of riders had gathered around a man who caught her eye. He was about her age, tall, with rough hair and an open shirt, and was wearing trousers with tool pockets. She could hear him speaking too and liked the sound of his voice. Blister whinnied, showing his impatience, and she knew she would have to get the horse up to the paddock before she could have a better look at the man.

By the time she came back he had disappeared and she dallied for a while. She found Beth and asked, 'Am I okay for next week?'

'Of course,' said Beth, 'especially if you take groups out for me.'

'Thanks,' said Lisa and headed for her car, annoyed at having missed this man.

Sonny

Who is this girl? Her energy and beauty have lifted my spirits. Why has this Lisa come into my story? Now I need a new sheet so that the story can continue. At last the pictures have more colour and I can relax.

I began this story because it's been building inside me for a while now. I need to get it on paper. I have blamed a lot of people in my life for my problems when deep down I know they are my fault. I live alone and avoid people. How did I end up here? I'm older now and facing the prospect of living out my days forgotten by everyone.

'Max' made my career with his cartoon strip. I've been drawing him for more than forty years and signing myself 'Sonny' but there have been strong hints from the editor that Max has had his day; which means me. Delivering my artwork is the one time when I meet people and the rest of the staff are the friendly faces who reassure me that I am okay. Over the years they've changed, but they've always given me a welcome and are often asking:

'Where do you get the ideas for Max, Sonny?' or 'How do you keep having new ideas?'

It's my little secret. I'll never tell them. It's too simple, too boring. If I told them they wouldn't believe it. I listen to the chatter on a radio station talking about the day's hot topics. I don't even tune to the same station

9

every day, but that's where my pencil finds something for Max to joke about. Take today's frame, straight off the radio.

My pencil draws Elsa in the first frame. She is a friend of Max's. She asks Max:

'Have you heard this thing about mindfulness?'

In the second frame the pencil draws Terry – another friend – who says, 'I hear it's a sort of Buddhist meditation technique.'

In the third box the pencil draws Elsa again. 'Helps you keep yourself in focus.'

And as usual Max gets the punchline. 'I'll have to think about it.'

Max was born by accident, helped by an older cousin of mine who worked on newspapers. My cousin knew that I had done cartoon strips for college papers and other small-circulation publications. I still have the letter he wrote telling me to visit him urgently. We met in a pub.

'Sit down, while I get the beer,' he said.

He put the two pints in front of us and started straight in.

'You need to create a cartoon strip and draw about twenty examples, now!'

'Why?' I asked.

'Alfie, from the Daily … has died, and they are looking to replace him.'

'But I can't draw his people. I mean that's not my style.'

'You don't have to. You can do whatever you want. But quickly.'

'How do I know what to joke about? I mean what will the editor be looking for?'

'I don't know. Read the papers? Make sure it's topical. You're the cartoonist, not me. I'll make sure they end up on the right desk.'

I remember taking him the first twenty Max strips about a week later.

'Brilliant. These'll do, and right up to date. How did you manage that? This stuff isn't all in the papers. Is it?'

'I don't really read papers. I got the ideas from the radio.'

'Good idea. It works – and it's not obvious.'

'I listen to it while I am drawing, and the pencil picks up the ideas.'

'If you keep doing that Max will always be topical. I like it. Never tell anyone! Let me take these, and I'll see you same time tomorrow night.'

I had a worrying day but the next day we met again.

'It's all good. I've arranged for you to meet them tomorrow morning.'

'What do I have to do? I haven't a clue about what happens next.'

'Just go to the meeting and they'll tell you. If you're worried about it, I've got a friend who works in an agency. Once you are accepted by the paper, we can get them to look after your affairs.'

'I won't be able to afford an agent.'

'Don't worry. They'll make sure you can! That's how they make their money. One more thing – get a name.'

'I've always been Sonny in my freelance stuff, can't I just carry on?'

'No point in changing something that works.'

In a few hectic and exciting weeks, I had left behind the precarious life of freelance artwork in books and magazines for the security of work on a national daily paper.

Max soon became such an institution that now I'm simply Sonny. I don't court publicity though. I never have, and the agency protects my privacy and looks after my public image. Max merchandise has been around for many years, and Max has been syndicated in publications all over the world.

I live in my studio. I don't get visitors to this nest away from the world, and I like it this way. My living room is my studio with a whole wall covered by a soft board on which I pin pictures and ideas. In the centre of the room – where the light falls from a dormer window – is my drawing board. It sits next to a small table where I keep the tools of my trade (pencils and the like) and the radio; my inspiration. I keep the rest of the room tidy, retreating into the world of Max by turning on the radio and settling on the high stool at the drawing board with my pencil and frames.

I have two large filing cabinets; special ones with shallow drawers where I keep rough ideas and new sheets of paper. To start with I kept my original final artwork, but it became too much. Now the agency stores my originals somewhere safe and fireproof. I like to check that Max never does a joke twice, and now I refer to his previous adventures on the internet. In the late nineties my agent convinced me to change my drawing style.

'Sonny, once you have a style that suits the world wide web, we can sell Max all over the world.'

I had been drawing Max over twenty years by then and teaching my pencil new tricks had been hard. I say teaching the pencil, as you have to understand that Max comes from the pencil. Until I have it in my hand nothing happens; I have no ideas and can get a bit stressed when I have impending print deadlines. It's silly, as when my pencil is on a roll it can provide ideas for several days in one sitting, so I aim to have two or three weeks of work ready at any time.

What I'm drawing now is different. I have started building this new storyline as Max is not going to carry on much longer. I don't know where this will lead me, so I just have to follow the pencil. I start the same way I do with Max; sharpening my pencil and setting the frames.

The pencil draws a tidy kitchen in a modern house with wood effect fitted units and a full range of appliances. Off to one side sits Tony at a table reading the paper and with an empty mug beside him.

Tony 12th October 2011

Tony was at home. A week had passed since the funeral, his family had gone home again and the house was quiet. He couldn't focus on anything and was sitting in the kitchen staring at the newspaper but taking nothing in. The doorbell rang. What now?

Betsan 12th October 2011

Betsan, Mrs Adams (from the choir) had called with her husband Ray, who rang the bell and stood back. Ray always let Betsan do the talking when they were together. The door opened and Tony stood on the doorstep, looking forlorn and unsure how to greet them.

'Would you like a cup of tea?' he asked.

'Oh, thank you,' Betsan said. 'I don't seem to have stopped today.'

He led them in, pausing to push the lounge door open.

'Why don't you sit in there while I fetch the tea?'

He went off to the kitchen while they went to find a seat.

'I don't know what I am supposed to say,' said Ray.

'No need to say anything.' replied Betsan.

They stood in silence taking in the room. They were familiar with it, but now Karen's energy had gone Betsan looked at it properly for the first time.

'Why two pianos?' said Ray.

'I don't know. I thought she went out to teach,' replied Betsan.

'And it looks like there are two pieces of every score.' Ray said.

Above the pianos shelving was packed with piano music of all types.

Sheets and scores were carefully organised, with cards that stuck out so you could find what you were looking for. The music dominated the rest of the room, leaving little space for the three-piece. A glass-fronted cabinet was full of jugs collected by Karen.

A plastic folder containing a choral score Betsan recognised was on one piano. She knew that Karen was fanatical about putting things back in their place on the shelf. *'We'll be up to our necks in music if we're not careful,'* she used to say. They sat down; Betsan behind a small coffee table.

Tony came back in with the tea and cups which he put on the table. He disappeared again and came back with a cake on a plate and a knife. 'Would you like a piece of cake?' he asked.

'Yes please,' they both replied. Tony cut three pieces and went and sat across the room, leaving the teapot to Betsan. She remembered that Karen poured the tea, and said nothing but set out the cups and poured three.

There was a moment of awkwardness when she realised she would have to get up and take the tea over to Tony, but he got up.

'Help yourself,' he said, taking a piece of cake and his tea and going back to his seat.

Tony hadn't brought plates for the cake, and Ray and Betsan looked at each other. Betsan had never let Ray eat anything without a plate to prevent crumbs dropping on the carpet and he didn't know what to do.

'Please eat some cake. There's more out in the kitchen.' said Tony. Ray took a piece, thanked him and tried to eat it so any crumbs would drop in his hand.

They retreated into their cake.

'Thank you for arranging the music at the funeral.' Tony didn't feel like talking.

Ray spoke. 'Tony, you should come and sit in at the choir practices with me. You enjoy it more than me. And we can have a pint on the way home.'

'Yes,' said Tony in a way that could have meant anything. 'I'd forgotten about the choir. There's a lot of music here for that …'

Betsan rescued him. 'Don't worry about that for a week or two – unless it's in the way. I've got the current stuff we're playing. I haven't thought … I mean … It's been such a shock. Now we need an accompanist, but I don't know where we will find anyone with so much talent.' Even Betsan shied away from saying Karen.

'She was so good …' Tony tailed off as memory of her playing hit him.

'Oh dear, I'm sorry.' Ever practical, Betsan spotted the tissues out of his reach and took them to him while Ray fidgeted. He was tone deaf, but even he had developed an understanding of Karen's musical talent.

Tony pulled himself together then gestured towards the piano.

'She left that score on the piano. She must have known.' Tony said.

'Known what?' Betsan asked.

'Known … she wasn't coming back.' Tony folded up in grief.

Betsan understood then. The music was one of the choir's favourites and she knew it well, 'Anfonaf angel' ('I'll send an angel').

'Oh …' Betsan tried to deal with the shock of this revelation as Tony sobbed. She could feel the sting beginning in her own eyes.

Tony spoke again. 'I had to tell someone.' This time he wept floods of tears, and Betsan got up and put her hand on his arm.

Ray poured Tony a new cup of tea with a big spoonful of sugar. He stirred it in and took it over. 'Drink some of that, mate. You'll feel better.'

Betsan gave Ray a look, but activity helped Tony and he sipped the tea.

'Too sweet.'

'You need it,' said Ray

Tony wiped his eyes and drank the tea. Nobody said anything.

'Thanks. I'll be alright now.'

'We'd better be off. Can I see to the cups?' said Betsan.

'No. I can do that. Thank you for coming. Honestly, I'll be better now.' said Tony.

'Come to a choir practice sometime. We can go for a pint.' Ray repeated, as they stood in the doorway.

'Do you have the schedule?' Betsan asked.

'It's on the fridge.' Tony faltered.

Now Tony wanted them to leave, and he closed the door on them rather abruptly, stood with his back to it and took a deep breath. He went back to the lounge and looked at the dirty cups but then turned to the pianos. He sat down in front of the piano with the folder on it, sighed, opened the piano lid and began to play.

He didn't look at the music; he didn't need to. He softly sang some of the words.

'am eiliad rydw i'n credu dy fod yma.' ('for a second I think you are here.')

14

Liz 12th November 2011

It was over a month later, and Liz Stephens had watched Tony as he drifted through the days. He had come back to work fairly soon as the academic year had started and that was his routine. But now his clothes had lost the smartness Karen had prided herself on and colleagues didn't know what to say to him. The talk amongst the students was that his lectures were rubbish.

One morning she saw Tony walking back to the office block from the lecture theatre and blocked his way.

'Good Morning, Tony. How are you?'

'Oh, hello Liz. Mustn't complain.'

'Have you got time for a cup of tea?' she asked.

'I suppose so,' Tony said. She saw that his inclination was to avoid her, but he followed her back to her office via the tea room. He sat down facing her desk, but she pulled up a chair next to him on his side of the desk. She had started out as a botanist and her office was full of plants. She had moved over to a career in personnel management and part of her work was helping people keep their personal problems from affecting the success of the university.

Liz was a long-time friend of Karen, Tony and their children, so she knew that Tony wouldn't open up easily. She prattled on with small talk about this and that in the university.

Jessica had called her at home the previous evening.

'I'm worried about Dad. He hasn't called me and seems to have lost interest in Mary and Paddy.' Her children, his grandchildren, whose arrival had given Karen and Tony a whole new lease of life. Until now.

Liz had been watching him at work but now that she knew Tony was struggling at home too, she had to do something.

As they chatted, Liz sensed Tony beginning to relax.

'What do you do in the evenings? Is there somewhere you can go?'

'I have to shop.'

'That's not seeing people. You need to get among people Tony. What else do you do?' She was persistent.

'Nothing much. I cook and wash up and watch telly. I play the piano; it helps me.'

Liz remembered years ago, before Tony and Karen had children, they had performed together on the piano. She knew Karen had supported the choir for years. 'Have you thought of playing with the choir? I expect they want an accompanist?'

'They don't know I play the piano. I was babysitting at the start. I'm not much of a singer so I went along to listen and have a pint afterwards.'

'You can help them Tony. They're your friends, aren't they?'

Liz backed off realising that Tony was starting to look a bit trapped. She took a sip of tea and waited for minute or two.

'How are Mary and Paddy doing?'

Tony looked uncomfortable again. 'I haven't seen them since …' He stopped as he didn't want to say the word. Liz took his hand.

'Tony, go and see them, they should be your life now. You were so proud when they were born.'

'I'm frightened that they will ask me where she is.'

'If you can't tell them the truth, tell them a lie. Say she's on holiday or something. They can deal with it when they get older.'

Tony was silent.

'What's the problem?' Liz asked.

'Jessica. Jessica wants to take me on as one of her projects. If I give her half a chance she'll come to the house and clear Karen's stuff, and I'm not ready for that. She thinks I need organising.'

Liz was surprised when he said Karen's name. She saw that maybe there was a chance to help him to move forward.

'You'll have to go and see them, she's worried about you. Remember she's lost her mother too. What are you doing this weekend?'

'Nothing. What is there to do?'

'Why don't you go to City, see Paddy and Mary and sort out what you are going to do for Christmas?'

'Christmas?'

'Yes, it's a little over a month till Christmas.' Liz watched Tony take in this new suggestion and decided that he had enough ideas for one day.

'Thank you for the tea,' he said.

'It's my pleasure. Come again, Tony. One thing you must do is to sort out your laundry and ironing. People are starting to notice.'

He looked her straight in the eye for the first time.

'It's that bad, is it?'

'I'm afraid it is.'

'Thanks, Liz.'

Tony 12th November 2011

Later that evening he faced the phone and resolved to ring Jessica – as Liz had suggested. He should go and see them this weekend; after all he didn't have anything else to do. He dialled.

'Hello Jessica, Dad here.'

'Hello. How are you doing?'

'I've made some soup without setting fire to the kitchen. I might come and see you on Friday. I can bring some with me.'

'That's tomorrow.'

'Oh, yes. Would you like me to come?'

'Of course. We've got to take the kids to a birthday party on Saturday but apart from that we're doing the usual.'

'I'll see you about six.'

'Lovely. Is everything else alright?'

'No. You have to explain to me how to work the washing machine. It's getting rather tatty round here and I think some people are avoiding me because I am a bit smelly.'

'Haven't you ever washed anything in it before?'

'Yes, but your mother worked the buttons. She was organised. She rather spoiled me you know.'

And so, Tony began to take steps to sort himself out.

Sonny

What a relief. At last I see a glimmer of hope for Tony; time I did some more work on Max and leave this.

When I come back to it, I wonder where the pencil is going to take me next. As I watch, Tony's kitchen unfolds and he is cooking.

Tony 15th November 2011

The next Tuesday Tony cooked bacon and egg for his tea and sat in the kitchen thinking about Liz and what she'd said. He had a feeling that he would spend the evening losing himself in the piano. But he looked at the choir schedule on the fridge and there was a practice that evening.

He was a quarter of an hour late but that was good, as he was able to slide into the seat next to Ray without having to greet people who were trying to be sympathetic. The village hall was tired and needed paint, and the curtains on the windows hung sadly; their lengths no longer consistent as hooks had fallen out and tapes had stretched unevenly. The choir had an arc of chairs in front of the stage and an upright piano was off to the right, set so the pianist could see both choir and conductor. Since the choir filled the space the piano was a bit behind the conductor's position. A music stand for the conductor was in front of the choir and then several rows of chairs filled the space before the back row, where Tony and Ray sat.

'Hi, good to see you,' whispered Ray.

They sat and listened while the choir finished its warm-up routines. Betsan stood at the piano and gave them the notes.

'Tonight, we are preparing for our Christmas concert again. We can start off with the hymns we are going to cover. Teresa, can you play for us please?'

Betsan went back to the podium and called the hymn number while a chorister came out to the piano. Tony knew she was one of the stronger altos and that the choir wasn't blessed with many. Teresa played the piano mechanically and they worked their way through the hymns. A number of times Tony cringed as Teresa approximated what was on the page. From listening to her playing he knew she was out of her depth.

Sonny

I stop the pencil for a moment in surprise. A woman has appeared in the picture standing behind Tony, and she is transparent. She's average height, slim and has a confidence and neatness about her that suggest she is the person who filed the scores above Karen and Tony's pianos. She looks younger than I expect. It's Karen and she is talking to Tony. I let the pencil carry on.

Tony 15th November 2011

'Tony, do it. You know you can and Teresa will never be a pianist.' Karen said.

But it reminds me of you all the time, replied Tony, silently within his own thoughts.

'I'll help you. We've talked loads about playing the piano. You are as good as I was. Do it.'

The silent conversation played out as the choir finished the latest hymn, and Betsan started to look at the music in her folder.

'Now we'd better start the other pieces. Can we start with "Anfonaf

Angel" please?' Betsan was unaware that Tony was sat at the back. Tony resisted as Karen's voice pushed him. *'Go on, it's the last piece you played.'*

Teresa set off into the intro and although she managed to keep going, that was all she could do. The sopranos started the first verse and they kept going until Teresa had to turn the page and then it came apart. Betsan gripped the podium and looked down at her music long and hard.

'I'll get some tape and fix the pages so I don't have to turn them,' said Teresa as she knocked the score off the piano altogether.

'Let's try again from the beginning.' said Betsan, seeing the disturbance in the choir. She turned to see Tony stood by the piano.

'Here. Let me. The choir needs altos,' he said to Teresa. Her music was in chaos. She got up to pick up the sheets and started sorting it into page order. Tony sat down at the piano. 'Don't worry,' he said.

'Don't you need it?' Teresa said.

'No,' he replied softly. Teresa went back to her place in the choir. As Tony had guessed, no one knew what to say now he was here for the first time after Karen's death.

'Right. Can we start again, please? From the beginning.' Tony knew Betsan was unsure whether he could play. She counted the tempo to him and he played. Once he had started, he watched Betsan and gave the piece every ounce of emotion he had, the choir picking up on his feeling too. For both the choir and Tony, the safest place was immersed in the music.

Karen, as though her hand was on his shoulder, whispered, *'Remember the choir like it if you put a little emphasis on their cues to help where they come in.'* He played it as she would have.

He saw Betsan was weeping as she conducted. He too felt the tribute the choir was paying Karen through their performance. They would never sing the piece that well ever again.

The piece ended and Ray, three or four other hangers on and the hall caretaker spontaneously burst into applause. The choir joined in.

'Tony, you never told me.' said Betsan as she wiped away her tears.

'You never asked.' For a moment Tony was tempted to play a little jazz to show off how accomplished he was, but again Karen was speaking to him: *'No. Wait. You've shocked them enough tonight, and you know the rules we agree; never play a piece without practice unless you have the music.'*

'Can you play for us at the concert?' said Betsan in disbelief.

'I suppose so. If Teresa doesn't mind.'

Later, Tony relaxed in the pub with his beer. He remembered Karen's earlier advice and stayed away from the pub piano. Somehow hearing Karen had helped his confidence, although he avoided saying her name. Betsan and Ray quizzed him on his piano playing.

'Is that why there are two pianos in your living room?' asked Betsan.

'Of course, and that's why there are two copies of most of the music. We played a lot together.'

'I thought that was so she could teach at home? Didn't she?'

'Not much. She usually went and taught in the schools and colleges.'

'What I can't understand is why you never played here before?'

'In the beginning we had the kids. I used to come later as an excuse for a pint with Ray in the pub. Somehow it never came up. This was ...' he stalled as he almost said her name, '... her domain.'

Ray and Betsan quizzed him some more and eventually he told them how he and Karen had met at a college competition in a pub to find who could play 'The Dambusters March' fastest and most accurately. He had to admit that while his rendition had been in the fastest time – and Karen had been a fraction slower – her performance had been deemed most accurate. Tony said, 'It was a moot point all these years, it had to be a fix. How can you tell who was most accurate when the piano was played at that speed?'

'But I was.'

Sonny

The pencil stops again. It amazes me how it has a mind of its own and has found these characters somewhere. As I draw them they are becoming real and I wonder how their lives are linked; their well-being is becoming important to me.

I haven't got into the habit of writing my great work yet – or should I say draw? The drawing part is easy for me, but I'm out of practice with filling in colours. I've never done that with Max, just the occasional shadow. I'm finding too that the frames I use for Max are not suitable for this and have had to make new ones. Christmas has passed since I last worked on this, and when I start again and the pencil takes me back into the kitchen of Tony's house, Radio 4 is playing the breakfast news.

Tony 14th January 2012

Tony was eating a piece of toast at the breakfast table. His leg was fidgeting under the table and he was unsettled. Over Christmas, while staying with Jessica, she had made him promise to clear out Karen's clothing from the cupboards in what was now his bedroom.

'I can come on a Saturday. David can look after the children and we can sort it out and bag it up. I expect most of it will need to go to a charity shop. Easy.' Jessica had said.

Now, Tony wasn't so sure. Memories of Karen ambushed him when he least expected it – although Jessica had told him there might be good memories in the cupboards as well.

He was eating his toast when the doorbell rang. He went to answer it.

'Hello Dad. Your door was locked and I've left my key at home.'

'Hello Jess. I'm having breakfast. Would you like some coffee?'

'No. Let's get started, I'm not sure how David is going to survive. I'd like to get home.'

'I'll finish my toast,' said Tony as they reached the kitchen. 'What have you brought with you?'

'Bags. I didn't know what you'd have here. Can I go up?'

'Yes. Give me a moment.'

Tony reflected on Jessica's determination to get on and guessed she had brought bags in case he would make that an excuse for leaving clothes in the cupboards. He finished the toast and reluctantly climbed the stairs.

Jessica was standing with the doors of the cupboards open, her hands on her hips and her back to the door when Tony came in. For a tiny moment Tony saw her stance as characteristic of Karen. *Ah well,* he thought.

'We can shut these two, that's my stuff.'

'There's nothing of hers there then?'

'No, it's all mine.' Tony had noticed that Jessica said her, not Mam. Jessica was finding this hard too.

Karen was in his head. *Do the easy stuff first Tony. Once you've started it won't be so bad.'*

Ever practical, thought Tony.

'Let's do the drawers first. I don't think anything there is worth keeping.'

The first drawer was full of stockings and tights of many colours and styles. *'Sorry about the tangles,'* said Karen. *'I didn't expect you to go through this stuff.'*

They emptied the drawer straight into one of the plastic sacks. Among the tights there were two packets unopened.

'Why would she keep unopened packets of tights?' asked Tony.

'All women do. It's in case they can't find a pair that isn't damaged.' said Jessica. 'Don't worry, I'll have those.'

The unopened tights disappeared into a soft suitcase that Jessica had brought the bags in.

She's figured this out, thought Tony.

'What do you expect?' said Karen. *'She's my daughter.'*

Next, they encountered underwear.

'No one wants Mam's second-hand knickers; they can go with the tights, but the bras should be kept apart as they are worth something.'

They pulled the stuff out and Tony held the sack open as Jessica stuffed the knickers in. They got another sack for the bras. Jessica looked at Tony who avoided her gaze.

'Coo, some of this stuff she wore was quite racy. Reds, blacks and even lacy stuff. I never knew.'

'Don't you say anything,' said Karen in Tony's ear. *'Don't even smile. It's our secret.'*

They moved on to a drawer of socks, rather worn in Tony's view. There were various items of gym and running kit as well. He shuddered at how much exercise she'd done. He could remember her saying *'It'll stop me getting osteoporotic in my old age.'*

What old age? he thought. Into the bag it went.

'Oh wow, look at these scarves,' Jessica started dragging them out onto the bed. All sorts of different types: silk, wool and knitted. 'I'll have some of these. They're too good for the charity shop. Look, some of these are like new.'

'She liked the idea of a scarf, but you know how practical she was. She would get one out to take with her and then leave it at home in case she left it behind when we came home,' Tony said.

'Here's her college scarf at the bottom of the pile, I've never seen that before. Can I keep this?' said Jessica.

But Tony was thinking as he ran some of the more modern silk scarves through his hands. Two particularly appealed to him and he pulled them out of the pile and put them on his dressing table. 'I'll give these to Liz; she's been good to me these last few months.'

Jessica looked at him and nodded. She kept the college scarf in her bag and they looked at the rest. She picked a second, but in the end they stuffed the rest in a bag for the charity shop.

Another drawer held jewellery and again Tony looked at it and closed it. Much of it he had bought with Karen, or as presents, and now wasn't the time to explore those memories.

'There's a great big pile of vests, nightwear and slips in the airing cupboard, you can give them to the charity shop. I don't think there's anything of value there.' Jessica went off to fetch them while Tony closed the drawers. He remembered that Karen had a stock of toiletries in a cupboard in the bathroom which he would never use, and went to fetch a box to put them in for Jessica. As he went down the stairs, Jessica called. 'Are you all right Dad?'

Karen followed him down. *'Keep going Tony. You're doing okay.'*

'Yes, don't worry. I'm not running away,' he called.

While Jessica reorganised the sacks and cleared the bed, Tony looked with foreboding at the big built-in wardrobes. *The drawers weren't so bad, were they?'* Karen said, in his head. They opened the first, and Jessica's eyes widened upon seeing the seven long black dresses at one end of the hanging rail which set out a history of dress fashion for the last thirty-five years. Apart from being black, all had high neck lines and backs.

'Wow,' she said.

'She needed them for concerts,' said Tony. 'She liked a bit of variety when they had a run of performances.'

Jessica pulled them out onto the bed and studied them. 'Did you know that she was the same size for all those years?'

'That's why we had those diet fads and that gym kit.'

'You lying sod, you liked me being fit. And furthermore, if I hadn't done you would be pie shaped by now.' He could hear Karen's voice from the past again.

As they cleared the rest of the hanging rail onto the bed, he had a few fleeting memories of parties and events that he had attended with Karen, but they were good memories. In the bottom of the cupboard there were shoes. *'You never noticed my shoes'* Karen said. Jessica and Tony worked through them bagging them together in pairs. Karen was wrong, he had noticed her white knee length boots from their first meeting. He set them to one side and said nothing.

With a sense of relief that nothing had given him any bad memories, Tony opened the next cupboard. First, Jessica pulled out a smock dress with wide shoulder straps and then a top with bold colours in a big square pattern.

'Wowee, I thought at first this was a top. Did she wear this? It isn't long enough to be decent!' Jessica was holding it against herself and seeing where the bottom hem reached. 'Dad, Dad, sorry, are you okay?'

Tears welled up in Tony's eyes as he watched her. Tears of happiness. He saw Jessica as a young Karen as he had first met her. He remembered now. Karen had talked of getting rid of this dress in the past but had kept it because of its special association. He took the dress from Jessica and felt the material.

'Tell me,' Jessica said.

'It's okay, Jessie. Your Mam kept it. I knew. She was wearing it the night we played in "The Dambusters March" competition – when I met her. It goes with those boots.'

'I'm not surprised she caught your eye wearing a dress that short.'

'She often wore dresses that short in those days. All the girls did – when they weren't wearing long floaty things that I hated.'

'Oh Dad, can I try it? Can I keep it? It's historic.'

Tony looked at her and was happy. Jessica was the little girl he remembered asking him to fix something she had broken, with the absolute faith of a child even though the toy was beyond repair.

'Of course you can, Jessie love. I can't wear it can I? Nor can Matt for that matter. Keep the boots too.' They both laughed as Jessica folded the dress and put it in her bag.

Their mood uplifted, they went at it clearing the rest of the hanging clothes and laughed again at some items. Soon there was no room to move with the plastic bags they had filled. In the bottom of the cupboard there were no shoes, but there were three metal baskets on runners with jumpers, T-shirts and other tops.

'We'd better take some of these to the car before we empty the baskets.' said Tony. With Tony's car rather full, they stopped and had a cup of coffee.

Tony had relaxed. The end was in sight, and he had enjoyed Jessica's company because she hadn't pushed him as he had expected.

They returned to the T-shirts. Karen had bought some on family holidays that they had enjoyed while others she had collected at half marathons she had run. There were even a couple from musical events she had been involved in.

In the bottom basket – under everything – there was a bright pink shell suit. Jessica dragged it out and held it up.

'God, did she wear this? It's vile.'

'Yes. It made her feel young or something. She was wearing it that day when we were at the beach and there was that fight. Don't you remember?'

Tony watched Jessica as she looked at the shell suit. Their eyes came together and they both laughed.

'Yes. Yes, I remember that day. It must have been about 1986. I was about six and Matt was about three. All that fighting. Mam watched it for a bit and decided we should go home, even though it was early.'

'The police were called and it was very unpleasant,' Tony said. 'Two men were fighting because one of them had brought a dog to the beach, and it had made a mess and then the man didn't clear it up. I suppose people didn't clear dog poo in those days. Others joined in and people got arrested and taken to court.'

'I didn't know it went to court. Mam didn't say. I never understood that.'

'What do you mean by "she didn't say"?' Tony asked.

'You were reading and we went off to look in the rock pools with Mam. In this pink shell suit.' They laughed again, 'Remember that Matt was three at the time and he hated wearing bathers. Mam decided that he was okay to go naked as long as he wore a T-shirt. Somewhere near the rock pools he did the poo. Mam said, 'come on, we'll go and have a little paddle in the sea.' I guess she wanted Matt to wash a bit and to get away from it. We were coming back to you as the men started fighting. That's what I couldn't understand. Mam never said anything. She did laugh a lot though.'

'I remember you coming back. She had tears in her eyes, like she'd been crying, but it must have been she was laughing at those men. She hated dogs you know. She must have thought the man had it coming to him for taking the dog on the beach in the first place with so many people around. But I never knew Matt had caused it.'

25

'People ended up in court and got fined, and Mam never told us.' said Jessica.

'She didn't even tell me. I expect that the longer she left it the worse it was, and then the police came. That must be why she hustled us home; she wanted to get further away.'

'I'll keep it and show it to Matt. I bet he'd love to see it and have a laugh!'

Jessica tucked the shell suit into her bag while Tony had a private smile to himself that she hadn't tried it on. As he did so, Karen said to him: *'I bet if our roles had been reversed, and you had been with the children and I had been reading, you would have kept knowledge of where the poo came from to yourself too!'* Tony chuckled again. He wouldn't have been wearing a bright pink shell suit, whatever had happened.

Soon the cupboard was empty and the clothes bagged up. Tony sat down on the bed as Jessica finished up. From where he was sitting, he could see for the first time that some sort of bag had fallen down behind the trays in the cupboard.

'Jessica. Can you reach that bag out, then the cupboard will be clear,' Jessica had to hunker down and reach past the half open bottom tray, pulling out a bag which looked like a small laundry bag from years gone by.

'What on earth is that?' asked Tony.

Jessica opened the draw string and pulled out a little bundle of material. She dropped the bag and unfolded what she was holding. A small pair of knitted baby bootees dropped to the floor. She was holding a tiny vest and a blue baby sleepsuit. There was a blue knitted cardigan as well.

'Where did these come from?' she said, 'They're lovely.' She didn't look at Tony, whose eyes were full of tears. He sobbed.

'What? Dad, What?' She put the baby clothing on the bed, sat down next to him and rubbed his back as the tears began to run down his face. A few minutes passed. *'She's never seen you crying like this before. Don't be too hard on her. Tell her the story.'* Karen was in his head. She had been the strong one. *'Go on, tell her.'* Tony found a handkerchief, cleared the tears from his wet eyes and blew his nose.

'Jessie, love. You wouldn't have been the eldest.'

'What do you mean?'

26

'There was a baby before you, but he died. There was something wrong and he died a day after he was born. There was nothing they could do.'

'You never said. I didn't know.'

'Yes. After the baby died your Mam went into an awful depression that lasted for ages. We didn't talk. We wanted him so much and he lived for a day. It was terrible, and I suppose I was sad as well. That was the first time that Liz helped us.'

'Oh, Dad.' Jessica hugged him. 'You mean Mam hid this little bundle as the last connection to her lost baby? I'm so sorry. What happened?'

'Liz knew we both played the piano. She told me if we couldn't talk, we should play the piano together. Your Mam took comfort in the second movement of Beethoven's Fifth, so we started to play that whenever your Mam was sad. She never told me why, but it had brought her comfort when she was younger and took her out of her grief. As time went on we found hope in the last movement, and that helped too. I bought the second piano at that time.'

'I assumed that you always played that. You always have as far as I can remember. It was like your theme tune.'

'No. It started then. We had to do something. So, we did as Liz suggested. We played together and slowly your Mam came back to life.' Tony stopped and drew in a deep breath. 'When you play together like that you have to look at the other person now and then to make sure you keep in time. At the beginning she would only look at my hands, but one day she looked into my eyes again and things got better. Then you came along and we remembered the baby every time we played together. That's why we played a lot I suppose.'

For a while neither moved. *I'm with the baby now,*' Karen said in Tony's head. *'Remember us both when you play the piano.'*

Tony reached out and lifted Jessica's chin so he could straight at her.

'James. The name of lost people in my family.'

Sonny

The pencil stops abruptly. The final picture in the sequence has Tony and Jessica sitting on the bed. Jessica has an arm around Tony and is looking at him, while a younger Tony is looking at a ghostly figure of Karen holding a tiny baby. I don't want to see any more of this grief – a nightmare from years ago.

27

Once again, the pencil sketches Max in the margin of the sheet. He has a sad look too.

'Sonny, it's been very hard for Tony, but his life will get better. Keep going. '

I put away the sheet where I can't see Max. I can't understand how the pencil draws him like this, but it's a bit frightening. How does he know the future? This is the second time he's spoken to me like this. He's willing me to keep going and I'm finding it hard to resist, but I can't see what's in it for him.

When I start a new set of frames this is a new place. A line of terraced houses in Village on the edge of Town, where Tony lives. Some of the houses are tired and others have had makeovers but they show their origin in industrial age. The terrace is set back from the road and there is a bit of public grass to the front – once part of a tramway from a long-vanished pit. City is about twelve miles away down the valley. The pencil hasn't shown me the names of these places; they are just City, Town and Village.

The pencil takes me to the back of the houses, to parking spaces in what were once tiny gardens and backyards.

Elin 10th March 2012

Elin Paterson parked her car in her space behind the terrace, carried her shopping bags from the boot into her kitchen and dumped them on the table. With automatic movements she filled and set the kettle to boil. She went to the bottom of the stairs and yelled up to her daughter, Megan.

'Wyt ti moyn paned?' ('Do you want tea?')

'Ie plis, byddai lawr yn y munud.' ('Yes please, I'll be down in a minute.') The answer was muffled by the closed bedroom door, but Megan had been expecting the call. Often, she travelled home in the car from the school where she was a pupil and her mother a teacher, but today she had taken the bus as her mother had gone off to do the shopping. Elin knew Megan liked the bus and the journey was a social occasion.

Elin set out the mugs and the teapot and started the tedious process of putting away her shopping. Her purchases were essentials to get her and Megan through the week, carefully chosen to keep the cost to a minimum. Today – to cheer herself up – she had splashed out on a bottle of posh olive oil. Elin was struggling to make ends meet and somehow, whatever she did her meagre savings had dwindled.

She reflected on the difference Megan made to the cost of running the house. Megan was eating all the time now she was home full-time and had stopped staying with her father, Kevin. He had remarried, to Catherine, who Megan called 'Y Gath' ('The Cat'). Megan now had two half-sisters, twins under the age of five, who she called the Pom-Poms as that's how Y Gath seemed to dress them. Their arrival had made her father's house too small for her.

Elin had expected to start a better life after the horrible battles of her divorce from Kevin, but her parents' health had collapsed. Her father had suffered from a respiratory illness which may have come from his work, so he needed a lot of care in his last years. Elin suspected that he should have sought compensation, but he would have none of it. She could hear him: 'I owe everything to them; they were good to me.' She thought they had used him ruthlessly.

Her crisis had come when her mother had begun acting strangely. Soon it was clear her memory was deteriorating. Elin had had to find homes for them, and eventually many of the costs had been taken over by the state. But her savings had been eaten up by the constant driving to visit them and the late nights coming home when she had resorted to eating in the pub, as she was too tired to cook. She remembered too one night when she had visited them both separately, and when she had sat down exhausted, her mother had looked at her in a strange way and said, 'Nage chi yw Mama ife?' ('You're not mother, are you?') Her mother had never called her chi, always the more familiar ti.

She made and poured the tea.

'Mae e'n barod,' ('It's ready,') she called up the stairs before picking up her mug and going out to enjoy it in the sun on her bench behind the house. A blackbird was cheerfully stringing together random notes over the distant traffic, and the leaves on the tree by the back wall were moving slightly in a breeze. Even in March her little bench was in a sun trap.

Moments later her peace was rudely shattered by a van crunching to a halt next to her car.

'Where are you?' came an angry voice that she recognised.

Kevin's shout shocked her. She put down her mug and fled back into the kitchen as he came through the gate and followed her. He was a solid man, running to fat, wearing working clothes although his business was essentially clean. He blocked the light from the doorway into the room.

'Go away,' she said. 'There's a court order against you coming back here.'

He came through the door into the kitchen and stopped. Everything about his stance challenged her. She faced him across the table, wanting to get away; but this was her house and she had to defend it. Memories of previous battles filled her head, and she knew that the kitchen table was no defence if he decided to attack her. Her fear of physical attack from him was so strong that she didn't think of his other options.

'I came to bring you a letter. It's all finished between us.' He brandished a thick envelope of papers.

'It's been finished for years.' Elin was almost shaking.

'This is final. Megan is old enough so I don't need to pay any more maintenance. I've finished paying.' Kevin was playing reasonable with the confidence of knowing that he was in control.

'But you have to pay. The court said.'

'Not anymore, sunshine.'

He dropped the envelope onto the table.

'Get out!' Elin was frightened of him. He could be violent and more than once in the past he had hurt her.

'Go away Dada,' Megan had heard the commotion downstairs. She had come knowing that her father would be less aggressive to her mother if she was there. She had changed from her school uniform and her clothes matured her. She was nearly as tall as her father.

'How's my little girl?' he looked her up and down. 'Come over and see us sometime.'

'Whatever. Just go away. You upset Mama.'

'Well, she upsets me. I've cleared away the last legal stuff from the divorce. You should be very happy.'

Elin knew the little maintenance he did pay was a help and didn't want to give up without a fight.

'You have to carry on paying maintenance to Megan while she is in full time education. That's what the agreement says.'

'Megan is over sixteen. She's old enough to get a job if you can't make ends meet. Sort it out yourselves. I'll give her work on Saturday mornings. Do her good. Get some real experience. I'm off. The stuff's there. I can see myself out.' Kevin swept out, slamming the back door.

Elin understood that Kevin had guessed that she wasn't in a position to take him to court again, and Megan's age was against Elin now. What she didn't know was that Kevin lacked the skill in business to keep up with the competition and inexorably he was going under. His young family was costing more and Megan was a cost he could do without.

But in the meantime, Elin was going to find making ends meet a big challenge.

'Be' ni'n bwyta heno Mama?' ('What are we eating tonight Mama?')

Elin fetched her mug from the yard and refilled it from the pot. She had barely heard the question as she struggled with the insoluble imbalance between her income and her bills. She would have to go and beg the landlord in the Railway for some time behind the bar. Maybe a knight in shining armour would wander into the bar and rescue her. There was no chance of that in the Railway.

'Am I going to have to get a job?' Megan asked, forthright as usual.

'I don't know, cariad. Maybe I can work in the pub at weekends.'

'Why don't you sell some pictures?' Elin taught art and, in the past, had sold one or two items but through Megan's childhood, the divorce battles and the trials with her parents, that side of her life had fallen by the wayside.

'I'm not sure we can afford the materials; we spend enough already now you're doing art. Where would I sell them?'

'So, I might have to work.' said Megan again.

'So, you might have to work,' Elin looked at the bottle of olive oil and began to cry. 'Oh dear, not if I can help it.'

Sonny

I hate the sadness of this broken home. I reminds me of when I was a teenager. I had huge rows with my father that finally made me leave home. While my grandmother had been alive, she had calmed the arguments and controlled my father, who kept on at me to get a proper career. But she had died when I was seventeen.

'Drawing all day with your head in the clouds. You'll never make enough to buy pencils and paper. You need a proper career.' Dad had gone on and on at me.

My father had been a bus driver for the local bus company and believed he was the best bus driver in the world. I never understood it. He simply drove his bus round a fixed route in City for his shift while a clippie at the

31

back of the bus saw to the travellers. On Sundays he was in the Sêt Fawr – the seat where he sat with the other elders – trying to look important; although he was a bit too short for that.

Somehow he killed any interest I had in religion. The Sêt Fawr gave him a position in society that had nothing to do with any beliefs. He thought it gave him moral superiority and, to him, confirmed that his arguments were the only right and correct ones. He wouldn't listen. And Mam was no help, always saying, 'Father knows best.'

Even then, with my pencil in my hand and blank paper in front of me I could feel a magic that I can't explain. I had to be an artist. But this was the early sixties and pop art represented everything Dad disapproved of.

Mr Starkey in the school had watched me sketching my homework after school one day – I did my art homework there as taking the work home caused more trouble.

'Why don't you take it home son?' he asked, and I told him. How I would never be allowed to go to art college nor have the career I wanted. I was only alive with the pencil in my hand, and maybe it's still the same. He knew.

'Cool head boy, we'll find you a college. And once you are eighteen we'll get you a grant and you can plough your own furrow.'

I wonder what happened to Mr Starkey. He did loads for me until I could leave home, as the terrible rows with Dad continued while I waited for my exam results and my college place. After all the help he gave me, I decided I would do my best to pay back to others what he did for me.

I never went back. I doubt Mam and Dad ever knew that Max was my creation, but they may have read the newspaper.

Chapter 2: May 2012

Sonny

I set up the paper and take up the pencil. This is a new place, showing Tony making his way down a corridor. Occasional notices on doors display the words 'Quiet, please exams in progress.' This is a building from the 1960s. The rooms are partitioned from the corridor with aluminium-framed panels up to the concrete structure above. Some panels have windows that have been covered over from prying eyes by the occupants, the paper tired and wrinkled, the Sellotape discoloured and coming away.

The nature of the corridor changes. Now the walls are plastered and covered with pictures of gowned academics, neatly captioned to explain their special contribution to this institution.

Tony 8th May 2012

Tony arrived at the Vice Chancellor's office. He knocked and went in.

'Sit down, Tony.' The VC pointed to the chair in front of his desk. The VC's academic career had been in one of the humanities and Tony had never understood how anyone could go through life with so many opinions. In astrophysics, mathematics often provided a unique answer, and Tony liked things tidy that way.

Tony took in the emptiness of the desk and had an insight that this wasn't one of the usual discussions about departmental business. He looked again at the professor, who was concentrating on the sheaf of a few papers that remained in front of him. To Tony's astonishment he read from the paper.

'Tony, thank you for coming at this short notice. I am afraid that there is no easy way to say this, but because of the funding cuts we have been forced to close some departments in the university and we have decided to finish running our astrophysics course. As you know, to run the course effectively we have to carry some heavy costs for telescope time and we can no longer afford them.'

Tony was hardly listening. He knew that the writing had been on the wall for astrophysics for some time – more so since Karen had died. She had been his rock, helping him through his PhD and his teaching career. She had learned a lot about physics listening to him talk about it. Since her death, his enthusiasm and drive had dried up and he had found it hard to focus on his work. It didn't matter anymore. The terrible emptiness that had taken him over when Karen had died, rolled over him like a wave.

'At the end of this academic year we will have to let you go, but I have spoken to the HR department and they will let you have details of the package we can give you and the various options for taking or deferring your pension. We will of course help you if you choose to try for a post in another uni.'

Tony deplored the word 'uni'. He always had. The proper word was university and he thought the VC was demeaning himself by using the abbreviation. His other words felt irrelevant.

'I would like to thank you for the service that you have given to this institution over the last thirty years. We will of course arrange a reception for you, and some others who will also be leaving this year, to recognise your contribution.'

In the confusion of the return of his grief and with his mind adrift in thoughts he was trying to avoid, he heard that his career would be recognised by a reception. His wife was gone and now his work was gone. And he would have a reception. People who had avoided eye contact with him for months would come and make stupid speeches about what a wonderful chap he was. He laughed out loud.

The VC looked at him in alarm.

'Are you alright? I mean, err … is everything okay?'

Tony understood then how nervous the VC had been about making this speech. He wondered if he should make things awkward for the VC, but in his heart he knew that his teaching alone over the last year justified this interview.

'No. I'm fine. I um … no. I'm fine. What happens now?'

'You need to go down and talk to Liz Stephens in HR. She has the details of the package she's prepared with your options. She'll explain it. They suggest that you pick up the package, read it through and think about things for a few days before you talk to them about what you want to do.'

'Right. Thanks.'

Tony got up and shook the VC's hand. He wondered why he had bothered as he headed for the door. The man had sacked him and here he was being nice to him. He reached the door and turned.

'I don't think you need to arrange a reception. I can't stand that sympathy all over again.'

He left before the VC could say anything, or if he did he didn't hear it. As he progressed down to HR, he passed various people without noticing them. Somehow, he couldn't get a grip on any thought process. He knocked on her office door and heard Liz call, 'Come in!'

By the time he was seated again in front of her desk he understood that she had been waiting for him, like the VC. But she came out from behind the desk and pulled up a chair next to him. She had an envelope for him. She looked at him sympathetically.

'Tony, I have to give you ...' She tailed off and restarted. 'Tony, can I get you a cup of tea?'

'Yes please. A mug if you've got one. Milk but no sugar, you know, the usual, thanks.'

There was some comfort in Liz's office as they had met several times since Karen had died. He knew she had stopped him going off the rails altogether and helped him deal with some of the horror of the loss of his wife. As she went off on her errand he sat and stared out of the window, although he didn't notice the view. He began to wonder what on earth he was going to do in the empty house.

She put an arm on his shoulder and the hot mug into his hand.

'I'm sorry Tony. After everything you've gone through and now this.'

'I'm sorry too. The VC offered me a reception to "recognise my contribution." I told him not to bother. So here I am. I suppose you have the job of making my sacking legal and doing it as quietly as possible.'

'To be blunt, yes. Please don't call it sacking. It's better to retire. That way we preserve your dignity.'

'Do you know, I'm fifty-nine and Karen and I never talked about when I would retire, and since she ... well, I haven't thought about it. Retire. That's a laugh. The VC offered to help me find a post in a different university. Who would want a burnt-out old bum like me at fifty-nine? Perhaps retiring is what I should do.'

'You've got a lot to think about and I expect you are a bit shocked right now. What I have here is a package of the options you have with pensions and the like. You are entitled to some redundancy and because of your service, we are able to set up a full pension for you since this is a redundancy. I expect you won't be much worse off. If you want to find another job that would be fine too, your pension could carry on just the same.'

He took a sip of tea and thanked her for being so thoughtful.

'What happens now?' he added.

'I give you this letter and we arrange a time when I can talk to you about what's in it. It's not right to go through it yet, while you are digesting your discussion with the professor. Today is Thursday. I suggest that you go home and have a think about things and come to see me at ten o'clock on Tuesday.'

Tony leaned forward and looked her in the eye. He wanted to keep her as his friend.

'Liz, what about my students? I can't dump them.'

'The VC will have to make arrangements for them for the next few days but don't worry, you can look after them till the end of term once we've sorted out your future. Take the letter and go home. No one is expecting you to do anything here for the next few days. Just treat it as though you were away at a conference.'

He made a decision and stood up. He took the envelope from her in one hand, with the half-drunk tea in the other. He wavered.

She laughed sympathetically and stood up too.

'Tony. Go back to your office, get your stuff and go home. I'll see you next week. And you can bring back the mug. We'll be talking for a while about the various bits in that package so fill it with tea before you come.'

'Thanks Liz. I'm sorry that you have to do the execution.'

'Oh come on, you are retiring. A whole new world is in front of you. You can do whatever you like.'

As he thanked her again, she opened the door for him and he went out. He was retiring. He asked himself again; what on earth was he going to do now?

He walked past offices and people, unseeing, as he tried to find a sensible train of thought. After reaching his own office and slumping down in the chair, his eye came to rest on the picture of Karen smiling back at him. For a moment he wondered what she would say when he got home and told her he now had no job. Reality struck home and he reached out for the picture, studying it as his eyes threatened to water. He remembered the music left on the piano: 'Anfonaf Angel'. He could hear her saying it. Perhaps she'd send him another angel. His time with the choir had become a great comfort to him and had given new purpose to his piano playing. Karen shouldn't be there to watch him empty his office; so different from when he had moved in thirty years ago when he was full of hope. He put her picture carefully into his briefcase with the envelope from HR and looked to see what else he should take now.

Sitting there, he contemplated the textbooks he'd collected over the years. The life blood of his career. Often in the past, he'd come back to this office and reached out for one of these old friends to check some fact that a student had asked him about. There was nothing in them that could help now. They didn't matter. A new wave of grief threatened him.

He drank the cold tea and set off for the car park and home.

Sonny

I sit back and think about this latest disaster in Tony's life. I know that empty feeling of arriving home to a cold and silent house. I do it too. My contact with the outside word is limited to my shopping and visits to the editorial office to deliver my work. Max had been wrong. Tony's life had got much worse. Maybe Max doesn't know.

One day I was chatting with a friend in the office.

'What are you going to do when they lay us all off because the internet has taken over, Sonny?' he asked.

'I've no idea. I just expect life to carry on like this forever,' I said.

'It's coming sooner than you think. With your talent you should draw one of these graphic novels. They say they are taking over from the written word.'

He was the one who set me thinking about my retirement, and the future of the newspaper. Circulation has started to sag as he predicted, under pressure from the internet and perhaps, like Tony, they are about to call me to an office and tell me that Max is no longer required. Drawing my novel is filling more of my time so maybe there is life after Max. I reflect on what Liz Stephens said to Tony. 'It's better to retire. That way we preserve your dignity.' This novel is telling me something. I should try to go forward as well.

I don't drink cold tea like Tony, so I make a new mug before setting my frames. The pencil draws the riding stables. There is life here in the energy of the horses and the people. I can see that this is a happy place with its smells and comings and goings.

Guy Barnes 12th May 2012

Guy Barnes was at the stables. He wasn't a huge fan of riding but it made a good excuse when he was invited to play golf, and at the stables he could watch the young women in their tight trousers. One girl stood out and he had hoped to meet her, but she rode a big fast horse with more experienced groups than his. He only saw her from a distance or as she passed through the yard on her way in or out. Even so, she seemed familiar for some reason.

This morning he encountered her unexpectedly around a corner.

'Oh, hello Mister Barnes. Lovely day for a ride.'

He was taken totally aback. She was stunning to look at, but more than that she knew his name. He would have to reply. He didn't like women being forward.

'Hello, yes. It's nice,' he said, and pulled himself together. 'Do I know you? Wait, are you Lisa?'

'Yes. I work in the reconciliation section at the brokers. I've seen you about.'

'Right, right.'

'I've got to go. My group's just leaving,' she said. 'Have a good day.'

She passed him and headed towards the saddled horses in the yard. He watched her walking away. *What a figure,* he thought.

Guy Barnes was a small man in every sense of the word and had a Napoleon complex. He was sure of his opinions and used his loud voice to spread them. He liked to control the people around him and to dominate. Despite this, many of his clients appreciated the work he did for them and he was successful; making them money and in the process gaining bonuses for himself. As a result, he was a team leader in the brokers' office.

Later, when driving home he thought more about the girl in the stables and the vacancy on his team. He should check her qualifications and see if he could recruit her. Then he would be able to watch her every day, and even take her out.

Sonny

My pencil stops for a moment, although I will carry on today. I suppose
Lisa's career could benefit from meeting that man, but I don't see him as
a partner for her. He's unpleasant and he has a nasty way of looking at her.

The pencil hurries on and draws a big room in an office, broken up
with partitioning high enough so only the heads of the workers and the
tops of a couple of plants can be seen above the grey panels. I have the
impression that it's cheerful and well-lit, and it would be neat if it wasn't
for bits of paper with names or notices pinned here and there. Individual
workers' cubicles would all be the same if the occupants hadn't
personalised them with plants, pictures and posters. The room has big
windows on the long sides; one looking onto the backs of other buildings
covered with ducts and pipes while the other looks out at offices and
shops.

Lisa 14th May 2012

Lisa was wondering about her encounter with Mr Barnes on Monday
afternoon, when she was interrupted.

'Seems like you are going to get your big chance.' Eric sounded a bit
jealous as he stood over Lisa at her desk. Eric was her supervisor, who
didn't understand the job as well as she did and did less than anyone in the
office. He was in his fifties and had been working in the brokers since he
had left school, or more likely as Lisa thought, he had been thrown out of
school. Everything about him was tired, and she wished he would wash
his hair more often. He smelt of tobacco – although she sometimes
thought that was better than other things he could have smelt of. He met
her definition of a creep.

Unconsciously, she moved to make sure he couldn't see her cleavage.
The cubicle she worked in didn't give her scope to move; it was the
minimum size a chair would fit into with the worktop, computer and
simple cupboards. Her colleagues called them pig-pens – the name fitted.

'What do you mean?' she asked. She knew this wasn't the place for this
discussion, but in this firm the culture for dealing with staff was feudal.
Others around her were listening.

'I have a letter here for you offering you a position in the brokerage
and betting department. It seems someone thinks you are efficient.' Eric
never praised anyone, ever.

'If it's addressed to me shouldn't you give it to me?' Lisa said.

'Here. But I want to know if I am going to lose you. I want an answer.' He gave her the letter and waited. Lisa read it.

'It says I have to go for an interview. So how do I know if they are going to offer me anything? You won't get an answer from me today anyway.'

'Tell me what happens, alright?' Eric gave her a strange look and turned away. *Randy old goat*, she thought.

She read the letter. They wanted to see her tomorrow. It said that the main interviewer would be Guy Barnes as he was the team leader in the section she was being considered for. She needed to know more about him.

She sent the email confirming that she would be at the interview and went back to her work.

The next day she wore a skirt as it was a better option for an interview. She had been trying to dress down because some of the men seemed to think she should be dressed up like a model all the time, even though they didn't. Lisa could probably win Miss World, and she had been aware for years that she attracted attention. She was twenty-five and in her prime.

At the appointed time she went up in the lift, past the floor where the Human Resources and other corporate sections operated, to the top floor where the traders worked.

The interview panel consisted of three men. Guy Barnes was leading the interview, together with his manager Bob Sullivan and someone called Mike Penshirst from the HR department; to whom she'd never spoken. She was surprised how easy the discussions were, although somehow Guy Barnes's eyes disturbed her.

'I see you have an MBA from our university here in City. I hope we can make better use of that than in your current position.' Bob Sullivan said. She had seen him around and now knew he was quite high up the firm, although his appearance was nondescript. He wore ties and rather worn suits – like most of the men – but rarely had his jacket on. He was a bit nervous about her.

'Yes. I am hoping to develop my career so this is a good opportunity for me to learn more. Over the last three years I have tried to understand the processes in my current role, and I hope I can prove that I know how they work and how to use them.' Lisa said. She was ambitious and had been preparing for this kind of chance to move on. To her surprise, after a short discussion Bob Sullivan told her she would be offered the job.

Mike from HR explained how her pay would change. She could see he was smarter than the other two, although this might be due to his position with public relations responsibilities. He was in his mid-forties and kept fit. She got the impression from his body language that he was uncomfortable with the other two men.

'We will continue to pay you the same as you are receiving now until your performance review in October, and you will also receive a bonus based on your sales value. The formula is a bit complicated but is based on the fees that we charge your clients. With bets, it also relates to their profits.'

Bob Sullivan added, 'Initially your bonus will be ten percent until you have proved yourself, and we will review that in the new year. The secret of a good bonus is finding yourself clients who make money. I'm afraid that very few people trading or spread betting on the stock market make much money, so you will have to work hard to pick some winners. But, don't forget we like the losers too if they do a lot of trading and pay their fees.'

They talked some more about details of the job and how the markets worked, and she agreed to start by being introduced at the departmental meeting on Friday. They thanked her for coming and she left the room. To her surprise, Mike from HR followed her out and once the door was shut, he said, 'Can I have a word?'

'Of course.' she said and stopped.

'Can you come down to HR? We're better talking there.' He was almost furtive.

'Of course.' she said again. He avoided the lift and they went in silence down the flight of stairs to the HR offices.

He took her into his office and shut the door. He was likeable enough, but she was starting to worry about what this meant.

The wall behind him had a lot of books on employment law and a window looking out over the street. She could see the river and the sight of water calmed her.

'I have a problem that you should know about,' he said. 'Do you know about Chantelle Wright? She worked in that department until recently.'

Lisa had heard that someone had gone but now was putting two and two together. He went on.

'I want to warn you about what happened so that you don't fall into the same trap. Chantelle was complaining of sexual harassment. Somehow, she was tricked into doing something unethical with some clients, and we had to sack her. She appears to have genuinely felt that she was wrong and accepted that she had to leave, so she didn't pursue her grievance about the harassment. I can't prove a thing, but I think she was stitched up.'

Lisa was a scared by this. 'What are you saying?' she said, carefully.

'Watch out,' he said, then looked out of the window away from her. 'I don't want to see your career wrecked like hers. You are an attractive young lady and that place is a bear pit. I suggest you start keeping a private diary of what goes on.'

She remembered Eric positioning himself to look down her cleavage the day before. So, the rumours she had heard could be true.

'A private diary?' Lisa repeated what Mike from HR had said.

'It doesn't matter what form it takes, but you should keep little file notes on any incident that bothers you. Dates and times, who said what; that sort of thing. That way if it comes to an argument we will have something to go on. Chantelle had nothing, and that was her downfall because it was her word against theirs. Of course, I am here if you need to come to discuss things, or you may prefer to get a friend outside of the company to use as a sounding board.'

'It seemed okay in the interview today.' Lisa said.

'Yes, it was bound to. They don't trust me and that's why I suggest you get a friend outside and keep clear of me. Unless of course, things get bad.'

'Thank you. I'd better go.' Lisa set off back to her cubicle with her head in turmoil. If she was going to move out of her mother's flat, she needed the extra money but would it be worth it? She had no idea of how much bonus she could expect, so she didn't know if the move was worth anything.

Heading back, she wondered what the real motives of the man from HR were. Making her way through the partitions, she remembered Eric. She would have to go and tell him what had happened rather than leave him to find her; that way he would be sitting and she would be standing. She decided he could wait a bit as he didn't know when the interview would finish.

Later she met Gareth Jenkins by the photocopier. He was in his sixties and grey, but she had noticed that he had a sharp eye and didn't miss much. He was a sort of janitor, although he did a lot more than just cleaning and could be relied on to fix things as well. To her he was more like a father figure than a colleague.

'How's tricks, Lisa?' he asked.

'Can't complain. I'm being moved up to the B & B, so I might be able to move on a bit.'

'B & B. Watch your back! They aren't a very nice bunch, although you should be able to make some bonus there. Do you know about Chantelle?' he said.

'Not really. I never met her. What happened?'

'I can't tell you now. Someone may come,' he said. 'But if you ever need help just give me a call.'

Lisa moved onto safer ground.

'Thanks Gareth. How did you end up doing this job? You could surely find something better?'

'I'm retired. Didn't you know? I was a clerk of works for a big building contractor. I have my pension but I get bored at home. I couldn't be bothered with those programmes on the TV valuing people's houses, antiques and rubbish. They don't pay me much here, but I don't have any responsibility and they don't expect much either. It does mean that I get out and meet people though.'

She had finished her papers and knew that Eric would be waiting if she wasn't careful.

'Thanks again.' She set off back to her workstation and sorted her paperwork. Some had to go into the office post so she picked that up, used it to cover her chest and headed for Eric's cubicle. His pig-pen was no bigger than hers. He didn't seem occupied, but did he ever? She knocked his partition.

'Oh, it's you,' Eric turned to face her. 'I gather you are going to desert us here.'

'Yes Eric. Time to move on and try something else. You'll have to do without me.'

'When are you going? Have you finished those period end transfer completions? Is my ledger up to date?'

'I start with them on Friday. I should manage most of the completions, but there will be some left which I will bring you on Friday morning. Otherwise it's business as usual.'

'Can't you work late and finish them on Thursday?'

'No, I can't.' They both knew that Eric would have to do the outstanding work, and she knew that he was very lazy and dumped stuff on his team that he should be doing himself. Perhaps they knew that upstairs and were moving her to put pressure on Eric. The thought made her smile.

'So, it's funny to leave me in the shit is it?' Eric wanted to get up but he couldn't unless she moved as the cubicle was too small. While she was standing, she had him at a disadvantage and the letters she had to post made a good barrier across her chest.

'Not particularly Eric, I just want to get on. I'll give you what's left on Friday.' She'd decided to finish the work as otherwise Eric would dump it on Debbie who was quite slow and got overloaded easily. She went back to her desk and got stuck in.

Both the man from HR and Gareth had warned her. What was that about?

Sonny

I put down the pencil. Why they are warning her? On the face of it this is a good move for Lisa. She's such a cheerful and likeable character, I want her story to end happily but at present it looks as though she is heading from one unsavoury character to a group of unpleasant people.

Lisa 18th May 2012

Lisa's first Friday meeting was a daunting prospect. She had come in a little earlier than usual to find her new desk and move her stuff from her pig-pen. As it happened, she bumped into a friend on the way who wanted to know about her move. So, she arrived at the same time as Bob Sullivan.

'Morning Lisa, come in and meet the team.' he said as he pushed past her through the swing door. A gentleman would have better manners; she'd noticed too that he never met her eyes.

'Morning Sir.'

'Lisa, take a seat,' Bob Sullivan sat at the head of the table and his team leaders were near the top with him. Her place was at the bottom, and she was one of very few women in the room. The firm had an organisational chart with pictures so she had been able to get the names sorted out in her head in advance.

Bob Sullivan introduced her and explained her new role in the team, the others in the room grunting their greetings. She wondered if it was her imagination but she had a feeling someone said, 'Nice to have a young wench in the meeting.' Before Bob Sullivan could move on to the agenda, George Nelson – the other team leader – said clearly, 'It's a blue day today.' The room full of men laughed, but it went over her head.

The meeting was over without her having to make any contribution, but she was relieved that she understood the discussions and felt encouraged.

As they left the room, Guy Barnes held the spring door for her and she thanked him but as she passed, she sensed his hand stroking her back and bum. *Or did he?'* She didn't know but it unnerved her. *'Was the man from HR right?'* When she got to her desk, she wrote it down.

The arrangement in this office was different from the pig-pens downstairs as this was a trading floor. She had been allocated a hanging locker near the entrance to the wide-open room. This was quite generous compared to what she was used to, so she would be able to leave odd items of clothing here. That hadn't been possible in the pig-pens; which had made after-work activities difficult when there wasn't time to go home to change.

Her desk was in a wide-open part of the floor. The open plan was intended to enable the team to hear each other's conversations so that they could contribute if they had relevant trading information. The L-shaped desks were loosely arranged and she wasn't comfortable with the way she faced one of the fairways down the room, especially as the filing cabinets were arranged on the wall behind her so people tended to come past to go to them quite often. After sitting down, she moved her computer screens to block them off. She wasn't too far from the window though so she could see the river; something she enjoyed looking at when she was in the middle of a phone conversation and facing the other leg of the desk. The man from HR must be below her on the next floor down.

Guy Barnes had given her a list of people whose accounts had been dormant for a while to help her get started, and she was working down the list phoning people to see why. This could yield some work for her but being on the phone meant she missed incoming calls. As she worked her way through the list, she wondered how she was going to get around that problem.

On her way home from work she called in at the supermarket.

Sonny

The Lisa in the story reminds me of Jen.

Jen is Jennifer, my daughter who lives and works in London, quite near my studio. Jen is thirty and I see her every two or three months. She is single, which I find sad. Some man would appreciate her if the way she treats me is anything to go by.

I have to confess that I never talk to Jen about her mother, and Jen doesn't know I am still married. She never raises the subject. I remember the final rows with Gabby and the feeling that I had to leave; that something was wrong with me. Max had come between us but he was our income, so I fled to London from the family home. Gabby had tried to get me to come back a few times in the early months, but I refused to meet her and devoted myself to Max. I have thought through this over the years and come back to wanting the security and comfort of my pencil – and Max. I know I abandoned the little girl and walked away from her childhood, but my parents cut me off too and I thought she'd grow up stronger without me.

Max became successful, paying Gabby's mortgage and a bit more. It's all done through an agent though, so I have no contact with her.

Jen had been five and a half when I had left, but she had been old enough to know that I drew, and tucked away in her memory she had an idea that I was something to do with Max. Gabby had done a good job with Jen, who had got a place at London University. As part of registering she had to produce her birth certificate and found my name on it. She hunted me down through the newspaper.

I remembered the phone call from the editorial office. 'A woman called Jennifer came and wanted to talk to you, can we give her your address?' I didn't know who she was at first.

'She's about twenty, pretty, and she says she's your daughter. I don't remember you had a family.'

I was shocked by the rush of emotion as the voice said 'family'.

46

'Did she leave any details?'

And so, I'd got her address and gone to see her. Without a phone number, I went to her flat and knocked on the door one evening, guessing that she would be out in the daytime. It had taken me a few days to work up the courage to re-open this door into my past, and I had no idea what to expect.

'Hello, can I help you?' she had asked when she opened the door. I suppose it could have been a flatmate, but I knew it was her straight away.

I wanted to run away.

'Jen.' She had known who I was before I had said it.

'Daddy! Come in, come in.' I was surprised. She took me in without question. She never judged me and it was as though I had never been away.

Since then we've built a relationship and enjoy one another's company. Jen doesn't go home often so we don't talk about Gabby, and I don't know why Jen left home but it suits me to stay away from the subject. I remembered how Mr Starkey helped me, so I helped Jen with her college costs and got her onto the property ladder.

When I start again the pencil draws Tony's house, but this is a new room where Tony has his computer. It's a workspace with reference books carefully organised on shelves. In front of the books are pictures in frames, pots with pencils, paperclips and the other paraphernalia of an office; with everything in its place. The computer desk is in front of a great black leather effect swinging chair, and in addition to the keyboard and screen there is a printer and telephone. Through the window I can see that this is an upstairs room.

Tony 19th May 2012

Tony is at home. For him Friday had come and mostly gone in a blur. For a while Tony had been very angry about his so-called retirement and had started to type ranting letters to all and sundry. Eventually the rage blew itself out. He heard Karen saying, *'Well done. Got that off your chest. Now delete it all in case you do something you will regret in future.'* So, Tony deleted everything. That evening he discovered he needed to talk to someone and rang Matthew because he lived closer.

'Hi Dad, what's up?'

'How did you know something was up?'

'I didn't. It's just a saying. So, something is up?'

Tony blurted it out. 'I lost my job. They've closed my department. No more astrophysics in the university. I have till the end of term and then nothing.'

The line went silent and Tony guessed that Matthew was thinking about the loss of his mother. Matthew had said previously that he had moments when he expected her to say something or he wanted to say something to her. They had shared the pain that she would never be there again.

'I'm so sorry' said Matthew. 'Why don't you come here tomorrow morning? We can go for a walk and get some lunch. I'll be on my own. Nothing like some fresh air to make the world look better.'

'Yes, yes, that would be good. Have you got anyone there with you?'

'Not tomorrow. Natasha has a course.'

'Right. I'll see you in the morning.'

'Dad, have you told Jessica yet?'

'No. I don't want to upset her as she is so busy and will want to come here and make a fuss of me. I decided to leave that till during the week when she won't be able to.'

'Okay, I hear you. I'll see you then.'

Tony breathed a sigh of relief. His children were so busy that he didn't like to interfere, although he enjoyed helping with his two little grandchildren in City. Matthew was harder to tie down, and while Natasha was more or less permanent now, Matthew had previously had several girlfriends. Tony instinctively knew he would be needing his children for the next few weeks, in the same way they had pulled together after Karen had died.

Matthew greeted him the next day. 'Hello Dad! Can I put my stuff in your car? Mine's a bit of a problem.'

They set off down to the coast, away from the built-up areas for a walk and some lunch. The conversation was tentative at first. Matthew explained how he had bought an old Morris 1000 and while the substance was good, some things under the bonnet were tired and unreliable.

'You could buy an old car too. It would give you something to do. Go out to rallies and that, meet a lot of new people.'

'I don't know. The choir takes up quite a bit of time. I never thought about retiring. What do people do?'

'I have no idea. I'm in my twenties for goodness sake, I haven't thought

48

about it either! I suppose it depends how much money you have. Do you have to get another job?'

'I read the stuff they gave me and as far as I can see I have some choices about lump sums and deferring pensions, but I should be able to live okay. Once you two had finished college, the mortgage came to an end and I have that money from your mother's life insurance. I won't have to work. And who would want me at my age?'

'They're looking for people to teach physics, but if you don't have to why bother? Take the money and go and enjoy it I say. You can spend more time with Paddy and Mary; time you should have spent with Jessica and me.'

'Ouch. Okay, point taken. Even if I don't work, I will have to do something. I was worrying a bit about money though as everything is earning useless interest in building societies.'

'Try betting some on the stock market. You might make some more!'

This was another of Matthew's jokes. He talked about the stock market as a betting shop. But this time Tony was being serious and took him literally. What did Matthew mean by 'betting on the stock market'? Tony was aware that in his academic ivory tower a lot of life had passed him by, but he was not going to show his ignorance by asking.

When Tony got home, he googled 'betting on the stock market' and discovered that there was a whole world of stuff going on that he knew nothing about. He knew about his own investments in the stock market made with Karen. She had had a better idea about companies than him, and although they had never lost money, the gains had been steady. That was investing. He had heard Matthew say 'betting'. He had a quarter of a million pounds earning very little interest that had come to him from Karen's life insurances. Maybe he should take some risk.

As the days went by, he sorted out the end of his career and his redundancy and began to think about the problem of how to win on the stock market. He cleared his office sadly, while remembering moving in, all those years ago, full of hope and ambition.

Sitting in his den a few days later he opened a box of files from his research years ago and flicked through some of the pages. The printouts contained many data points recorded from a radio telescope surveying the sky for radio waves. His desktop computer contained more computing power than the machine that had made these printouts. He had based his career as an astrophysicist on his skills as an analyst of vast quantities of data. Could he beat the stock market gamblers with scientific analysis rather than gut feeling that everyone else used? He packed away the old files with a new sense of purpose.

Sonny

I don't do computers. That stuff Tony is doing is a bit of a mystery to me. Now the pencil takes me to a pub. On the face of it this is a traditional pub, but a larger conservatory-like extension has been added at the back where the tables are laid out for dining. There are some tables occupied by people drinking teas and coffees or finishing their meals while soft background music plays. In the bar some staff are splitting money from a jug marked 'for the staff' and Elin takes her share. She has her coat on and heads out into the cold with the usual pleasantries to the others.

The pub is on the side of a valley and on the edge of Village, which is full of terraces of old houses – evidence of an explosion of industry many years ago. Here and there buddleia sprouted from gutters and chimney pots and weeds grew along the edges of the pavements. One or two houses are boarded up, with very old 'for sale' signs outside, looking as worn as the houses themselves. As she walks back to her house, I can see that this is a sad community whose only reason to exist is the people who stubbornly remain.

Elin 26th May 2012

Saturday lunchtime in the pub had been busy and the tips had cheered Elin up. Any money coming in was going to make a difference. She hung her coat on the hook and went to the kitchen.

'Hello Mama,' Megan said. 'What are we eating today?'

'I haven't a clue. What is there?'

'Nothing. Nothing I like. Some old tins. We're running out of breakfast as well.'

'I'll go to the shops this afternoon, when I've had a minute. I've got to be back in the pub by seven.'

Elin sat down at the kitchen table and started making a list; she dreaded going to the shops. Food always cost more than she expected and she had to keep putting stuff back on the shelves – and Megan ate so much.

'Mama, I need more titanium white. Can I have ten pounds?'

Elin's heart sank. Each week Megan needed more materials which nibbled into the limited cash she had.

'Okay.' Elin knew from experience that painting needed lots of white.

The job in the pub was taking up her spare time and wasn't helping much. Elin stared at her shopping list to see where she could save the money and resisted the urge to cry. She couldn't see how she was going to get out of the trap.

Sonny

I put the pencil down. What I don't understand is what Elin and Megan are doing in my story. I thought Lisa and Tony would be enough for a story, and I don't know how they are connected, but now I have Elin as well. And I wish that the story didn't have the shadow of the murder in the park hanging over it. I hope the pencil knows where it's going.

Chapter 3: June 2012

Lisa 4th June 2012

During the morning meeting the following week, Bob Sullivan announced that as they had a new member of department they should stop on the way home for a drink.

'It will be good to get the team together away from the formalities of the office. Is that okay for everyone? Which night?'

Someone suggested Thursday. One or two people said they had other engagements but most were clear that night and so the decision was made. As the meeting broke up Lisa became aware that Jeremy, a young man from the nearest desk to her, was standing rather close to her. Naturally she was nervous about him, but somehow he blocked her from the wandering hands of other members of the team.

'See you later,' he said and winked.

She watched him as he walked back to his desk. She could see that he was attractive. He was approaching six foot three inches tall and clearly worked out a lot. She knew Jeremy Dudley was the latest addition to the team before her, and that he stayed away from the banter that went round the office. When she thought about it she realised that she hadn't noticed him, but this morning he had neatly shielded her from Guy Barnes on the way out of the meeting.

Lisa 7th June 2012

On Thursday she was uncertain what to expect, but to her relief it was Jeremy who came and stood over her desk.

'Time to finish. Close up and get your coat; I'll show you the way.' As she cleared her papers away others passed on their way out. 'Come on, last one buys,' someone said.

The pub wasn't far from the office and Lisa decided that she would stay safe with soft drinks, so that she could take her car home. Most of the team were stood at one end of the bar, while Bob Sullivan was buying a round. She felt very exposed as she walked through the room towards them; even in her coat. Somehow a pint of lemonade appeared in Jeremy's hand next to her, but no one asked her what she wanted – and everyone else had a drink.

Then Guy Barnes was next to her. 'Sorry Lisa, we only buy pints. Girls shouldn't drink them, should they?' The audience laughed and Lisa felt even more uncomfortable. She pushed up to the bar and dithered. The woman waited.

'Can I get a cup of tea?' she asked. The woman moved away and returned holding a cup and a mug. 'Which size do you want?'

'The big one, thanks.'

'Do you want milk? Sugar's over there.' She pointed to a small station with cutlery and serviettes.

'Yes, milk please.'

The woman brought her a little tray with a pot of tea, the mug and a small jug of milk.

Lisa paid her and poured the tea.

'I've never been in a pub where someone drank tea,' Guy Barnes said.

'I've never been alone in a pub with a group of men who didn't offer me a drink.'

Bob Sullivan broke the tension.

'So, Lisa. What do you do with your spare time?'

They discussed riding – of which Lisa knew a lot and the rest knew practically nothing. A splinter group formed, discussing the national rugby team and the next match of their tour in Australia. Someone was trying to sort out a sweepstake based on the final scores but there was no agreement about how to run it. Lisa poured more tea and found Jeremy standing next to her.

'Jeremy, what do you do with your spare time?' She decided the risk was worth it. Besides she felt Jeremy was safer than the rest of the men, even though most of them were married.

'Play rugby and keep fit. Keeps me out of mischief.'

'Shouldn't you be discussing the big game with that lot?'

'They know as much about rugby as they do about riding.'

Lisa was surprised. It was a long sentence for Jeremy.

The party was breaking up as Guy Barnes broke in again. 'Fancy a bite to eat?' He ignored Jeremy.

'No. I've stuff to do at home tonight.'

'Another time then.' Lisa didn't think so.

Jeremy broke in. 'I'm off. Are you walking to the car park?'

'Yes, thanks Jeremy,' she said, then turned to the others. 'See you tomorrow.'

Among the remaining men a voice said, 'Two young love birds.' They all sniggered.

So they set off together along the short length of street, in silence. As she walked Lisa felt safe with Jeremy and suddenly knew why. Jeremy was gay. His car was first and as he opened the door there was no one nearby.

'Jeremy, are you, er ...' She didn't know how to finish it. He turned; his face fierce.

'Lisa. Don't ever say it. Very few people know. You are quite safe with me. I saw what they did to Chantelle. I couldn't help her and you need to watch your back. I'll help if I can but you have to keep my secret.'

She put her hand on his arm and looked at him. 'We've never had this conversation.'

He smiled and got into his car as she walked across to hers. She knew what sort of men she worked with and was prepared to fight her corner. She could imagine what life for Jeremy would be like if his secret emerged.

As she drove home, she thought about the man at the stables. The glimpses she'd had of him served to increase her interest.

Sonny

Now my story has another vulnerable character who I will worry about. I can't imagine living with a secret that if it comes out could destroy me. Living all the time hoping that someone isn't going to casually say something, assuming everyone knows. Having a secret so damaging that someone could blackmail you to keep it hidden.

Gabby is a secret that I don't tell anyone, but the way I live there are very few people in my life who would be interested. This reminds me what a sad lonely man I am. No one would care if I came out gay or anything else. I put down the pencil and leave the drawing board. I am comfortable and safe in my flat, but now I feel a need to get out and be among people.

It's warm and dry and I don't even need a coat. I go to the park for a walk and to have a quiet pint in my local where, who knows, I might meet an acquaintance for a chat.

Later the pencil moves to a new place; a picturesque pub called the Ketch and Tender by the seaside, nestling under a cliff, facing south and with a bit of a curving beach to one side. There are arrangements for diners to eat outside on a terrace overlooking the sand.

Tony 21st July 2012

'Got a girlfriend yet?' Matthew asked Tony as they ate lunch. This was his way of trying to wind his father up.

'You always were a cheeky little so and so. No, I haven't and it's none of your business.'

'Yes, it is. I want to know when I'm getting a wicked stepmother; like in the pantomimes.'

'When I have something to tell you, I expect you will be the first to hear. Until then fear the worst – only I haven't met anyone with horns who can work magic on horrid little boys.' Tony was relaxed and trying to give as good as he got. They prattled on together.

'So how have you been spending your time?' Matthew had at last plucked up the courage to broach the subject his sister had been nagging him to raise.

'Unpacking my old office and sorting the house out. I hadn't realised how many places there were in the house where your mother kept things. I know we've cleared most of her clothes out but that still leaves a lot of other nests; like her sewing box and sewing machine, for example. You never know – I might have to sew a button on but they don't need to take up that corner of the dining room. And there are other things like that.'

'Don't chuck anything away. Even Jessica may want some of it. Most things can be eBayed or car booted, so you could make a bit of money.'

'Oh, I don't need money. I've got more from my pension than I expected and now I don't have to pay pension payments and National Insurance, so I'm getting nearly the same as before. I have a plan for making money too.'

'What's that?'

'I haven't fully worked it out yet. I'm just researching ideas.'

'Tell me. I might be able to help.'

'No. I'll tell you later when I'm happier with the idea.' Tony was not going to tell Matthew that since he had Googled spread betting, he had thought about little else.

Prices of stocks and shares, and the indexes like the FTSE are moving all the time as people buy and sell. Spread betting is a way of betting on these movements. The advantage is that there is no need to actually buy anything so there is no need for a large capital outlay, but the downside is that prices can go up or down, and so you can lose as well. The key to winning is to understand in detail what is causing the movements, and to be able to predict what is going to happen.

Tony had started a massive analysis of stock market data worldwide to see whether he could spot any way to forecast movements. He had been looking for a more powerful PC to handle the analysis.

'Tell me about this car thing. What do I have to do?' Tony changed the subject.

'Oh. If you can come home with me and leave your car with us, you can drive my Morris to that garage down the road from you where Dick works. I've spoken to him and he has agreed to give it a service and sort out the performance and reliability under the bonnet. He's expecting it in the morning. There isn't much wrong so it will only need a couple of days, then you can bring it back next weekend.'

'You've got me all organised haven't you! Lucky I haven't got around to selling your mother's car.'

'Don't sell that! Natasha might like it if her latest project goes ahead.' Matthew's life was full of new ideas.

'Right now, what is worrying me is whether that car will get me home.' While Tony knew how to keep cars running, he didn't want the hassle. They got up from the table and Matthew paid at the bar.

'Thanks for lunch, Matthew.' Tony said.

'It's my pleasure. You did it enough times when I was a student. I'll see you at home.'

They drove to Matthew's house where Tony got into the Morris and started it. Everything seemed okay and the car was still warm from Matthew's trip.

'Hang on, we need to make sure you have enough water. Can you open the bonnet and switch off?' Matthew fetched the watering can and a rag, which he used to take the radiator cap off. At that moment Natasha came out of the house.

'Hello Tony, how are you?'

'Fine thank you. Have you finished for the day? You missed a good lunch down at the Ketch and Tender.' Tony said.

'I've had a miserable sandwich; don't rub it in. Yes, I'm done for today. I was hoping Matthew would come and take some air with me. How about it, Matt?' Natasha said.

Matthew looked up from his task of filling the radiator. The rag slipped off the top of the radiator and down into the engine bay. He replied to Natasha.

'No probs. I'm here just for you. Once Dad's gone, I'm ready.' He screwed the cap back onto the radiator, closed the bonnet and turned to his father.

'There you are. Dick should be able to fix that and we'll see you next week.'

'I'm off then. Abyssinia.' Tony used the old family joke. He set off home in the somewhat dishevelled car. Matthew hadn't said what he should do if he broke down, but it was too late now. He drove on, gaining confidence as the car settled down and he got more used to it. But he relaxed too soon.

A huge bang came from under the bonnet, followed by an extraordinary rhythmic crashing. The ignition light had come on so he pulled in and switched off. Now what?

He was in Village, about three miles from home. Town – where he lived – was once a village like this one, but it had flourished and grown so that now it would have swallowed this one if it wasn't for the hillsides. Tony regarded this as the poor end of Town. He couldn't think of anyone he knew who lived nearby.

Just my luck, he thought. *No tools and no friends.*

He opened the bonnet to see that the rag that Matthew had dropped was tied up in the fan belt; together with a lot of wires which it had collected as it had whipped around. He looked at his clothes, rolled his sleeves up and started on the messy job of pulling it off.

Most of the wires were for the front lights of the car so if he could tie them safe, he could drive the few miles home. He found the wiring for the dynamo and could see that it could be put back. He started to hunt the car for tools but knew instinctively that Matthew wouldn't have left anything like that. It was too late to ask him now.

What was he going to do?

Sonny

I put my pencil down for a moment. I don't have a car so I've never learned about them. I am surprised that the pencil has drawn this, but it understands what Tony does on his computer so I shouldn't be surprised. I hope it doesn't expect me to know how to fix this broken car. I pick up the pencil again. This time it draws Elin's terraced house where she's sitting at a small table in her front room. Behind her is a sofa and a comfortable chair, while opposite is a television and some bookshelves; rather untidily loaded with art books that are too big for the shelves.

Elin 21ˢᵗ July 2012

Through the open window Elin had a view across the valley. Once this view had been industrial, with a pit and other associated works and railways, but that all went years ago and trees were starting to turn the valley green again.

She was going through her bank statements and adding up the bills she had. With careful husbanding of her income – and no disasters – she was managing to keep afloat. Her parents' illnesses had wiped out her savings and they had left her nothing. When their situation was at its worst, Elin had increased her mortgage to tide things over, but this had been a step too far. The job in the Railway would let her build a little buffer. She thought sadly about Megan, knowing there was no chance of a holiday for either of them.

A strange bang and odd rattling noise broke her concentration, and she looked up. A rather battered Morris Minor came to a stop across the rough grass in front of the house. *Pity the council only mow it four times a year,* she thought, *but that might increase the rates.*

The man who got out didn't fit the car. He opened the bonnet and peered inside. He was too smart and his actions indicated that he didn't want to get his hands dirty. He looked around to see if there was anyone to help but decided that he had to do something himself.

He's older than me, she thought. *But he looks after himself. He keeps himself fit.*

He hunted through the car and the boot.

He needs tools. She smiled at her cleverness, relieved to be taken out of her financial misery.

She got up and went out across the grass, watching for dog poo.

58

'Can I help?' she asked.

'Do you have a pair of pliers?' he asked. 'And a screwdriver. It's my son's car and he has sent me off without any tools.' He didn't notice her.

'Give me a minute, I have a little box of tricks with that sort of thing,' she said and went to get them. Getting up close to him had surprised her. He sounded nice.

She fetched her little toolbox and gave it to him.

'Do you mind?' he said.

'No. You carry on. Can I make you a cup of tea?' she said.

'Are you sure?' He was ferreting in the toolbox and picked out a pair of pliers.

'It's no trouble. How do you like it?' she asked. He hadn't looked at her.

'Milk please. I don't take sugar, thank you.' Now that he had the tools to repair the car, he got on with it.

She headed back to the house and made the tea. She wondered about him. He hadn't even looked at her and that bothered her. Was she so invisible? Is this what happens to middle aged women?

She yelled to Megan. 'Megs, do you want a cup of tea?'

'No.' She barely heard the reply. Megan could be a bit of a recluse with her art and her music. As her mother taught art this was one subject where they could be quite at odds with each other. Elin had never quite got used to allowing Megan full freedom with her materials, since her early attempts with paint had been so messy and needed a lot of supervision.

She made the two cups and went back carefully across the grass to where he was standing up looking at his hands. He picked up the cause of his problems and began wiping the oil and mud off, while trying to avoid his clothes.

'Oh dear me, you need to wash. Why don't you come back into the house and get cleaned up?' Elin said, still holding both cups.

'Oh sorry. What a mess. Let me check that the car will go and I'll take you up on that offer.' He got into the car and started it. Everything sounded sweet, and he switched off again.

He shut the bonnet and started to put the pliers and screwdriver back in their box. She stopped him.

'Are you going to get home alright? Why don't you take it with you in case you have a problem again?' she said.

59

'Thanks. I'm afraid that might be a good idea the way this car is.' He put the pliers and screwdriver in the car and locked it before picking up her toolbox.

As they walked to the house across the grass, she warned him.

'Lot of dogs around here, mind you don't get caught.'

'In the park near us they put up notices about bagging dog poo but it made no difference. Some man came in a fluorescent jacket with "dog warden" on the back for one day and since then people keep it tidy.'

Tony, 21ˢᵗ July 2012

As they walked back to the house, he studied it for the first time and began to take in the lack of maintenance compared to some others in the row. Karen's voice broke in. *'She's helped you out, and you haven't noticed her. She's going to need thanking properly.'*

Tony looked at the woman for the first time as she led the way into the house. He could see she had a look of defeat about her posture; a sort of careworn tiredness, but despite that he could see she was still attractive.

'You'd better come to the kitchen sink and do a proper job.' she said.

He followed her to the sink and she gestured to the soap with one of the cups of tea, went to the table and put them down.

'I'm sorry, can you roll this sleeve up again for me, please?' One of Tony's sleeves was falling down into the danger area. She came over and rolled it for him. Her hands brushed his forearm and their eyes met. He saw hers were an emerald colour and heard Karen again, *'You never notice anything about people.'*

'Thank you.' Tony got on with washing his hands, noticing how happy he felt to have company. He turned to see her sitting at the table – which was rather cramped in the small kitchen. There were only two chairs so he sat at the spare one.

He took a sip of the tea. Immediately she started to talk.

'Is it warm enough? By now it's been on its travels!'

He sipped again. 'No, it's fine. When I was working, I often drank it cold because of the distractions.'

'What did you do?' Elin asked.

'I teach astrophysics at the university. Actually, not true, I finished at the end of the last term.'

'You should talk to Megan; she's doing physics at A level and she finds some of it hard. No one has properly explained to her the difference between mass and weight, and it's beyond me!' This was introducing something he didn't know to the conversation. 'Megan's my daughter. You can hear the music upstairs.'

'Oh, are you married? I gathered from your treatment of the tools that they were yours.'

'No, I am divorced. Megan is the only good thing to come out of it.' Elin added, bitterly.

Tony stopped himself from prying further as he heard Karen say, *Talk about yourself, she needs to know more about you.*

'My wife Karen died last year rather suddenly. I have a daughter, Jessica, who lives in City. She's married with two little ones. The car belongs to my son Matthew and I was doing him a favour by taking it the garage, but it looks like I have wrecked it for him.' Tony remembered the damaged car. 'I wonder if I should set off, the car has no working lights anymore. I just hope it gets me home.'

'Is it going to take you that long?' They both laughed. 'Do you want another cup before you go?' Elin asked.

'Yes, okay. That would be lovely but haven't you done enough? I haven't thanked you for your help and the first cup yet.' He passed her the cup. As she put the milk back in the fridge Tony saw that it didn't have much food in it. Karen had kept the house well stocked – especially when they had teenagers – and the habit had continued since she'd died; although he had been throwing some food away.

Elin was less depressed than when he had first seen her, but he couldn't remember how he knew that. She was standing straighter and her eyes were smiling. Her emerald eyes. What would Karen think?

They drank the second cup together and carried on exchanging details of their lives. Elin kept clear of her money woes and Tony avoided his plan to make money by betting on the stock market.

'Now I do have to go,' said Tony as he got up from his seat, 'and I can't thank you enough for your help. I hope I haven't kept you from something important.'

He thought Elin winced a little. 'No. I've enjoyed our little chat.'

61

Elin, 21ˢᵗ July 2012

Elin showed him to the door while he continued to thank her, and she watched him pick his way across the grass to the car. It started and he waved and drove away.

What a nice man, she thought as she closed the front door. She turned and came face to face with Megan.

'Who was that man, Mama? He looked nice to me.' Megan had always been forthright.

'A passing motorist,' said Elin. 'He broke down and I lent him some tools.'

'You were very chummy in the kitchen.'

'Were you spying on us?' Elin was sharp.

'Only a little. I forgot that he was here and nearly walked in on you.'

'Why didn't you?'

You were so cosy; I didn't want to break it up.' Megan's comment prompted Elin to remember that she had no idea who he was or where he lived or anything. Just that he had a dead wife called Karen. *How stupid can I be?* she thought.

'What have you been doing then?' Elin said, changing the subject.

Sonny

This reminds me of my life with Gabby. What happened was all my fault, as I should have given up Max and looked for something else to do. The trouble was I so loved it when the pencil drew him. I pay her an allowance and we're still married. I wonder how she is.

I met her when I was thirty-five. She was doing a college course with a mutual friend and had come to one of his parties. At that time she had been developing her skills as a beautician and kept herself presentable. In my eyes she was beautiful even without make up. The trouble was I let Max fill my life.

Maybe Gabby fell in love with the glamour of Max. He was established by then and I was already just known as Sonny. As I reflect on what might have been if I had been more attentive to Gabby, I have a pencil in my hand and Max appears on the paper in one of his characteristic strips.

In the first box Max is gazing straight out of the frame at me with fierce eyes that I can't escape. There is no background to the picture and Max is looking serious. 'What?' Max says.

Max turns away in contemplation. 'Do you mean you didn't know?' he says. I can't believe this; Max is speaking to me again. He's my creation. He isn't supposed to have a mind of his own.

Max turns back to me. 'You should have asked me. I knew all along.' Max is sad now.

The fourth and final box of the strip shows Max making his revelation, looking at me mournfully.

'She's still in love with you, you know.'

I almost throw the pencil away. What does Max know?

'She's still in love with you, you know.' The words are there on the page in front of me. I don't understand. Why 'still'? Why the present tense? Does Gabby still love me? She's never wanted a divorce. Would she have me back? Has she never found anyone else? I'm taken aback by the way Max is getting under my skin.

I wonder about when I left her. Having Jen had forced a break in her career before she had been able to start out on her own as she had wanted. She said that Max was in the way, but I thought it was Jen. One row had led to another and I had run away to hide with Max.

'She's still in love with you, you know.'

The pencil hurries on again, this time outside the sacred frame; breaking the rules. Max speaks again.

'She reads me every day. She tries to find something of you.' He looks away, as though I am beneath his contempt. He turns back to me again.

'You draw Elsa like her you know.' I put the pencil down, frightened to carry on with this conversation, frightened that Elsa might join in as well.

I didn't know Elsa looked like Gabby. Am I still in love with her?

When I come back to it later, Lisa is at the stables.

Chapter 4: July 2012

Lisa 21ˢᵗ July 2012

The same day, Lisa was hoping that the man would be at the stables. Being apparently unobtainable was making him more attractive. As luck would have it, when she drove up to the stables the next morning he was driving away in a big white van. His hair was unmissable. On a whim she waved. He didn't wave back, but then he might not have had time.

The stables were quite extensive with two quadrangles of loose boxes for the horses. Beyond these were the paddocks and other fields where the horses were allowed to graze and run free. Apart from the lane leading into the stables, a gallop led away into some common land that was wooded and criss-crossed with bridleways for riders to explore.

She parked her car in the rough ground by one of the paddocks and took her kitbag from the boot. She walked over to where she could see Beth and asked her who the man was in the white van.

'What? The man in the white van? That's Rhodri, Mrs Howells's son. He doesn't live here with her but he comes to help with odd jobs. I think he's a kitchen fitter by trade, or a carpenter. I came on to him once and he laughed at me! Nicely. He said he wasn't interested. He isn't seeing anyone and Mrs Howells is worrying about him.'

Beth prattled on about him as they saddled up. 'He went away to university and got a law degree, but after a year in an office he chucked it in and set up as a carpenter.' She didn't notice how Lisa was lapping it up.

Others joined them on horseback and they set off into the woodlands.

Lisa's horse had picked up her high spirits, so he too was full of himself and on his toes. The ride was exhilarating. Lisa was feeling on top of the world and her face showed it with some colouring from the sun and wind, and her eyes sparkling.

The trek finished on a track and in her high spirits she galloped down, making a bit of a display. She let the horse walk a little to cool down as the rest of the group came up behind her.

As she rode into the yard, she saw that the white van was back. She wasn't so sure that her little wave had been the best plan.

She hopped down from the saddle and began the process of taking the saddle off. She heard him behind her; a quiet, confident, warm voice saying, 'Hello, did you wave at me this morning?' But as she turned a brash voice cut across,

'My God, it really is you. Morning Lisa, that's a hell of a ride you were having back there.'

'Morning Guy,' she said, 'I was getting some exercise.' She immediately regretted it. She should have called him Mr Barnes.

Guy came up and the horse skittered a little. She reached up to calm the animal, saying, 'Whoa there, Blister.' Guy moved back nervously and she sensed that he was no rider.

'He's huge,' he said, 'I couldn't even get onto something that tall.'

'I've been doing it a long time,' she said. 'He's a bit highly strung so you have to get his confidence, but he's great.' She was patting the horse's neck and talking to him. Blister pulled away from Guy again and she had to struggle to control him.

'Do you come here often?' he said.

'Did you really say that?'

'Oh god, yes I did.'

'After a week in the office, this is where I blow the cobwebs away.' He didn't seem quite so bad out of the office environment. Perhaps he was afraid of the horses and wasn't in control. She had to turn to calm the horse again and noticed that the white van was moving away. Guy was a pain in the arse.

'Anyway,' he said, 'what are you doing for lunch?'

'I have to hose this fellow down and then I'm meeting a friend from college. She doesn't come home very often so I want to see her.' For once she was grateful for an excuse and made a mental note to think of excuses for future use.

Beth came over to tell Guy that his ride was ready and he went off. Beth came back to help her sort out Blister.

'Do you know Mr Barnes?' she asked.

'Yes, worse luck. I work with him.'

'The girls don't like him. He's made some unwelcome passes and comments at some of them. He treats them like dirt, but the boss has told

65

us not to upset him as he pays well. We have to give him the safest rides too. He's so bad at riding I wonder why he comes.'

Lisa knew. Guy couldn't play golf and came to the stables to avoid having to admit this to the golfing set.

'Did you get a word with Rhodri?' Beth asked.

'No.' Lisa didn't want it rubbing in and didn't want to talk about it.

Sonny

I'm sorry Lisa missed meeting Rhodri because of Guy Barnes. The more I hear about Guy, the less I like him. I want to write a happy story about appealing characters, but first there's a murderer – presumably a man – then there's Kevin Paterson, who's just plain nasty, and now Guy Barnes. Until they came along I hadn't encountered anybody like them.

The pencil starts again and to my relief it draws Tony driving Matthew's battered car. He's driving from Elin's house through Village; sad with its boarded-up shops. He drove into Town and immediately saw the contrast of brightly coloured shop fronts. Past the village hall where the choir met and the adjacent playing field, and on he goes down the shopping street. The dual carriageway up the valley has been kind to Town and it can cope with the traffic. His house is on a mature estate on the far side from Elin's house – about three miles distant.

Tony 21st July 2012

Tony drove home with a song in his heart. Breaking down hadn't been such a problem after all. He called Matthew to thank him for lunch and tell him he'd arrived home at last.

'What did you have to do to get it sorted?' asked Matthew.

'Mainly I had to pull the rag out from the fan belt. The problem was the dynamo. I had to borrow tools to remake the wiring.' Tony didn't want to talk about the nice lady who had helped him. 'Luckily I was able to get some help but none of the lights work now.'

'I'll phone Dick in the morning and ask him to add it to the list. I am sorry to spoil your afternoon like that, especially after we had such a good lunch.'

'No one got hurt and I wasn't planning anything important.' Tony felt happier now the conversation had moved away from who had lent him the tools.

'Thanks Dad, I guess I owe you one after today.'

'How's your sister? Did you see her at the weekend?'

'She's worried about you. You should go and see her. You haven't seen the little ones for a few weeks. Give her a call.'

'I should, but she tells me what I should be doing. I don't need her to tell me how to run my life.' Tony said.

'She's thinking of you; it's her way of letting you know she loves you. She bosses the hell out of me too.'

There was a silence as they both thought of Karen, who had been head to head with Jessica all along. Since her death Jessica had somehow decided that it was her place to organise them, except she didn't have the subtlety of Karen.

'Let me know when Dick's finished and I'll go and see him.' Tony said, keen to get away from the sensitive ground of Karen.

They finished the conversation.

Tony had set up his PC and now carried on studying stock market prices. He guessed that he would have to devise a programme to analyse them. He knew how to set a computer up to filter incoming data from a radio telescope and this was very similar, so he looked in his physics files to work out how to approach it. Whatever he did, he needed stock market data first in order to know what format his program would have to take.

He looked online at various companies who supplied stock market data and found that he would have to pay. He knew that he would need some kind of broker to set up a betting account so searched the net again. There was so much choice he was confused but found a firm of brokers nearby who appeared to do what he wanted. He resolved to ring them in the morning for advice.

What he was doing was an excuse for avoiding ringing Jessica, and now it was nearly too late to ring.

'Hello Dad, I was just going to ring you. How did you know?'

'Know what? Is everything alright?' Tony asked.

'Yes, everything's fine, but I need some help. Nia, who does the childcare, has to go to look after her sick mother. I'm stuck for someone to help for the next couple of days while I sort something out.'

So all Tony's plans for the next day were put on hold.

Sonny

The pencil stops, and I leave my story for a couple of weeks. When it restarts, the pencil draws the entrance to the broker's office where staff with indoor clothes are running to escape from unseasonal wind and rain. Inside the office the pencil takes me to a conference room where Bob Sullivan is holding his morning meeting.

Lisa 23rd July 2012

This morning's meeting had been short and uneventful, although apparently it was a red day today. Lisa wondered why some days had colours.

As they were about to get up, Guy spoke. 'I met Lisa at the stables on Saturday, she was going a hundred miles an hour on a massive horse. Quite a sight.'

'Blister is a thoroughbred so he's like one of your expensive cars – fast but temperamental. But as you say, goes at a hundred miles an hour,' Lisa said.

'Lisa was dressed up for riding in tight breeches. I was most impressed.'

'I'm sorry I missed that,' said George Nelson.

'I didn't think my trousers were on the agenda here,' said Lisa.

'A figure like yours is always on the agenda at these meetings.' said Guy.

Lisa left the meeting as quickly as she could and wrote the exchange down in her book once back at her desk What did 'always on the agenda' mean? Was this something to do with the colours?

Concentrate, she was thinking when the phone rang. *Now what?*

She answered, surprised that it was an outside call. Everyone else must have been busy and the call had come through to her. Here was a chance for her to get a client of her own.

'Er … Hello, my name is Tony Jones. I need some advice about betting and how I set about doing it. Am I talking to the right person?' He sounded very nervous.

'Of course. I should be able to answer your questions – and don't worry, if I can't, I'll come back to you with what you need.' Lisa knew that she could handle this.

'What I think I need is an account so that I can do some betting. Do you do that?'

'Yes, I can set that up for you. We will have to carry out some security checks for the money laundering regulations, and you will need to deposit some money with us before you can start.' Lisa set about explaining her company's requirements.

'So, you can send me the forms I have to sign and we can set it up as easily as that?' Tony had been surprised that he had hit the right person first time.

'Yes. No problem.' Lisa got his name and address from him and started an account reference. 'Have you got any other questions?'

'Yes, actually. I'd like access to stock market data. How do I get that?'

'We have data on our website for the UK but if you wanted to go further afield, I suppose you would have to set up an account with someone like Bloomberg to be able to access their system. We advise any clients who want worldwide data to do that, and I can set that up and take the fees as part of our service if that is what you want.' Lisa ticked the box in the automatic mailing system to add those forms to the package he would receive. 'Is there anything else, Mr Jones?'

'I've never done anything like this before, so I was rather hoping you could give me a bit of advice about how to go about it.' Tony sounded insecure, although Lisa sensed he'd relaxed somewhat.

'One thing we advise clients to do is to try a bit of paper trading first. You can get the feel of how it works without getting your fingers burnt, as it were.'

'What do you mean by paper trading?' Tony asked.

'Paper trading is when you place trades or bets in our paper trading system and see how they perform. There's no money involved so you can do it without any cost. That way you can learn about it without losing any money. Our paper trading system is a sort of a dummy market although it does use the real pricing that is in the marketplace at any time.' Lisa explained that Tony didn't need to sign the client registration forms to do some paper trading; she could set it up for him then and there.

George Nelson was walking towards her. He avoided her eyes and seemed to be looking under her desk. *Come to think of it, they all do that,* she thought.

'That sounds like a good idea, I'll do that. Thanks for the advice.' They did what was necessary for Tony to start paper trading straight away, and Lisa promised to send him the forms. 'Is that everything?' she said.

'Not quite,' said Tony. 'We need to go right back to the beginning and you need to tell me your name again – and your private line – so I can get you again when I need your advice.'

They finished the call and Lisa rang off. She made sure that the right boxes were ticked in the client record and that the correct forms would get to Tony as soon as possible. He was a real client of her own, and she sat back and prayed that he would earn her some bonus.

Lisa 25th July 2012

The next entry in her diary was later in the week when some clients came in for a meeting and coffee and cakes were provided by a caterer. As they were sitting down, Guy Barnes said to her, 'Can the little lady do the honours with the coffee?'

As the business progressed, she noticed one of the younger visitors was watching her. He appeared sympathetic. She ignored it until the end of the meeting when they were standing around, comfortable that the meeting had been a success. Once again Guy Barnes said, 'Thank you gentlemen. We'll be in touch. And now can I ask our little lady to show you out?'

Lisa led them to the lift without a word. In the lift the younger man asked, 'Do they always call you the 'little lady'?'

'Occasionally.'

'It would never be allowed in our firm.' The other men nodded. 'Nor would expecting you to serve the coffee in those terms.'

The lift doors opened and the men went and signed the book at reception. The younger man held back. 'You should complain.'

'And give up my job? I need the money unfortunately, but I keep a record of the little incidents. Maybe someday I will use it.'

'I'll make a record in my file. If you ever need a witness, call me.'

'Come on Barry,' another man called to him, 'we haven't got all day.'

They made their farewells and left. She wondered what to make of his offer and went back to her desk to keep her own record. She was surprised how she was accepting the little comments without noting them. She was getting used to it.

That evening she had to sort out her laundry. As she was sorting her underwear, she looked at the pile of knickers and the assortment of colours. The colour of the day was the colour of her knickers, she was sure. But how did they know?

Her first reaction was extreme rage, but she needed this job so once she had calmed down, she resolved to prove her theory. She picked a gingham pair from the pile for the next day.

Sonny

To my great relief the people in my story are starting to link together. Lisa's situation is worrying. She said she needed the money, but could she find another job? The pencil draws the twilight of the July evening. There's still a glow in the west from the setting sun over one of the parks.

Man 27ᵗʰ July 2012

In the park, the man was waiting. It was late on Friday evening. In theory the park was closed, although getting over the fence was easy enough if you knew the right places. Now that the pubs were emptying out there was a good chance that a girl would come into the park – maybe just for a pee – and if he was patient, he would be lucky. He had been surprised how few women reported assaults and this was making him bolder.

He had no luck that night; there were no loners out for him to prey on, so he slipped out of the park and walked back to his flat. *That park is too close to home,* he thought as he reached his flat. *I should be working further away.*

He had been in a few relationships but none of them had lasted as he had fixed ideas about how women should behave, what work they should be allowed to do and what work they should not be allowed to do. He lived alone, satisfying his sexual desire by stalking drunken revellers late at night. He remembered the night when he had murdered one. The memory of it excited him, especially as the police had got nowhere and the press had gone quiet. He'd always been careful. Seeing police gave him a lift as well; they weren't as clever as him and he knew things they didn't.

Sonny

I don't like this man and can't understand why the pencil has decided to bring him into my story. The others in the story are becoming friends to me and I don't want to see them hurt. Is that what happens in my story? Does one of the women get caught by this stalker? I have to leave it for some weeks to calm my fears.

When I restart, Elin is in her front room doing sums again and looking grim.

Elin and Tony 22nd August 2012

Despite her work in the Railway on top of her teaching job, this week Elin didn't have enough money. Worse still she now had no time to do the housework and shopping, so everything was falling behind. Maybe Kevin was right and Megan would have to go out to work. Would it be right to take her money to pay the bills?

Her mind went back to the uncomfortable feeling in the car on the way home from shopping last Tuesday, and Megan's exclamation:

'Mama, something's wrong with the car!'

She had stopped and they had both got out to look at the flat tyre. The man at the tyre centre had been sympathetic, but the tyre had been wrecked. The money she'd saved from the pub had nearly gone in a moment.

Now they would have a week of eating porridge to try to avoid going into debt; something her father had drummed into her. 'Never a borrower or a lender be'

A strange car pulled up in the street outside. Initially she paid it no attention as she rarely had visitors these days. It was more likely to be someone for Megan. When she glanced up, she saw the man from the broken-down car. He had a package and was carefully crossing the rough grass. *Avoiding the dog mess, no doubt,* she thought.

She got up and opened the door as he rang the bell.

'Hello, I've brought your tools back,' he said offering her the package.

'Come in out of the rain. Thank you, you shouldn't have bothered; I don't use them.'

'You'll need them next time I break down outside your door,' he said pulling off his waterproof.

'Right,' she laughed before leading him into the front room and offering him the sofa facing the gas fire. Near the window was a table with a scattering of bills. She saw him looking at the books and wished they didn't look so untidy. He remained standing, waiting to be asked to sit.

'Can I get you a mug of tea?' she asked. 'Just milk if I remember right.'

'That would be lovely, thank you.'

Elin left the room to put the kettle on. She looked in the fridge for milk and wondered where it had gone. Having an idea as to where it might have gone, she called up the stairs.

'Megs, ti eisiau paned?' ('do you want a cup of tea?') Tony heard movement upstairs and a voice called down.

'I've had a drink, thanks.'

'What's happened to the milk?' Elin called back.

'I drank it. That's all there was. The tea's nearly finished too. You need to do the shopping.'

Tony was standing and sneaked a look at the papers on the table. He didn't see the detail but could see straight away that she had been adding up her bills. He moved away before she came back.

'I'm afraid that Megan has finished the milk, so unless you want it without, tea's off. Have a seat.' She plonked down one end of the sofa and Tony had no option but to sit next to her.

'It's alright, I came to see you. We have some unfinished business. I need to introduce myself to you. I'm Tony. Tony Jones.'

'I'm Elin. Elin Paterson. And that's Megan you heard upstairs, who is a teenager and eating me out of house and home.'

He told her where he lived and gave her his phone number which she wrote in a little book she fetched from the table by the window.

'Now you have to tell me how I can return the favour you did me.' Tony said.

'You don't have to do anything, honestly. I'm fine.' But it wasn't alright and she turned away from him and burst into tears. He reached out for her forearm.

'What have I done to upset you?' he asked. He wished Karen was here. She knew how to deal with this kind of situation.

'Nothing.'

'It's got to be something.' Tony said. She faced him again, so his hand came off her arm and he picked up hers. She sobbed again. Tony carried on. 'Tell me about it. Maybe I can help. I owe you a favour.'

'My ex has stopped paying. He says Megan's old enough to work, and I can't make ends meet.' She sobbed again, 'Megan's a teenager, she eats all the time and needs clothes. I don't know how to feed her. And to cap it all I had a puncture and had to buy a new tyre.'

'It sounds like we need to go and buy milk and tea at least. Where do you shop?'

'In Tesco's in Town.'

'I've got the car. Have you got time to come now?'

'I'm working at six in the Railway. But I can't shop until he pays me and that's not until tomorrow.'

Tony made his mind up. 'I'll pay, don't worry. We can be there and back easily by six. Get your coat.'

'I can't. How can I pay you back?'

'It'll be me paying you back. One good turn et cetera. Don't worry. Now dry your eyes and off we go.'

Elin looked at him. He seemed so genuine and she was desperate. The truth was that there was no food in the house. She blew her nose and decided.

'Okay, it would be very kind of you. I don't know what to say.'

'Don't say anything. Just get your coat.' Tony said.

'I'll have to tell Megan,' she left the room and shouted up the stairs again. 'Megan, I'm going to Tesco. Is there anything you want?'

'I need hair shampoo and stuff.' Megan was coming down the stairs, 'Aren't you going to work at six? I thought you hadn't any money.'

'Come in here. Megan, this is Tony. He was here before, you remember. Tony, this is Megan.'

'Hi' he said while Megan looked him over.

'Is he going to take you?'

'Yes, he is.' Elin said. 'Now what is it we need to get you?'

'Can I come too?' Megan said. Tony was surprised at how forward this girl was but there were enough seats in the car.

'Yes of course, let's go. You'll need a coat.'

Tony waited as Elin and Megan got their coats and bags and went out to the car.

At Tesco, Tony expected Megan would go off on her own but she stayed with him and Elin and pushed the trolley. They went to the milk first and Elin picked a small bottle off the shelf.

'That'll never be enough,' he said. 'Get what you need.'

Megan changed the bottle for the biggest size. He winked at her as Elin looked worried. Megan clearly understood that here was an opportunity to be grabbed and as they went around the shop, Elin tentatively suggested things but Megan confidently filled the trolley with a full selection of food for a week. Occasionally, Tony asked Elin if she liked something and added it to the trolley as well.

'Who's going to pay for this?' said Elin, looking at the mounting pile of food in the trolley.

'I am,' said Tony, 'I haven't enjoyed going to a supermarket so much in years.'

As they were nearing the checkout Tony remembered that Megan had said she needed shampoo or something, and they only had food in the trolley.

'Megan, did you need shampoo?' he asked.

'Not really. I can probably manage,' she said. Elin was relieved as the bill for the trolley was going to be bigger than she had ever paid. 'But we need washing up liquid.'

'Megan!' said Elin. 'We can't take any more.'

'Yes you can,' said Tony. 'Fetch whatever you need.'

Megan went off and fetched her shampoo and some other cleaning products. Tony saw a bottle of red wine on offer and added it to the trolley when she came back.

They drove back to Elin's house, and she directed him into the lane behind the terrace so that he could park in the space behind the house. They carried everything into the house and piled it on the kitchen table. Elin put the kettle on while Megan started packing things into their cupboards.

'You can't refuse a cup of tea now,' she said. 'How am I ever going to thank you for this?'

'A cup of tea will be enough,' he said, sitting down on a kitchen chair.

'You can't sit there, you're in the way,' said Megan. He got up and moved back by the kitchen door.

'Megan. He's a guest. You should have a bit more respect – especially after what he's done this afternoon.'

'Sorry Tony,' Megan said. 'For a moment I thought you were a member of the family! All this food is amazing.'

'Megan, Tony came to give me back the tools I lent him when he broke down.' Elin was on the defensive as usual. How had Megan decided that Tony was family so quickly? She'd only glimpsed Tony once. The cupboards in the kitchen had never been so full.

'Whatever,' said Megan.

Elin made the tea and poured a mug for Megan, who collected it together with her shampoo and conditioner and turned to Tony.

75

'I'll leave you to it. I have a picture to finish. Thank you again for this stuff.' She waved the shampoo as she left, and Tony thought the mug of tea was about to end up on the floor.

'Bye Megan,' he called after her, and said to Elin, 'Am I allowed to sit down now?'

'Of course you are. I'm sorry she's like that. Says what she thinks.' Elin passed him his mug of tea. She hadn't asked him how he liked it. They chatted and Elin explained her school job and the evenings in the Railway.

'I need to get on. I have to get to work at six.'

'Can I drop in again?'

'I suppose so but best to call first as I'm often out.'

She fetched her coat and bag and went back the stairs, yelling up to Megan to feed herself and the voice came back, 'Dim problem.' ('No problem.')

Tony dropped Elin off at the Railway and drove home later than he intended.

Sonny

Are these two meant for each other? I don't know. From what I have seen they are both avoiding any line of conversation which could open up where their relationship is headed. This reminds me of how the pencil helped Tony repair the broken-down car. As with that, the way their friendship is developing is outside my normal experience. Each time I see people getting on in my story it reminds me of how big a hole there will be in my life when Max finishes.

Tony 22nd August 2012

Tony's answerphone greeted him with a flashing light and he called up the messages. 'It's me. Where are you Dad? You never go out. I'm worried about you. Call me please.' Jessica never left her name.

He rang her after his breakfast next morning. She was typically abrupt.

'Where have you been Dad? I needed to talk to you.'

'If you remember, Matt's car broke down and I had to borrow tools to get it home. I just took them back.'

'You were out a long time. I need help again. Could you come and babysit for me on the evening of Thursday 6th September? That's in two weeks. We've got theatre tickets with friends so there's no one to babysit.'

When she was alive, he and Karen had been quite regular at Jessica's to help with the little ones. Now they were both in school. Tony nearly said that he would have to look in his diary, but he knew that Thursday was free. Since he had retired, he was always free.

'Yes. That should be fine,' he said.

'Come down on Thursday morning; we can have lunch together and you can tell me what you are doing with your time.' Jessica was organising him. He smiled.

'Okay, it's a deal. I'll let you know when I'm coming. '

'Aren't you always free now Dad?'

'Not always. Anyway, if I come to City there's someone else I'd like to see as well. Like there was yesterday.' He regretted the last remark straight away, and of course she jumped straight onto it.

'I thought you took some tools back. Where did you go? All the way to Birmingham?'

'No. Look, I'll see you on the 6th.'

'Okay thanks, it's good of you.'

He had a bad feeling that he would have to explain about Elin to Jessica. He wondered what Karen would have told him to do. But Karen's voice was in his ear: *'No need to tell Jessica yet. She can find out in due course.'*

Next day, Tony had a look at the papers that Lisa had sent him about setting up an account and decided that he should meet her. He could hear Karen in his ear telling him that he knew nothing about her. He also needed to give her the references so that so could set up the account, and he decided that he could kill two birds with one stone. He emailed her:

Lisa,

Can we meet up to sort out my references and chat about things? I can do most days with a little notice. I'll be in City for the morning of 6th September.

Tony Jones

She replied practically straight away:

Dear Mr Jones,

Of course we can meet. Why don't you come to our offices at about 10:30 on Thursday 6th September? I'll send you details of where to park and how to find us. That will give you time to read what I sent and you can see what questions you have. If you come to our offices I can photocopy your originals for the money laundering regulations for our files, and we can sign the necessary papers. Afterwards we could have a cup of coffee somewhere nearby as it's easier than in our offices.

Best regards,

Lisa

Tony answered to say that would be okay. Now he had his meeting set up he decided to be positive with Jessica, so he texted her next:

Have a meeting in City in the morning of 6th. Can we meet for lunch when I've finished? Dad

Once he was committed to seeing Jessica, he knew he would enjoy it and knew Jessica would answer later as she was busy. So now he was looking forward to his trip to City.

Now he had an appointment with Lisa set up, Tony began to read in more detail the pages that she'd sent him. He filled in all the forms and found the identification papers she had asked him for. Then he spent the rest of the day working out how to get a data table of prices for the London Stock Exchange together in a form which he could use. He left his PC at the end of the day well satisfied with what he had learned.

Next day, Tony carried on his hermit-like existence. This time he read what Lisa had sent on spread betting. There were plenty of warnings about how easy it was to lose a lot of money quickly, but by the end of the weekend he had worked out how the paper trading system worked. It only worked when the markets were open, so he would have to wait until sometime in the week.

Over the weekend he also wrote little search routines and let them loose on historical London stock price data. He could see that some days the FTSE 100 had distinct rises or falls but nothing gave him a clue what was driving the moves. If he could predict these movements, he would have a basis for some proper betting but nothing showed up. It looked to him as though stock price movements were random.

Chapter 5: Early September 2012

Sonny

When I ran away from my wife I was on the crest of a wave with Max and too busy to notice what my life was like. I had a rented flat which was rather dark, and after a few years I began to feel the pressure of being a cartoonist. Every waking hour I scanned the world around me for ideas for Max's next strip, and as the deadlines approached the pressure grew. It was relentless and I had no one to help me.

People ask me, 'What do you do?'

'I'm a cartoonist.'

'I couldn't do that. I can't draw.'

What they don't understand is that the drawing is a small part of being a cartoonist. Most people can draw well enough to be a cartoonist; they just don't try. The real challenge is being funny.

The editor chooses a strip from a number of my rough ideas. Then I do the finished artwork on the one he has chosen. Partly this is to do with making sure that Max keeps up with the rest of the paper, but sometimes my humour misses the mark. Back then it was like being in a competition where I had to be the winner every day, as people only remember the last one.

This perpetual hunt never went away. I would sit by the radio analysing each conversation and trying to find an angle.

Inexorably the pressure and the loneliness closed in on me.

Externally I was fine. I managed to move myself into the flat I have now, which is lighter and close to the park where I could get out and walk. But finding humour was hard. Somehow Max carried on and I eventually admitted to myself that I was depressed but had no idea what to do.

Behind reception in the agent's office there's a small kitchen and sitting area. One day I had a coffee while I was waiting to see my agent and two people I know by sight were chatting there.

'Wow, you're brown.'

'Yes, we went to Majorca for a fortnight. Brilliant. It didn't rain once and we could swim every day.'

'I wish I could do that. We go to the West Country because we can take the dogs too.'

He saw I was listening. 'Where do you go, Sonny?'

The questioned floored me. 'I haven't had a holiday for years.'

'You should. Maybe Max would find a new angle. He could get a tan.' We laughed.

My agent arrived. 'Sorry about that. Telephones should be banned. Come and have a seat.' she said.

But I was miles away, wondering whether a holiday would help my apathy.

Tony 6th September 2012

Thursday 6th came and Tony packed his bags and set off into City. Lisa's directions were good so he arrived at the offices in good time.

The receptionist in the brokers was professional and friendly. He signed the sheet in the book, and she showed him to a chair where he could wait. She offered him coffee but he decided to wait until Lisa came.

The lift bell sounded and the door opened. Tony was struck by the beauty of the woman who walked out. She looked around and walked straight to him. He stood up.

'Good morning,' she said. 'I'm Lisa.'

'Tony. Good morning,' he replied and they shook hands.

'No trouble getting here I hope?' She said.

'None at all. Your directions were good.'

'Why don't we have a seat here while we sort the papers? There's a photocopier in the offices behind here so we don't need to go any further.'

The chairs where they were sitting were discreetly around the corner from the receptionist and provided some privacy for a conversation – so long as no one was waiting for the lifts.

He produced the utility bills and passport that she had asked for, and she thanked him before briefly checking her papers.

'Mr Jones. Is it all right if I take these to the photocopier?' she asked.

'Yes, carry on. By the way, I prefer Tony. I'm Doctor Jones but call me Tony.'

'Oh! I'm sorry. Is that on your forms? Oh I see it now; I am sorry. I won't be long.'

'Take your time, I've plenty.'

She wiped her pass on a sensor and disappeared through a door at the end of the hallway. She was younger than Jessica and quite a looker. For a short moment he wished he was younger, but in his head he heard Karen laughing and saying, *'Don't be an old fool!'* For once he agreed.

Lisa 6th September 2012

Lisa took the papers into the office where she had worked previously. She wasn't having a good day and meeting Tony was a relief as it had taken her out of the atmosphere on the trading floor.

The meeting that morning had been a nightmare. Recently she had realised that every time someone passed her desk, their eyes didn't look at her; they looked under it. There was no front to her desk, and she knew that when she was absorbed in her work she never gave a moment's thought to where her legs were going, and at times her skirt rode up. Over the last few days she had guessed that they knew the colour of her underwear when she wore a skirt because of where they were looking.

As the meeting drew to a close someone had announced that it was a blue day, and the others had laughed. She'd reacted rather badly.

'You're disgusting. What sort of joke is that? Half are you are married men. What would your wives say? I want a board on the front of my desk immediately.'

Bob Sullivan looked at her. 'I'm sorry. What on earth are you on about? If we don't have a bit of humour in the office it would get very hard; we can't be serious all the time.'

'That's not humour. At least it might be schoolboy humour. It's harassment and it's revolting. I want a board please.'

The other men were avoiding eye contact with Lisa. Bob Sullivan didn't seem to know what this was about. There was silence.

Bob Sullivan said, 'Lisa, we don't need any more outbursts like that. That item's closed and this meeting's over.'

As they scattered back to their desks Lisa had asked Guy Barnes how to get her desk modified. He smiled rather scarily and said, 'You heard what the man said.'

She went back to her desk and wrote down what'd happened. At least that helped her to calm down.

Now she was watching the photocopier and wondering what to do next when Gareth Jenkins came in.

'Hello Lisa. How's things? You don't look happy.' Lisa realised that here was someone who would understand and who could help her.

'Hello Gareth. Could be happier. Can you do something for me?'

'If I can.'

'I need a board on the front of my desk so that the men can't see up my skirt. Those animals think it's a huge joke knowing what colour knickers I have on. They make bets on it every day.'

'Don't those desks have boards on? Or has someone taken the board away?'

'I don't know. That's how it was. It's taken me until now to work out what the colour of the day meant.'

The photocopier finished and she picked up the papers.

'I have to go as I have a client. Can you fix it for me?'

He smiled at her. 'Go and sort your client out. I'll get someone to fix your desk.'

She thanked him and hurried back to where Tony was waiting.

'All done. Here are your originals" she handed back his passport and bills. 'Please can I have the signed copies of the forms I sent? Do you have questions about what you've read?'

Tony sorted out the forms she needed.

'Thanks. Your instructions were fine. The problem now is to work out how to win some bets.'

'I have to set up your account first. I'm afraid you'll have to put some money in it before you do any betting.'

'It's okay. I've read the guidelines on that and I have some put by for starters. I'll do it when I can beat the paper trader.'

'Would you like a coffee?' she asked. 'We could go round the corner and sit in Costa. I can leave my file with Sue on reception.'

'I have to meet my daughter at noon. I'll suggest she comes to Costa.'

They left the office and headed off to the coffee shop where they found a table. Tony texted Jessica about where she could come to meet him.

'Sugar?' Lisa asks.

'No. I've never taken it.'

'Now we've done the paperwork what are you going to do?' asked Lisa.

'I thought I'd have a go at spread betting. I don't do anything exciting in my life, and my son suggested it.' That was what Tony had heard Matthew say.

'Dodgy business spread betting. About one person in six makes any money at it and some lose a lot. We get the fees and the bets are placed with another company. Wouldn't you be better playing the market? You can look at any market you know; one of the growing economies may give better chances of making a reasonable return. Less glamorous but a lot less risky. I can do that for you if you want.' She was aware that he knew little about the market and she worried he could lose a lot of money.

'I told you, I'm a Doctor. One of my specialities was the analysis of radio data from telescopes and satellites. I was going to use my mathematical and data processing knowledge to try to spot where to make bets. Don't worry, if I can't back a certainty I won't risk my money. I've played with the paper trader so I'm learning about the risks.' Tony warmed to his subject and they discussed what he had in mind.

Lisa stayed sceptical. 'You need to learn about stop losses. They won't matter when you are paper trading, but they are an important tool to close a position if it's going against you. As well as that you will normally be required to hold enough on the account to cover losses. We will automatically close a losing position according to our rules depending how much you have deposited.'

'Before I get into that I need to work out how to forecast a winner.'

Jessica's text sounded on Tony's phone and he saw that she had accepted his suggestion. 'My daughter is coming here.'

Somehow the discussion moved away from his ideas and Lisa started talking about herself.

'I don't have a boyfriend at present. There's someone I've got my eye on, but I haven't managed to meet him properly yet,' she said. She was surprised that she felt comfortable talking to the older man. She felt safe with him, as she did with Gareth Jenkins.

'I would have thought a beautiful girl like you would have loads of suitors,' Tony said.

'Oh, I have men who chase after me but none that I like. There's one in the office who would like to take me for a meal, but he's a creep. Most of the men in the office regard women as lesser beings.'

'What do you mean?'

'I get called "the little lady" and they expect me to pour the tea; that sort of thing.'

'The women I encountered in the university would put them right. They made sure that equality ruled,' said Tony.

'It's even worse than that,' Lisa explained the problem with her desk. Tony was shocked and encouraged her to be careful. She told him she was keeping a record in her book, and that she could see herself leaving the job sooner or later because of the atmosphere.

Tony and Lisa had hit it off and were both leaning forward across the table over their empty cups of coffee.

'You make sure you have solid evidence and keep it somewhere safe. You'll have no case without evidence. I've had evidence of stars and pulsars, but when it came to the test it wouldn't bear examination. It's just wasted work then.'

'If I have to leave, I will take some of them down,' she said. 'Don't worry.'

Tony 6th September 2012

'What would you do?' asked Tony.

'Set up a riding school. I live for horses. I ride every week if I can and the troubles of the week are wiped away. There's a big thoroughbred called Blister who I've been riding for a while; he's incredible. That's why I have to do well in this job, to save enough money.'

'Hello, Dad. Who's this?' Jessica sat down beside them.

'Oh hello Jessica. This is Lisa. Lisa, I did tell you. This is Jessica. I've promised her lunch.'

'Lord! Is that the time already? I need to get back to the office. Jessica, it's lovely to meet you but I have to go. Doesn't time fly?' Lisa was putting her things together as she spoke and got up to leave.

'You don't have to go because of me, honestly. He's my father.'

'Really Jessica,' Tony broke in, 'Lisa is helping me with investments, she works at the brokers around the corner.'

'Ooops,' Jessica reddened.

'I have to go,' said Lisa, 'you can keep in touch by email or phone.'

'Thanks for everything. I'll be in touch.' Tony replied, but Lisa was halfway out of the café.

'Sorry. I couldn't believe you were being so intimate with such a beautiful girl.'

'Neither could I,' Tony said and got up to kiss his daughter, 'How are you? Let's go and get some lunch. What do you fancy?'

At lunch Jessica quizzed Tony about what he was doing with his time.

'Dad, you never ring. You must be doing something.'

'I'm trying to decide how to invest the little bits of pieces of money that I have left after giving loads of it to you and Matthew. You can't have it all.'

'No. Okay. You have to live too.'

'By the way, your Mam's car has gone to Matthew for now because he or Natasha needs it. I'll have it back some time.'

'That's fine by me, we don't need it. Now, you should be out trying to find a rich widow to take you around the world. Staying at home won't get you company.' Jessica was pushing him.

Tony gave in. 'I have met someone. That's where I was last week when you rang. She's an art teacher.'

'You old rogue, you never said a word.'

'There's nothing to say.'

'Tell me more.'

'She's divorced and a bit younger than me, and she's nice.'

Jessica kept pushing but she got no more from him over lunch. Eventually they had to go to rescue Paddy and Mary from their primary school.

Tony slept well on Thursday night and once he got home, resolved to spend Friday continuing his hunt for an answer to winning a bet. He poked about in the stock market figures in the London markets, and then found he had access to all the stock markets in the world, as Lisa had said.

He thought about the days he'd already identified where the FTSE 100 index had risen and fallen. To make a bet on them he would have to know to place the bet before the market moved. Looking at the London data was too late but the Far Eastern markets were operating in the night, so if something moved there it could give him the clue he needed.

As he had with the London data, he extracted a set of history from the Hong Kong market to see if anything tied in with movements in the London market. He set up his search engine and left it to run. *This was going to take a lot of studying,* he thought.

Sonny

The pencil has returned to the brokers' office. Behind reception is a little room, long and quite narrow with enough width to squeeze past the desk and chair against the wall to one side. At the far end are couple of metal lockers and a sluice. The walls are unplastered block work – although partly hidden by a large noticeboard full of business cards and other letters, pinned haphazardly. At the chair sits Gareth Jenkins.

Gareth 6ᵗʰ September 2012

Gareth thought all day about what Lisa had said about her desk. He knew that he was invisible to the men in the office. He was just an old man who came at their beck and call when they needed things moving or fixing.

He had seen Chantelle get caught up with the predatory males in B & B and had tried to warn her, but she appeared to accept that a girl in her position was treated like a decoration. Now Lisa was heading in the same direction.

He called his wife as the day was drawing to an end in the office and people were going home. 'I have something I need to attend to this evening so I'm going to be late.'

'There's nothing special on here tonight so take your time,' she replied. 'Just let me know when you leave so I can put tea on.'

He thanked her for being understanding and privately rejoiced in his luck at having such an understanding partner. *She must be due a bunch of flowers,* he thought.

He went to check Lisa's desk. He hadn't understood what she had said as the desks had front panels as far as he could remember. Hence his need to find out the truth of what she'd said.

As he had hoped there was no one left in the open plan office, and he moved quickly to look at Lisa's desk. Her's was at the end of the large room and had been subtly moved from the normal pattern so that the side under the computer faced the open aisle between the other desks. He saw that what she had said was true. He knelt down closer and saw how the front panel had been cut up alongside the two side pedestals and the middle section removed. The work was quite crude but whoever had done it had finished off the raw edge so that it didn't look wrong.

Lisa was being harassed. Maybe even Chantelle had been a victim of this and just hadn't realised.

Gareth was angry. He had a daughter a bit older than Lisa and if she had been in this position, he could imagine feeling murderous. He knelt on the floor with his thoughts in turmoil.

He calmed himself down and went to sit in a chair to think what to do next. One thing was for certain; the desk had to be fixed. He could make a fuss, but that wouldn't do any good as he could lose his job and Lisa would be left without help. The best thing was to fix the desk and see what happened.

He could fix the desk himself but decided that an outsider would be a better bet as it would be harder for the people in the office to stop. He knew a young carpenter who had done jobs for him before, and he liked him. They had first met on a building site a few years ago when the young man was starting out, and he had thought that the boy would do well.

He pulled his mobile from his pocket and rang.

'Hello Rhodri.'

'Hello Gareth. How're you doing?' The cheerful voice made it easy for Gareth.

'I need a little job doing quite quickly. When can you give me a morning?'

'Of course, Gar. A morning but no more or I'll have to break a promise.'

'It won't take a whole morning. It's simple. I need a piece of veneered board fixing across the front of a young woman's desk to stop men looking up her skirt. It has to be an outsider otherwise they will stop it.'

'Have you measured it?' Rhodri asked.

'No. You'll have to come and look to make sure that you have the right colour.'

'Okay, I'll aim for next Tuesday.'

'No problem. Thanks Rhodri.'

They chatted about what Rhodri had been doing and after they'd finished their call, Gareth rang off and called his wife. He hoped this wouldn't harm Lisa.

Tony 8th September 2012

On Saturday morning Tony was lonely and wondered about Elin, so he phoned her.

'Hi, it's me, Tony, how are you?'

'Oh hi, I'm okay.' Elin was brief.

'Can I take you for lunch?' Tony asked hopefully.

'No. I have to be in work at eleven thirty, and I don't finish till two thirty.'

'How about dinner?' Tony persisted.

'No can't do that either as I have to work from six thirty till nine thirty.'

'I suppose that only leaves tea; how about that?'

'Oh Tony! I promised Megan that I would buy her shoes this week and we have to do it today. I just can't.'

Tony could hear Karen telling him that he hated shopping.

'Elin, can I come and be the taxi for you?' There was a pause at the other end of the line and Tony guessed that Elin was talking to Megan.

'Okay. Yes. Megan says that's okay.' Elin said.

Tony nearly asked if Megan was the boss.

'Can I pick you up from the Railway at two thirty?'

Elin had got her composure back together now. Tony's call had broken in on her depression. 'Yes, please, that would give us more time for tea.'

So, Tony picked Elin up from the Railway and Megan from the house. The three set off to the shops. Megan knew what she wanted and they were quickly bought. Tony was close enough to see Elin wince at the price.

Tony suggested an old family tea room nearby. Megan replied, 'No. I don't need tea, you two go. I'm going to have a mooch around and see who I can meet.' Her mobile was in her hand and it was clear she had a meeting arranged.

'We'll be going back to the house at about five. Do you want a lift?' asked Elin.

'I'll text,' said Megan, 'Can you take my shoes home? Thanks.' She skipped off down the arcade.

'Typical,' said Elin. 'Come on let's have that cup of tea. I'm starving too.'

'Haven't you had lunch?'

'No. We were too busy today. I didn't get a chance.' The truth was that Elin hadn't had time for a sandwich in the pub.

They got themselves settled at a table in the tea shop and Tony ordered sandwiches and cake for Elin.

'You shouldn't,' said Elin. 'I can manage you know.'

'Are you sure?' said Tony. 'You look to me like you are going under. I came to ask you if I can help. Do we need to go around the supermarket again?'

'No, we're fine. I restocked yesterday.' Which was almost true. Elin had done some shopping but the prospect of buying Megan's shoes had hung like a black cloud over the shopping list.

Tony looked at her. He didn't know what to say, but he was certain that she was desperate and too proud to admit it. Their eyes met across the table as he wondered what to do, but before he could decide she burst into tears and buried her head in her hands.

He could hear Karen in his head. *'Don't say a word. Just get up and go and rub her back and wait.'* And so he did. He saw there were paper napkins in the middle of the table. One hand rubbed her back while the other reached out for the napkin. Her head rose and she took the napkin. As she leaned back, he took his hand out from behind her.

'It's okay. You can sit down again, I'll be okay.' Elin said as she pulled herself together.

'Will you? Are you sure? I came to ask you if I could help.'

The waitress came with the tea and food and laid it out on the table.

'Can we talk about it later?' Elin replied.

'Of course. I think the waitress wants to listen in!' Tony said, smiling as he poured tea and arranged the plates. Elin started into the sandwiches and they sat in silence while she ate them all. Tony took one piece of cake and Elin ate the rest. It wasn't even four o'clock and they only had cups of tea to finish.

'Can we leave Megan in town and take you home?' said Tony.

'Yes, she's got the money for the bus fare, but I have an idea she's meeting a school friend to go to the pictures. I'll text her.' Elin found her mobile phone and texted Megan.

In no time she had an answer back. 'She's set up with her friends for the evening, so I expect she'll get dropped off later. Her friends' mothers have been helping since I've been working stupid hours.'

They drank their tea. Tony paid the bill and they set off back to Elin's house. On the way Tony asked again, 'Are you sure you don't want to call in at Tesco's on the way?'

'No.' Elin said and lowered her head again. 'Yes. I can't manage anymore. Those shoes were the last straw. How do I thank you?'

'You don't have to thank me. You helped me when I was in trouble, and I like you. Shall we stop at Tesco's?'

'Yes.' Elin didn't know what to say.

As before, Tony made sure that she was well stocked up with everything and paid at the checkout. She looked small and frightened, and he didn't know what to say. They drove back to her house and unloaded everything into the kitchen. Once things were sorted out she made more tea. Tony could hear Karen in the back of his head. *Don't tell her off now. Let her get it off her chest. Just listen.'* He took his tea, led her into the sitting room, sat her down on the sofa and set a chair so he could face her.

'Elin. Can I help? Tell me about it.'

'I can't afford my mortgage, and I can't sell the house as it isn't worth enough to pay it off. Last month a puncture left me on my uppers and you had to rescue me. Now, buying that pair of shoes for Megan has used up this month's spare cash.' Elin had been hiding her worries somewhere inside and this kind man had broken her resolve and opened the floodgates. She told Tony of the disasters that had befallen her and more than once had to stop to wipe away the tears. Tony held one of her hands and listened, aware of the advice Karen would give him. Eventually Elin sat back and shuddered. 'I don't know what to do.'

'Elin, I have a friend called Liz Stephens. She's helped me a lot over the years. Why don't you let me get her to come and talk things through with you? She's experienced with these things.'

'But when can I do it? I'm either doing school work or serving in the pub.'

'Don't you have any evenings free?'

'I suppose so, but right now I have to go to work.'

'I'll talk to her and see what she suggests.'

Sonny

I'm watching Elin living hand to mouth. How does the pencil know this stuff? Since Max became a success I've never had to worry about money. There's enough for my living expenses, some to pay Gabby and some left over. Occasionally, programmes on the radio explore the lives of people where money is tight so I expect it comes from there.

Meanwhile the idea of Max getting a tan had stayed with me. I needed a break from the pressure, and I had the money. I couldn't see how

90

though. If I stopped would my followers leave me? Initially I ignored the suggestion, but it nagged at me.

Months later I was sitting with my agent.

'Sonny. I've been meaning to ask. What happens to the reject roughs?'

These submissions were not finished artwork – but they were ideas – and the next day they would be forgotten. I had kept them all.

'I've got them in a filing cabinet at home. Not well organised, but I have them all.'

'What, going back to when Max started?'

'Yes. Pretty much.' I said.

'Sonny, what are you going to do with them? You could have some gems.'

'I hadn't thought. They were rejected.'

'Have a think about it. The editor only picks the one he wants that day. It doesn't mean the others are rubbish.'

We talked some more and I went home and had a look in the file. I saw what she meant. There were some turkeys of course but there were good ideas too that had not seen the light of day. As the weeks went by it dawned on me that among the roughs there was enough material for me to be able to take time off with a bit of planning.

I start a new frame.

Lisa 11th September 2012

The next Tuesday Lisa was in the morning meeting as usual. She was wearing trousers to avoid a discussion about colours, but Guy followed her into the meeting.

'I prefer tight trousers on a girl,' he said. 'They show your anatomy better.'

She stopped at her chair to allow him to pass and he groped her. No one noticed so she said nothing and resolved to note it later. The meeting was unremarkable, but she managed to avoid getting too close to Guy on the way back to her desk – even though he followed her. She could feel his eyes on her bottom.

To her surprise, the man from the riding stables was on his knees in front of her desk with a new wooden board which he was fixing across the gap.

'Hello,' she said. 'Thank you for doing that for me.'

Before the man could speak, Guy butted in. 'What are you doing? No one has authorised work on any desks in this office. Take it away now.'

Lisa looked at Guy and said, 'I didn't think my modesty was a matter for discussion. The boss said, "item closed" so I arranged to get it closed.'

'He meant the subject was closed.' *Guy was losing it,* she thought.

'I was told to put something here to stop men looking up the lady's skirt when she's working here. It's a very reasonable idea and all the other desks have them. Who are you anyway? I have a proper order number for the work and intend to finish as I have been asked.' Lisa saw that the man was shocked by Guy's attitude.

'Who do you think you are talking to me like that? I'm a manager in this office and I decide what goes on. I don't want that board there so take it away now.' Guy stood over the man as he knelt in front of the desk. Lisa wanted to intervene but somehow the man had drawn Guy's attention.

'I take it that you like looking up skirts?' As Lisa watched, the man stood up. He was a big man at over six foot and well developed from the physical work he did. Seeing him so close for the first time, Lisa felt as if a set of prickles had gently dusted over her body. She hoped she hadn't blushed. She had a new feeling now; this would be her man. The man towered over Guy and looked down at him.

Guy said, 'Oh, do it if you must,' as he went off to his desk and the man watched him go. Behind him Lisa breathed a sigh of relief. 'Thank you for helping.'

'I can quite see why you need this fixing up. You go to the stables with him, do you?'

'Yes, I go to the stables but not with him. He's my boss. Sorry, I'm Lisa.'

'Lisa. Yes, I know, my mother talks about you. You ride Blister, don't you? I'm Rhodri Howells and Mrs Howells is my mother.'

Lisa saw Guy nearby watching this exchange. 'You'd better finish and go as I have work to do. Can I call you later?'

Rhodri looked around at the other people in the office and said, 'No problem, I understand.' He fixed the board and Lisa was able to sit down again at her desk. Rhodri cleared away his tools and swept up the small amount of dust from holes he had drilled. As he got up to go, unseen by others he deftly dropped a business card onto her desk.

'Thank you,' she said, but he left without looking back.

92

She picked up the card and just held it for a long moment. It was like her first physical contact with Rhodri. Then she recorded the events of the morning and tidied the book away.

She checked her activities log and noticed that Tony Jones had made a successful paper bet. His previous efforts had all been failures.

Before she left the office, Lisa entered Rhodri's number into her phone and once she was safe in her car, she rang him. She was unsure what reaction she would get from a cold call like this.

'Hi, It's Lisa here. You know, from the brokers this morning.'

'You certainly work in a bear pit. I wanted to thump your boss.'

'What do you know about it?' Lisa asked.

'Oh, Gareth filled me in. I've worked with him on a few sites. He's a good man.'

'I need to thank you properly; can I buy you dinner sometime?' Lisa was shocked at how forward she was being.

'You don't owe me anything. Are you riding the Saturday after next? I will be at the stables as I have a little job to do for my mother. I'll meet you and we can sort something out after your ride.'

'I didn't know you were connected to the stables until you said. I've only seen you there once.' This was a lie as Beth had told her about him.

'I've had a contract for ages where the work has to be done when the place is empty and that meant working evenings and Saturdays, but this is the last week.'

They finished the call and Lisa sat back and relaxed. At last something was going right. Even better, she could wear skirts without worrying that someone was looking up them.

During the next few days Lisa noticed that Guy was preoccupied and avoiding her. She decided that he was embarrassed about the incident with the board and regretted what he had said. She couldn't have been more wrong, and a week later at the morning meeting she had the shock of her life when someone announced that it was a black day. The men in the meeting laughed long and hard and she felt humiliated.

When she went back to her desk the board had been discreetly cut again so that her legs were in full view. She kept her cool and wrote it down. At lunchtime she told them that she was nipping out for a sandwich, and on her way out of the building slipped into Gareth's little workroom.

93

'Hello Lisa. What brings you here.'

'Hello Gareth. I never thanked you for fixing my desk.'

'You needn't worry; it's the least we can do to be civilised.'

'The thing is – last night the desk was cut again.'

'You're joking.' She saw Gareth jerk into a different level of awareness. He wavered for a time. 'You've got a problem, haven't you lass? I'll get Rhodri to fix it again.'

'It won't work, they'll just cut it again.'

'Don't worry. I'll get Rhodri to fix a sheet of something a bit more difficult to cut. He told me what happened last time, so we'll do it one evening when no one's about. You'll have to give me the keys to your desk when we do it so we can bolt behind the drawers and make it a solid job. Unbelievable.'

'Gareth, you need to keep the paperwork for the jobs so we have evidence when I go public.'

'What do you mean?'

'If I just leave, they will employ another woman and play power games with her until she leaves too. We have to fix it. But for that I need the evidence.'

Sonny

Poor girl, having to fight like that all the time. I want to help her, but at the same time I am frightened where this story is going and want to stop it altogether.

Max pops up on the side of the sheet and points a finger at me: 'You can't run away from this as well. You have to keep going till the end.'

He appears a second time, not so accusing. 'It's not all bad you know. She's met her man.'

I want to thank him for cheering me up. Max is confusing me though. This story is part of my plan to retire. But if I retire Max will finish. So what's driving him?

I carry on with a new sheet.

This is somewhere the pencil has not been before; the lobby of a modern hotel. Glass and shiny marble everywhere with a dead tree trying to be a sculpture to make it less severe. There's a sofa – one of those square low ones designed by someone who didn't want you to sit for long. Through the glass opposite the check-in desk is a bar with low tables laid out in geometric rows, each with four equally uncomfortable chairs. From speakers hidden in the ceiling plays the sort of music you would never play yourself.

The bar is quiet. Six businessmen have moved chairs to be together, which breaks up the pattern, while in another part parents are trying to control two small children while they have tea.

At a third table Elin and Liz are also having tea.

Elin 14th September 2012

True to his word, Tony had spoken to Liz Stephens and arranged for her to visit Elin. He had wanted to come as well, but Liz had sent him packing. 'This isn't a physics problem,' she had told him.

'Typical man,' Liz smiled. 'As soon as he's faced with a problem, he calls in someone else.'

'Oh! I didn't think he meant it like that. He's trying to help. He's helped me a bit already. He was nice.'

'He told me you'd helped him.'

'I suppose I did. Gave him a cup of tea. I've served him two by now if that's helping!'

'So, what did he do for you?'

'He did the shopping. Actually, he's done it twice. It was so unexpected. I don't just mean he did the shopping; he paid for it. Loads. I was worrying we would have to eat porridge for a week until I could earn a bit more.'

'How do you earn it?'

And so Liz started teasing Elin's problems out. Liz was skilled at dealing with people and Elin was soon opening up to her.

'Why are you doing this for me? You don't know me.'

'Tony's a good friend to me and he's had a very bad time. Did he tell you?'

'A bit. He didn't make a big deal of it.'

'No. Take it from me, he's had it rough. Now let's get back to you.'

'I just wish I could get some savings behind me so I don't have to keep spending money stupidly. If I had a bit more I could stock up when things are on offer. I don't think I'm too far from being balanced – I don't know though. If I had more money, I would tidy the house up a bit but I'm scared of getting into a spiral of debt. I read about someone in the paper who owed thousands just because of the interest.'

95

'You're right. There is one thing you can do. Why don't you go and talk to your mortgage company? You may be able to get a better deal, or if you explain your situation they may be able to let you have an interest holiday for a few months. Then you can build that cushion you need.'

'Will they do that? I didn't know. I'm scared to talk to them in case they start worrying that I won't pay.'

'They don't want that either so helping you is protecting them. See what they say, and if you think they are being awkward get a go-between. Come back to me or ask Tony.' she laughed. 'Although he would probably come back to me!'

'I can't keep asking you and Tony for help though.' Elin was avoiding her eyes and fidgeting. She worried that Liz could see the battle between her pride and her desperate hunt for a way out of her predicament. Elin didn't know if Liz would be able to relate to her situation.

As if reading Elin's mind Liz added, 'Getting help is not weakness. The thing about a go-between is that they don't have the same emotional commitment to the outcome of discussions, so they don't get focussed on the wrong issues. When you do it yourself it's hard to do it dispassionately and get the best deal.'

'I'll talk to them. Thank you.'

'You should do something else too; give yourself some time off. You've come tonight, can you do that every week?'

'I suppose so. What do you mean?'

'You need to get a hobby and get out of your rut, frankly.' Elin showed in her face she'd been taken by surprise.

'Go to keep fit, start swimming or go to an evening class. Do you sing? Why don't you join a choir? That way you meet people and can forget this money stuff for a few hours a week.'

'But there's Megan ...'

'From what I hear Megan is capable of looking after herself. Does she get away at all?'

'Often, now you mention it – in town with her friends – I've tried to keep her in pocket money. Now you've got me worried where she's going.'

'Whoops,' said Liz. 'Anyway, get away from your worries a bit. It'll make you feel better. And now I'm afraid I have to go.'

They got up, sorted their coats and headed out of the hotel.

'Thank you for listening to me, I do feel better honestly. I'll call the mortgage company as soon as I have a minute.'

'It's been a pleasure to try to help. Don't forget to find a distraction. I'll call you in a couple of weeks and see how it's going.'

Elin headed for her car. She wondered if Liz Stephens had been sent to check her out as she had known Tony for a long time. Was there more to this than helping her out?

Chapter 6: Late September 2012

Sonny

I wonder where this is going. But for now I'm planning my holiday. I had found I could use the roughs to build a backlog of cartoons with the editor that enabled me to get away. Then I evolved a system to keep ahead and now I no longer have the constant pressure. Slowly, I beat my depression and found time to relax and ideas for Max came easier to find.

My holidays are generally the same every time. I find a bed and breakfast somewhere in the country and spend a few days walking the area. I generally try to get away around the middle of October to take advantage of the autumn colours – and avoid the summer crowds.

I like hills and views, but I like old buildings too. Over the years I have been in a lot of country churches. Just every now and then I have come across one that has a special atmosphere of peace – better than most others – and to discover one of these is a treat.

What I don't understand is what gives one church this magic while other similar ones are ordinary. Is it the ventilation and smell? The design of the lighting and the windows? The state of the paintwork and what was built originally? Or is the pictures and clutter that decorate the walls? As I grow older my holidays have been spent trying to work out an answer to this question.

I get back to Max. The paper won't be sympathetic if their supply of Max strips dries up.

But in the strip I'm drawing, Max is talking to me with a look of contempt.

'You don't want to find the nicest church ambience.'

I want to tell him that I do. I've had many good holidays searching; away from it all in beautiful places and scenery.

'That's right. Away from it all.'

What does he mean? Why is Elsa watching me from behind him?

'You're not looking for anything.'

How can he say that? I've searched around and been to some delightful places.

'It's an excuse. You're running away. Like you always run away.'

I think of Elin and her responsibilities. How she is trying to find a way out of her predicament. I think of how Lisa is being treated, and how she is looking for a way forward.

Then I think of me and Gabby. Like Elsa she could stand and watch, not saying anything. I ran away from her like a coward. I didn't help. Max is right, I'm hiding. I can't face Max again now, so I seek refuge in the park. But as I walk away from the flat, I can't help but remember Max's words. 'You're running away. Like you always run away.' I wonder where this is going.

When I come back, I start a new frame.

Lisa 22ⁿᵈ September 2012

That Saturday Lisa's ride on Blister was everything it should have been, as Blister sensed her happy mood. The weather was cool and damp as autumn was setting in, while underfoot the ground was soft and the rain was just staying off. She didn't notice and neither did the horse – Blister sensed her mood and was full of life.

It was a different matter back at the stables though. She was impatient to meet Rhodri but there was no escaping the work of rubbing the horse down. She couldn't see Rhodri's van anywhere so she started getting nervous.

With Blister back in the stable, she put the tack away and went to find Beth

'There you are,' said Beth. 'I've a message for you.'

Her heart sank. 'What?'

'Cheer up! It's good news. Rhodri asked me to tell you that he's with his mother in the house and you should go up and join them. Did you meet him?'

Lisa ignored the question. 'Thank you, can I use the shower?' She hurried off to get changed out of the damp and rather smelly riding gear. She was annoyed as she would have taken less time with Blister if she'd known that Rhodri was here all along.

She rang the bell at the front door and Mrs Howells greeted her.

'Hello Lisa. You've no need to ring, I know you well enough now. How was your ride?'

'Blister's amazing. Have you ridden him? He's got such style and character; he beats the rest at everything.'

'He likes you,' said Mrs Howells. 'He's a bit of a handful for me. Now, do you want a coffee?' For a moment Lisa wondered whether she was talking about Rhodri or Blister.

'I'd love one. Milk, no sugar please,' said Lisa. She wondered where Rhodri was. Mrs Howells guessed her thought.

'He's finishing a little job for me upstairs. He's ordered his coffee already.'

They talked some more about the horses while Mrs Howells made the coffee. As she poured the two cups, in walked Rhodri.

'All done, Mum. You'll have to test it and see if it suits you.'

'Thanks Rhodri. I'll let you know. Now why don't you two go and sit in the sun lounge where you can get a bit of peace. I've got work to do.'

They carried their coffee to the conservatory.

They talked about where to eat and agreed on a pub close by.

Rhodri added, 'There's a gallery near the pub where they've got an exhibition of pictures by Fiona Wainhouse, and I wanted to go. You don't have to rush off this afternoon, do you? You can tell me what you think.'

'No. I've nothing planned this afternoon. Fiona Wainhouse is the one who designed the sets for the opera last year, isn't she?'

'Yes,' answered Rhodri, and Lisa was relieved that she had remembered that.

'I'm under false pretences. My van had to go to the garage and won't be back till Monday, so I was rather hoping you could chauffeur me around.'

So, Lisa took Rhodri to lunch and to the gallery where she enjoyed it far more than her limited experience of art would have suggested. Somehow or other they ended up in a restaurant having dinner together. During dinner Rhodri brought up the subject of Guy Barnes.

'Do you have to put up with that creep? He took five minutes to get right up my nose.'

'Yes. I have to put up with him but it's a constant battle. Would you believe that the board you put on the front of the desk has been cut again? I can't sit down without worrying about who's looking at what.'

'Cut again!' Rhodri was outraged. 'Did he do it?'

'How am I supposed to know? One day it was as you left it and the next someone had cut it.'

Rhodri made all sorts of threats, so Lisa calmed him down.

'Look, don't do anything until Gareth calls you again. Then you can brick the gap up if you want.'

'I don't do brickwork,' he said. They both laughed and the mood lightened again.

Later Lisa offered to run him home, but Rhodri was adamant that he would save her the journey to his flat, and that he would take a taxi.

On the pavement next to her car, she thanked him for her day and he kissed her on the cheek. She reluctantly got into the car – this marked the end of a wonderful day – but he leaned over her as she sat into the seat.

'Don't worry, I'll call you in the week.' He kissed her again.

'Thanks Rhodri, it's been brilliant.'

Sonny

This couple have cheered me up no end. The life in Lisa reminds me of when Gabby and I were first together. Gabby had a sparkle in her eye and put energy into everything she did. Like Elsa she watched a situation and contributed when she had something to say. I had learned early on to listen to what she said.

Gabby was an only child and had grown up without needing to be entertained all the time. Her parents had been alive after I left and I guess they had given her support with bringing up Jen. From the newspapers I had seen that both her parents were now dead. Her father had been a joiner and from laying floors for people his knees had been a problem when I knew him. Gabby had taken on his skills from watching him work and had a practical streak that kept our home running.

I don't know where she got her eye for colour, but she was always cleverly coordinated; hence too her skills as a make-up artist. I've been doing cartoons without colour for so long that I can imagine asking her for advice with this new project of mine – which needs a better eye for colour than mine – in the same way that she would ask me about design.

My train of thought stops abruptly as I realise I'm imagining being back with Gabby. I take the pencil and restart, careful to avoid letting Max comment.

Gareth 25th September 2012

Gareth stayed on late one evening in the office to meet Rhodri. He'd called him first thing on Monday to set up the new repair for the desk. As he expected, Rhodri rang him from outside the office at six-thirty.

'Rhodri here. The door's locked.'

'Give me a moment and I'll open it. Have you got a sheet?'

'Yes, it's heavy and I'm likely to blow away in this wind if you don't hurry,' Rhodri joshed good-naturedly.

Gareth tripped the switch for the office door and let Rhodri in; holding the door for Rhodri to bring the sheet in. Gareth could see that Rhodri had put fixings on the sheet to make it difficult to remove.

They took it up in the lift and onto the trading floor. Gareth hoped that the office would be empty but to his dismay one desk was occupied. He decided to carry on as though the job was nothing out of the ordinary.

'Have you got the desk key?' asked Rhodri.

'Here, I had it from Lisa earlier.' Gareth undid the desk locks and pulled the drawers out. He was amused to see Rhodri's business card was on top of some personal-looking stuff in one of the drawers.

They measured the sheet and drilled the holes so that the sheet could be bolted into the desk with the fixings hidden. Gareth was impressed by the preparations that Rhodri had made. The steel sheet he had chosen had a sort of plastic coating on the outside face to make it appear like a piece of wood, so it wouldn't look out of place. Along the bottom there was a thicker piece of steel.

'If someone tries to cut that they'll need a decent saw and it will be a lot harder to cut it without making a real mess. The wood was too easy,' said Rhodri.

Jeremy, the remaining worker on the floor, was now packing up to go. He came over.

'Hello Gareth, trying again I see,' he said. Gareth could see now who it was. Jeremy was about the same age as Lisa and had been in the firm about the same length of time, although he had been trading for longer than Lisa. Probably, Gareth guessed, because he was a man.

'Yes. We're trying again. Who does it? Do you know?'

'I should imagine it's Mr Barnes. He controls everything around here. He has little man syndrome.' His remark surprised Gareth. Jeremy went on, 'I watch what goes on and wonder why Mr Sullivan doesn't stop it but for some reason he won't go against Mr Barnes, even though he's the boss. I'm amazed Lisa hasn't reacted more.'

'What do you mean?' Gareth was canny enough to keep asking questions rather than venturing his own opinion. He sensed that though Rhodri carried on with fitting the sheet, he was listening intently too.

'Mr Barnes continually finds ways to belittle her. It's like she's treated as a clerk or something. This desk thing gives them a private joke. I can't understand why.'

'Why don't you say something?'

'I did. I spoke to George Nelson and he just laughed at me. He told me that women shouldn't work in a male environment and that they are there for the men. He warned me off and told me that I should toe the line or my cards would get marked. I have, although I don't like it.'

'If you think it's wrong, keep a record of those things. That's what Lisa's doing. Building a file of evidence so that when the fight starts for real, she's got some ammunition. That's where Chantelle went wrong; she had no evidence to prove anything.'

Jeremy looked surprised. As the janitor, Gareth guessed he was invisible and Jeremy hadn't thought about him.

'I didn't know,' said Jeremy. Gareth supposed that no one had told Jeremy about Chantelle, so he probably didn't know what had gone on.

'Talk to Lisa, she'll tell you. Help her. Now go on home,' said Gareth. He sensed that Jeremy was nervous about Rhodri listening into the conversation. Jeremy fled.

'I thought this desk nonsense was bad enough.' Rhodri said. 'It sounds as though she's being got at all the time. I could come in here and box some heads.'

'Cool head, lad. Lisa's pretty capable. Now let's get finished up here.'

'You know that policy notice we put up in reception last year? This company is an equal opportunities employer and all that stuff? I wonder if anyone has read it. Why did we bother?' said Rhodri.

Gareth shrugged. 'No one does anything about it. It's a bit like the hospital. The managers stick up a notice laying down some rule or other and think they've done the job, but no one actually reads them.'

They checked that the panel was securely in place and Gareth started replacing the drawers.

'Your card's in here; did you know?'

Rhodri didn't reply and their eyes met. Rhodri coloured.

'I suppose she could do worse,' said Gareth.

'Yes,' was all Rhodri could say.

'She's a very special girl in a hell hole. Don't make matters more difficult for her, or I'll come after you.'

'I won't. Honest. I just hope that this steel plate won't create a problem for her.'

They collected up the tools, cleaned away the sawdust and headed for the lift.

Sonny

The more I see of Rhodri the happier I am that he is getting on with Lisa. He got on with fixing the desk without any nonsense and has clearly made a good impression with the older man. That kind of respect does not come easily.

Lisa and Rhodri 25th September 2012

That evening Rhodri walked to the pub, where he told Lisa that his business would fold if he ever lost his licence. *How sensible,* she thought. They met outside and went in to get their drinks. As they walked over to a free table, Rhodri became aware that all the eyes in the bar were following her. She was stunning even when dressed casually.

Once they were sat down Rhodri studied the menu on the table. 'I'm starving; do you want anything?'

'No. I ate at home but don't let me stop you,' she replied. He went back to the bar and ordered. As he walked over to the bar and back, she had a chance to study him and saw what a handsome man he was. For the first time in ages she sat back into her chair and felt at ease.

She chuckled as she remembered when he had phoned. She had looked at the screen on the phone: 'Rhodri.' Her heart had lifted.

'Hello,' she had said.

'Hello you. Do you fancy a pint?'

'I don't do pints.'

'Oh sorry, I forgot that you were a proper lady.'

'If you're asking if I would like a drink in your company this evening, I shall have to check my social calendar. This evening. Laundry. Ironing. Putting the rubbish out.'

He'd laughed. 'Do you want to come for a drink?'

'Of course I do. The rest of the list is even more boring.'

So here they were together in the pub.

'Why haven't you eaten?' She asked as he sat down again. 'It's late?'

'I've been doing your job. I have to tell you something,' he started. She sensed that he was nervous.

'What?' she prompted.

'I've been with Gareth in your office fixing your desk again. We did it late to avoid that man I met before. You know, the one who comes to the stables. We've put a proper piece of sheet steel on the front of it. I hope they don't succeed in cutting a hole in that.'

'Thank you. I wonder what the animals will make of that.'

'There's more. A young man was at his desk when we arrived. Jeremy, I think Gareth called him. Gareth talked to him.'

'Yes, Jeremy sits at the next desk.'

'You've got it. He sounded as though he thinks that what you are experiencing is beyond the pale. You've got an ally there. Gareth told him to keep a record of what he sees if he wants to help you.'

'Yes, I keep a record but I've no idea how it will help because the bosses are in it together. In the end I'll have to find a new job. Jeremy's okay though, but I don't think he'll say anything because he's scared for his own position.'

The waiter arrived with food for Rhodri and Lisa saw how good it looked. She started pinching chips from him and they relaxed.

Later they both realised they had working days in the morning, so Rhodri arranged a taxi for Lisa.

'How are you getting home?'

'I'll walk, it's not far. Call me,' he said and kissed her gently. She got into the taxi and waved him another kiss, and he watched her leave.

Lisa 26th September 2012

The day after the desk was repaired Lisa got to work on time as usual; although she felt tired. She walked into the office and met Guy Barnes by her desk.

'Good morning,' he said, 'how's your armoured bunker today?'

'What do you mean?' She was avoiding getting to close to him while she took off her coat.

105

'Have a look at your desk. Not many girls in this country have to have armour plating on their desk because they are shy.'

'Item closed is the expression that Mr Sullivan used. Item closed.' She wanted to sit down but knew that he would come and stand behind her and then who knew where his hands might go.

'Whatever. The time has come for your probationary period to end, so we need to meet Bob Sullivan on the 9th October at eleven. Can you come please? Your diary is free, I checked.' This was her electronic diary in the system.

'Yes, fine. I'll be there.' Lisa hoped he would go away, and luckily someone called him from the other side of the office and he went. She rang Gareth immediately.

'I spoke to Rhodri last night.'

'There's a surprise. He's a good lad, Lisa. He's given me lots of help in the past.'

'Thank you for getting him to fix my desk. I don't know what I'd do without you.'

'You run along now and get on with your work.'

She rang off and recorded Guy Barnes' comments about the armoured desk. After a while she emailed Mike from HR and asked him if he was coming to her probationary review.

Do you want me there? he replied.

Yes, I do. Lisa sent back.

I'll come then. Do you want to tell me about it beforehand? he wrote.

No. Let it come out in the discussions. She told him where and when again.

For Lisa the morning meetings were like running the gauntlet, with Guy Barnes and George Nelson both having jokes at her expense. The remarks always went into her record afterwards.

'How's the armour drama queen this morning? Well protected? The most expensive desk in the company I should think.'

'Bob, do I have to put up with this? I thought you said the item was closed last time we spoke about it.' Lisa had appealed to Bob Sullivan at one meeting. She couldn't believe that he was so detached from the issue.

'With that piece of armour plating it certainly is now,' said Guy Barnes. He was making a bit of a joke about it, but she worried that he was making such an issue out of it that he would find a way to come back at her. Apart from George Nelson – the other team leader – the men in the room were avoiding eye contact.

Bob Sullivan had called the meeting to order, and they talked through the business.

Elin 1st and 2nd October 2012

Elin was sitting in the front room of her house and fidgeting. She'd found the phone number for the lady from the choir but hesitated about taking the plunge. Less than two weeks had passed since she had spoken to Liz Stephens, and she had the idea she should do something about finding a hobby before Liz rang back.

Her discussion with the building society had been a bit depressing. It sounded as though she would have to fill loads of forms and be interviewed before they would be prepared to talk about what they called 'her options'. Meanwhile, a colleague at the school who she had confided in had suggested that the Citizen's Advice might be able to help her too – which had been encouraging. Somehow she felt it would be wrong to go back to Liz Stephens.

She remembered the conversation with Megan when she had come home that night.

'How did it go, Mama, was she nice?'

'She was very helpful and yes, she was nice,' Elin paused. 'But somehow I sort of felt I was being interviewed for a job.'

'What job? Would it pay more?'

'No. Not a job,' Elin remembered the clarity she'd had on her way home the night before. 'More like, "Was I fit to be a friend of Tony's?" She's known him and his wife for thirty years or more.'

'Did you pass the exam?'

'Good question – I don't know.'

She had hoped that Liz Stephens's offer to ring again was a good sign. In her heart of hearts, she had felt that the advice she had received had been what she needed, so she decided to take the plunge.

'Hello, is that Betsan Adams?'

'Speaking.'

'Have you a moment to talk? It's just that I was given your name for the choir. Have I got the right person?'

'Yes, carry on.'

'My name is Elin Paterson. I used to sing many years ago but after my daughter was born, I was too busy. I thought I might try and come back to it. I also played the piano as a child so I can read music.'

'What voice do you have?'

'I'm an alto.'

'So you can read music and you're an alto. Please come and join us for a trial. A trial for you and a trial for the choir. We have to make sure your voice suits our sound and you have to decide if you like us. We practice on Tuesdays at eight in the hall, and we have the occasional concert. Can you come tomorrow?'

'Yes. Tuesdays are usually free. What sort of music do you sing?'

They discussed the choir's repertoire. Elin had heard some of the pieces being sung in the school, and Betsan Adams sounded nice. The call had been easier than she expected.

The next evening, Elin ate with Megan and explained she was off out to join a choir.

'I didn't know you sang Mama. I mean properly. I know you sang a lot of nursery rhymes.'

'You don't know me. I was going to be an opera singer and this horrible little baby came and spoiled my plans.'

'Really?'

'No. But I sang in a choir in college and thought it would be nice to get back to it sometime. I played the piano too but as we've never had room for one, I'm afraid that's gone by the wayside.'

'Who's the dark horse?' said Megan. 'I never knew.'

Elin set off to the choir with a spring in her step.

She was early. Other choir members were moving chairs and chatting. She walked to the lectern where two women were talking:

'Excuse me. I'm Elin Paterson'.

'Ah, Elin. I'm Betsan and this is Teresa. Teresa, this is Elin who I was telling you about. She's hoping to join us.'

'What do you sing?' asked Teresa.

'Alto, but I'm quite rusty I'm afraid.'

'Great. We need more altos; you are most welcome. Don't worry, if you've sung before it's like riding a bicycle, it comes back in no time. I'm an alto too. Come and sit with me.'

Elin was hugely encouraged by the welcome and followed Teresa to her seat. Teresa handed a her a folder with music. 'Here, this is for you. We ask our members to only mark scores with pencil.'

As if by magic, the chaotic chair moving and milling bodies resolved into a seated choir and Betsan addressed them.

'We are on trial to night tonight with Elin who is with Teresa and the other altos. Look after her please; we need altos!'

Elin hadn't seen Tony when he walked up to the piano from where he had been talking at the back of the hall. So, when the choir had an interval, he surprised her when he came and asked her how she was.

'I've been hiding behind the piano watching you,' he said. Elin was taken aback.

'That sounds sinister.'

Before Tony could correct his error, Teresa butted in. 'Have you met Elin? She's got a good voice and is picking up the music very quickly.'

But Elin was glad for the interruption. She was feeling a bit ambushed by Tony. Had Liz Stephens been pushing her into his arms? Was she being set up? Tony's presence in the choir was too convenient, and the meeting with Liz Stephens had been like a job interview.

Others joined in the chat to welcome Elin, and Tony was pushed away. Betsan called them all together again to carry on the rehearsal.

Tony caught Elin again as she went back to her seat.

'Will you come to the pub after so we can talk some more?' he asked.

'No. I have to work tomorrow. I need to get home.' She went back to her seat.

The choir finished their rehearsal and broke up, some heading home, some heading for a drink. Betsan went to Elin as she was starting to leave.

'Will you be joining us?' Betsan asked.

'No. I have to get home.'

'Okay, I understand that. Most of our members who work go straight home. I meant; how did it go? Will you be coming next week again?'

Elin paused. She was a bit confused about what she felt for Tony and still had an uneasy feeling about what had happened. On the other hand, she had enjoyed the evening and knew she wanted to come back. Both Teresa and Betsan had been welcoming, and she had found her voice again.

'Very likely I'll be joining you. I'd like to reflect on how the choir's schedule will fit my other commitments first though.'

'Oh good, we would so like to have you – altos who can read music are rare. We often get people who say they can sing alto and who sing everything a third below the soprano line, so please come if you can.'

'I'll try. I have evening events at the school over the next two weeks. Do you practice at half term? I'll be free from then. I usually am on a Tuesday.'

'No. Half term is left clear as quite a few members are away that week. We'll see you in November.'

Betsan thanked her again, and Elin watched as Betsan made a note in her diary. Now Elin needed to get home as tomorrow would be a long day, so without a backward glance she headed out of the hall.

She walked home humming a tune she'd learned and thinking about Tony. Having played the piano to a decent grade in her teens, she could appreciate that he was a talented player. Somehow that added to his plus points and she liked him, but she was worried that she was being herded into a corner, and she didn't like the feeling.

Sonny

I pause the pencil for a moment and reflect on Elin's confusion. I didn't think that Tony had asked Liz Stephens to check out Elin, and Liz didn't steer Elin to this particular choir, so what has happened is a surprise. Am I naïve about how people interact?

I've made a couple of false starts recently where the pencil has drawn Tony intently working at his computer. I don't understand what he's doing but the screen is always full of figures. I can't see any reason to keep these images; there's no life or action in them.

This time, when I start a new frame Tony is in the hall at the piano tidying up his papers after the practice. Standing behind him is the shadowy figure of Karen. She's often behind Tony when he's with the choir.

Tony 2nd October 2012

Tony watched Elin leave the hall. He had to collect up the scores and keep his music tidy. He remembered how he had joshed Karen for being the last out of a practice and last into the pub.

'Now you know why I was last out,' said Karen.

Tony almost turned. She seemed so real. He smiled to himself. *Touché,* he thought and went back to collecting up the scores.

'As a chat up line that one takes some beating,' Karen said. *'I've been hiding behind the piano watching you. Rather creepy, don't you think?'*

Tony squirmed at the memory. This was the first time he had encountered Elin in company, and he had botched it totally.

'She's okay you know,' said Karen. *'She's trying hard to give her daughter and herself a better life. You like her, I can tell.'*

Tony did like Elin and he was hating his total ineptitude. She had left without a word to him at the end. Would she come back? Did she care about him? He didn't know.

'I think she'll come back,' said Karen. *'She looked as though she was enjoying the singing and Betsan and Teresa were nice to her; unlike someone I know.'* As usual Karen was right as she dug away at his conscience. *'You'll have to find a way to sort that out.'*

He put away the scores and walked over to the pub, mulling over what had happened. Elin had cut him dead. No matter how he tried there was no explanation for what had happened.

As he arrived at the pub, he resolved to see if he could clear the air with Elin at the next choir practice.

Lisa 9th October 2012

At the end of the morning meeting; Bob Sullivan said to Lisa, 'We'll see you at eleven in my office?'

'Yes,' she said but no one was listening. She had no intention of being early now she had invited Mike from HR. Back at her desk she was working through her job list when the phone rang.

'Good morning Lisa.' It was Tony.

'Good morning, how are you?'

Tony and Lisa talked about the progress that they had made investing his and Karen's money. Tony was happy that Lisa was handling his work most professionally.

'Have you done any paper trading?'

'Not stocks and shares,' said Tony. 'I've had a look at the spread betting, but I'm still looking at the share data you made available to me. It's going to take a while to get my head around all the different systems.'

'Remember what I said. Only a few people make much money spread betting. Go very carefully.'

'Don't worry, I heard you.' Tony respected her advice. He couldn't argue with any of the advice she had given him about the investments he had made. They rang off and she carried on with her list.

At eleven o'clock she joined Mike from HR outside Bob Sullivan's office. She knocked and went in. Guy Barnes was already there.

'I didn't know Mike was coming,' said Guy Barnes.

'I invited him,' said Lisa. 'I need him to clarify some issues that I want to raise.' She wanted Guy Barnes on the defensive, and to her surprise Bob Sullivan appeared taken aback. But he accepted Mike's presence – which had been her biggest worry.

They sorted out their chairs, and Bob Sullivan showed Lisa that he had the assessment form in front of him; which set the agenda. Initially it was all good, as Lisa had made some of the original dormant accounts that she had been given productive again, so she was 'on track' as he put it.

She glanced at Mike from HR, guessing he must be wondering why he had bothered to come to this meeting, and hoped she could keep her nerve. She knew that there was a section on the form for her comments. Bob Sullivan was speaking again.

'It says on the form that we should ask you if you have any issues you want to raise with us before we finish the interview.'

'I'd like it noted that I have been referred to as "the little lady" on a number of occasions and in particular in front of visitors from the bank, who expressed surprise. I was expected to "play mother" and pour the coffee. I don't expect better treatment than the men, but I object to being used as a waitress.'

'Come on Lisa, you were the most junior person in the room. We had to start somewhere,' said Guy.

'If I hadn't been there it would have been every man for himself to get his own coffee, or we all would have looked after the guests. It didn't feel like I was doing it because I was junior.'

Guy was getting annoyed.

'We don't write that sort of thing on these assessment forms. You need to grow up.'

Mike from HR became alert. This is why Lisa had invited him to the meeting.

'What are you saying Lisa?' he asked.

'I thought the company had policies about diversity. Belittling women by expecting them to serve coffee goes against that policy, and furthermore I expect calling me a "little lady" falls into a category of bullying, and the company has policies about that too.'

'What action would you expect us to take?' asked Bob Sullivan.

'I don't want to be treated like this again.'

'It's a tough world. If you can't stand the stress, move on.' Guy was steaming.

'I want something on that form,' Lisa said.

'I suggest Bob writes on the form that we will review this again at your next assessment. In the meantime, I will print the relevant policies and Bob can circulate them.' Mike from HR seemed to be trying to avoid direct confrontation with Guy Barnes.

'Good suggestion,' Bob Sullivan said before Guy could say anymore. Bob filled in the form. 'Right. Is that it now?'

'No,' she said. 'I would like it recorded that I have had to arrange on two occasions to have a board put across the front of my desk to preserve my modesty. The second time was because the first one was vandalised. I should also like it recorded that I resent any reference to colour being raised in the morning meeting and ask that following this meeting, that should never happen again.'

'Get real,' said Guy. 'What sort of joke is this? I thought we were here to review her performance on the trading floor.'

'The assessment process allows me to raise any issues I have. That's what I'm doing.'

'What colour?' asked Mike from HR. 'What's this about?'

'As far as I can tell, there is a running book on what colour my underwear is. The board on the front of the desk is one part of stopping that nonsense. My desk was set up without a front so any person walking through the office can have a look underneath.'

'It's just a bit of fun. You can't seriously want that on the form as well,' said Guy.

'Guy, that's enough.' said Bob Sullivan, realising he too was complicit.

'Is this true?' Mike from HR was in disbelief. This was new to him. No wonder Chantelle had lost the plot. He wondered what she had been putting up with.

Lisa didn't answer the question; she waited to see what the two managers would say. Privately, she thought she had gone too far.

'Lisa,' said Bob Sullivan. 'I agree we should stop it. What are we going to write?'

Guy Barnes was silent at last; recognising the danger in the look Bob Sullivan had given him.

'Bob,' said Mike. 'If we're talking about sexual harassment, it has to stop now. If Lisa wants it on the form then it goes on the form.'

'Guy. Sort it please. Alright Mike,' said Bob Sullivan. 'I'll add that to the form. Is there anything else you want to raise?'

'No. Thank you,' Lisa said.

Bob Sullivan filled in the rest of the form and passed it over to Lisa to check. She read it and passed it over to Mike from HR. He read it without comment and gave it back. She signed it.

'Do I get a copy of that?' asked Lisa.

'No!' said Guy Barnes. But Mike from HR faced up to him. 'She has a right to any entries in her file; with a few exceptions.'

'I'll arrange it,' said Bob Sullivan. 'Thank you, Lisa.' He seemed quite comfortable with the things that Lisa had raised – unlike Guy Barnes. Bob Sullivan seemed almost happy with the outcome of the meeting, something which was at odds with her previous experiences.

The meeting was over, so Lisa got up and left. Mike from HR stayed behind. She wanted to hear that conversation, but she had done her bit and won the battle that needed winning.

She had a bad feeling that battles with Guy Barnes would continue. He had appeared to resent her for the whole meeting. No doubt his need to control would show up in some new form.

Mike from HR came by her desk later to give her a copy of the form. He looked at the front of her desk but was lost for words.

'Thank you for coming,' said Lisa. 'I needed you there.'

'Thank you for inviting me. Any other bombshells in your cupboard?'

'As you advised, I record every event. Mostly to do with the colour of the day and the desk. I'm afraid you'll have to find out if anything similar is happening to the women in George Nelson's group.'

'Yes, I'll do that – although Bob Sullivan should sort that out now. Keep in touch.'

Sonny

I think about my visits to the agency. Mind you, there are as many men as women there and they are very equality minded. It strikes me how old-fashioned the attitudes of the men are in the brokers. Max appears in the margin, looking smug.

'Elsa keeps me in line.'

Maybe Gabby kept me in line too. I wanted everything she wanted until it came to Max, and then I stopped listening and expected everything to be okay. Max reminds me of how a journalist at the newspaper had explained a case in a London office where a woman had taken her employer to court.

'They had one of those fancy policy statements on the wall. Remember what it said about management in that other report years ago,' said Max.

As it happens, I do remember: 'It would seem that they confined themselves to a false belief that the instruction was being implemented in spirit. Such a belief had about it little more than a pious hope and had nothing to do with good management.' The 'pious hope' had stuck in my mind after someone in the editorial office had pointed it out to me.

'Bob Sullivan isn't managing,' said Max.

'Yes, but why?'

Tony 9th October

Tony came early to the choir practice. As was his habit he sorted out the scores as Betsan had requested him earlier that day. He sat down at the piano and played the pieces that were newer to him than the others. No problems there anyhow.

The choir assembled, sorted the chairs and gossiped. As usual Betsan called them together and the rehearsal started. Tony spied over the piano expecting to see Elin with Teresa in the altos as she had been the previous week, but she wasn't there.

Karen spoke to him. *'Well, you wrecked that, didn't you? She won't come back now.'*

The turmoil that had accompanied him home the previous week re-awakened. He played the pieces as Betsan called them but without his usual extra musicality. Away off in his own confusion he failed to sense how his mood – apparent in his playing – was showing in the singing.

'Okay, we'll take a break,' called Betsan, and came over to the piano.

115

'What's wrong Tony? You don't seem to be with us today.'

'Oh, sorry, my mind was elsewhere.'

'You're right there.' Betsan was acid. 'Do you think you can join us during the second half?'

'Honestly Betsan, I'll try to do better.' Tony took the plunge. 'I was going to ask you; did Elin Paterson say she was coming back?'

'Yes, she did; after half term so gave her apologies. What's that got to do with you?'

'Nothing. I'm sorry. I'll pull myself together. What's next?' Tony looked miserable but Betsan didn't push it. He knew she had seen what he had been through. He knew too that she was no fool and would put the pieces together.

Betsan went off to resolve some other issue she was worrying about and Tony sorted his scores. Karen was behind him again.

'Another week when you say something stupid.'

He buried his head in his hands and pulled himself together. *Go away*, he thought.

'Only if you play properly,' said Karen.

So Tony focussed on Betsan and played his heart out. She turned to him and raised an eyebrow. 'Y Tangnefeddwyr' was one of the choir's favourites and this time he made sure he played it properly.

'She's sussed you out,' said Karen. *'She knows that Elin is important to you.'*

But Tony wasn't worried about Betsan. There were other gossips in the choir who might be more of a problem, but Tony didn't think that they knew enough to draw any conclusions.

'You'd better talk to Elin before she comes again,' said Karen, always practical.

Tony shuddered. When would he ever be free of Karen? He knew she was his voice of reason, but every time he heard her in his head a great well of grief opened up inside him. Why couldn't she be there for real?

Sonny

It looks to me like Tony has no idea what he has to do. I would have had no idea either. I'm married but I haven't seen Gabby for about twenty-five years, and since then I have had no involvement with the opposite sex.

I start a new frame. Today I have to make sure that there is enough backlog of Max strips to tide me over so that I can get away next week. I have some ideas from a radio show over the weekend but – as has been my habit since the idea was suggested – I have a look back at some of the rejects. Here's one the editor rejected after the talk about holidays.

Elsa is brown from her holiday and says to Max, 'Where did you go for your holiday Max?'
Max replies, 'Much Wenlock.'
Elsa says, 'Is there much in Much Wenlock?'
Max replies, 'I don't do much on holiday,' and adds: 'It puts me on edge.'

It made me laugh, but the editor didn't know that there was a Wenlock Edge so it was wasted on him. I suppose Elsa could have said, 'If you don't do much, why go to Much Wenlock.' But the pencil gives Max most of the punchlines.

When I think about it, I notice that Elsa went on holiday on her own and so did Max. They've been an item in Max's strip for as long as I've been doing it. Are they still that far apart? What does that say about me?

Chapter 7: October 2012

Sonny

My holiday has been good this year. Now I'm sitting in a church about three quarters of the way back, soaking in the atmosphere. Someone has thoughtfully put cushions on these pews to make longer sermons more bearable. It's quiet. I can hear some birds outside but otherwise nothing. There is no smell of damp; this church has been well maintained, and there are subtle signs that when the interior was painted other work minimised any ornamentation. Behind me is an oak and glass room filled with toys and books for younger worshippers, and behind that toilets and a kitchen. This church isn't a temple to the past; it's alive now.

On a wall near me is a small plaque to a Lt F Crosbie R N, killed by enemy action in 1916. He was thirty-one when he died. Nothing more. What horror brought his end? Who put it up? At that age he should have had a girlfriend or wife and even children. What happened to them that they should leave this simple memorial? Did the people who placed this here expect some traveller to gaze on it and to wonder about the stories behind it? I like reading memorials but they cause more questions than answers.

This church is light and cheerful – unlike many dark, damp and depressing others. I will come here again.

While I sit here for a few precious moments, I am able to forget the pressures in my life and feel at peace. But with this thought I am taken back to thinking about Max and what he might be doing. My mental clock is counting the days till the stock of strips for the paper needs filling up again.

My mental clock reminds me too that I must catch the bus back to where I am staying if I am to be in time for dinner. The spell is broken.

After a few days of eating cooked breakfasts I return to my drawing board. Max has to catch up. After all the walking my joints are telling me that they are not as young as they used to be. When I am at home, I don't do enough walking. I need to get round the park more regularly.

Max appears in the margin, contemptuous.

'The trouble with you is that you are bound up with self-pity.'

'What do you mean, self-pity?'

'Look it up. An excessive, self-absorbed unhappiness over one's own troubles.'

'That's not true.'

'Let's face it. You are a miserable old bloke and my royalties give you an income for life, so you haven't got any troubles.'

I put down the pencil. Max is right. What have I got to complain about?

Now I have enough Max strips and can get back to my story. I set a new sheet and pick up the pencil.

Elin 25th October 2012

Elin got a letter back from her mortgage provider, with forms and small print. After work one evening she made a cup of tea and sat down to read them. Liz had suggested that a mortgage holiday would provide her with a way of helping her money situation, and she had built up a bit of hope that this gave her an answer. Together with her visit to the choir she had started to think that things could get better.

When she read the papers laid out before her, her worst fears came back again. The company was quite clear:

'Your mortgage must be less than eighty percent of the value of your home at the end of your payment holiday.'

She knew that this was impossible and furthermore, she knew from borrowing more when her parents were ill that any changes to her mortgage would involve fees. Elin guessed that before the process started, she would have to pay for a valuation of the house.

She hunted for a ray of sunshine in the papers but came up with a blank.

Just then, Megan came in looking cheerful.

'Do you need more tea from the pot, Mama?'

Elin's head was buried in her hands.

Megan sat down next to her so she could reach the cup across the papers. Elin stopped her.

119

'There's no more milk.'

'What's this stuff?'

'I thought it might be a way of making our money situation better but it's hopeless.'

'Ask Tony, he'd love to help. Chat him up.'

Elin sobbed. 'Last time I saw him I froze him out. I thought he was being rude. Now I think it was a misunderstanding and he took it the wrong way.'

'Ring him up. Owain was like that with me but he came round quick enough.'

Elin looked at her. Her daughter never ceased to amaze her. Megan had a direct answer to everything and usually she was right. Elin didn't like the idea of sponging off Tony, but he was a friend.

Elin picked up the papers and stuffed them back in the envelope.

'We'll forget that idea. Perhaps you're right, I should be friendly to Tony.'

'You should. He didn't enjoy shopping till he met you.'

Elin was silently thinking about Tony. Megan left with her empty mug, and Elin wondered what to say to Tony. She listened for Megan going upstairs again, heard her door closing and reached for the phone.

Tony 25th October 2012

Tony was playing the piano while he tried to decide what he was going to cook that evening. He'd had enough of searching the stock market data for the day and this was his reward. He rationalised it by telling himself that he had to practice to keep up his skills.

The ringing phone broke into his reverie. He stopped and went to pick it up.

'Tony Jones.'

'Hello, err … Elin here.'

Tony was taken aback. By playing the piano he was avoiding the issue of Elin and how he would smooth out his previous ineptitude. More than once he had heard Karen telling him he needed to do something.

'Tony, are you there?'

'Yes. Elin, I'm so, so sorry. I was meaning to ring you to say sorry for my stupid remark at the choir. I was going to do it this week at the practice but you didn't come.'

'No. I couldn't. I had a meeting in school.'

'So, you're coming next week?'

'I hope so.'

'I'll see you there.'

'No. Wait. I was going to ask you to come and have some tea with me on Saturday. I'm afraid that's the best I can do between shifts in the pub. I should apologise too. I left a bit abruptly but the practice goes quite late, and I had to work in the morning.'

'So now we've both apologised. In that case I'll pick you up on Saturday. When do you get off?'

'Two-thirty. You know where I work?'

'Yes. You can come and have a cuppa here if you like. If you don't mind?'

Karen said in Tony's head, *That's pretty bold of you. Does she trust you that much?*

'I guess so. If you have enough milk.'

They both laughed and it was agreed. Tony went back to the piano and played a few bars before going to the kitchen and looking in the freezer to see which of the endless supply of cakes that Jessica gave him would suit Elin. Decision made, he tidied up and fed himself.

Elin 27th October 2012

Elin left the pub a bit flustered just after two-thirty, putting her coat on as she came. It was colder outside than she'd expected. The car park had a fair number of cars in it. To her relief Tony was there and drove over to pick her up. Her lunchtime had been hectic with no time to eat. For a change the tips had been quite good, but now she was starving. She'd had little breakfast as she and Megan had run out of essential food, especially – and ironically, considering her conversation with Tony a couple of days earlier – milk. Now she had agreed to spend the afternoon with Tony, she would be short of time to shop.

'Hello. Thanks for picking me up.'

'My pleasure. Are you alright to come back to our house?'

'Of course.'

Tony drove them to his home while Elin wondered why he had said 'our house'. She was regretting this arrangement already. She sensed that although they had apologised on the phone to each other, it was unfinished and the silence in the car as Tony drove underlined it. She had a huge uncertainty about the nature of their relationship. But so far he had been a perfect gentleman, and she had to admit that the visits to the shops with him had helped her over the last two months.

They drove into the drive of a modern house among others of a similar age, although they were old enough to have established trees and bushes. To the right of the house there was a car parked in front of a garage. The house itself had big windows and to Elin it felt welcoming. The autumn leaves had mostly been cleared up but there were some blowing around in little flurries along the tarmac of the drive.

'Is someone else here?' she said.

'No. Why do you ask?' Tony replied.

'It's just there's a car here.' Elin knew this was wrong as soon as she said it. Tony had paused.

'It's my wife's car. My son uses it but he's away.'

Elin touched his arm before they both got out and let Tony lead her to the front door.

As she stood in the hallway, Tony took her coat and carelessly hung it on the bottom of the bannisters. She took in a sense of neatness and could tell that the watercolours were of local scenes – even in the dull autumn light from a window by the front door. Straight through from the front door she could see the kitchen as that door was ajar. To the right was a closed door and the staircase.

Tony opened the door to the left and led her into what she supposed was the sitting room.

'Have a seat while I put the kettle on,' he said.

Elin didn't sit immediately. Waiting alone in this room was wrong in the context of the unresolved nature of their relationship. As she looked around at the two pianos and the music on the shelves, she also had a strong feeling that this room was stamped with another personality. She sensed that she shouldn't be here on her own. Turning away from the pianos, she saw a small table over by the front window with some family photographs in frames. The largest frame held a picture of a striking woman smiling at the camera. Instinctively she guessed this was Tony's dead wife. She wanted to pick it up and study it but didn't want to be caught by Tony holding it.

As a child she had played the piano seriously but had given it up. She walked over to look at the score neatly placed on the open piano, ready to play. 'Anfonaf Angel'. This was a new piece to her, although she remembered that the choir had sung it on her first outing there. *When she and Tony had got it wrong somehow,* she thought.

On an impulse, she picked out the notes of the melody on the piano as Tony came in with a big tray with the mugs, teapot and an un-iced chocolate sponge cake.

'Sorry, do you mind ...' she tailed off. *He does mind; musical instruments can be very personal,* she thought. *I should have asked him first. Why do I keep doing this wrong?*

Sonny

The pencil stops for a few moments while I take in this scene. When the picture restarts, the ghostly figure of Karen is sitting at the other piano.

Tony 27th October 2012

Even a few notes on the piano – picking out the tune that Karen had left him – brought Tony up with a jerk. He was getting better at dealing with the random grief that hit him when he least expected it; brought on by a sound, a smell or a view. He put the tray down on the table.

'What are you doing? How dare you bring her into my living room and let her play your piano? And that tune,' Karen filled his head. Also, Elin had played his piano and not the other one. Tony was acutely aware that he had brought a woman into the house unchaperoned. His father would have been shocked. *Well, she's here now,* he thought.

'You don't take sugar, do you?' said Tony. For him, Karen was filling the room. *'She remembered how you took your tea. Didn't she?'* And he could see her sitting at the piano, facing away from him like that sad time when she wouldn't look at him; full of grief.

'Are you all right?' said Elin. Tony was going through the motions of pouring the tea like a puppet. He pulled himself together.

'Yes. It's that tune, it has memories.' *'Damn right it has, I left that score for you,'* said Karen.

'Oh, I'm so sorry.'

'Never mind. Why don't you have a piece of cake?'

'Yes, please.'

'It's one of Jessica's – my daughter. She's worried that I will starve living alone like this so she makes me cakes, but I don't eat them and they fill my freezer.' Tony felt he was rabbiting on to fill the space created by the tension in the room. *'Shut up you stupid man and get on with it. Get her out of my room.'* He cut a piece and handed it to Elin.

He watched to see if she liked it and was surprised how quickly it went.

'Tony, you idiot. She's starving and needs more than cake.' Karen's voice had changed to one of concern. Tony knew she had never held onto a grudge for long and was relieved that the voice had changed.

'Elin, I'm so sorry. I should have made you a proper tea. Have you had lunch even? I should have asked.' *'Too right.'*

Elin looked at him.

'No, I didn't have lunch. I hate to admit it, but I'm starving.'

'Take her to the kitchen, feed her properly and get her out of my living room. Don't worry, I'll stay in here.'

Tony picked up Elin's mug and put it back on the tray, desperate now to get away from Karen.

'Come on, let's go to the kitchen and you can have a proper meal. There's no rule that says you have to have the cake after the sandwiches.'

'Are you sure?'

The kitchen was neat and tidy and had a small breakfast table with two chairs against one wall.

'It's no problem, sit you down there. As I said, I've got too much food because Jessica worries about me!'

Tony opened the fridge to see what he had to make a sandwich, but there was a shepherd's pie that Jessica had given him when he had helped with the children on Thursday.

'There's a pie here, how does that suit you? Come on, I'll heat it in the microwave and have an early supper with your late dinner.' Tony started warming the pie and fetched some frozen peas so that there was a bit of green. He was relaxing now he was active and out of the sitting room.

'You don't have to do this,' said Elin.

'I do. It's nice to help and truthfully, it's nice to have someone to have a meal with. I sometimes miss meals for that reason. You don't mind eating in here, do you?' He switched the oven on to heat the plates, laid the table and measured out the peas. When he turned around Elin was quietly crying.

124

'Now what have I done?' he said. 'It's here anyway.'

'Oh Tony, I'm sorry. Life is so hard; every bill is a worry and everything seems against me. Liz Stephens offered me a lifeline with the mortgage company but it won't work because of their rules. Then I come here and look at you, helping at every turn.' She took a tissue from a box on the sideboard.

'You helped me when I was stuck,' he said. Karen was in his ear again. *'Hold her hand, Tony. She needs comfort.'*

Waiting for the ping of the microwave, Tony sat down opposite Elin and took her hand in both of his.

'How bad is it? Are you in debt?' asked Tony, gently.

'No – apart from the mortgage but that's a fluke. If I have an extra bill then I'm in trouble.'

The microwave interrupted them. Tony moved the pie to the oven and heated the peas. He brought a water jug and was about to offer her water, but she stalled him,

'No, it's okay. I have tea, thanks.'

'Thanks for reminding me. That's the story of my life; forgetting mugs of tea until they've gone cold.' They both laughed.

Tony served the pie when the peas were ready and they talked about the choir. He explained how it was Karen's thing, but that he had reluctantly taken it on after she had died as the choir had been struggling. 'I suppose I was too and Liz suggested it. I quite enjoy it now as it gets me out.'

They finished their plates, and Tony cleared them away and put the sponge cake back in front of Elin.

'I couldn't possibly,' she said and burst out laughing. 'I'd love a piece. Funny thing, someone's been at it already!'

Tony gave her a new piece and took one himself. Karen was in his ear again. *'Tony, she was starving. I bet there's no food in her house till the end of the month. You have to take her to Tesco when you take her back.'*

As they were heading back to the car, Elin was thanking Tony profusely. He said nothing for a while as he drove to Tesco but then started:

'Elin, I am sorry about being a bit dull in the choir the other day, please do come along. I understand if you have to head home straight after because you are working the next day.'

125

'Tony. Where are you going?' Elin asked.

'Tesco. You need to stock up. Jessica made that pie. You can't rely on me to produce food for you. You'll have to make some of your own. What's Megan eating?'

'Megan's eating me out of house and home. But Tony, you don't have to do this.'

'I do. It's my pleasure.'

They did the shopping, and Tony took Elin home where Megan came out and helped empty the car and put everything away. Tony saw her looking at him and Elin with a strange expression, and he wondered what she was thinking.

'Oh golly. I have to go back to the pub. I'm on again this evening,' said Elin.

'I'll drop you. I have to go that way to get home.'

'I usually walk. But thanks.'

Tony dropped Elin off where he had picked her up earlier in the day and as she left the car, she squeezed his hand on the steering wheel and said, 'Thank you, Tony. I don't know what I would do without you.'

Before he could reply, she dashed into the pub.

He drove home thinking what a good afternoon it had been. Karen appeared there beside him. *Tony Jones. Are you sure you know what you are doing? You can't play at this you know. She's a grown woman with plenty of issues, and she doesn't want you as a problem too. You've taken her to Tesco three times now. You've got to decide how far you want to go.'*

But Tony was wondering about the piece of music again. 'Anfonaf Angel'. Was Elin the angel that had been sent?

Sonny

Elin and Tony are settling into being friends while Karen is asking Tony searching questions. I've had a holiday. I'm happy with these two. Life is looking up.

The pencil has drawn some more sessions with Tony at his computer. There are differences in these scenes due to the time of day or the clothes Tony is wearing. I was on the verge of throwing the work away – something I rarely do – but after one of these false starts Max appears in the margin. As usual he has a look of despair about how thick I am being, but I can't understand why.

126

'You have to keep them, they're important.'

'Why?' I want to say.

'You'll have to wait and see.'

This time when I restart, the pencil sketches an office that I have not seen before. It's a rather depressing place with tired paint and several old wooden desks in a large room lined with filing cabinets. After a while I recognise Cheryl, the PC. She's just coming on shift.

Cheryl 9th November 2012

'Cheryl, we've had a report of a predator in the park. There's a young woman downstairs having a cup of tea in the canteen who would like to make a statement. Can you take it please?' Mike Townsend, her sergeant, handed her a report form. 'Call me if you need help.'

Cheryl made her way down to the canteen. As the sergeant had said, a woman was sitting off to one side with an empty cup of tea. She went over and dropped the papers on the table.

'I'm Constable Cheryl Carter and I've been asked to talk to you. Do you mind if I get myself a cup of tea first? Do you want another one?'

The woman nodded. Cheryl picked up the empty cup and fetched two cups of tea.

'Sugar?' Cheryl knew that starting a conversation was easier if you stayed off the point.

'No thanks – actually, can I change my mind? Yes please.'

'Here. Barbara is it?'

'Thanks. Yes, but everyone calls me Babs.'

'Right, Babs. Do you have somewhere you have to go?'

'No. I don't start till later – I do shifts in the bakery.'

'So, we aren't in a rush?' said Cheryl.

'No. But I would like to be out of here soon as it makes me nervous.'

'Helping the police with their inquiries. It's okay. Please feel relaxed. You can walk out of here at any time. All I have to do now is hear your story and we'll decide what to do next.'

'I was out late after the shift finished at ten last night. I take Beaker – my dog – to the park; I know it's closed but he needs a run if he's shut in all afternoon. My flatmate feeds him and lets him out for a short while at about six, but he wants more than that and I've been taking him for years. I'll have to think about it now though.'

'What happened?'

'We slipped into the park as usual, and I headed up the path to the top of the hill as I like to look at the view while he runs around. Most of the time he doesn't go that far from me, so he's sort of company.'

'What sort of dog is he?'

'A mongrel – without the intelligence bred out of him. Beaker's a mix of a Jack Russell and a bigger dog; some kind of hound. Anyway, last night he followed a scent he liked for longer than usual and I couldn't hear him. Before I called, a man appeared but I don't think he knew that my dog was with me. He was friendly, but I was wary. We've been warned, haven't we? We discussed the lights of City you can see from up there, which building was which and the like. Then he said it was a cold night out and asked would I like a nip from his hip flask'.

'Did you drink?'

'No. I don't ever drink spirits as they don't agree with me. I suppose we'd been there about ten minutes, with him standing beside me looking towards the centre of City, when he moved a bit closer and I started to wonder if this was a sensible place to be. I couldn't see him properly and got frightened.'

'It's okay, take your time. It can be hard going back over things, and I expect you are blaming yourself for being a fool. Don't. It's non-productive.'

'Yes, sorry. Anyway, I decided I should head home and get away from him but before I could do anything, he grabbed my arm. I don't know what the man intended but Beaker must have come back quietly. He must have sensed that I was frightened. When the man touched me, Beaker let out a ferocious growl. The man let go and moved away from me saying, "no, no, no," or something like that.'

'Beaker was pretty well hidden in the dark and so the man didn't know what was out there. It was calm and cold with no moon, so Beaker could have been a Rottweiler for the noise he made. I'm so proud of him. He's never made a noise like that before.'

'What can you tell me about the man?'

'It was dark. I don't know. He was the same height as me but that's all I know. Oh, and he had gloves on.'

Cheryl asked her for any other details she could think of. Among her papers Cheryl had a six-inch scale map of the park, and she took Babs along the route she had taken and where she thought the man had come from – and gone to. She wrote up Babs's statement and asked her to check and sign it.

'We may have to talk to you again. We are grateful that you have come and talked to us today. For now, you can leave. I'll see you out. You'll be fine. Will you be okay getting home?'

'Yes, it's only a short step.'

Cheryl saw her out and went back to the office.

'Sarge, I've got a statement, but she didn't see anything. She was lucky her dog frightened him away.'

'Where is she now?' asked the sergeant.

'I sent her on her way. I thought I had everything.'

'You'd better run after her and fetch her back then; we've got another body.'

Cheryl's hand went to her mouth as she gasped. But she saw the concern in his eyes.

'You're kidding me. I don't believe it.'

'Yes, it's real. Go quickly, she's a key witness.'

Sonny

After the last few scenes where Tony's friendship with Elin has survived a little hiccup, and I thought Lisa had got Guy sorted out, this latest event in my novel has given me a scare. Something could happen to any of the women. Apart from Lisa and Elin, there is also Jessica, Megan and Cheryl. I'm almost scared to carry on as I have no idea where this story is leading, and I don't want a bad outcome for any of them as they are becoming my friends.

I leave it for almost two weeks with all the worry of what might happen, and when the pencil restarts, Lisa is at her desk.

Lisa 21ˢᵗ November 2012

Lisa was recording her experiences in her little book more and more. Since her meeting with Bob Sullivan, Guy Barnes and George Nelson seemed to have developed some kind of competition to see who could get their hands on her more. Just seeing them made her nervous and she had to manage her moves about the office to avoid them, especially when they felt unwatched – at least by anyone who mattered. The staff on their two teams appeared uninterested in her plight, and Lisa suspected that there were implicit threats that any comment would have consequences for the individual concerned.

One morning she had greeted the receptionist cheerfully, walked straight into the lift and found herself facing Guy Barnes. In the limited space she had available she stepped back only to hear George Nelson wish her good morning and place his hand firmly over one of her buttocks.

'Good morning,' said Guy Barnes, stepping closer and putting a hand on her breast. She froze, paralysed and somehow unable to think. Why did her body always react this way? She was utterly trapped. The lift seemed to take forever.

'Well Lisa, I must say, we enjoyed this ride,' said Guy Barnes as the doors opened and the two men stepped away from her. Lisa said nothing and walked to her desk. As she filled her little book, she understood how Guy Barnes had misinterpreted her freezing up and her lack of objection to their behaviour as tacit approval – or even enjoyment – as he had said. She felt a shudder of hate and discomfort. But she didn't know what to do to stop them; knowing that Guy Barnes would belittle her for being a little girl in a man's world. 'Can't you take the pace?' she could almost hear him saying.

Her body was developing its own reaction, going completely still. *Like a rabbit caught in headlights,* she thought. *When did that start?* Even back in September she had been relaxed with Rhodri and took comfort in holding his hand when they were out, but now she was starting to avoid even that.

This morning Guy had called a meeting to discuss some changes to procedures and – as was the usual for this type of meeting – tea, coffee and biscuits were provided at the back of the room. Lisa sat at the end of the table with her back to the door, with Jeremy to her right. The table had been moved over to enable the use of the electronic projector and a flip chart, so Jeremy's back was quite close to the wall.

Frank came in a rush. He usually was last in.

'Sorry I'm late,' said Frank, pushing past Jeremy to get to a free chair.

Frank completely misjudged how small the gap was and as Jeremy tried to move to make more space, Frank spilled most of his coffee over Jeremy's shoulders and back.

Jeremy screamed and leapt from the chair, ripping his shirt off to try to remove the hot liquid from his skin. In a moment he was standing naked

130

to the waist towelling himself off with the remains of his shirt. Lisa was left looking up at the tight six pack and the chest muscles perfected by hours in the gym. She gasped at the speed it happened.

'Sorry, I'm so sorry,' said Frank.

'Can you find a shirt and come back please? Sit down Frank, before you do any other damage. The little lady will get you a new cup.' Guy was all business and efficiency.

As the meeting finished and everyone was standing up, she was next to Guy with his evil smile. 'That must have been a wonderful experience for you seeing that magnificent body so close. You gave quite a gasp. Did it make you wet?'

The remark was too unexpected, and in her confusion it took her a moment to understand what he had said. She shuddered.

'You don't need to say anything. I understand,' he said, laughing.

She went back to her desk and filled in the little book about having to get a cup of tea for Frank; only then realising that Guy had called her the little lady again. Her contributions to the meeting were clearly going unheard.

Chapter 8: Christmas 2012

Sonny

When I start again the pencil draws Elin's kitchen. She is unsettled, flitting around moving things and then moving them back again.

Elin 20th December 2012

Elin was at home on Thursday evening. She was expecting Megan back; who had refused a lift home so that she could attend some event to do with Owain's rugby club. Megan had promised she would be on the bus at ten past six and Elin could see it was later than that, which was worrying her. Megan usually texted when she was late, but she was growing up and had recently become attached to Owain.

She automatically made another mug of tea and thought gloomily about Christmas. There was no plan at the moment and she didn't know what was going to happen. She hadn't even enough money to have extra food for the next week, as they were approaching the end of the month again and things were tight as usual. She stood clutching her mug of tea. What she really wanted was for Megan to come home so that she didn't feel lonely.

The bus would have dropped Megan at the front of the house, but Elin could hear excitement at the back of the house and there were voices. She instinctively knew it was something to do with Megan, as the neighbours were rarely active at this time of the evening.

She got up and opened the back door. Megan was standing there with a great box with Christmas wrapping paper on it. Elin could see someone else behind her, so she stood back as the words of reproach she had prepared died on her lips.

'Hello Megs. What's going on?'

Megan dropped the box on the table, and pushed it forward to make room for the second one that Owain was bringing in.

'Noswaith dda, ('Good evening,') Mrs Paterson. We've brought you a Merry Christmas!' Owain said. She knew he played rugby successfully but she had never been this close to him before. He was as tall a man as she had ever met and unnaturally wide, but so was his smile whenever she had seen him. With the two boxes on the kitchen table, and now Megan and Owain, the kitchen was full.

'How did you get here?'

'My Mum brought us. She had to, to carry this lot.'

'Is she coming in? Do you need a cuppa?'

Unasked, Megan filled the kettle and switched it on.

'I don't know. I'll go and ask her.' Owain vanished out the back door.

'Now Megs, tell me what's this stuff? Who's going to pay for it?'

Megan came face to face with her mother and took a hand. 'I'm sorry Mama. I wasted some of my money on the raffle at the bazaar, but I won it! It says it's everything we need for Christmas dinner – including the crackers. It also says we should unpack it immediately, as some of the contents need refrigerating.'

Elin sat down. She was confused by the turn of events. Only minutes ago she had been worrying about Megan as well as how she was going to pay for food for Christmas. Now the kitchen was full of food and people.

Owain's mother came in with the great bear that was her son, who filled the doorway behind her. 'Looks like Megan was the lucky one this year, right enough. I hope you haven't done too much food shopping. Those hampers are filled to the top.'

'Come on now, who wants a mug of tea?' said Megan, beside the now boiling kettle.

'We should be getting back – but go on, it's Christmas,' said Mrs Lloyd.

'It's only us at home Mum so there's no rush.' Owain was happy staying near Megan, that was obvious.

Tea was made and so Megan began unpacking the first hamper. All sorts of nuts, mandarin oranges, mince pies, and a Christmas pudding came out; along with two bottles of wine, liqueur chocolates, candles and crackers. There were even Christmas paper table napkins. Elin watched in disbelief. There was enough here for at least six people. The rest of the food was in the other hamper – the whole main course. Even some smoked salmon for starters and sheets of paper setting out how it should be prepared.

'Who's going to eat all this?' Elin asked.

'You, me, Owain and Mrs Lloyd. And Mrs Lloyd can invite her Gary.' Megan said.

'My Gary's invited already,' said Mrs Lloyd. 'He'll do what he's told.' Her Gary was a constant partner but had never moved in with her and Owain.

'That's five,' said Elin. 'Where can we sit down? We won't be able to cook in this kitchen and sit at the table, it's too small.' She was looking at how Owain was filling one end of the room on his own.

'Our house isn't any bigger either,' said Owain. 'We haven't got a dining room.'

But Elin's mind was elsewhere. She'd like to invite Tony to pay him back for his kindnesses, but she didn't know how to do it. That would be six. They'd have to find a way. She didn't want to say anything to Megan till she had thought this one out.

'Megan and I will sort it out,' she said and let the conversation move on to other news that had come from the bazaar. Megan was full of who was going with whom, but also wanted to plan when she could see Owain over the holiday period.

'I hope someone is going to get some of their homework done before their exams in January,' Mrs Lloyd said and winked at Elin.

Elin 21ˢᵗ December 2012

The next night was the choir's big Christmas concert. Elin decided that this would be her chance to talk to Tony about what he was doing for Christmas, and to invite him to join Megan and her.

But what with one thing and another she got to the concert just in time to take her place. She saw that Tony was busy with his music and talking to other people, and she couldn't see how she was going to catch his eye.

She made cups of tea for herself and Teresa at the interval because the singing was making her thirsty. The hall was warmer than usual, filled with the choir and the audience. By the time she started looking for Tony he had disappeared to talk to Betsan about encores or something. This was making her worry more about what he would say.

Fortunately, there were pieces that she enjoyed during the second half of the concert, so her worries were drowned by the needs of the singing. As Tony had said to her a fortnight before the concert, 'The audience don't appear to enjoy the concert but demand lots of encores. I've never understood it.' She could see what he meant as the evening finally drew to a close.

Afterwards, Tony was busy again clearing up the music and making sure that it was kept as it should be. The hall was almost empty by the time he was finishing, and other people had had their little chats with him. *No more excuses,* she thought and went over to join him.

'I bet you're tired after that,' she said.

'Strange,' said Tony, 'but I find playing the piano energising. Tomorrow I'll be tired but right now I'm fired up. How are you?'

'Good. I preferred the second half to the first, and I see what you mean about the encores now.'

'Yes, that is a bit mad. Are you coming to the pub?'

'Yes, quickly. I've no work tomorrow; that's what I wanted to talk to you about. I have to sort out Christmas and I wondered what you were doing. You've been very generous to me over the last few months and I should be paying you back. What are you doing on Christmas day?'

Tony 21st December 2012

Tony wasn't sure what he was doing for Christmas. Last year he had gone to stay with Jessica to get away from the newly empty house, but this year Jessica was taking her children to David's parents. His plan had been to stay at home, and Matt was going to join him with his Natasha. But a few days previously Matt had called him.

'Hi Dad. I'm afraid I've got some bad news.'

'What's that?'

'Tasha has arranged for us to spend our Christmas in Southern Spain. She didn't know that you would be home alone and went and booked it before I could talk to her. I hope it isn't too late for you to arrange something.'

'I'll work it out. Have a good trip.'

'I'll bring Mam's car back after the holiday. I've got a new contract now and I'll have a car or van with that. I might even have a Christmas present for you then!'

Since the call Tony had kept himself busy with the concert.

So, Tony replied to Elin. 'I've no idea.' He stopped what he was doing and sat down, so Elin could come and sit by him.

'What about your family?' she asked.

'Last year I went to Jessica's and Matt joined us there but this year they've gone their separate ways. I've been avoiding thinking about it to be honest.'

'Well you must come to us. We'll wine, dine and entertain you – at least Megan and Owain will.'

'Who's Owain?'

'Megan's boyfriend. It's got more serious recently.'

Tony looked at her and saw how eager she was. Karen said, *'Go on Tony; don't dither, she's trying to be nice to you.'*

'I'd like that,' he said. 'You'll have to tell me what to bring. Or should we go round Tesco tomorrow and make sure we have everything?' As he said it, he heard Karen again. *'You stupid man. She's trying to pay you back.'*

'No,' said Elin, 'Megan and I will do it as our treat. In truth, Megan's done it already. She's won Christmas dinner in a raffle, and we need someone to share it with. Owain and his mother – and probably his mother's boyfriend Gary – will be there too.'

'Thank you. I'd love to come. Gracious, six of us, and I hadn't expected more than me. How nice of you.'

'Yes, six of us. It's going to be a bit of a squeeze. Owain is huge!'

'You don't have a dining room, do you?'

'No. It'll be a scrum. Cooking and eating in the same room with six of us will need a bit of planning. I may have to ask you to bring a couple of chairs.'

'No problem.'

The caretaker's voice broke across their discussion as some of the hall lights went out.

'I'm locking up. Do you want to spend the night in here?'

Tony and Elin grabbed their things and headed out. As they were going Karen was talking to Tony. *'Tony, why don't you invite them to our house? There's plenty of room there and the dining room is never used now. They can cook in our kitchen.'*

'Elin, I have a dining room I never use. I could bring chairs but why don't you come to my house? There's more space, and you can bring the food and cook it.'

Elin 21st December 2012

This was an option that hadn't crossed Elin's mind. She had never seen Tony's dining room. But she had been struggling with trying to work out how to fit six people into her kitchen and cook, or the alternative which was Christmas dinner on people's knees in her sitting room. It was a sensible solution but the idea was too sudden for her.

'But Tony – think of the mess that will make, and we'll be cooking on a cooker we don't know and won't be able to find anything.'

'If it's like last Easter when the family came, you'll help with the washing up and I won't be able to find anything after you've all gone.'

They laughed. 'Anyway,' said Tony, 'sleep on it. You don't have to decide tonight. See what Megan says and call me in the morning. Now let's go and have a sing song in the pub.' Tony took her arm and they walked the hundred yards to the pub. This would be the first time that Elin had done this after a choir evening.

'Sing song? I thought we'd had the concert.'

'You'll see. They'll have me playing the piano again, so this may be a mistake. I'm going to have to play for the rest of the evening. There's no need for you to stay till the bitter end; just go home when you've had enough and call me in the morning.'

As they walked into the pub – as Tony predicted – a voice said, 'Here he is. Come on Tony, we need you at the piano.' So, Elin lost him for the rest of the evening; but before she had a chance to think Teresa grabbed her and took her to the bar. 'What do you want?' she asked Elin.

'You don't have to do this,' Elin replied.

'I do. You got the tea, and I want a word. We've never had a chance to chat. What'll it be?'

'A pint of lemonade would be lovely. My throat needs it.'

Tony had started playing some of the songs that the choir knew and many responded by singing, but when Teresa came back from the bar with Elin's lemonade they went and sat away from the piano so that they could talk. They talked about the concert and how it had gone, but Elin sensed that Teresa wanted to change the subject.

Quite suddenly Teresa asked her: 'Are you and Tony an item?'

The question – out of the blue – took Elin by surprise. *Were they an item?* She hadn't thought about it, trapped as she was in the private hell of her finances. She decided to hedge her bets.

'What an idea. I've seen him about five times; mainly at the choir. I met him completely by accident when his car broke down outside my house.'

Elin looked at her afresh. Was Teresa competition? While they'd been talking, she'd seen how Teresa watched Tony as he played.

'You always have a word with him at practice. I was being nosey.'

'He's the only person in the choir I knew when I joined, so he's a friendly face to me.'

'I wondered what you knew about him. He's had a rough time for the last couple of years and none of us want to see him hurt.'

You don't know what my life's been like, thought Elin. *At least Tony has understood that.*

While they had been talking there had been a pause in the singing. Elin could only see Tony if she half turned around and that was a bit pointed, given the conversation she'd just had. She didn't know what to say to Teresa.

Tony started playing again, and this time Elin felt a bit of a reaction in the room. Teresa looked up at Tony with a start.

'What? What's happened?' Elin asked. Teresa said nothing.

Tony was playing 'A Nightingale Sang in Berkeley Square.' Elin didn't see anything odd about it to start with. Some people were singing it softly or humming, but this was quiet compared to the singing from the choir's repertoire. The atmosphere in the pub was transformed from the rowdy to the romantic. Elin knew from Teresa's reaction that she hadn't seen this before.

Tony was sending her a message.

The piano moved on without a pause to 'Some Enchanted Evening'. The soft singing in the pub carried on; no one daring to let their voice be heard above the others. Elin was driven back to Teresa's question. 'Are you and Tony an item?' The gesture Tony made had swept her away with the magic of the moment. And it was for her. She'd never had a message like this before and sat totally still; terrified that moving would break the spell.

Tony 21st December 2012

At the piano, Tony was surprised by the reaction in the room to his change of mood. As he came to the end of the piece he was tempted to run on into 'There's a Place for Us'. But Karen was there as usual. *No. You've sent a powerful message, don't overdo it.'* He ended there and waited. Spontaneous applause came from the crowd, and he moved on to play a medley of Christmas songs; with which everyone joined in loudly.

At the end of one song – while the next was being chosen – Tony looked across to where Elin had been sitting and could see that both she and Teresa had left. He hoped that the morning's phone call brought the answer he wanted.

As he left the pub another thought struck him. Karen's voice had changed its attitude. She was encouraging him now whereas before she had been defending her space. He wondered what it meant.

Sonny

Tony seems to me to be accepting that Karen is no longer with him and is becoming able to look forward to having a new friend. I'm relieved about this change. But this scene has reminded me that I will be alone for Christmas.

I take up my pencil again to see what else is going on in the lead up to Christmas. I draw Lisa in a taxi dressed up to go out, but she doesn't look happy.

Lisa 21st December 2012

Lisa sat in the back of the taxi as it parked on the side of a busy street in the middle of City. When the whole subject of the staff Christmas party had come up she had stayed quiet and listened, all the time thinking about ways she could avoid going. She guessed that an evening out with Guy would be a trial and was having enough harrassment in the office without putting herself in a position where it could be worse. Then Bob Sullivan had spoken to her one day where others were listening.

'Lisa, I hope you will be able to come to our Christmas function. I'm always very keen to see members of my groups getting together out of work. It particularly helps the younger and newer members get to know people they don't speak to much in the office.'

It had caught her by surprise. 'Of course. I'm looking forward to it.'

Somehow her answer had committed her, and she hadn't been able to find a convincing excuse. She had told herself that for the good of her career, she couldn't step too far out of line. But now – for the umpteenth time – she wondered whether this was a mistake, and whether she should ask the driver to take her home again. But they'd arrived and the cab driver wanted his fare.

'Can I take your card please?' she said. 'I'll call you when I need to go home.'

'What time will it be love? It gets busy at this time of year with office parties and that.'

'That's where I'm going. I'll be finished by about eleven. Can you come back here then?'

'Better you give me a call or text about ten-thirty and I'll give you a time.'

'Thanks,' she said, taking the driver's card and putting it in her bag.

She walked along the street to the restaurant where the office had decided to have their Christmas dinner. She had big misgivings about this, as Guy Barnes had told her in no uncertain terms how he expected her to 'Strut your stuff on the dance floor with me'. She wanted to avoid that at all costs; guessing that he would prefer a slow number where his hands could go for a wander.

She pushed her way into the restaurant, gave up her coat and headed into the private dining room. She disliked the low ceiling and feeling of claustrophobia that the low mood lighting gave the room. She stood for a moment in the doorway as her eyes adjusted.

'Hi, what can I get you?' asked Jeremy, to her great relief. She had thought about this and decided to avoid strong drinks and stay on water while eating. But she would have something to start with.

'Can I have a bottle of Becks please?'

She followed Jeremy to the bar, sensing he had approached her out of his understanding for her need for protection in this predatory crowd.

At the bar Jeremy was served by a mixed-race barman. Lisa watched. The barman was obviously gay, but she saw him give Jeremy a look and guessed that the barman somehow knew that Jeremy was gay as well. She recognised the danger to Jeremy that he could be outed by some casual comment by the barman, and she saw how quickly Jeremy moved away from the bar to bring her the bottle.

'You don't want a glass?' he asked.

'No. It's easier to keep the drugs out that way,' she said, holding the bottle with her thumb in the top.

'Do you think someone would try that here?' Jeremy was surprised.

'Some of these animals are capable of anything, even if they are married.'

Jeremy shook his head. 'That's awful.'

'We'll see. Let's join that group over there,' she said, heading towards some of the younger members of George Nelson's group, where the other two women in this otherwise-male party were.

The group let them in, and they made inconsequential small talk about what people had planned for Christmas until the time came to sit for the food. Although Jeremy and Lisa tried to get themselves onto the table with the group they had been with, Guy Barnes dragged them away to sit with his group.

'Come on you two, it's time for my team to socialise together.'

So, the unspoken plan that Lisa and Jeremy had to avoid exactly that situation was defeated. They were forced to sit where Guy made them sit, and he insisted Lisa sat next to him. For a moment she remembered the thought she'd had in the taxi to turn around and go home. She was committed now.

To her relief there was a jug of water on the table.

'What are you doing later? We thought we'd go to a club and take in some of the night scene.' Guy Barnes started in as soon as they were sat down.

'I'm taking a group riding in the morning and need my sleep.' Lisa said.

'Riding this close to Christmas? When do you do your shopping?' Guy clearly intended to talk to her all evening.

'I've done it already. With riding I have so little time to shop that I did it on the internet last month.'

The conversation struggled on for a while, with Lisa facing a barrage of questions intended to find a weak spot that Guy Barnes could use. Fortunately, the restaurant staff arrived with the food and for a while it was chaotic as each person tried to remember what starter they had ordered. People settled to eat and Guy Barnes backed off; letting Lisa relax until the next trial.

The gay barman became the wine waiter, asking each diner which wine they preferred, sorting out the glasses and pouring each person's choice. As she was the only woman, he started with Lisa, who opted for a glass of white wine; knowing that she could keep it topped up with water without being too obvious. The barman carried on around the table. She looked across at Jeremy – who appeared engrossed in his starter – and avoiding eye contact. She knew there was little she could do to help him if something unfortunate was said, but the waiter was a professional and the dangerous moment passed.

The barman reached Guy Barnes and asked him what he would have.

'I'll have the red please, boy.' He said, using the insult from the slave states. The waiter stiffened while three of the older staff at the table giggled. The waiter kept his dignity and poured Guy Barnes his wine.

'Thank you, boy,' said Guy.

The barman left, and Lisa watched as Guy Barnes and the giggling three began a bragging session, each telling a more outrageous story about how they had misbehaved with anyone who wasn't a fit and healthy white male. She had nothing to offer this conversation. It looked like an inept attempt to impress her with their skills as macho men. She watched the staff clear away the first course and thought about how long the meal going to be; planning to make her escape as soon as possible after the last course.

Lisa noted that the other four members didn't say much, although they occasionally smiled. She couldn't understand why this group sat and watched her being abused in the office and never said anything. Guy Barnes must have cowed them into silence somehow.

A different wine waiter appeared and had to check what each choice had been. She waved him away and discreetly topped her glass up with water. She caught Jeremy's eye and recognised the signs that he was thinking the same thing. He smiled briefly. The bragging conversation had moved onto sports, so Jeremy had an opening.

'What did you play Guy?' he asked.

'Rugby,' said Guy. Lisa saw the difficulty that Guy was in. He wanted to be the macho man but hadn't any sporting talent. She had seen him riding and guessed his lack of control of horses stemmed from a general lack of sporting ability.

'What position?' Jeremy set the trap.

But one of the giggling three butted in.

'Guy had a trial to play linesman for the school third team but didn't get selected.'

She didn't join the laughter, although Jeremy couldn't avoid smiling. Lisa watched the giggler realise his mistake of showing Guy up and quickly said, 'What position do you play, Jeremy?'

'Wing forward. At the moment I have been playing for the City team. But I'll have to give up because so far, I've been lucky but picking up an injury could affect my attendance record at work.'

Lisa knew that Jeremy's attendance was better than anyone's.

'What sort of season are they having?'

'We're fourth in the league and the next few games are against teams at the bottom of the table, so we are hoping to move up.'

The discussion moved onto the fortunes of the City rugby team – which was followed by some of the less vocal people at the table – and while the main course was served the conversation revolved around some of the team's characters. It bored Lisa but was a safe topic, and she was surprised that they didn't talk about it in the office. Jeremy's place in the team came as a surprise to some of them. But she reflected that this was a result of the atmosphere in the office, and she knew how quiet Jeremy was at work.

Lisa sensed Guy looking at her and his brooding stare frightened her. She guessed he may easily have failed a trial as a linesman, but he was a poor loser and would plan a way of getting back at his detractor.

The rugby talk continued through the main course, but when the staff came to clear their plates the barman was among them.

'Oh, the boy's come back again, has he?' said Guy Barnes, cutting across the other conversation. Everyone went silent and the staff left. Lisa wanted to tell Guy Barnes to grow up but knew this would be an excuse for getting at her again. No one else knew what to say, so Guy Barnes started a new topic.

'Anyone know any good limericks?'

A number of the men produced offerings which Lisa judged mediocre. None of them were even risky. One of the gigglers produced one:

'On the breast of a barmaid from Sale

Was tattooed the prices of ale,

And on her behind,

For the sake of the blind

Was the same information in Braille.'

Lisa laughed with the rest of them, seeing it as quite a clever little rhyme. When the laughter finished, Guy Barnes turned to her:

'Do your breasts display the prices of ale, or are they more sophisticated and into the FTSE 100 or share prices?'

143

'No good tattooing share prices,' said a giggler. 'They move around too much. Mind you so do breasts when they're on the loose.'

'What would you tattoo on your breasts, Lisa?'

Lisa became the focus of everyone's gaze – although Jeremy looked down at his hands which he had on the table, fidgeting with his dessert knife and fork. Lisa was glad that she had chosen a dress with a high neckline. Even so she reddened.

'I don't want to talk about it,' she said.

Guy Barnes brayed at her. 'Can't keep up in the real world? We like talking about them. Don't we boys?'

Amid the laughter, Lisa sensed that it was for the benefit of Guy Barnes and was nervous – rather than genuine – amusement. But that didn't help her find a formula for shutting him up.

'I like trying to read the Braille with my hands too. What prices do you keep there?'

'I try to keep my hands to myself in the office, unlike some people,' she said.

'Oooooooh!' Guy Barnes was enjoying this. 'We'll keep that till when we go dancing later.'

To Lisa's relief the restaurant staff appeared with the dessert course and sorted out who was having what. The table had gone silent again, and she prayed for a new topic of conversation.

The barman reappeared and asked, 'Who wants coffee or tea, and does anyone want a liqueur with their coffee?'

Lisa told him she would like a pot of mint tea if they had some.

'I don't suppose the boy serves mint tea at an event like this – which is for proper business-people,' said Guy Barnes.

'We have mint tea, Madam,' said the barman.

'Thank you,' said Lisa.

The barman ignored Guy Barnes and went around the table the other way. When he had taken the orders from the other eight people, and reached Guy Barnes, he ignored him and went off.

'Come back, boy,' Guy Barnes yelled, fortified with wine.

The head waiter appeared like magic behind Guy Barnes's seat and asked, 'Is there a problem sir?'

'There certainly is,' said Guy Barnes. 'The boy didn't serve me.'

'We have a policy here to treat everyone as equals. That waiter is a very capable member of my staff.'

'He ignored me. I want a cup of coffee and a large brandy please.'

'I'm sorry sir. You've had enough to drink. I will not have a member of my staff abused. If you don't like that sir, I suggest you leave.'

Guy Barnes was red with anger but could see that if he had to leave, he was in danger of losing a lot of face.

'Okay. Please can you bring me a cup of black coffee?'

'Certainly sir,' said the head waiter and left. Quickly the staff finished serving the tables.

Lisa had not been to one of these evenings before so was unsure what to expect. She had expected a disco to start up and a battle to avoid being handled by Guy Barnes but there was no music. Instead Bob Sullivan stood up and made a speech about company performance and how everyone was doing a fine job. Lisa decided that it was brilliant for someone who was collecting management clichés, and little else.

'And now we come to the awards section.' Bob moved to a table behind him that Lisa had not spotted before. It had a number of neatly wrapped Christmas presents.

Various people were called out for different contributions to the office performance. There was a mixture; some for genuine successes such as landing the client who paid the most fees. Others were more tongue in cheek, such as a bottle of tomato sauce dressed with a bow for a broker who was always saying that he was trying to 'ketchup'. Jeremy won a prize for having the best attendance record.

'I have a prize too for the newest member of our team, Lisa, for having reactivated the highest number of dormant accounts.'

As the applause started, Lisa heard Guy Barnes say to the table, 'It's a pair of armoured plated knickers.' She stood up, and on impulse picked up her bag as she headed over to collect her prize. Bob Sullivan gave her a wrapped present as the applause died down.

'Well done Lisa, well done indeed. I've looked back five years and you have done better than any of the previous winners.'

'Thank you.'

'Stay here,' said Bob Sullivan. 'We are going to have a photo of the winners for the company magazine.'

She joined the group of winners with their wrapped presents while Bob finished his list.

'Thank you again everyone – now please enjoy the rest of the evening.' A man appeared and took the microphone from him, and Bob Sullivan walked over to the group of winners. 'The photographer's in the lobby where the company logo has been erected.'

They shuffled out of the room and photographs were taken. It was past ten and Lisa grabbed her chance, fetching her coat and heading out with Jeremy to find a taxi before she could suffer anymore. *What a good thing I didn't leave my bag behind*, she thought.

Once in the taxi she rang Rhodri.

'How did it go?' he asked.

'As you might have expected,' she said.

'How did you escape so soon?'

'Pure luck. I won a prize and they took us out of the dining room for a picture. It gave me a chance to leave without a scene.'

'Are you riding tomorrow?' she heard the hope in his voice.

'Yes. I'm doing Beth a favour so she can get off early to go shopping. I should be finished about half four.'

'I'll be there.'

Lisa sat back and closed her eyes. She had survived the evening without having to face the roving hands and as she relaxed, became aware of how keyed up she had been. She shuddered. Tomorrow was a better prospect.

Elin 22nd December 2012

Next morning Elin and Megan were sat at the breakfast table. Elin was a bit nervous about how to bring up the topic of Christmas but as usual, Megan weighed in first.

'How was your concert last night? You were out quite late.'

'It was good, really enjoyable. Odd though, the audience didn't appear impressed for most of the concert but wanted loads of encores at the end.' It struck Elin that she had been able to forget about her troubles for a few hours. Almost.

'So, when did it finish?'

'We went to the pub afterwards and had a sing song there. It's amazing how everyone knows so many words.'

146

'That must be the first time you've been to the pub for a drink for ages.'

'Yes. Come to think of it, I don't see the point of spending what I haven't got. Neither should you till we work out how we are going to survive.'

'I bought a couple of tickets. Everyone did. I didn't want to look tight to my friends and I did win the hamper.'

Elin had known that it was only a matter of time before the hamper came up.

'Yes, you won the hamper. I asked Tony to join us for Christmas, and he told me how his family had other plans and will be happy to come. I told him he would have to bring chairs so we would have somewhere to sit. He said ...' Elin tailed off, forgetting what he had said but remembering how he had played a love song to her in the pub. She smiled.

'What's going on Mama? What happened? What did he do?' Megan said, and Elin saw that Megan had spotted that there was more to the evening than she was letting on. She avoided the subject.

'He said he had a whole dining room that he didn't use and suggested we spend Christmas in his house.'

'What did you say?'

'He said I wasn't to worry about it till I had a chance to talk to you. What do you think?'

'What's his kitchen like? Will we be able to do it?'

'It's bigger than ours and has all mod cons. We would have to check he has a pan big enough for the turkey but everything else should be there.'

'What time should we eat? Lunchtime is best for Owain. He wants to do something with his Dad in the evening. Mind you, Tony lives quite close to Owain so it would be convenient for them.'

They both wondered what to do. Megan spoke first.

'How long will the bird take to cook? It'll need starting quite early to be ready by lunch. Who's going to do that.'

'We can ask Tony. I don't know how much of a cook he is. He gave me stuff his daughter had cooked when I went there, but he did heat it up.' Elin wondered why Megan put her on the defensive.

'Ring him up and tell him we'll come to him. Then we can work out how we cook everything.'

Elin felt nervous about ringing Tony with Megan listening but there was no way out that she could see. So she called him.

147

'Morning Tony. How are you?'

'Tired out. I always am.'

'Your fault for being the life and soul of the party. I enjoyed it a lot. It'll take me years to learn the words and tunes to those songs that they sang in the pub last night.'

'You were sitting in the wrong place. The other side from where you were there are boards with the words on that we made up years ago. That's how they know the words. It's sort of karaoke.'

'I didn't know they were cheating!' Elin said, and went on quickly before Tony got onto 'The Nightingale Singing in Berkeley Square'. 'I've got Megan here and she agrees that it would be nice to have a proper dining room for our Christmas party. We'll have to have Christmas lunch as Megan's Owain has to leave by four to go to his Dad's. So, the turkey has to go in the oven at about seven in the morning because it's quite big.'

Tony was silent.

'Tony, are you there?'

'Yes, I was thinking. Why don't you and Megan come and sleep here? Then it won't be a rush. There are spare bedrooms for both of you. You could stay till Boxing Day too. You won't have to drive home if you have a glass of wine.'

'Wait. I'll have to ask to Megs.' Elin turned to Megan. 'Tony suggests we sleep there for two nights so I can enjoy a drink. What do you think?'

'Novel,' said Megan, smiling. 'A holiday. When did we last have one of them?'

'Do I take that as a yes?'

'Yes. It'll be easy to join Owain from there on Boxing Day. He has a stunt that the rugby club are doing that he wants to me to go and watch.'

'Tony, did you hear any of that?'

'Yes. Do I take that as a yes?'

'Yes, thank you. We'll come after lunch on Christmas Eve and stay till after breakfast on Boxing day. I have to work in the pub that day.'

Elin and Tony discussed the details of what was needed before ringing off. Elin was relieved that Tony had kept away from what had happened the night before. She didn't know why she didn't want Megan to know and needed to think about it. But there was no way to get past two nights with Tony at Christmas without Megan saying something. Right now, she had to prepare for her shift in the Railway.

Sonny

I watch as Tony first cleans his house and then shops among the crowds to be ready in time for the arrival of Elin, Megan and the others. He understands that although they are bringing Christmas lunch, there are other meals to be eaten. When the pencil sketches Elin's car pulling into the drive, Tony's worn out. It strikes me that if I were preparing to spend Christmas with someone else in my flat, I would be too.

Tony 24th December 2012

Tony opened his front door and went out to meet Elin and Megan as they got out of the car. He had a moment to look up at the clear sky. *My stars will soon be out,* he thought. Father Christmas was going to have a cold night.

Elin pulled two bags from the boot of the car, while Megan had got out but then turned back to get one of the hampers of food from the back seat.

'I'll take those if you like,' said Tony to Elin. 'You can help Megan. I'll be back in a moment.'

Tony took the two bags into the house and put them at the bottom of the stairs. He returned to see Elin struggling with a heavy box.

'Here, let me,' he said and took the box from her.

'Thanks Tony. I was about to drop it.'

Tony went to the kitchen and left the box on the table. He looked for the umpteenth time to see that it was okay, as Karen said in his ear, *'put the kettle on. It's cold outside.'*

He went back to the front door, but Megan was coming in carrying the other box and trying to see past it to avoid tripping over the doorstep.

'Can I take it?' he asked.

'No. I'm okay. Lead the way.'

Tony led her into the kitchen and showed her where to put the box on the table, whereupon Megan plonked the box down and straightened up. Tony was amused as Megan started to inspect the kitchen. He heard the front door closing and called to Elin. 'We're in the kitchen.'

Elin walked in.

'Let me take your coats and I'll show you round.'

Elin took off her coat and scarf, gave them to him and followed him out to see where he put them in the cupboard under the stairs. She then went back into the kitchen.

'Come on Megs. We can look at the kitchen in a minute.'

Tony waited in the hall as Megan took off her coat, and Elin hung it on a peg and closed the cupboard door. He picked up the two bags and headed up the stairs. The bathroom faced them at the top of the stairs, and Tony turned left towards that end of the landing – where one door faced them – while a second was off to the right towards the back of the house.

'You can take your pick; they're both made up.' He put the bags down and Elin and Megan each went into a bedroom.

From the back bedroom came Megan's voice. 'I've got the boy's room. Some of these books are pretty geeky!'

Tony smiled. Matt had a fine collection of fantasy novels and quite a few science fiction ones as well. He stuck his head round the other door.

'Okay?' he asked.

Elin had opened her bag and was putting on a pair of slippers. She straightened up and looked him straight in the eye.

'Yes. I'm good,' she said. 'I've left my troubles behind.' She pointed towards the room Megan was in and whispered. 'She's got all her senses tuned on to working out what's going on between us.'

Tony laughed out loud. 'I know, I know. Now come and have a cuppa.'

'Yes,' she came to the doorway, but Tony didn't move. Elin touched Tony gently on the hand. 'We have to sort out those boxes in the kitchen.'

Tony set off down the stairs with Elin following behind. The simple touch on the hand had lifted his heart. He wasn't alone now. *'You've left your troubles behind too,'* said Karen.

Sonny

I watch more of this scene as they finish in the kitchen and Tony takes tea into the living room. To my amusement Megan is trying to have a good poke into the cupboards without being too obvious, although I can see she's got one eye on the interaction between her mother and Tony. At the same time they are trying hard to act as though there's nothing between them.

Tony 24th December 2012

'Come on, there's time enough for the kitchen; let's stop for a minute for tea.' Tony called them from the living room.

Elin came in. She had been in this room before and settled onto the sofa. Tony had found the old Christmas decorations and bought a Christmas tree since the phone call. Megan followed and stood in the doorway.

'Tony. Did you do the decorations yourself?' She was smiling.

'Yes, why? Jessica would have reorganised it by now. Don't tell me you are going to change things.'

'Who's Jessica?' asked Megan. She sorted of squinted at the tree from by the door where she had been taking in the two pianos and the music.

'My daughter,' said Tony. 'She lives in City and has a husband, David, and two little ones – as you can see in the pictures over there. They've gone for Christmas with David's parents.'

Megan studied the pictures. Tony was frightened she would ask about Karen, but she said nothing. He guessed that Elin may have explained his situation to Megan before they'd come.

'Do you mind if I re-do the decorations a bit?' asked Megan.

'She's an artist, Tony. She's got an eye for arrangements.'

'So have you, Mama. You would be doing it if you hadn't sat down.'

Tony laughs. 'Do whatever you want,' he says. 'It's the same every year. But before you do, let's sort out how you want your tea.'

Tony and Elin sat together on the sofa while Megan confidently moved things around on the Christmas tree to her satisfaction. Tony watched – thinking of how Karen would have done the same – but Karen would have taken a lot of stuff off the tree first. He had to admit that Megan made a good job of it.

Megan sat down, sipped her tea and looked about.

'Why are there two pianos? Can you play all that music?' Tony felt Elin stiffen. Megan had strayed into Karen's area. But somehow her innocent approach wasn't threatening.

'We used to play together. I can't play all of the music, although I probably could sight read most of it. There are some bits here that I don't think anyone could play.'

'Megs, Tony played at the concert and in the pub afterwards. He's good.'

'Owain plays the piano pretty well. It surprises me because his fingers look too big, but he has big hands and can reach miles with one hand.'

Tony could see Karen sitting at her piano facing outwards and watching the conversation. She wasn't upset like she had been when he had brought Elin in here the first time. *'Ask questions, Tony. It will take the focus away from you, and people like talking about themselves,'* said Karen.

'Do you play?' asked Tony. 'Or is there another instrument you like?'

Megan was quiet for a minute. 'I gave up. It was either art or music, and I couldn't do both; there isn't enough time. For art A-level they expect you to produce a massive portfolio of stuff and everything has to meet the standard. The sketches are mostly scrap as each piece in the portfolio has several false starts behind it.'

'Megan sets a high standard, so she makes quite a lot of what she calls scrap; although I don't agree.'

'You do it too, Mama.'

'Do you paint?' asked Tony, turning to Elin.

'She did,' said Megan. 'She teaches art, but since Mamgu and Tadcu got sick she's stopped doing her own stuff.'

'The truth is I spent too much on their illness and can't afford the materials, especially while Megs needs them for her exams.'

Tony said nothing. Elin couldn't afford materials to paint and by the sound of it she couldn't afford music lessons for Megan either. He remembered how sometimes they couldn't afford food even. Were Elin's difficulties the reason why he felt the urge to help her, or was it because he liked her company? He looked at her sat next to him. She had changed since the car had broken down that day he had met her. Now there was more confidence in the way she held herself, and she had made an effort to smarten up so she seemed younger.

He expected Karen to say something, but she was silent.

Megan finished her tea, stood up and walked over to the piano and looked at the single score.

'Oh, cool. "Anfonaf Angel". We sang that in the school choir.'

'We sing it in the choir too,' said Elin. 'It's one of their favourites. We sang it the other night. I thought you didn't need music for that, Tony?'

'I need music when I practice at home to make sure I'm doing it correctly. If I play too often without music little errors start to creep in.'

But Tony was thinking about how Karen had been silent, and Megan had picked that moment to talk about 'Anfonaf Angel'. He wondered what that meant. *You're getting in too deep here Tony, change the subject,* he thought.

He finished his tea and said, 'What preparations do we have to make tonight to make tomorrow a success?'. So they set off to the kitchen to plan the party.

Sonny

Christmas Eve in Tony's house is a quiet affair as I watch Tony, Elin and Megan with their individual agendas. Tony and Elin are trying to avoid giving away to Megan that their relationship is moving to a new level. Megan meanwhile is revelling in watching them both.

Elin 25th December 2012

Elin got up early and put the turkey into the oven, stuffed according the instructions that had come with it. She was glad to be alone for a minute. The combination of Tony and Megan was rather wearing. At a quarter to eight she decided that instead of going back to bed, she would make a pot of tea and read the rest of the instructions for 'The Perfect Christmas Lunch'. She wanted to check they hadn't missed something before it was too late to fix.

'Good morning!' Tony had come in behind her. 'Is the oven doing what you expected?'

'Oh, Happy Christmas, Tony. Yes, the oven's doing fine and the tea is freshly made.' They were both in dressing gowns, she noted. She poured him a cup of tea.

She turned so she could watch the doorway, in case Megan walked in on them.

'Thank you,' said Tony. 'How long will sleeping beauty take to wake?'

'If I know her, fairly soon I expect.'

'Thank you for coming. It has made a huge difference to my Christmas already. I wouldn't have bothered with a tree and decorations if it had been only me.'

'Thank you for asking us and for playing the "Nightingale" after the concert. I take it that was for me?'

'Yes. But I didn't expect the people in the pub to react like that.'

'Very strange, especially as Teresa had just asked me if we were an item.'

'How is it that I am the last to find out?' laughed Tony. 'But to go back to your question, the answer is yes. This is very hard; I was with Karen for so long that I've forgotten how these things are supposed to work.'

Now Elin laughed. 'So have I. You came out of the blue with a broken car and later rescued me in Tesco's. Until Teresa said it and you played the "Nightingale", I was rather locked into my worries.'

'And I was rather lonely and had a lot of fun taking you shopping.'

She reached across the table, took his hand and held it. She saw how his eyes were looking at her with a warmth that spread inside her.

'You can play the "Nightingale" again for me sometime,' she said, and he smiled.

'Happy Christmas.' Tony said. He disappeared into the utility room, returning with two old rugby socks stuffed with odd shapes and with items in Christmas wrapping paper reaching well out of the top.

'I didn't think anyone should go into your bedroom – or Megan's – so I told the old man to leave them down here.'

He studied the two socks and handed one to Elin.

'Someone's coming,' he said.

Into the kitchen walked Megan in her pyjamas, scratching her head and looking sleepy.

'What are you two up to?' Megan asked. She stood next to Elin who stood up and kissed her. 'Bore da, cariad, Nadolig Llawen.'

'Dolig Llawen, Mama. Is there a chance of a cuppa?' Megan turned to Tony. 'Happy Christmas'.

Tony handed her the second sock and replied, 'Happy Christmas, I'm afraid that we've drunk the tea. I'll make some more.'

Megan looked around the kitchen for somewhere to sit, and Tony told her to sit in his chair.

'I'll get another one,' he said and went out.

'What's going on Mama?'

Elin saw the way Megan was looking at her and knew that it would be better if they were honest with Megan; otherwise she would be constantly asking. Tony came back in with a chair and sat in it at the end of the table. Elin saw him watching the two of them with concern, so she reached over and took his hand again.

'Megan, fach. Tony and I are a bit more than just good friends but it's early days, so we are feeling our way.'

'I wondered what we were doing,' said Megan, 'staying here over Christmas.' She looked at Tony. 'Don't upset my Mama, she's very precious to me. Now, where's that cup of tea?' They laughed and while

154

Tony made the tea, Elin and Megan set to with the socks to see what Father Christmas had brought them.

In no time the table was covered with torn and scrunched-up wrapping paper.

'How did you work out what we would like?' asked Megan.

'I cheated,' said Tony. 'Jessica told me what I should get, and now I've got a massive job to explain to her why I've got two women staying with me for Christmas.'

Sonny

I watch as they happily clear away the mess and get breakfast. They set to work on making the lunch: boiling the Christmas pudding, setting the table, preparing the vegetables and the other jobs that go into setting up a lunch party.

I keep on drawing to cover up my own loneliness. Just after eleven o'clock they stop to have a cup of coffee.

Tony 25th December 2012

'It's a good thing we don't have to cook like this every day,' said Megan. 'We'd never get anything else done!'

Tony sat down with his coffee at the breakfast table – which by now scarcely had room for his mug. He sat back and watched as Megan and Elin finished cutting the Brussels sprouts, washed their hands and sat down as well.

The doorbell rang and Tony went to answer it.

Mrs Lloyd and Gary stood in the doorway with Owain blocking out the light behind them.

'Happy Christmas, Mr Jones. We thought we'd better come early to help get things ready, and we've one or two things with us as well.' Mrs Lloyd didn't have a hand free to shake Tony's hand, but he saw that she would have. 'By the way, this is Gary.' She pointed an elbow.

'Happy Christmas, Gary. I'm Tony.'

Gary nodded in return.

By now Elin and Megan were in the hallway as well, so it was difficult for the newcomers to get in out of the rain. It definitely wasn't a white Christmas.

There was a sort of mad dance while coats were taken off and put to hang, bags of food were taken to the kitchen and presents taken to the living room. Owain was standing like an obstacle in the middle of the hallway.

'I've been here before.' he said. Megan was standing next to Owain.

'You never told me you knew Mr Jones,' she said.

'I don't. I used to come here for piano lessons with Mrs Jones. In that room there.' He pointed.

At mention of Mrs Jones, Karen, nobody spoke. Tony had a vision of Karen thrust into his consciousness. Her unexpected arrival caught him unawares and threatened to plunge him into grief. He wanted to be angry that all these people had come in and invaded his peace, but Karen spoke to him. *'Calm down Tony. They're guests. Say something.'*

'Are you okay Tony?' asked Elin.

'Yes. Yes, I'm fine. She had loads of pupils over the years and I didn't meet half of them.'

'I'm sorry Mr Jones.' said Owain.

'No. Owain, that's fine, and please call me Tony.'

Everyone moved into the kitchen to carry on with the preparations. Tony was uncertain what he was expected to do as Elin and Megan had a word with Mrs Lloyd, and the three women were quickly occupied. Gary had managed to sit down, but there was no chair for Owain who filled the middle of the room.

'You men,' said Elin.

Mrs Lloyd handed Gary a bag of carrots and a peeler. 'Come on Gary, make yourself useful. And Owain. We haven't got room for you here.'

Tony had been thinking. He remembered now how Karen had talked about how talented Owain was at the piano. *'Take him to play,'* she said. He imagined her sitting at the piano and the idea of Owain sitting there seemed somehow wrong. *'Let him do it Tony. Someone will have to play that piano again someday.'* He took a deep breath.

'Owain, why don't you play the piano?'

Owain looked at him and smiled. 'I get in the way in the kitchen. Sorry.'

Tony led Owain into the living room where the two pianos sat under the shelves of music.

'Which one did you play when you were here?' asked Tony.

'The one in the corner. She played that one – or just listened.'

'You played duets with her?'

'Yes, sometimes. Some days when I came, she'd had enough of teaching and wanted to play. I enjoyed it. She was a better timekeeper than I am!'

Tony went through a range of emotions. Pupils had sat at her piano, and she had played his. He had never expected that. She played together with someone else too – not just him. It was as though she'd been unfaithful, as they had played together so much after the baby had died. *'You're wrong. I never let anyone play your piano. That would have been betrayal. That's the piano we bought then.'* Karen's voice helped him settle. He understood now why he had been so affected when Elin had played the few notes on his piano.

Owain sat down at the piano and opened the score on it. 'Anfonaf Angel'. He started playing, and Tony sat down and joined in when he heard how accomplished Owain was. *'You hide in the music too; like me,'* said Karen, and Tony relaxed into the familiarity of the keys. He could hear Elin and Megan singing the words in the kitchen, and his mood lifted. He was having a good Christmas.

Sonny

I put down the pencil and look around my room. I don't want to watch my characters enjoying themselves together. They are all enjoying their Christmases with laughter, music and activity filling their houses. My room has no movement.

I don't like the Christmas radio repeating Noddy Holder, Bing Crosby and all those other Christmas hits over and over, so I turn it off. My room becomes quiet.

I stay in my room, away from the park where family groups, parents, children, friends and dogs are getting some fresh air. Among them I feel more alone. Each child will be trying their new bicycle or scooter – often wearing bright new helmets, gloves and jackets that they've been given by Father Christmas.

It makes me think of Gabby. I wonder what she'll be doing with Jen. I could be there too if Max retires. But if I gave up Max, I would lose the company of the editorial office. There's something comforting about being in the middle of all that news gathering, and hearing about things before they've even been on the radio from people who will talk to me.

157

There at least I can feel part of something. Today though they are closed. My pencil has been working at my cartoon story and now I've had enough, but as I sit on my stool at the drawing board Max pops up in the margin.

'Happy Christmas.' he says. He's dressed like Father Christmas.

Not you, I'm thinking.

'Ho, Ho. Yes, it's me. If I didn't come and talk to you today, you wouldn't talk to anyone.'

True.

'Never mind, next Christmas will be different.'

Why should it be any different from this Christmas? I'll probably still be writing this.

'Wait and see how different. You have to finish the story.'

I step away from the board, not wanting to let Max get further under my skin; he's annoyed me enough. I'm writing my story because I want to do something different. There isn't much humour in it and I'm worried for all of the women who are in it. Worse still it hasn't improved my life at all. And why Max wants me to finish makes no sense, as then Max will end and I can't understand why he wants that. Why's he driving me on?

The urge to write my story came from wanting to try something new – and to get away from Max – but now I am jealous of the fun that my characters are having in their separate parties. My room is emptier and quieter than ever before and the walls close in on me; a prison of my own making.

The pencil starts in again at the stables a few days later.

Lisa 29ᵗʰ December 2012

On the Saturday after Christmas Lisa wanted to ride as usual, but Mrs Howells had phoned her the day before.

'Hi, Lisa.'

'Hello Mrs Howells.'

'Lisa, things are a bit chaotic here because of the Christmas holidays. Can I ask you a favour?'

'Of course, what can I do?'

'We've got a gang of school children from a home in Croydon. They're orphans and we've promised to take them riding on Saturday morning. It's been booked for a while, but I didn't know that some are going to need to be on a lead rein and I need everyone I can get to help.'

'I'll help. What time?'

'Oh thanks. From nine if you can manage it, and we should be finished by one. You can ride Blister in the afternoon if you want.'

So, Lisa had spent Saturday morning among the riders leading two girls who had barely been out in the country before; let alone got so close to animals. Their naivety delighted Lisa and she had to smile when she discovered Rhodri had been roped in by his mother too.

Afterwards Lisa and Rhodri had their lunch together in a pub they had come to frequent.

'Are you going back to the stables?' asked Rhodri.

'I'll have to silly, to fetch my car. I'd also like a run out with Blister before dark. It'll be nice to ride instead of walk!'

'I know what you mean, I haven't walked that far in ages. I hadn't realised how much I just jump into the van.'

They talked away about the clash of cultures between city children and the countryside. Coffee came and Lisa idly stirred the cup. She was relaxed, her hand resting on the table. Rhodri took in her beauty and gently reached over to stroke her hand.

She reacted as though he had given her an electric shock. Lisa's hand jerked off the table and out of sight as if it had a mind of its own. She kept her eyes on her hands under the table, hiding them from Rhodri and trying to understand what had happened.

They didn't speak as they made their way back to the stables. When they arrived, Rhodri went off to fix some issue with a stable door as Lisa set off on Blister.

Lisa was confused and upset. Everything about Rhodri made her happy. More and more she wanted his company. But she had developed a reaction to all the creepy hands at work, and now she found it was the same with any small touch from Rhodri. It was like a poison growing between them and this time it seemed worse. They'd had such a perfect morning and lunch.

Blister made a dive for a tussock of grass at the side of the track and Lisa nearly slipped off. She got his head up and encouraged him to walk forward. He responded and she recovered her concentration. Blister seemed distracted and not his normal self, so Lisa forgot her gnawing worry and focussed on the horse.

She patted his neck and talked to him but he seemed to ignore her, pushing so that he could get to more grass on the side of the track.

'What's wrong with you?' she said.

Blister had picked up her mood. Now she understood that riding him any further was not going to be fun, so she walked him back to the stables.

She was spoiling her relationship with Rhodri, and now with the horse as well.

Sonny

Since Max's comment about next Christmas being different, I've been a bit frightened to come back to this and have kept away. I've had to prepare Max as usual, but each time he gets into the margin he tells me to keep going. He's starting to annoy me. I thought he was my friend.

When I come back to my story it's January, and Elin is at home.

Chapter 9: January 2013

Elin 4th Jan 2013

Lifted by the break she'd had at Christmas – and also by the tips that she had earned in the Railway during the holidays – Elin started the new year in better spirits than she'd been in for a while. She and Tony had a couple of afternoons out walking as well, which she found relaxing as they discussed what they should be doing. She chuckled as she remembered Tony and Owain playing the pianos together. Life was good.

Until that is, she phoned the garage to ask if her car was ready for collection from its annual service and MOT test.

'How is it?' She asked the service manager.

'A fail. The brakes and brake discs have to be changed on the front axle, and you need two new tyres. To put it right will cost four hundred and eighty pounds.'

'Oh. Is there anything else I should worry about?'

'We should change the exhaust pipe if you want to keep running the car, as it is about to drop off. That could be another two hundred and fifty. Don't forget you will have the service to pay on top – and there's the fee for the MOT. Total bill will be around nine hundred and thirty to nine hundred and fifty, depending on the price of some of the parts.'

Elin wondered where she was going to find nine hundred and fifty pounds to keep her car running, on top of the car tax that was also coming due shortly. That meant that this month she needed more than a thousand pounds above her other carefully husbanded outgoings.

'What do you want to do?' The service manager cut into her thoughts.

'I don't know. I'll have to think. What's the car worth?'

'You'll be lucky to get five hundred cash but without an MOT certificate you wouldn't be able to sell it.'

'What would you do if it was your car?'

'Scrap it and start again. Seriously love, it's dangerous as it is and we can't let it go like that. Better make the decision before we run up any

161

more charges than the MOT. Mind you, if we scrap it, I'll waive that charge.'

'Don't do anything yet. I'll call you back.' Elin rang off, realising that instantly she had no car anymore. She and Megan would have to catch the bus to work and for other essential journeys – unless they could walk – while she worked out how she could afford another car. She sat staring at the turned-off television, doing rough sums in her head and felt the tears start to well up in her eyes; before rather ineffectively wiping them away with her hands. The only way forward was to borrow. She gave her eyes another rub.

She heard the front door. It was Megan, home from wherever she had been with Owain. She came into the room.

'Hi Mama, sut wyt ti?' ('How are you?') Megan cheerily came around the chair and stood in front of her.

'Uffernol,' ('Hellish,') replied Elin. 'The car's failed its MOT and needs a thousand pounds to repair it. We don't have it.'

'Oh. Mama, I'm sorry. After such a good Christmas and holiday.'

Elin looked at her, alive with love and enthusiasm. She had to keep going for the sake of Megan. Something in the way Megan stood suggested to her that she should be remembering something.

'Megs fach, I forgot. How did your paper go today? I didn't see you afterwards.'

'No. We went straight for tea. I think I did okay. Some of the comments by other people suggested that they hadn't understood the questions, and I think I did.'

'No use worrying about it now it's done. I hope all the students get a good result in the January exams. It gives them confidence for the May papers.'

'I'm sorry about the car, I'll make the meal if you like. I haven't any more papers this week.'

'It's alright. I'll come and join you.' Elin marvelled at the way she could work with Megan in the kitchen. During the later stages of her marriage Kevin never offered to help and expected his food as of right; one of the many reasons she'd had to end it. But now with Megan she was starting to enjoy the kitchen again. She thought about how they'd cooked Christmas dinner together at Tony's, with the pianos in the background and had a small smile before remembering the disaster that had befallen the car.

Megan was taking the raw components of the meal out of the fridge when Elin entered the kitchen, picked up the potatoes and took them to the sink to peel them. But as soon as her hands were wet the phone rang. She put down the potato and the peeler and washed her hands under the tap, grabbed the towel and ran to the front room. Picking up the phone with the towel she breathlessly answered.

'Elin Paterson,' she said

'Tony here, you sound a bit rushed.'

'Hello Tony, I was up to my elbow in potato peelings. How are you?'

'I'm good. Matt came last night. Brown as brown; he only has to look at the sun. He and Natasha had a good trip, and now he's had time to call in. He's got some new job. Oh, I told you that at Christmas. Anyhow, he was feeling guilty for letting me down, and Jessica had given him chapter and verse on how selfish he had been.'

'What did you tell him?'

'I rubbed it in as hard as I could for a little – from the moral high ground – and he was looking more and more like a sad dog with its tail between its legs!'

'That was cruel!'

'I couldn't keep it up. He was so sad. I had to tell him that we had a super Christmas. He could see the Christmas tree and the decorations, so he was starting to work it out.'

'I rang you last night to see if the choir restarts next week or the week after. I'm in a bit of a muddle ... Did you go out?'

'I had to take Matt home. He brought Karen's car back as he and Natasha don't need it anymore "cos he has a car with his new project".'

Elin went silent. Tony now had a spare car sat on his drive. She was torn between the realisation that here was a solution to her problem, and how she would ask Tony if she could borrow it. He didn't need it; she had heard him say before that he didn't need two cars.

'Elin, are you still there?'

'Yes. Sorry Tony. I ...'

'What's happened?'

'Tony. I wasn't having a wonderful evening. That is, at least, until you rang.'

'Elin. Tell me. What can I do?'

'Oh Tony, my car failed its MOT. From what the man said it's scrap. I had a nightmare phone conversation.'

'Never mind. You can have this one here. It's about four years old and I made Matt get it serviced and tested while he had it.' Elin sensed Tony had made the decision instantly.

'I can't. I'm always taking stuff from you, and I never give anything back.'

'Yes, you can. You have to. What else am I going to do with it? Come to that you did give me something. I had a wonderful Christmas and before you made your suggestion I was going to be home by myself, sad and lonely.'

'But you made Christmas a success by letting us use your house.'

'You and Megan did it. As I remember I spent most of the time playing the piano with Owain. The decision is made. You can have this car as soon as I sort out the insurance with Matt and get it over to you.'

'I've got insurance for several months. I could put it on that. I insist.' Elin was relieved that at last she had something she could offer. It didn't all have to come from Tony.

'Okay. We'll talk about that again when it runs out.'

They talked on about the detail of the transfer of the car to Elin and what they would do on Saturday afternoon. They were still talking when Elin heard Megan call.

'Mae bwyd yn barod.' ('The food's ready.')

'I have to go Tony. I was supposed to help Megan make food and now it's ready. Thank you for being there for me.'

'You're there for me as well.' Tony's words made her feel warm and happy.

They finished the call and she went back to join Megan.

'Who was that?'

'Tony. Oh Megs, I'm so glad he came along.'

'Mama, you're in love. What's happened now?'

'His son had been using his wife's car and now he's brought it back. Tony says we can have it. As long as I pay the insurance that is, I insisted on that.'

'Can you afford it?'

'Yes. It's paid up till August already.'

'How old is it? Is it a wreck like ours was?'

164

'No. It's about four years old. It hasn't been used much since she died. Tony says it should be good for a few years.'

'You know Mama, borrowing a car from someone adds a bit to the relationship.'

'I know Megs. He's very kind. I don't know where it's going.'

They sat in silence, tucking into the food that Megan had made, and Elin reflected on how her life was better at last. She didn't want to take advantage of Tony or upset him.

The next day Tony picked Elin and Megan up from school and drove them home.

'Do you need to call at Tesco's?' asked Tony.

'No, we're okay,' replied Megan, before Elin could say anything. Tony drove them home.

'Do you want a cup of tea? Megan asked.

'No,' said Elin. 'We haven't got time. I've got to take Tony home and go to work.'

'I'll see you later then,' said Megan and set off into the house alone. Tony set off again to take Elin to his house so she could keep the car.

'Are you sure about this?' asked Elin.

'Yes, certain. The car will sit and rot otherwise; or I could sell it. This way it's being used.'

'Tony. Where are we going?'

'Elin, I didn't know how lonely I was till I met you. I was hiding it from myself. I like your company and I'd like to be with you more.'

'I know what you mean, but there is a problem.'

'What's that?' As usual the implications of getting closer to Elin were lost on Tony. He was just happy she was in the car with him, but now she sounded a bit as though she was about to end their relationship. He had hoped that their Christmas success was making things a bit more permanent, but now she was back pedalling.

'Megan. I know she's growing up and has a great deal of self-confidence, but she's still my daughter and I'm a one-parent family for her. I don't want to upset her while she's in the middle of her exams, and her last papers are in May. I don't want to rock the boat until she's safely past them.'

'Ah, I had forgotten her exams. How's she doing?'

165

'Okay. She's certainly done the coursework well, but she deserves a stable period from now on'.

'What are you saying?'

'I like you a lot Tony and you've made a big difference to my life, but right now I have to stay living at home with Megan. Once she gets a place in a college and I become an empty nester; then things could change.'

'You'll still be coming to the choir and we can still have outings on Saturday afternoon?'

'Of course, but I need to stay with Megan and support her for now.'

Tony thought about it. He remembered Jessica and Matt in their teens, how they were full of confidence at one minute and full of insecurity the next. He had his own life unplanned before him and hadn't thought of the implications for Elin of the next steps in their relationship. Curiously, Karen stayed silent. He wondered what that meant.

'Oh! I'm sorry. I guess my mouth is writing cheques that I haven't thought through. Elin don't worry. You can have the car. It's something I can do for you. Take it with no strings attached.'

'Thank you. Now I have to get a move on. I'll see you on Saturday for a cuppa.'

Tony got out of the car and held the door open as Elin came to the driver's side. While he was thinking about making sure she understood the eccentricities of this particular model, unintentionally he must have looked a bit serious. But Elin didn't get into the car, she hugged him and kissed him. He was taken by surprise.

'Tony, thank you for this. Megan's exams will be over in five months and we can work out what happens next. I like you and want your company. Please don't take this the wrong way.'

The hug and kiss she gave him told him what he wanted to feel; she wasn't giving him the push she was being practical. Elin got into the driver's seat and Tony explained the controls. Tony was happy now; he leaned in and kissed her.

'You'd better go or you never will!' he said.

She laughed and started the engine, adjusted the mirrors and reversed out of the drive. With a hoot of the horn she drove off. Tony stood for a while mulling it over. He thought back to the time before he knew Karen, when he had been looking for a life partner and remembered how inexperienced he had been then. Karen had been the one to move things

166

on; he had happily followed. He had no idea how these matters of the heart were organised and felt vulnerable to making a mistake and spoiling it. He was reliving the feeling of inadequacy from his time in college. It made him feel young again and sometime, he would have to tell Elin.

Lisa 9th January 2013

One morning, the new year seemed a long way off to Lisa when it became clear that a problem with a vexatious client needed to be resolved. Bob Sullivan told Guy Barnes to 'get with Jeremy and Lisa and fix it.' So that afternoon Lisa met the two of them in the conference room.

Guy Barnes was focussed on the matter in hand and the three of them discussed the different options for dealing with the client – and the potential risks and advantages of the different approaches. Lisa enjoyed the exercise as it crossed into areas which she had not previously experienced. After three quarters of an hour they had agreed a plan of action and were packing up their files.

'You're happy to write that letter now?' Guy asked.

'Yes,' said Lisa. 'It's all here. It just needs the words now.'

'Let me see it before it goes out.'

'Of course.'

Lisa sensed Guy the experienced broker and manager switch off, and Guy the predator appeared.

'I was going to ask you two what happened at the Christmas dinner,' he said. 'Where did you disappear to?'

'I went home.' Lisa said.

'On your own?' Guy asked. 'I was hoping to dance with you.'

'I don't think my life outside the office is any of your business.'

Guy turned to Jeremy. 'Did you go with her?'

Jeremy hesitated. 'No,' he said, but Lisa saw that the damage had been done.

'You're unsure. You're lying. Did he go with you Lisa?'

'Do you mean did we share a taxi? Yes, we did. Did we go to someone's home together? No. We did not.' Lisa was annoyed and forthright while Jeremy stayed silent.

'I'm concerned to know if two people in my department are having an affair. If you didn't go to someone's home, did you go somewhere else together?'

'No. We did not. We are not having an affair. We are not an item. End of story.' Lisa said.

'But you fancy Lisa don't you Jeremy?' said Guy. 'I've noticed a few times when you've pushed in between me and her.'

'Excuse me?' said Jeremy.

'Since you lost your shirt in the meeting, Lisa's been watching you. Admit it. You fancy her too. You've been getting close to her.'

'What if I do? Lisa's got her own boyfriend. I respect that.'

'I've had enough of this conversation,' said Lisa. 'I'm going back to my desk.

'I have too,' said Jeremy. 'I don't …'

'You know, if you can't stand the pace here you can leave.'

'I don't like the tone of this,' said Jeremy.

Lisa sensed another change in Guy Barnes. His voice went lower and filled with menace.

'What I'm trying to show you both is that I hold all the cards here. I can make your lives as miserable as you like. So, if you want to have an easy time and the good money here, then you know what to do. Or you can leave. That includes letting me get to know you a bit better Lisa, without Jeremy getting in the way. And no more clever stunts in assessment meetings or Christmas parties.'

'That's outrageous,' Lisa wanted to say, but she had frozen up; in that way her body did when Guy was touching her.

'That's the way it is. I'm watching you. Everyone else toes the line. Now be a good girl and sort that letter out.'

He stood up but clearly expected them to leave before he did, so they couldn't talk together.

Lisa went back to her desk in disbelief and typed up the client letter – after filling in her notebook.

Sonny

I have to leave this now. I want to throw the whole project in a skip, but Max has warned me I must carry on. I'm a cartoonist and yet here I am writing a nightmare story. Why should I keep going? It's supposed to be a hobby for pleasure, but I'm more and more frightened that something bad will happen to Lisa.

I try to start again a couple of times in January, and all I get is more pictures of Tony working at his computer. He rings Lisa too to talk about investment stuff I'm not interested in. Max has told me I should keep these too but there's nothing new to show.

The pencil draws something different.

Gareth 23rd January 2013

Gareth watched Jeremy walk into his little cubby hole behind reception early one morning. The space was cramped and he didn't get up.

'Can I talk to you?' Jeremy closed the door.

'Of course, what's up?'

'It's Lisa. I don't know how to help her. It's horrible and it's starting to give me sleepless nights so what it's doing to her I can't imagine. She's a public plaything up there.'

'Why do you think I can help?'

'I don't want to be seen talking to her. I've been warned off taking her side. I need someone to ask her what I can do to help without giving myself away.'

'What am I supposed to do?' Gareth was wary. He hardly knew this young man.

'You know her boyfriend, the carpenter guy. Talk to him, ask him if there's any way I can help.'

'You could talk to Mike Penshirst in HR.'

'Yes, but they'll know.'

Jeremy sat down on a rather battered chair next to the little table that held Gareth's cup of tea.

'She'll have her meeting with the managers again next month – we all will. I hoped I could do something about that.'

'Why then?' Gareth was curious.

'When Lisa had her probationary assessment meeting, she must have done something. After that the board on the desk was never mentioned again. I don't know how she did it, but I was hoping I could find something to give her to help the next meeting.'

Gareth saw that Jeremy was genuinely keen to help.

'What's the purpose of the meeting at this time of year?'

'They tell us what our bonus for the year will be based on.'

Gareth sat back, sipped his tea and came to a decision.

'One thing that got up Chantelle's nose was the bonus arrangements, but I don't know what. Is there a difference between what the men and women get?

'Oh God. Is it as simple as that?' Jeremy said. 'Don't you know about the bonus thing? Does Lisa?'

'What bonus thing? Why should I?' asked Gareth.

'The bonus scheme in this office is based on an individual's fee earnings once they get over a certain level. The men get fifty percent of the income over that threshold. As far as I can tell women only get a maximum bonus of twenty-five. Worse than that, the difference between their bonus and the fifty percent mark is divided among the managers i.e., Mr Sullivan, Mr Barnes and Mr Nelson.'

Gareth felt the need to stand up. He was clearly upset. 'I thought this was an equal opportunity employer. I put up a notice for HR to that effect in reception.'

'Some are more equal than others,' said Jeremy, almost to himself. He stood up and the two men struggled to find space between the chairs in the tiny room. 'I need to go.'

'Thank you for that. You'd better leave it to me,' said Gareth. He sensed that Jeremy was nervous that somehow, he had said too much. Jeremy fled.

Gareth sat down again and drank the rest of his tea. He got up and closed the door again, looked at his watch and reached for the phone.

'Rhodri. I hope this isn't too early for you.'

'Cheeky sod. I've been at work for ages.'

'As if I believe that.'

'How dare you.'

'Rhodri. How are you getting on with Lisa? Are you still together?'

'Honestly Gareth, I don't know. She's distant all the time. Like she's not interested, but she is. I'm very confused.'

'In that case you and I need a pint tonight in the Dragon. Can you finish by six? You late starters have to work later too.'

'I guess I should be able to skive off by then. What's it about?'

'Lisa. Let's talk about it in the pub.'

'What?—'

'Tonight. I can't talk here, you know that.'

'Okay. Thanks Gar.'

Rhodri 23rd January 2013

Rhodri was in the Dragon when Gareth arrived.

'What'll you have, Gareth?'

'A pint of that, please,' pointing to a pump. 'I'll find somewhere to sit.'

Rhodri knew that Gareth liked to stand at the bar, as he had a number of acquaintances who called in at this time of day. If he wanted to sit this was something serious.

They sat opposite each other and each took a sip.

'You remember that boy Jeremy who works with Lisa?'

'Yes, he's okay. I've seen him in the gym a couple of times, and he generally says hello.'

'He came to see me. He wanted to ask my advice.'

Gareth explained what Jeremy had told him about how the women in the brokers had a lower bonus than the men, and how Chantelle had left because of it.

'Who's Chantelle?' asked Rhodri.

'She worked next to Jeremy for a couple of years, and when she left Lisa had her desk. I don't know what went on altogether, but she was sacked and left – all in a day. She suffered in the same way as Lisa and did something stupid, so they had to throw her out.'

'So, nothing was done about "the animals" as Lisa calls them?'

'No. But I think the guy from HR is trying to help. He must suspect something.'

'It's hearsay and speculation. Nothing much to help Lisa.'

'I'm afraid so. Cool head now Rhodri; this is a battle Lisa wants to win.'

'I'd better go and talk to her. Thanks for that Gareth. I'll see you.' Rhodri drained his pint and left.

Moments later he was sat in his van talking to Lisa.

'Have you eaten?' he asked.

'No, not yet.'

'I'll pick you up.'

He picked a Chinese restaurant where he hoped no one would know them, and as they ate he explained what he had been told about the bonuses.

He watched her as she digested his message. She put the fork down on the plate and her mouth fell open. She was silent for a time and he wanted to touch and comfort her. But he knew that was a mistake. Lisa was upset by physical contact. He knew that if he reached across a table to hold her hand it would quickly retreat out of reach.

'Why doesn't Jeremy say something?' Rhodri asked.

'He's frightened they'll start harassing him,' she had returned to the conversation. She looked at the half-eaten food and pushed it away a bit. 'I don't believe this.'

'He could help you.'

'Rhodri. Jeremy's gay. He has managed to hide it from them so far, but with their prejudices he will be ostracised – or worse. I worked it out, and he asked me to keep quiet about it.'

'He's gay? I was worried he fancied you. With a body like that he could be serious competition.'

'No. He protects me quite a bit in the office, and we have allowed them to build the idea that we could be an item to protect his position. But he's been warned off helping me. Never fear, there's no competition from Jeremy.'

'Why am I the last to notice? I had no idea.'

Talk about Jeremy calmed Lisa and she started to eat again. For a while she ignored Rhodri altogether as she finished her food.

'Cool head, Lisa,' she said. 'Next month's assessment meeting will be rather exciting.'

Rhodri drove her home, and from the way she sat he knew that she didn't want to talk. As they arrived back, he wanted to hold her but she leaned across the van and stole a kiss on his cheek before jumping out – too quick for him. She stood in the van door facing him as he ached to hold her.

'Thanks, Rhodri. It has to get better soon and this will help.'

Lisa 8–15th February 2013

Two week later at the end of a morning meeting, Lisa was preparing to get up when Bob Sullivan said, 'Lisa, can you wait?'

'Yes, of course.'

'It won't take a moment. When everyone has gone.'

The rest of the people in the meeting left, unsurprised. Bob did this quite often; normally with Guy Barnes or George Nelson but occasionally with others as well. Lisa saw Guy Barnes look a little sharply at Bob Sullivan and left.

'Lisa, we have to have your bonus assessment next week. Would you like me to arrange a time to suit Mike Penshirst?'

'Yes, please.'

'Is it going to be like the last one? Have you been having more problems?'

Lisa was about to speak and stopped. She had to decide how much to give away now and what to leave till the meeting. For a while she had seen that Guy Barnes had avoided any contact with her whenever Bob Sullivan was nearby. Since the meeting with Jeremy though, whenever he had a chance, he was revoltingly physical and warning or not, she had to do something. This unexpected discussion with Bob Sullivan suggested that he knew more than he was letting on.

'Yes, there are some things I will want written on the form – as last time. Things may look okay to you, but my life can be quite unpleasant at times.'

'Stop right there. We should close this discussion now and have it with Guy and Mike present. I'll arrange a suitable time.'

Bob Sullivan got to his feet, collected his papers and they headed back to the trading floor.

As she sat back at her desk Lisa reflected on this turn of events. For the first time in a long while she had a feeling that there was a possibility Bob Sullivan was sympathetic. She noted the meeting in her little book.

At the time arranged for the assessment Lisa was careful to arrive slightly late so that Mike from HR would be there before her. As she entered the room – clutching the form from the previous meeting – she was relieved to see him there.

'Morning Lisa,' said Bob Sullivan, even though he had seen her that morning.

'Morning,' she replied, and took her seat. The meeting followed the boxes on the form as before, and her performance points were all complimented.

Now Guy Barnes moved onto the subject she had been waiting for. 'Now we come to the percentage of bonus you will receive. Your performance, as we have heard, has been excellent and from this meeting you are no longer probationary. Congratulations.'

'Thank you,' said Lisa. In preparing what she had to say, she had forgotten that this was a significant step forward for her career. She barely heard what Guy said next.

'As you are no longer probationary, we will move you onto your normal bonus rate for a full member of this team; which will be twenty-five percent.'

For a moment Lisa stayed silent but remembered that this was her cue.

'Excuse me? I thought that the normal rate in this group was fifty percent. Is there some reason why I don't get the same rate as the men?' The bored Mike from HR came awake with a start, but he didn't speak.

Bob Sullivan sought help from Guy Barnes.

'It's always been the case that younger members get a lower percentage,' said Guy.

'There are younger people than me,' said Lisa. 'Is it because I'm a woman?'

'But you have less experience than the others,' replied Guy.

'But Mr Sullivan has set out that I have been doing a good job. You have just told me I am a full member of the team and no longer probationary. What's the difference between me and the others? After all, I will only get a bonus if I earn it.' Lisa was leaning forward slightly; just enough to show some cleavage to the two men facing her, something she avoided normally. She could see Guy Barnes's eyes were being drawn.

Again, Bob Sullivan looked at Guy Barnes for help. They were both dithering. Lisa looked at Mike from HR, sat off to one side.

'How is the bonus scheme supposed to work? Who administers it?' She knew the answer but wanted to hear it in front of her two managers.

'Administration of the bonus scheme is a matter for the department. The sum available is calculated by the accounting group based on fifty percent of eligible fees, and the distribution is arranged by departmental heads. By Mr Sullivan.' Mike from HR could see where Lisa was going but had not quite understood.

'So, after everyone has been allocated their fifty percent share there will be some left over. That is, the gap between my allocation and the fifty percent that the accounting groups calculates. Where does that go?'

'I don't know. Bob, can you tell us?' asked Mike

'As probationers are being closely supervised, the excess is split among the departmental leaders – Guy, myself and George Nelson. That's the way it's always been done.'

'So, if you give me a twenty-five percent bonus and the men get fifty percent, you three will get the other twenty-five percent between you?' Lisa was relaxed; she had thought this through. Guy Barnes was furious though, as he could see that the presence of Mike from HR in this meeting was ensuring that Bob Sullivan would have no option but to give her fifty percent. Bob Sullivan decided to try to bluster his way out.

'Lisa, I see your point. But we'd better take this discussion outside of this meeting to resolve the issue in case there are implications in what you are suggesting.'

'Mr Sullivan, with due respect it says in the lobby of this building that this company is an equal opportunity employer and will diligently strive to work fairly with all employees. You are discriminating against me as a woman, and I want that noted on the form. And I want the fifty percent bonus like the men.' Lisa sat back. Her cleavage had done its bit to disrupt the discussions. She wondered if Mike from HR had seen the irony of what she had done. He could now carry on the fight for her.

'Bob, you have to do as she says or I will have to take advice on this matter from the group HR in London. Please can you note her comment on the form.'

'Right,' said Bob Sullivan, writing the comments into the form. 'Thank you for bringing this matter up with us Lisa, I am sure that this was an oversight.'

'Thank you,' she said.

There was silence while Bob Sullivan finished filling in the relevant section of the form and noted that Lisa was due the full fifty percent bonus. 'Are there any other issues that you want to raise with us before we finish the interview?'

'Yes. On the previous form it says I asked not to be referred to as the little lady again; nor asked to serve coffee and tea.'

'Yes,' said Bob Sullivan. 'So what?'

'Despite that, on the 21st of November in a meeting I was told 'the little lady will get you another cup'. I believe that request fails on both counts. There wasn't even a please.'

Mike from HR leaned forward and took Bob Sullivan's attention.

'Who was that?'

'Guy, do you know?' asked Bob Sullivan.

'Excuse me. Why don't you men get the message?' Lisa butted in. 'I'm in the room. You've told me I am a full member of this team. The answer to the question is that Mr Barnes said it. What just happened is one of the problems I face working here. We are back to the notice in the lobby again. Women in this organisation are invisible except as sex objects.'

'Easy Lisa,' said Mike from HR.

Lisa was wound up now, but his intervention brought her to her senses. Alienating him was the last thing she wanted.

'Sorry, but you see how it is.' Lisa replied calmly but firmly.

'Yes. I'm sorry too. Bob, you have to note this discussion on the form.'

'Certainly Mike. I'll write it up and you and Lisa can check it before it gets signed. Have we finished now, Lisa?'

'No. According to my records, between the last assessment meeting and today, I have been physically groped on sixty-nine occasions – in the lift, by the photocopier, after meetings, even at my desk.'

'What do you mean groped?' asked Mike from HR.

'One of the men in this department has run his hand – or hands – over some part of my anatomy.'

'Sixty-nine? You can't be serious,' said Bob Sullivan.

'I am serious. It's noted in my book, which for now I'm keeping. I'm not naming names, but I can.'

'Bob, have you seen evidence of this?' Mike from HR asked.

'No. Never. There may have been one or two sniggers in meetings, but apart from that I thought that Lisa was getting on okay.'

'It's never happened anywhere near Mr Sullivan.' said Lisa, wondering whether she had gone too far. She glanced at Guy Barnes who had gone silent.

'So, what do we do now Lisa?' asked Mike from HR.

'I've thought about this. I want it noted on the form. I want it made clear by Mr Sullivan to all staff that it's unacceptable behaviour. And I have acquired a rape alarm. From now on whenever it happens, I will set off the alarm if I am able to and expect the company to make a specific investigation of that event.'

Bob Sullivan looked at Mike from HR.

'Bob. Lisa has made a fair offer. We have to sort this now. Otherwise someone will sound a rape alarm in this office and then it's out of our hands.'

Bob Sullivan sat and stared at his paper for a while.

'Lisa, thank you. I will accept that as an action plan and note it on the form. Mike, we'll have to see if that's sufficient in view of the allegation Lisa has just made.' Bob Sullivan was shaking his head. 'I'm scared to ask now. Is there anything else you want on the form?'

Lisa realised that she hadn't discussed the meeting where she had been threatened by Guy Barnes with Jeremy and didn't want to raise it without his involvement.

'No, Mr Sullivan. If I can check the form and have a copy, I expect it will meet my needs.'

'Thank you, Lisa.' Mr Sullivan turned to Mike from HR. 'Mike, is this going to be okay? Can we let it go at that?'

'Bob, you know I have to take this higher and take advice on that question. For now, if Lisa is prepared to accept this as an action plan to deal with the problem, we should review it in six months. Unless of course, Lisa sounds the alarm in the meantime. But if it's on the form, you will have to notify – in print – everyone in the office as a minimum, and I'd like to see the wording of that. Or if you prefer, I'll suggest a draft to you. Now Lisa, are you okay?'

Lisa took a deep breath. 'Yes, thank you.'

'Lisa. If you need to come and talk to any of us, please let us know. We can get this group together anytime. We prefer that to letting a problem fester any longer, don't we Bob?' Mike from HR said.

'Yes, yes of course. Now, if we've finished you can leave us and we'll bring you a copy of the form when it's complete.'

'Thank you, Mr Sullivan.' Lisa got up and left the room and went back to her desk. She'd wanted to listen at the door as she knew there would be a heated discussion with Guy Barnes.

Lisa 19ᵗʰ February 2013

Four days later at the morning meeting after Bob Sullivan dealt with the business of the day, he asked them to wait a moment.

He turned and dialled a number on the phone behind him.

'Mike, can you come in please?'

A few moments later Mike from HR walked into the meeting and stood at the back of the room. Lisa guessed this was for her benefit.

Bob Sullivan started. 'We have a situation in this department that stops right now. I have written to you and the letters are available to you on the table behind me. You will each take a copy, and before you leave this room you will sign the receipt inside to confirm that you have received the letter and have read it and understand it. If you don't understand it, you must say here and now.'

Mike from HR stood by the table with the letters, behind Bob Sullivan who continued, 'Quite simply, I will not have sexual harassment in this department. No one will do any inappropriate touching of other members of staff. It has come to my notice that women in these offices are regarded as fair game by some of the men working here and that is unacceptable. It constitutes gross misconduct and thus carries the possibility of instant dismissal. It stops now. As a move to show how seriously I take this, we will be issuing rape alarms to all female members of staff and will set out in the letter instructions to them as to when they should set them off. If an alarm goes off Mike and I will interview those involved and consider what action is called for; as I said, up to and including dismissal.'

Lisa looked round the room, but all eyes were on Mike and Bob at the head of the table. Guy Barnes had his arms folded defensively across his chest. She remembered how he had changed his tactics against her after her first assessment meeting. *What would be his next line of attack?* Lisa thought. *I'm tired of this constant warfare.*

Mike from HR handed out letters to each person, and each read the letter and signed their receipt. Lisa was impressed. The letter set out definitions for more than she had asked for, and also set out definitions of workplace bullying and other examples of poor behaviour.

The receipts were collected up and Bob Sullivan spoke again.

'Is everyone quite clear what company policy is on these matters? Have you any questions?'

No one was prepared to venture a comment in the frosty atmosphere, and most people were eager to escape back to their workplace.

'I don't want to hear any more nonsense. Now get out.'

As they all left the room Lisa met Guy Barnes in the doorway. He stood back to let her out – with bad grace rather than good manners. She left the room thinking, *oh dear, what have I started now?*

Somehow Jeremy was alongside her as she neared their desks. He took out his mobile phone as he split off to his own desk.

At her desk she started noting the meeting in her book. As she was doing it a text rang in her mobile phone. It was from Jeremy.

I'm afraid you've declared war. I'm on your side. Let me know if you need anything. J

Lisa looked up and smiled at him. He winked. She finished the entry in the little book. If Bob Sullivan's edict worked, she shouldn't have to use her book again so dropped it into her handbag to take it home out of harm's way.

Sonny

The pencil continues to draw Tony working away at his computer. One day I notice that he is staring at it and not moving. This is different. He picks up the phone and makes a call.

Tony 5th March 2013

'Morning Lisa, how are you?'

'Hello Dr Jones. Fine, I suppose.'

'You're sounding a bit uncertain.'

'I haven't had my best few weeks. The riding's a bit less fun when the weather's been like it has and to be honest, this place is getting on my nerves.'

Tony's surprised. Lisa has never been anything other than courteous and cheerful.

'I hope better weather's on the way. Anyway, there's something I was meaning to ask you.' Tony explained an issue with one of his investments and Lisa went through the details of the papers that had been sent to him.

'Once you understand the jargon it makes sense,' she said.

'Thanks for that. No need to do anything,' he said.

'No. We'll let you know when there is. Now, how's the betting going? I hope you haven't done anything rash.'

'I win some, I lose some; but I'm learning all the time. I'm tracking markets in the far east and Dubai to see if they have any correlation with rises and falls in the FTSE. It's complicated, but I have won one or two on paper that make sense. All on paper though so no big risk. I'll only try ones that I'm sure about till I see if my system has any value at all.'

'Be very careful. It would be sad to throw away all the money you've invested.'

'Don't worry, I'm scared enough making paper bets. I'm sure the bar will be higher when it comes to placing a real bet.'

'I'm glad to hear it.'

The call ends. Tony gets up and makes a note in a file and goes back to his screen again.

Liz 14th March 2013

Liz Stephens was sitting among the flowers in her office. It was coming to the end of the day and she decided that there was a chance that Elin would be at home, so she called. Although she had spoken to her a few times on the phone, and Elin had told her that she was coping, she wasn't sure how true this was. Liz wanted to see her.

'Elin Paterson.'

'Elin, Liz Stephens here. I hadn't called for a while and I wondered how you were?'

'I'm good thanks. We're good. I've started sketching again.' They exchanged pleasantries and Liz was struck by how cheerful Elin sounded.

'Would you like to meet again for a chat?'

'Yes. Any day other than Tuesday.'

'How about Wednesday?'

So they agreed to meet as before in the lounge in the big hotel in City.

Liz 20th March 2013

Liz got there first and found a seat where she could see Elin when she walked in. She remembered the frightened-looking woman who she had met here before but failed completely to see Elin this time.

'Hello Liz,' said Elin, who had walked right up to her.

Liz was astonished in the change in Elin since September. She was altogether younger and smarter and held herself with confidence.

'Golly look at you. I didn't recognise you. How embarrassing.' She stood up while Elin sorted out her coat and chair. 'What can I get you?' Liz asked.

'Just ordinary breakfast tea would be lovely thanks. It's been a bit of a rush and I missed my afternoon cuppa.'

Liz sorted out tea for them both and they settled down. She was going to ask Elin how she was but the question was superfluous. Elin was exuding happiness at every pore, and her face glowed.

'I'm sorry to drag you all this way, but I wanted to make sure everything was going alright. I promised Tony.'

'Don't worry,' said Elin. 'The shops are open late and I don't often get the chance for a bit of a mooch around; even if I don't buy anything. I do need a present though. Maybe you can help.'

'How?' Liz was mystified.

'Tony's birthday. I have no idea what to buy him. He seems to have everything he needs. I had thought about buying him some music but that would be like taking ice to an Eskimo.'

Liz thought about the last time she had spoken to Tony. He had talked freely about Jessica and his days babysitting with Paddy and Mary, and how they were growing. He had talked too about Matthew and his strange relationship with Natasha, as they both had careers that involved lots of travel. She realised that he hadn't said much about himself or the choir, although he had seemed happy.

'Elin, are you seeing much of Tony? He hasn't said anything.'

'Men are like that aren't they?' Elin smiled. 'Has he even told you about Christmas yet?'

'No. He said nothing. I assumed he'd been to Jessica's.'

'No. Jessica went off to David's parents. At the last minute, Megan and I went to Tony's.'

Elin explained about the hamper and how they had ended up in Tony's house.

'Do you know about Megan? She's just eighteen. She says what she thinks and has decided to organise me. Tony and I failed completely to hide anything from her. We had to own up to her that we had something going, as a result of which we had to admit it to each other.'

'Gosh. He never said a word.'

'You knew Karen. He may have thought that you would think he was betraying her. She lives in his head you know.'

'What do you mean?'

'When he's uncertain, her voice speaks to him. I'm not sure if he likes it, but he seems to need it.'

'He's never said anything to me. What … I mean … ?' Liz didn't know how to ask where Elin and Tony's relationship was.

'Liz, Tony and I are doing fine. We meet every week at the choir practice and most Saturdays we get together when we can. Sometimes he's babysitting, and sometimes I'm working. I'm not prepared to go any further than that until Megan's finished her exams; her life has been wrecked enough by my divorce. Tony's happy enough with that. We're both a bit inexperienced.'

'You're obviously happy. I'm so glad. I completely missed you when you walked in. You look so different. While I was getting tea, I was wondering what had happened.'

'The Tony Jones effect!' Elin chuckled. 'Liz, I feel loads better.' She paused. 'The truth is I haven't come on for twelve years because of the stress of Kevin, then my parents, then worrying about money, but I've restarted. I assumed I was too old.'

Elin talked happily to Liz about Megan's affairs, about Karen's car and how Tony was keeping her afloat by helping with the shopping.

'Which is why I need to get him a decent birthday present.'

Liz looked at her watch and thought for a moment.

'I've got a bit of time. Would you like me to come with you?'

They finished their tea and set off to the shops where Elin bought a blank canvas and resolved to paint a present for Tony.

Lisa 13th April 2013

Lisa's days in the office had improved a bit as since Bob Sullivan had issued his warning, and she was no longer continually subjected to random hands. She had her alarm to hand but from habit continued to avoid compromising situations. But Guy Barnes was watching her and most likely planning to take his revenge.

One morning she attended the meeting and took her usual seat at the bottom of the table.

Guy Barnes took the meeting. 'Bob Sullivan is away this week having his Easter holiday and I will be taking the meetings this week.'

The usual business was conducted and Lisa expected the meeting to finish, but to her surprise Guy Barnes had added a new item.

'I have to tell you about some changes we are making in our work here in the office. In future, accounts worth more than half a million pounds will be handled by senior members of teams. I have been working with George here to re-assign accounts so that the workloads remain reasonable, and we will get that list to you after this meeting.'

Back at her desk Lisa was relaxed about this as she had few accounts over that sum. But when the email appeared in her inbox and she started to study it, she discovered that she had lost three accounts which were those most likely to cross the bonus threshold; while she had been allocated a number of accounts which she knew from experience were moribund. Jeremy was the other junior in the team.

She called across to her colleague, 'Jeremy, how's your list?'

'Pretty okay. I didn't have any big ones. I've had some smaller ones added.'

'Are those active?'

'Yes, a little,' he said but then his phone rang and the conversation was killed.

Ever the professional – and out of courtesy – Lisa rang the three clients she had lost to explain that their accounts were now being handled by others. The third one was the one she least wanted to lose as she had opened his account, and by helping him she had managed to get the funds on the company's books up above the half million-pound mark. She liked Tony and didn't want to lose him as a client.

'Dr Jones. Lisa here from the brokers.'

'Morning Lisa.'

'How's it going? Still trying to find the magic bet?'

'I've stopped paper trading for now as my system seems to work. I'm waiting for the right conditions when I can try a real bet. There have been a few I could have tried, but I've made the standard that the indicators have to reach more severe. So far those conditions have not happened.'

'I hope it works Tony. Spread betting is an easy way to lose a fortune. I have some news for you. We will be writing to you in due course to explain the details but I thought it polite to let you know myself.'

'What's that?'

'According to some rules in this office I am a junior member of staff and cannot handle accounts over half a million. Your account is being transferred to Mr Barnes who is a much more experienced account manager than I am, so I hope he will be able to help you.'

'I doubt he will be as good as you Lisa. Nothing seems too much trouble for you. Can I write to them and ask them to leave me with you? I don't see the point of change for change's sake.'

'I suppose you could do that but please don't say that I was any part of that process.'

'Why not? What's going on? Is there something you're not telling me?'

'Loads, but I can't talk about it here.'

'Okay. Who do I write to?'

'Mr Bob Sullivan – at this address – would be a place to start. Do me a favour though, send me a copy in an envelope marked for my specific attention.'

'Right, I will. Thank you for everything you've done Lisa. I may bypass Mr Barnes occasionally if that's allowed.'

'I couldn't possibly say what rules govern client behaviour!'

They both laughed and the call ended. Lisa had thought about the implications of the change that Guy Barnes had announced. Jeremy was unaffected. It was only her. Bob Sullivan was away and normally he announced such changes. The more she thought about it, the more she understood this was payback for her winning the fight in the assessment meeting. She was unlikely to get a bonus now anyway.

The battle with Guy Barnes was getting nastier.

That evening Lisa was doing her ironing and realised that she had no future at the brokers. Once again, she wished she knew what had happened with Chantelle. She appeared to have been sacked; although if Chantelle's life had been anything like her own, she had probably wanted to get out anyway.

Her mobile rang. She had hoped that Rhodri would call. She had a bad feeling about things with Rhodri – and worse –something in her was causing the problem. She had to find a way to stop her reaction to physical contact. She needed to make a special effort, as she knew he was the one for her.

To her surprise it was Tony. 'Evening Lisa.'

'Evening, Dr Jones. I didn't expect a call from you?'

'No. I'm afraid I'm not ringing to ask you out for dinner or anything, but I've been thinking about our call earlier today. To be honest I was a bit shocked. As far as I am concerned the service you have provided has been first class and one of the reasons why I have given my business all to you. If I took some of my money out and put it elsewhere, would that change things?'

'I doubt it.'

'I didn't want to ask you while you were at work but can we talk frankly now? What have you done to merit this treatment?'

'Bluntly, a number of men have been sexually harassing me, so in a performance assessment meeting I asked the boss to get it stopped. I told him that the next time someone physically touched me I would set off a rape alarm in the office. This change has been to get back at me.'

'Physically? You mean touching you?'

'Yes. I told the boss that I had been touched sixty-nine times according to the little diary I keep of what happens to me.'

'sixty-nine! You're joking?'

'Yes, sixty-nine. I record it every time.'

'I don't know what to say. That sort of behaviour should get someone sacked.'

'Mr Barnes is a control freak who has somehow blackmailed the boss to protect him and turn a blind eye.'

'Lisa, the reason why I rang is that my wife's brother is a specialist in employment law; you may need proper advice.'

'I was wondering if I can carry on to be honest. They've started to attack me in every way they can. I was thinking tonight I may have to find a new job.'

'Do I have your permission to ring him? I'm sure if he's free he'll ring you back tonight. He can get quite aggressive about injustice, and I'm sure he'd like to hear your story. He's called Alistair.'

'Are you sure?'

'Yes. I'll give him a ring. If he can't call you back, I'll ring myself. Don't go anywhere.'

'Thanks Tony.'

Lisa put her phone down and carried on ironing her pile of clothes. He was right. Even with the help of Mike from HR she was out of her depth. Maybe her approach to her assessment meeting had been over the top, but she had been driven to it.

The phone rang again.

'Hello, is that Lisa? It's Alistair here. Tony Jones suggested I give you a call.'

'Yes, this is Lisa.'

'Lisa. Can I call you Lisa? Please call me Alistair. I specialise in employment law – especially unfair dismissal – and from what Tony says, you are in a bad place.'

Alistair went on to explain what he did and how he worked.

'Don't worry about the costs at this stage. I'll tell you if your case is not worth pursuing and there won't be any costs. If you have a case, we'll do our best to pass the costs on.'

'Thanks.'

'You have to tell me what's been going on. That way I can get a feel for the situation.'

'I'd already thought before Tony spoke to me that I was in too deep. I'm not sure what to do next. Maybe the best thing is to resign and find another job and save a lot of bother.'

'I've got time to listen now if you want to tell me what has been going on.'

Lisa had a moment of doubt about talking to a stranger down the phone about her troubles but she was friends with Tony, and Alistair sounded nice. He must be Tony's brother-in-law. She had nothing to lose talking to him at this stage. The ironing could wait so she unplugged the iron and sat down.

'If you've got time. It started when I had a new job, June 2012.'

She went on to explain about the harassment and sexism that was rife in the office, her first assessment, the treatment of her desk and being referred to as the little lady.

He interrupted. 'How was that meeting recorded?'

'On a company form. I made them put the details on the form and we signed it.'

'Do you have a copy?'

'Yes.'

'Where?'

'Locked in my desk drawer with my other employment papers.'

'Can I suggest you bring all your papers home and keep them somewhere safe? You could even make copies and send them to me. If things start to get ugly your desk is vulnerable.'

Lisa went on to explain the second meeting, the bonuses and the physical assaults.

'You've got the record for that as well?'

'Of course.'

'How do you know you've been touched up that many times?'

'I kept a book in my desk and recorded everything that I considered inappropriate. Verbal stuff as well as the physical things.'

'Lisa. That book's dynamite. I suppose it's in your desk now?'

'No. I brought it home when I got the rape alarm and told them I would set it off if there is any trouble. I was hoping not to have to write in it again. I've got one in my desk in case; which so far is empty. I wrote this last stuff about bonuses in my book here at home.'

'Right. Keep it out of the office and away from anyone who could get hold of it. You have to make a copy and send it to me. If you have to make an entry at work, make a copy at home as well.'

'Why is it so important?'

'From what you have said to me you can sue the brokers for unfair dismissal and other workplace offences. If you do leave their employment because of this, you could get substantial damages for loss of earnings. Apart from that the company is facing potentially huge reputational issues, so your little book may be worth millions to them. Does the book name individuals?'

'Yes. It has to, to make sense.'

'So apart from the company position, there are individuals who presumably face ruin. Get me a copy as soon as you can.'

'Thank you, I will. What should I do? Resign or what? It's a big decision.'

'I know. If you enjoy the work and you are reasonably paid that's hard to give up. But there's no point in being miserable. By the way, why were you speaking to Tony this evening? That's the bit I couldn't understand.'

Lisa explained about the business of the rape alarm and how the accounts had been moved to get back at her and her bonus.

'If you think the rape alarm will do it, stick with it. You are going to end up leaving them, and so you should plan for that now. Whatever you do, keep your records safe or they will vanish.'

They talked some more about Alistair's address and how she could contact him, and she thanked him and rang off.

Lisa sat for a while after ending the call and reflected on Alistair's comments. She could survive for a few months without a job, but he was right. Her career as a broker in this company was finished. It was simply a matter of when. She thought again about Chantelle. *What had happened to her?*

Sonny

The pencil stops again. Is this the way out? Will Lisa just leave?

Max pops up in the margin. He's more conciliatory than usual.

'Keep going. She's a fighter.'

I'm scared of what could happen to her. That Barnes man is a fighter too and doesn't care how he wins.

'The crisis is coming. You haven't got far to go,' Max said.

How does Max know?

'It's like my strips in the paper. The good guy always wins.'

That's because I write it. Real life isn't like that.

'It's your story.'

As usual Max leaves me wondering. If it's my story it should end the way I want. But when the pencil is in my hand it has a mind of its own, and I don't feel as though I guide it. Very perplexing.

Lisa 1ˢᵗ May 2013

Some weeks after the changes to the client lists, Lisa was again in the morning meeting and now Bob Sullivan was back in the chair. After the usual business Bob Sullivan got on to changes that had come from head office.

Lisa followed the detail of the changes that the company was making to their trading arrangements – and the reasons why – and didn't see anything controversial. One change, however, surprised her.

'Now we come on to the spread betting arrangements. For some time now we have been researching people's betting habits. Only a small proportion of bets are placed under one pound and these bets attract a disproportionate cost for administration. In order to discourage this, we have decided to modify the company spread betting website, take away the pennies in the bet value and require entry of pounds only.'

There was some discussion about what this meant, but Bob Sullivan cut it off.

'Listen. It's being done as we speak. As soon as we can we will write to all our clients about the changes. Please can you check your client lists and make sure that everyone who is spread betting gets a call to let them know. We can't afford a client placing a bet without knowing this change has been made, especially if they lose heavily as a result. Please ring the active clients today.'

'Furthermore, I would like to remind you that deposit limits for spread betting are a requirement for all clients. All of them. They protect the clients and they protect us.'

'Go back to your desks and work through all your clients, ring those you have to and check that the deposit limits are set for all accounts.'

Lisa returned to her desk after the meeting and dutifully rang those clients who were spread betting to inform them of the change. She had a busy day with other things and realised on the way home that she had not called Tony – who she knew might place a bet at any time – even though he had not been active. She felt she had a special relationship with him as he was the first client she had ever signed up.

Tony's situation bothered her, so she rang him after she'd eaten – but she was not to know he was at the choir and there was no answer.

Lisa 11ᵗʰ May 2013

That Saturday Lisa went to the stables again, but this time after lunch as Rhodri had called Lisa earlier in the week and suggested that she change her riding time to two-thirty so he could join her.

'You don't ride do you? I've never seen you.'

'Actually, I do,' said Rhodri. 'You can't be brought up with horses around you without going for a ride occasionally. You've never seen me ride. If you think about it, you didn't even know I had any link with the stables till we first met.'

Lisa was surprised but knew that he was right. She wondered how good he was.

Rhodri continued, 'If we ride in the afternoon, I can finish the job I have to do on Saturday morning. Once we've been riding, we can then go to see "Silver Linings Playbook" – it won some Oscars, so they're showing it again. Unless you've seen it?'

'I haven't seen it. That sounds like a good plan. Two-thirty on Saturday.'

So it was they were together in the yard. While Lisa saddled Blister, Rhodri was getting one of the other horses ready – a big, rather docile mount called Rustle.

'My problem is that I've got a bit big for the more exciting horses,' said

189

Rhodri.

They headed off out of the yard with a wave to Beth who was sorting out some other riders. Blister was his usual cheerful self, pulling at the bit while Rhodri's horse liked a lazy walk and followed behind. Lisa turned Blister round and made him walk alongside Rustle so she could talk to Rhodri. Blister accepted the new pace and settled down.

'You can try Blister if you like,' she said to Rhodri, but he smiled at her. 'No. I'm confident enough but he's a real handful, and he's used to you. He might decide to try my limits out, and I could get into bother.'

The day was warm with enough breeze to keep them cool in the open and some white cotton-wool clouds dotting the sky. In among the trees it was warmer, and Lisa was glad that Rustle had chosen a less demanding pace than Blister liked.

Inevitably, Lisa talked to Rhodri about her workplace trials. She knew he was quite angry as he didn't say much. She had the feeling that if he was free to do so he would have murdered Guy Barnes.

After they finished riding and had sorted out the horses, they walked up to the house where Mrs Howells had thoughtfully put some lemonade in the fridge.

'I thought it would be too hot for tea,' she said as she poured them long glasses on the decking behind the house. 'How's your work going Lisa? Rhodri says very little about it, except that you have problems.'

'The truth is Mrs Howells that I don't think I can carry on, and I should be looking for another job. The behaviour of some of the men is outrageous.'

'Have you reported it?'

'Of course. But each time I have closed off one way they can get at me, they set up some other scheme to show me who's in control.'

'What are they trying to prove?'

'That a little girl can't do the business in a big man's world. A woman's place is filing and making tea and being a good little wife at home. When she's not being decorative in the office.'

'I thought that finished years ago. Mind when I first started, I had the feeling that some expected me to fail because I was a woman.'

'Didn't Dad help?' asked Rhodri.

'Of course, but he was off working a lot of the time.' She turned to Lisa who had never heard Rhodri's father mentioned before. 'He was in the merchant navy and was washed off a ship in a storm when Rhodri was ten. The stables were established by then, so I was able to cope. That's why Rhodri knows so much carpentry. I needed him to do the odd jobs!'

They talked on until Rhodri and Lisa headed into town to find something to eat and go to the cinema.

Lisa enjoyed the film. The leading man, Pat (played by the delicious Bradley Cooper!), was a pleasing hunk like Rhodri, and the character Tiffany – in her wild and determined way – pleased her too. Through the film Lisa held her handbag so Rhodri couldn't get hold of her hand, even though she sensed that after such a wonderful day he deserved to know that she wanted to be with him. But the poison of the men in the office was in her soul, and she had developed a horrible resistance to physical contact.

During the walk from the cinema to Rhodri's flat she had been wondering what her reaction would be if Rhodri wanted to be more physical with her. She wanted to be with him, but she was frightened of what her body's reaction would be.

He opened the door so she could go in. She'd been to his flat before to pick him up but this was her first chance to go inside. And although the outside had been rather unpromising, the inside was light with fresh paintwork. It was bigger than she expected as well, and she faced him as he closed the door.

'Would you like the guided tour?' he asked. She nodded, sensing herself tensing up. It was only Rhodri, but she was starting to feel trapped.

'This is the living room – complete with Xbox for bachelors – and my books and music.'

'Wow, you've got plenty of CDs. That must have cost a fortune,' she said.

'No. I cheat. I have a friend who does house clearances, and he lets me go through them before they go on general sale in a charity shop. I'm afraid some of the books are like that too. I haven't read them all.'

Among the books were quite a few non-fiction titles relating to design and construction. *No wonder he knew about building and design*, she thought. There were a number of boxes associated with the TV and a pile of remote controls. She dropped her bag on the sofa – part of a worn three-piece suite. She wondered if this was from a charity shop as well. Rhodri read

191

her mind.

'The three-piece was my mother's. Most of my furniture is from her or second hand. I spent my money on a decent sized flat. I did it up while it was empty because I could carry on living at the stables. I have my workshop at the stables still, although most of the time I work out on sites.'

He led her into the kitchen diner, which was larger than she expected, with modern units and in the dining area an out of place table and chairs.

'More hand me downs,' he said. 'They don't fit, do they?'

He smiled at her, as if showing her this was a bit embarrassing.

She saw that he had no pictures on the walls and filed it away as something she could give him, remembering how he had enjoyed their visits to galleries. She tried to think what sort of art he liked.

'While we're here would you like a cup of something?'

'No thanks. I'm not sure hot drinks at this time of night suit me.'

'Something cold?' he was eager to please.

'No. I'm okay. Thanks.'

They moved on to have a quick glance in the bathroom. It was clean and tidy but looked as though it hadn't changed since he'd bought the flat. Lisa wondered if he had cleaned up specially; in case she came back with him.

He came to a stop in the hallway and faced her.

'We'd better not go in my bedroom as I'm not sure how I left it. Things get a bit rough by the end of the week, and I try to clean up at the weekends but having to work this morning got in the way.'

He showed her the second bedroom, which was a mess of boxes, bits of furniture and even some used cans of paint.

'This is a workshop I'm afraid.'

Even so, Lisa thought the room was big enough for a double bed. They went back into the hall.

'Come back to the living room, and my little secret.'

She followed him past the furniture to the window, where she saw a door for the first time. He opened it and they went onto a balcony that had a view across City. The evening was still and she went to the rail and leaned on it, taking in the sounds of traffic. He stood next to her. For while they both took it in, and she understood what he meant when he said it was his little secret. She could imagine standing here after a day's work with a drink, letting the cares of the day drift away.

Her senses sharpened, bringing her back to the present. She felt vulnerable while at the same time wanting their first real kiss. Now they were facing each other, and she could see that he wanted it too. He reached out with both hands and very gently took her upper arms to pull her towards him. It was his mistake. The softness of his touch was identical to that Guy Barnes and others used when they had been feeling her up in the office.

Abruptly she stepped back away from him and shut out the feel of his touch. She saw the bewilderment in his face and knew her body had betrayed her. She felt frozen inside. She wanted him to hold her tight, but her action had broken the moment. An internal scream of pain filled her head and tears of grief for the lost chance filled her eyes. She had wrecked the magic. She knew she had to get away from the distress in his eyes and leave before something bad was said. It was her fault. She had to go.

Without a word she fetched her handbag and ran from the flat, down the two flights of stairs and out to the street, tears freely pouring down her face. She went to her car, but once she was behind the wheel – in her safe little private box – she stopped. It had happened so quickly that she hadn't thought out her reaction to the gentle hands on her upper arms. But now she realised that Rhodri had no idea of what he had done.

How was she going to explain to him something she did not understand? For a while she sat in the car and cried, gripped by the thought that she had wrecked the one bit of her life that had been good. Going back to Rhodri now was impossible. There was no way to rebuild that feeling of togetherness they had shared on the balcony before she had destroyed it. She drove home with tears pouring down her cheeks, knowing that the longer she left reconciliation the harder it would be.

Rhodri 11ᵗʰ May 2013

Rhodri was perplexed. The day had been so good. The ride in the woods, the meal together and the feel-good film. Now Lisa had pushed him away. The truth was he was starting to wonder if he should propose to her. In his eyes everything about her was perfect but now something had happened, and she had shut herself off from him.

He went over it in his mind. All he had done was try to kiss her, nothing more. Was there something about him that was putting her off? Though of course he had hoped it would lead to something more after the wonderful day they'd had together.

As soon as she had pushed him away, he had seen the tears in her eyes. What did it mean? He ran over the expression he had seen on her face trying to understand how it could be full of tears, and yet he had seen a longing in her eyes as though she had wanted the kiss as well.

The moment had seemed an age while they looked at each other, but Lisa had left the balcony, grabbed her handbag and fled. He knew that she wasn't going to go far before she broke down in tears. But why?

He didn't chase after her. The failed kiss had hurt him too and although he dithered for a while about going after her, he felt that his world had shifted. He went through the day in his mind again. She had been reluctant to hold his hand when they were out together and this had been a feature of their meetings, but he thought back to the first day he had taken her to the art gallery. Then she had been happy to walk hand in hand. Now physical contact was out. He began to get angry and slumped down in front of the TV to flick through the channels watching rubbish till the small hours.

Chapter 10: Early May 2013

Sonny

I've had a bit of time away from this but now set my drawing board for a new session with my story. I can't quite remember where I'd got to and look back at the previous scenes. My pencil is sharp and the frames are drawn. It no longer surprises me that I'm drawing a new venue.

The picture is quite dark, but I can see a young woman ranting at a man in a night club. I've seen her before in the newspaper when she won some prize in a judo competition. I can hear her shouting, even above the club disco playing Adele singing *'Don't you remember'*.

Woman 11ᵗʰ May 2013

'You are so totally dumped. I've never met anyone as annoying as you. Why should I always drive home so you can drink? Getting drunk doesn't do you any good. Every Tuesday night you have to go out to quiz night in the pub with your mates and you always come back smashed. On Thursdays it's something else. On Saturdays you have to take over the sofa for the football. And Monday mornings … 'Where's my clean shirts?' What do you think of women? As long as you have food, clean clothes, time for your drinking and your mates, you can be quite nice. Have you ever washed up in your life? Have you ever been shopping for food? You don't need a girlfriend; you need a mother. Clear your crap out of my flat tonight or I'll give it to the bin men.'

She turned away from him, picked up a jacket from a chair and headed for the bar. Her now ex-boyfriend watched her. For a moment it looked as though he was going to follow, but he shook his head and left.

She ordered an orange juice at the bar and drank it, watching herself in the mirror. She looked as though she might burst into tears.

Another man nearby was quietly observing. His hands fidgeted with a hip flask. He seemed indecisive – as though he thought to walk up to her – but then changed his mind.

'Can I get you anything else?' The barman was in front of her.

'Nothing thanks,' she said.

She looked back at the mirror, nursing her empty glass. She needed time to think before she drove home to see if her boyfriend had cleared out. She put on the jacket and headed out into the fresh air. Moments later the man followed.

Sonny

I like the spirit in this girl and now I am worried for her. I hate the threat hanging over the women in my story. I wish the pencil didn't have to carry on drawing a new frame, and I'm hoping that there isn't a bad outcome to this scene.

The new picture is dark. From the lights I can see this is a park in the centre of City. Now I can see better. The young woman from the club is sitting on a park bench at the side of a path, and she's staring out over the night-time city. I sense she has been crying, but she is over it now and the tears have finished.

Woman 11th May 2013

The man walked across the grass and came up to the park bench. He didn't hide his approach but came from behind. The woman turned and saw him against the sky, then went back to facing the front. He stopped beside her – about two yards away.

'What a lovely evening out here. You picked a good spot to sit,' he said. She found a handkerchief, wiped her face and blew her nose.

'I came for a bit of peace,' she said. He didn't take the hint and continued to stand beside her; as though looking at the view.

'Got a problem?' he asked, getting closer.

'I gave my boyfriend the heave-ho. I wanted some privacy to think.'

'I've got a flask if you want a drink.' At the mention of the flask he moved closer till he had a hand on the back of the bench to her right.

'No thanks, I came here to be alone.' His hand on the back of the bench was nearly on her shoulder. He still didn't go. She felt he was too close behind her and jumped up to face him. She stepped back to give herself space and unhurriedly moved her handbag to free both her arms.

'Why don't you come home with me?' he said. 'If you're feeling like that you should have company and break out of it.' She knew he would have preferred her sitting on the bench. She was much easier to restrain that way.

'Leave me alone. I'm not interested.'

He took her left hand with his right.

'Come. You'll be much better once we get somewhere comfortable.' He took her calm for the confusion of drink.

He jerked her towards him, anticipating resistance, but she was ready. She broke his grip, jumped forward and pushed. He was off balance and falling back. His left hand grabbed at whatever it could. His desperate fingers missed her jacket, tangled in a piece of her blouse, and he fell. Now she was braced in her fighting stance. Her blouse ripped as it dragged through his fingers, and he crashed onto the turf; narrowly missing the bench.

'You bitch. What have you done?' From what she could see he was clutching at his left hand and making no move to get up. 'Shit, I'm bleeding.' She stepped away and breathed easier. She knew he wasn't hurt badly. People who are hurt don't make much noise.

'You asked for it.' She turned and ran, confident that he would not follow.

He nursed his sore hand. Tough threads in the blouse had dug into one of his fingers. He looked about. He couldn't see any witnesses, but he needed to get away from here in case she went to the police. His muddy trousers were an obvious giveaway, so he fled home.

The young woman got over the fence out of the park and went looking for the police incident van parked in the centre of a nearby square. She had seen it when she was coming out of the nightclub earlier. The van was open – although the city centre had calmed down a lot.

She climbed the steps into the van. She was wary now, as she did not know what kind of reaction she would get and was feeling like a complete idiot. The news in the papers about attacks in the parks had been going on for a while and the police didn't have any leads.

Sonny

How relieved I am that this young woman is safe now. I relax and let the pencil hurry on as it draws the inside of the police van. I remember that the last time he was thwarted, he went on to find another victim. Did Lisa go home? Are any other women in my story – my friends – at risk? Is this the story? I have to carry on.

Cheryl 11th May 2013

At the counter was PC Cheryl Carter. She watched the woman come into the incident van.

The woman was breathing freely and her blouse showed some damage. Cheryl saw her relax and pull her jacket closed.

'Are you alright?' asked Cheryl.

'Yes, I'm fine. But I've had a little set to in the park with a man.'

'It would be better if you go and sit at the back where we won't be interrupted. I'll be along in a mo.'

Cheryl got on her radio and explained that she needed a hand on the desk in the van if someone wasn't busy. She made her way back to where the other woman was sitting. Cheryl sensed she was nervous.

Cheryl knew that taking notes at this stage may not be the best idea, so she decided to let the story come out first. For the first time she took a proper look at the woman and saw the face was familiar.

'Do I know you?' she asked.

'No. But I've been in the papers a bit recently as I won a medal in the judo championships. You know the headlines – "City girl throws them all". Loads of people think they know me now.'

'Oh yes, I remember. You did really well. But what were you doing in the park? We do advise people against that.'

'Yes. I know. It was silly. I dumped my boyfriend and had to get away to be alone. Some creep came and tried to get his hands on me. I fixed him though.'

'Did you throw him? Is he alright? Do I need to get someone into the park to find him? Is he injured?'

'Pride mainly. No. I didn't do what I wanted to. They train you to keep it to the dojo – that means staying in control. Last time I saw him he was sitting on the ground mouthing off. He was shorter than me and a bit fleshy; bit older too, thirty-something. I ran because I reckoned with my training he wouldn't be able to keep up.'

'How did you see him in the dark?'

'I didn't. It was more sensing. For a moment he was close to me.'

By now her jacket had fallen open again and Cheryl could see that her blouse was torn, so she had obviously been in some sort of tussle.

'So how did you get away from him in the park?'

'He pulled me towards him, so I stepped forward and gave him a little push. He didn't expect that and fell backwards on his arse. The bastard caught my blouse with his hand as he fell.'

'You're sure he's not there?'

'He won't be. He was clutching his hand and swearing.'

They both studied the damage to the blouse. From what Cheryl could see nothing was missing, but it was torn.

'Do you mind if I keep that? He may have cut himself. We've got T-shirts here.'

Cheryl went and fetched a T-shirt. 'I'll stand guard here while you change,' she said.

She put the blouse in a bag and they both sat down again.

'I'm going to have to take a formal statement from you as this could help us build our picture of what is going on.'

So, for the third time Cheryl was involved with the park murders and shuddered as she thought of what could have happened to this woman. She remembered the awful day she'd had in the park those months ago when the body had been found.

'I need a cup of tea,' she said. 'Would you like one?'

Sonny

The pencil stops for a moment and then restarts. Two days have passed and Cheryl and another policeman are by the park bench. No murders have been reported, so for now my women are safe.

Cheryl 13th May 2013

'This is the one she was sitting on Sarge. She described it exactly.'

'Sit down Cheryl. Let's see what happened.' The sergeant went behind her; studying the ground, expecting that any marks would have gone with rain and the traffic of dogs. But a smooth indentation in the mud next to the end of the bench showed where someone could have sat down heavily.

'That would have spoiled his trousers,' he said.

Cheryl stood as the girl would have stood. 'She had it worked out, didn't she? He was on the slippery mud and she was on the tarmac path.'

'It's pretty level though, as she said. So he was probably about the same height as her.'

They both sat down on the bench and studied the park around them. The trees were surrounded by bushes and there was plenty of cover close by to hide a body. The woman had been very lucky.

As they sat, she caught sight of a button with a little piece of thread and material attached. Once again, she relived the awful day when she had been at the site of the murder. The detached button suggested a much more unpleasant outcome. She bagged it.

'What do you think?' she said.

'You could be right. He had another go and picked the wrong woman. She's pretty well contained, that one. Now we have a clearer idea of his height, that will help once we find him.'

She studied the button in the bag.

'Cheryl are you okay?' he asked. 'You've gone a bit pale.'

'It brings it all back. There were buttons on the ground that time too.'

He took the bag from her and looked at it.

'We might get a little DNA off the blouse where it hurt his finger,' he said.

'He's hurt his hand. How are we going to find a man with a damaged finger Sarge?'

'I don't know. First we have to get you a cup of tea.'

Chapter 11: 14th May 2013

Sonny

From the scene in the park I get the feeling that the strands of this story are coming together. I want to finish the story somehow, but I am frightened. I avoid Max as he will just tell me to keep going.

When the pencil starts again I don't understand some of the things it draws for the story. For example, why is the Greek debt problem and the German response to it so important? And what has the growth rate in China got to do with it? My newspaper editor would like me to make cartoons of world events, but I have difficulty finding humour in politics in the UK. European politics is even more remote. Despite the editor's pleas, I have left all politics in his office.

I can't get away from it. I have to carry on, so I prepare the frames as usual and take up the pencil.

Tony Jones is at home working at his computer after having breakfast. I feel safe here.

Tony

Today's the day! For several months Tony had been playing with spread betting and now he had a feeling that he should be more positive about it. The stock market was unreasonably high, and the commentators sensed that the FTSE 100 had a fragility that it had not had for a while.

His own analysis of the Far East gave clues that the market was going down – although the London market had not made any early moves. Tony resolved to have a little bet on it going down.

He studied the bet entry page, which wasn't quite the same as he remembered for paper trading but had all the fields he expected. He entered the details as Lisa had explained and checked them over. He had decided to bet fifty pounds and entered the figures carefully; including the extra two zeroes for the pennies.

He pressed the confirm button and it asked for his password. The machine asked him to confirm that he accepted the terms and conditions and understood he would have to pay for any losses. He confirmed and sat back to watch the screen. For a few moments nothing happened.

To his utter horror a new screen appeared confirming that he had placed a bet for five thousand on the stock market going down in the next twenty-four hours. He stared at it in disbelief. What would Karen say if she knew that he had risked the money she had set aside for their retirement on a crazy bet like this? *'You need to take more care, Tony.'* He could hear her voice from right back at the beginning of their relationship when they had been at university and he had fouled up a calculation by simple errors with decimal points.

For a time he was paralysed. He saw a button on the screen which said, 'Watch the progress of your bet'. He clicked it and a new screen appeared showing the FTSE 100 index and calculating his bet. Already the index was creeping up and his bet was losing. Only a few points, but each point was worth five thousand.

He reached for the phone and dialled for Lisa. He had been told that since his holdings in the bank were now more than five hundred thousand pounds, his account had been moved to Guy Barnes. But Tony instinctively did not like Guy Barnes and in this crisis he needed to talk to someone he trusted.

His call was routed to a receptionist. 'I'm sorry, our account managers are in a meeting. They will be available after nine-thirty. Can I take a message?'

Tony had half an hour to wait, and he knew it would be a very long half hour.

Sonny

I see the losses on the bet creep up a little and set up a new frame. It shows the system in the brokers. From what I can see the bet has been accepted and automatically passed on to the bank, who work the spread betting market. So, the bet is out of the control of the brokers.

The pencil starts a new frame showing a different part of the brokerage. I don't remember this part of their building before, but I do recognise Gareth Jenkins. I don't understand why we are here as I don't think Gareth is an important part of the storyline, but I let the pencil continue.

Gareth

Gareth is on his mobile phone. 'Rhodri, you said you are coming over this morning. Are you still coming?'

'Yeah, don't worry. I've had to finish something, but I'm on my way. What have you got?'

'The people in HR want to move some of their partitions to create a bit of meeting space. It's straightforward.'

'I'll see you in half an hour.'

Gareth rang off. He'd rung Rhodri the day before.

'Rhodri. Can you give me some time tomorrow?'

'Yes, shouldn't be a problem but there's something I have to do first thing.'

'You'll be here by lunchtime, then.'

'Cheeky. Is about ten too early for you?'

'No, that's good. I was meaning to ask you – you got engaged yet?'

'To Lisa, you mean? Not much chance of that.'

'Why? Have you asked her?'

The joking Rhodri of a few moments before had disappeared.

'I don't know, Gareth. I like her, but I don't know.'

He hoped that Rhodri would see Lisa upstairs again. They were a natural couple and this worried Gareth. 'What had gone wrong?'

Sonny

The pencil returns to familiar territory and the meeting in the brokers is breaking up. I expect now we will get back to the meat of the story.

Lisa

In the manager's meeting Guy Barnes was full of himself, as usual. Lisa avoided him, and once it was over went back to her desk to look at the recent trade records. Her list had reduced since they had moved her bigger accounts, and she was angry. The ones she had been given in return were dormant.

Today she was angry too because of the mess she had made with Rhodri at the weekend. She had tried so hard, but Guy Barnes's creepy fingers had somehow poisoned her against any human contact. Once again she felt a sort of wave wash over her like spiders walking on her bare flesh, and shuddered. It had to end today.

Unconsciously, she slid her hand into the top drawer of her desk and fingered the little rape alarm she had decided to use next time Guy Barnes touched her. Unless she did something, nothing would change.

'Lisa, we have a problem.' Guy stood facing her over her desk.

'What?'

'I've got a red flag against that man Tony Jones whose account was transferred to me a month ago. He's placed a stupid bet.'

Lisa knew Tony wasn't a fool so she wondered what he had done.

'Can I see the trades?' She couldn't see the account now it had been moved to Guy, and he needed to enter his password.

He came around the desk and stood behind her. She had to move to the left –away from her precious top drawer and the rape alarm – so that Guy could get to the keyboard. He typed in his codes and stepped back to allowed Lisa to control the screen.

'Why would he do that? He hasn't done any spread betting trades before,' Guy said. For the moment Lisa sensed that Guy was fully engaged with his job.

She worked the keys and the computer found the records of Tony Jones's bet. The running bet came up on the screen and Lisa looked in disbelief. Tony's loss was near forty thousand pounds. Guy continued.

'It's worse than I thought. The master has set off the bet. We can't ring him up and cancel it. It's too late.' Lisa knew Guy was flailing round for an idea. She was worrying about Tony as if he had still been her client.

'He hasn't set a stop loss. I tell my clients they should always do that. You should have told him. It's your fault.'

'I did tell him,' Lisa said. 'I sent him the literature as well and told him to read it carefully.'

'Didn't he look at it?' said Guy. She knew he was wondering if there was a liability for the loss currently showing on the bet because of the change to the website. She also knew he was fanatical about his bonus – he was always bragging about how much it was.

'We won't know how bad this is until tomorrow morning; we're going to have to let the bet run on – it's up eight already. We might have to bankrupt him.' Guy said.

'How ethical would that be?'

'Never mind that. It can't be our fault.'

'He talked to me about it though. Let me bring up the paper trading.'

Again, she worked the keys while Guy looked over her shoulder.

'It's all fifty pounds. He never did anything else.' Lisa scrolled back through the record.

'So why would he suddenly make a bet of five thousand?' Guy asked.

'I told him that he had to remember to add the pennies into the bet. He hasn't done any paper trading since the change, so he's put the pennies in. Bob Sullivan told us in the meeting that we should contact all our clients and tell them that the pennies had been moved from the betting website.'

'I did. For the clients who were betting.' Guy was shaken. 'Dr Jones hasn't bet before.' Lisa now knew that this was Guy's fault. She flicked the screen back to look at the progress of the bet just as the loss jumped over forty-five thousand pounds.

'What level's been set for his deposit?' asked Lisa. 'That should kick in to stop the bet.' She worked the keyboard looking for the screen with Tony's data.

Guy had gone very quiet while the computer found that page.

Lisa thought she knew what was on it. To her surprise the deposit limit was blank.

'It's blank,' she said. 'How can that be?' She remembered Bob Sullivan's instruction to set a deposit limit for all clients. Lisa was shocked. She had been careful to put the limit on Tony's account as she didn't want him to lose too much. She sat back in the chair as the implication hit her.

'You deleted it. Why? It would have been alright if you hadn't taken him,' she said. 'You've deleted it to set me up for a disciplinary.' As soon as she said it, she knew it was a mistake. He had changed in an instant. His hand slid onto her shoulder and as usual her body froze at his touch.

'Please take your hand off me.'

Sonny

I look at the storyline. What can I do to help? I know that Max is off somewhere laughing at me, knowing I'm powerless. Even if I thought I was creating the story, I don't have any way to influence it. He says it's my story, but all I can do is keep setting the frames and hope it will get better.

The pencil draws the next desk where Jeremy Dudley is sitting. Can he can help Lisa?

Jeremy

Jeremy had seen Guy and Lisa having an animated discussion about something on the screen, and when Guy was near Lisa he was always concerned. He hated his inability to say something about it. His sexuality gave Guy a weapon against him too powerful to risk, and he knew now how Guy suppressed proper discussion about the culture in the office.

He noticed when Guy first tensed and then put his hand on Lisa's shoulder. For the first time Jeremy was in the right place. He grabbed his mobile phone and started filming what was going on. He didn't care who saw. His sympathy was with Lisa.

Sonny

I set a new frame and the pencil quickly brings me back to Lisa and Guy.

Lisa

'Please take your hand off me.'

'You love it. I can feel you react.' His voice had changed and was much lower. Aimed at her. She was unable to respond. Unable to move. No longer the brave and angry girl she had been even moments before.

His hand slipped down round her neck to the gap in her blouse, then under it. The fingers started to work their way under her bra. Lisa was still thinking about the betrayal that a disciplinary would be. Then she understood. He had been setting her up for blackmail. Like he was blackmailing all the others in the office, just so he could do what he liked. Whatever had frozen inside her was changed to hot anger in an instant and she reacted.

Her hand reached for the drawer where the rape alarm lay, but in doing so she had to push against Guy.

'See, you're enjoying it,' he said. She opened the drawer and by the rape alarm was the black book. To reach the alarm she would have to push him harder.

'Now I see it. You're going to fire off that alarm,' he said and pushed her back roughly so that he could stop her reaching the alarm.

Lisa had fallen from horses many times. She saw her chance to roll off the chair and out of his clutches as he shoved her to the left. Her blouse tore as she threw herself off the chair and his hand came free. Her plan would have worked except her head caught the wastepaper bin as she fell and she collapsed to the ground. She lay stunned but as sense came back, she understood that lying stunned was her best weapon if she couldn't sound the alarm.

Sonny

I desperately want to help. What can I do? Lisa is lying on the floor between the desk and the toppled chair. Guy appears distracted as Lisa's skirt has risen up in the fall, and her behind is uncovered.

Max appears in the margin.

'You've got to carry on. You can't stop now.'

'I know I have to carry on. I need to know she is alright, don't I?'

'Just do it,' he says.

The pencil hurries on to a new frame.

Jeremy

Jeremy jumped from his desk as soon as he saw Lisa fall to the floor. While his phone was still filming, he walked over to Guy and looked down at Lisa. Guy was about to take the black book from the drawer – guessing that this may be where Lisa had been keeping notes – but Jeremy slipped his phone into his pocket, lifted Guy bodily from behind and put him down away from the desk. It was no effort for him. He leant down and deftly flicked the skirt back to make Lisa decent.

'Stay down,' he whispered.

He showed Guy his phone. Jeremy had struggled with the office culture long enough too and saw that this could be the end for Guy. He faced him.

'I filmed that. You assaulted her, and now you've knocked her out.'

'No. She knocked herself out.' Jeremy was towering over Guy, physically threatening.

'Go and sit in the conference room and wait till we sort this out.'

'But what about …' Guy was thinking about the bet and his bonus.

'I'll look after her. You've done enough. Go to the conference room or I'll take you there in pieces. Do you want me to sound that alarm?'

Guy backed away from Jeremy to face Bob Sullivan, who had heard the end of the exchange.

'Guy, what have you done? What Jeremy suggests is for the best. I'll come with you. Jeremy, get help for Lisa please.'

Jeremy thought for a moment and then decided. As Bob Sullivan and Guy walked away, he dialled 999.

'Ambulance, please.'

'What's happened?'

'A girl has been assaulted and she's unconscious.'

'Assaulted? You need the police as well.'

Jeremy hadn't thought of that, but even in his anger he saw that for Lisa this was the best thing.

'Yes, please.'

He finished the call and bent over Lisa, keeping himself between her and others who were watching.

'Lisa are you okay?' he whispered, not wanting to touch her.

'I'll live,' she said softly. Jeremy wondered if his 999 call had been a good idea but ignored it. Someone had to do something.

'Are you comfortable? Do you want to get up or are you okay for a minute or two more?'

'I'll get up.'

Jeremy picked up the chair and set it on its wheels. He helped Lisa first to sit upright on the floor and then up into the chair. The side of her face by her cheekbone was bleeding slightly along the red mark left by top of the bin, and her eye was looking puffy.

'Call Mike Penshirst.' Lisa said.

'Yes, good idea.' Jeremy called HR.

Sonny

I am relieved that Guy is no longer near Lisa, but I am still worried for her. I set a new frame and the pencil draws the Human Resources office.

Mike Penshirst

'Penshirst,' he says.

'Mr Penshirst, you need to get up here. Guy Barnes has assaulted Lisa.'

'Lisa? Assaulted? Is she alright?'

'We've called an ambulance and the police may come. His behaviour has been beyond for ages, and you should have sorted it out before now. I captured it on my phone.'

'You've no business calling the police. That could have serious consequences.'

'This company's not going to fix it. It's your problem now.'

While he was talking, he noticed Gareth Jenkins and Rhodri listening to his side of the interchange as they moved the partitions by Mike's desk.

'I'll be up straight away.' He senses the anger in Jeremy and knows he's right. He rang off and got up, where he was faced by Rhodri.

'Is she alright? That's my girl you know.'

'I didn't know.'

'Can I come up with you?' Rhodri wanted to see her; that's why he had come to this job, but Mike was cautious.

'Perhaps when I know what the score is. It will get complicated if the police come.'

Gareth butted in. 'I've got my mobile Mike. Call me when Rhodri can come up.'

'Ok. Give me half an hour.' He rushed off.

Gareth

Rhodri turned to Gareth. 'She's hated that man ever since she's worked for him. She says he's a creep and a predator. She said he's got some hold on the managers she doesn't understand.'

Gareth nodded. He knew as well and hoped that Lisa had kept details of everything that had happened. He had a soft spot for Lisa too and replied, 'I hope she's not badly hurt. He said that the police may be involved.'

The two men carried on moving the partitions, but they were both more concerned with what they didn't know about the situation upstairs. Why would the police be called?

Cheryl

Out in a patrol car not far away, PC Cheryl Carter took the radio call. 'Can you go to the brokers and see what's going on. We've been told that a young woman has been assaulted in the office. An ambulance has been called as well. There's no rush.' She had to do a U-turn to head the right way but decided not to put on the flashing lights.

Sonny

I watch the pencil start again as it follows the news. This time the picture is in Syntagma Square in front of the Greek parliament building. I don't know why I am watching this. I want to know what's happening to Lisa. A spokesman talks to the press about how the parliament has rejected some of the demands from the European Community for financial controls.

Now my pencil has moved to a press conference where the German Chancellor is giving a reaction to the events in Greece. I don't understand this financial jargon – and I suspect the translator doesn't either – but a commentator breaks in to say the Germans have decided to withdraw their support for Greek funding from the European Central Bank. The German Chancellor is demanding development of a new economic structure. The commentator waffles on about the implications of this development leaving me none the wiser.

The pencil has moved on again to an announcement outside the stock exchange in London. Following a special inquiry into banking practices new rules limit the fees that can be charged for certain types of transaction. More jargon I cannot follow.

But the pencil carries on finding financial stories. Now a press conference talks about accountancy rules and how transactions by companies are reported. They say this is aimed at the hypermarkets and is intended to limit their scope for booking profits which are not real. The commentator says that with this announcement the market has started marking down some shares. I wonder what all these mean to my story.

The pencil returns to Lisa's desk.

Lisa

Jeremy had somehow found a can of cold Coca Cola, and Lisa was holding this with her right hand against the swelling on the side of her head.

'I'm not sure I need an ambulance. I should be fine.'

'You do, of course you do. You need to be as badly injured as possible. He had it coming to him and you need to make sure he gets it big time.'

Mike from HR arrived to ask how she is.

'I feel quite groggy and have a throbbing inside my head.'

'Can you tell me what happened?'

'Ask Jeremy. He saw it all.'

'Barnes stuck his hand inside Lisa's blouse and she went for the phone, but he shoved her away and the chair went over. I didn't see where she banged her head.'

'No. I went for the rape alarm. It's in the drawer. He saw it and pushed me away from it.'

Lisa turned her chair and with her left hand opened the drawer. She showed Mike from HR the alarm, but he picked up the black book.

'What's the book?' he asked.

'It's where I make records of what goes on in this office.'

Mike from HR took it from her and flicked the empty pages.

'But there's nothing in it?' he said.

'No,' replied Lisa. 'After Mr Sullivan made his speech about harassment, I took the original home and have made copies of it in case someone decided to pinch it and leave me with no evidence.'

'I'd like a copy if I may.'

'I'm not sure. I've been taking legal advice. How do I make a formal complaint of sexual harassment in this company? Or do I have to take a civil case in court for dismissal? I can't come into this office again.'

'Whoa, slow down.' But the receptionist was showing a green-uniformed paramedic into the room and pointing to them. To Lisa he was a big warm teddy bear of a man with an open honest face. He radiated care.

'Coo! You've been in the wars love. We'd better check you over. Can we go somewhere that's a bit more private?' He addressed the two men who were standing over Lisa.

'You'd better go down to HR. Clare can show you an interview room that you can use.'

'How far is that?'

'Down a stop in the lift.'

'We'll fetch a chair up. We don't want her walking too far until we know she's okay.'

The paramedic produced a radio and called his colleague who was below somewhere with the ambulance. Soon the receptionist appeared again with another paramedic, this time pushing a light wheelchair. This was a woman in a green uniform. To Lisa she was a bit severe on first impression and would have been better wearing a size bigger.

They gently settled her into the wheelchair and were about to start when the paramedic woman leaned forward and said softly into Lisa's ear, 'Have you got a cardigan or jacket we can use to hide that blouse?'

Lisa was instantly grateful because she was starting to feel cold and shivery as the shock of events began to set in.

She pointed to pegs on the wall and said, 'The blue cardie on the left.'

The paramedic fetched it. She draped the cardigan over Lisa's shoulders and buttoned it at the front. 'You can put it on properly once we've done some checks.'

'I'll be down in a minute.' said Mike from HR. His head was down as he went.

From her seat in the wheelchair, Lisa guided them to Clare in HR.

Sonny

Briefly the pencil goes back to the news again. Rumours of a bond default in Dubai were apparently hitting the stock market. The commentators were starting to talk about Black Tuesday. To my surprise the pencil does not go back to the saga in the brokers' office. It draws Tony in his home, a bit earlier that morning.

Tony

Tony had watched as his bet had gone negative in the early trading optimism. After nine-thirty he had phoned four times but no one had answered. The receptionist was patient with him, but even she had not answered the phone every time. He tried Lisa's number too, but that rang on till it asked for a message.

'Lisa, it's Tony Jones here. I've made a frightful cock up with a bet and I don't know how to stop it. Can you ring me.'

He couldn't bear to keep watching, so he decided to get the shopping done and come back to it later.

Mike

Mike Penshirst walked into the conference room where Bob Sullivan and Guy Barnes were sitting in silence. He sat down away from them.

'What are you going to do now?' Guy asked.

'You are going to resign,' Mike replied. 'Or we fire you. Gross misconduct is inevitably a sacking offence.'

'Bob, you can't let this happen.'

'Hold on a minute Mike,' said Bob. 'Aren't you being a bit hasty? We haven't had any investigation. We don't know the facts.'

'I'm telling you Bob. You can't let this happen,' Guy said.

Bob Sullivan went silent. Mike looked from one to the other and said, 'The facts are pretty straightforward. We've got a young lady on our staff who has collected a dossier of harassment in many forms over a long period. She's now developing a massive bruise and black eye, and for some reason her blouse has been badly torn. A member of our staff has made a film on his phone and will no doubt support the testimony in her file. We are going to face a serious legal situation I should imagine, and this will be accompanied by a great deal of bad press. Someone's going to have to ring head office and they will no doubt want to come and sort us out. Get real. The shit is going to start flying everywhere.'

Bob Sullivan was still silent. Mike looked at him and said, 'Come on Bob. You've got to get a grip.'

Bob Sullivan pulled himself together. 'Guy, it's over. You're finished. I should have dealt with you when Chantelle left. You can say whatever you like to whoever you like. I expect you've done for my career as well.'

'What's this?' said Mike to Bob.

'I've been defending him because I was stupid about Chantelle. We had a one-night stand, and Guy suggested he would tell my wife if I didn't look after him. But not anymore. We ruined Chantelle – and now Lisa. You've got to go.'

'Can't we deal with this in-house?' said Guy to Bob, but Mike answered.

'No chance. A senior broker with his hands in a subordinate's bra on the trading floor. Whatever way you put that in a newspaper it spells bad news for us. She's a pretty girl too, so her pictures will spice up the story. Are you going to resign Guy?'

'I need to think. I didn't realise. She needled me. I got annoyed.' Guy was pretty well grounded in his situation and was thinking about what he could salvage. But he knew time was short. Resigning was the best way out in terms of saving face, and he had to start building his bargaining position.

'One of the clients that was transferred to me made a mistake with a bet. She said it was my fault, that I should have told him about the changes in the spread betting rules. She said it wouldn't have happened if I hadn't taken over her client.'

'Did you take her client?' Mike was annoyed that Lisa had been treated this way.

'No. He was transferred to me because his holding had gone above half a million pounds. She's the most junior on the trading floor. We couldn't have her handling big accounts.'

'Since when was that a rule? Did she bring the client in?' Guy had forgotten that Mike had been on the trading floor before he had moved over to HR. Bob was staring at the floor, recognising another thing he had tacitly approved.

'Well, she's young and only a girl ...'

'Stop right there. Only a girl. She's as well qualified and capable as the rest of you and you know it. Her paperwork never has any mistakes – unlike some others. We don't discriminate in this company. That's another reason why you should leave.' Mike started to write on his pad.

'What are you writing?' asked Guy.

'I'm recording this conversation. If you need a sheet to write your resignation, you can have one,' said Mike.

As they began to argue about Guy's resignation, George Nelson came in without knocking:

'Bob, the markets are going mad and we need all hands on the trading floor. Can't you leave this till later?'

Mike Penshirst faced him. 'We've got a much bigger problem than that. Get out and deal with it – and next time knock.'

'Perhaps I'd better see what's going on,' said Bob Sullivan.

'No!' Mike Penshirst was angry now. 'Get on the phone to head office and start doing whatever damage limitation is needed with this situation.'

Bob left to call his boss; the set of his shoulders showing his dejection.

Lisa

The paramedics tapped Lisa's reflexes and measured pressures and temperatures. They sympathised with her as she went through the shivering and shock of understanding what had happened. They looked into Lisa's eyes and concluded that apart from the bruise on the side of her face, she was fit and healthy.

'I don't think you need to come with us,' said Bill. 'What do you think?'

'No. I'm fine apart from my new complexion. How long will that take?'

'Couple of weeks. There are various things that help with bruises like arnica cream and vitamin E. For the next two days, regular application of an ice pack – every hour if you can. Now how do we get out of here?'

'I'll take you to reception.'

'No. Phone down and ask someone to come and fetch us. That way you can have a bit of a sit and rest here far from the madding crowd.' The female paramedic was nice. Lisa had initially read her character wrongly.

'You could ask Clare. She's outside. She'll sort you out.'

Outside, Clare was talking to the receptionist who was asking:

'Where's Lisa? I've got a PC here who wants to talk to her.'

Clare explained which room they were in and they waited.

'Come on, you've been so nice. At least I can take you to the lift.' Lisa said.

She walked them into the office and Lisa came face to face with Rhodri, who'd been working with Gareth and waiting for news. This was the first time she had seen him since the night on the balcony, and she felt that whatever fear of contact the office harassment had caused was now broken and walked towards him. He had a worried look, and she knew he was about to start raining questions on her.

'Just hold me. Just hold me very tight.'

The two paramedics were a bit taken aback but saw the smile on the older man's face and guessed this was good news.

The hug went on a long time and the receptionist appeared with the uniformed Cheryl.

'Oh, hello Bill. How's the patient?' Cheryl asked.

'She'll live. By the look of things, she's doing all right!'

Rhodri and Lisa broke apart. Lisa reddened on the good side of her face and looked at the PC.

Rhodri stood back and looked at Lisa. He sensed that a huge barrier that he could not understand had broken inside Lisa and she had somehow changed from the girl he had seen in tears three days earlier. He felt his gnawing worries evaporating.

Sonny

What a relief. At last I can see hope of a happy ending to this story. Maybe Max is right after all. The pencil hurries on.

Cheryl

'Sorry,' Lisa said to Cheryl.

'Can we have a quick word? I'd like to understand what happened here.'

'Of course. There's an interview room we can use. Rhodri, thanks. I'll call your mobile when I'm free. I'm not doing any more work today.'

'I'll be waiting,' he said.

Lisa walked with Cheryl back to the interview room, where they sat down.

'I'm PC Cheryl Carter. I got a call that someone was assaulted, which was you judging by that shiner. How did you get that? Sorry, you'd better start with your name.'

'I'm Lisa.' Lisa described the events. Cheryl wondered if Lisa had injured herself falling off the chair accidentally and felt she had plenty of more worthy cases to pursue. Meanwhile Lisa was holding her cardigan tightly closed about her, but Cheryl didn't comment.

'I guess we'd better visit the scene of the crime if that's all right with you.'

'I'm not sure I want to do that; why don't you ask Clare?' Lisa wanted to sit down again. This was going too fast. 'I have a colleague who filmed the incident on his phone. He can confirm the story I expect.'

'Who's that?' Cheryl asked.

'Jeremy. Jeremy Dudley. His desk is next to mine.'

Clare and Cheryl went up in the lift and out onto the trading floor. Faces turned towards them, but no one made any moves; they were on their phones and busy. Clare took Cheryl over to Lisa's desk where Cheryl did a sketch in her book and came to a decision. 'I'll record the event for our files, and review it with the sergeant, but I don't imagine we'll take it further.' She packed away her notebook.

'You need to talk to someone in management, if you would be so kind. Jeremy,' Clare called. 'Where's Mike Penshirst?'

Jeremy looked up. 'He's in the conference room.' As Clare spoke to Jeremy, Cheryl had a look around. A button from Lisa's blouse was on the carpet. As Cheryl knelt down to pick it up, it was as though cold air was blowing over her. Slowly, she pulled her notebook and pen from her pocket again.

She said softly, 'Oh my god.' Could this be the same as the others?

Slowly Cheryl turned to Clare and said, 'I have to talk to my sergeant. Things may have changed. Can we go back to talk to Lisa?' She stood up – having made her decision – and they returned to the HR offices.

Cheryl thanked Clare and went back in to talk to Lisa.

'Can you let me see the damage to your blouse, please.'

Lisa did as she was asked and opened her cardigan so that Cheryl could see.

'His right hand, and your left breast?'

'Yes,' Lisa was looking bemused. Cheryl realised she was repeating herself.

'Can I use a phone please?'

'Of course, dial nine for a line.' Cheryl looked at Lisa. 'Perhaps I'd better do this somewhere else.' Cheryl left the room and asked Clare for a phone. Clare showed her a room identical to the one where Lisa was sitting.

'Dial nine for a line,' said Clare, and closed the door. Cheryl phoned the police station and got straight through to the inspector.

'Inspector, I'm in the brokers as a young woman has been attacked by a colleague. I thought I'd keep a record and do nothing, except the woman's blouse is the same as that woman in the park. It's even lost a button. That's what made me suspicious. Do you want me to talk to the guy who attacked her?' She waited for an answer.

'No, I'll come with the sergeant. Can you keep him there? We'll be about twenty minutes.'

'I can talk to someone from management, maybe he'll help us.'

'Keep him talking,' said the inspector.

'Okay.' Cheryl was surprised. It sounded as though the inspector bought her story. She hoped she was right.

She rang off then left the room and went back to Clare and asked, 'How can I arrange for Mr Barnes to be kept where he is?'

'We can talk to Mr Penshirst,' said Clare, and picked up her phone.

'Clare here, Mike. Can you have a word with the police?'

He replied. Clare answered again.

'No. You should be okay on the phone. Can I put her on please?'

Clare handed the phone to Cheryl. 'It's Mike Penshirst. He's the HR Manager.'

'Morning Mr Penshirst.'

'Good Morning Sergeant,' he said.

'Constable I'm afraid sir. Constable Cheryl Carter.'

'Mike Penshirst. I'm the HR Manager here. What can I do for you?'

'Lisa has been assaulted, and before we close the case my inspector would like to review the events with Lisa and Mr Barnes. I expect he'll be about twenty minutes getting here. Where is Mr Barnes now?'

'He's in the conference room here with me where he's been since the err ... since it happened. We've been discussing his future with this company, if you must know.'

'Can you keep him there until the inspector has had a chance to talk to him? Will that be alright?'

'Of course, whatever it takes.'

'I'll stay here with Lisa so she can rest while I wait for the inspector. We shouldn't be doing this in public.'

'Fine. Is she happy with that?'

'Yes. We'll contact you when the inspector is ready.'

Cheryl rang off.

'Is there tea anywhere here? I could murder a mug,' Cheryl asked.

Clare started, 'Yes, there's a kitchen. Help yourself.' Then, 'No, I'll bring mugs for you both. How do you like it?'

Lisa

Cheryl went back to Lisa in the interview room.

'How long will this take?' she asked Cheryl.

'Not long once he's here, if I know my boss. Probably less than an hour.'

'Do you mind if I text my boyfriend?'

'No. Carry on,' said Cheryl, who was checking her notes.

Lisa texted: We're going to be a bit longer. Lisa, XXX.

No problem, I'll be here. XX, came the answer.

I'll call you or find you. XXX, texted Lisa.

Clare brought the tea in. Lisa leaned back in the chair and took a sip. Relief. It was over. Now the company would have to do something. Her mind ran over the events of the morning and it all came back. Tony Jones's bet was running somewhere. What was the FTSE doing? There was no status board in these offices. The last time she could remember anything he had been heading for losses of fifty thousand pounds.

218

Knowing him as she did, she expected he would be frantic. She had to find out what was going on as soon as she could.

She turned to Cheryl: 'Do you mind if I make a call?'

'No. Carry on.'

She rang Jeremy. The first time it was engaged.

'Jeremy, Lisa here. What's the FTSE 100 doing?'

'Crashing. It's down nearly 130 points and it's still falling.'

'Crashing? But it was going up?'

'Crashing. The whole world has gone mad. We could use you, and even Guy on the floor right now. Anyhow, how are you?'

'Sore, but I'm okay thanks.'

'Listen, I've got to go. Talk to you again.' Jeremy rang off.

Lisa thought about the one hundred and thirty points. Tony's bet was now winning more than half a million pounds. Even so she knew that Tony would be in a state. At least her own positions had been lined up in case the market was going to fall.

She glanced at Cheryl again and dialled Tony's number.

Answerphone. 'Tony, Lisa here. I've seen the bet you made. How did you know the Footsie was going to crash? Keep a cool head and I expect it will be alright. We'll have to talk again tomorrow morning when the bet is closed. Don't ring here today. We've been having a bit of a do.'

Cheryl was interested. 'What did he do?' She didn't know anything about what went on in these offices.

'He made a very stupid bet. That was the reason I was arguing with Mr Barnes. The client made a small bet but the decimal point was wrong because our website has changed. Mr Barnes was supposed to tell him about the change but hadn't bothered. It could easily have bankrupted the client. But the index is crashing for some reason and he could stand to make a lot of money. Millions even. If he became bankrupt, he would've had a good case against us as we didn't provide him with the proper information. That's what I was talking to Mr Barnes about when he lost the plot.'

'But won't your firm lose millions if he wins?'

'No. We're an agency for another firm.'

Soon the receptionist appeared; this time with the inspector and another policeman. Lisa and Cheryl got up.

'Constable. Thank you for the call.'

'This is Lisa, sir. Lisa, this is Inspector Gregory and Sergeant Townsend.'

They sat down again to Lisa's relief, as they were big men and the room was rather small.

'This is the young lady who was attacked, I gather. How are you?'

'I'm fine. May need a paracetamol tonight for a sore head but the shock has passed now.'

'Would you like to tell us what happened?'

Lisa explained again what had gone on; as she had to Cheryl. She watched as Cheryl checked what she said against her notes. When she thought she had finished, the inspector said to Cheryl:

'Anything to add?'

'Well sir, I have sketched the arrangement of the desk and if it's important we can come back with a camera. The chair has been picked up since the assault.'

'Can you can prove this?'

'Someone filmed it on his phone camera sir. He'll make a good witness. I have not interviewed him formally.'

'Now, remind me why you called me, Carter?'

'I found this on the floor sir.' She put the blouse button onto the table. 'There was one in the park after the attempted assault. Lisa, do you mind showing us how your blouse is torn?' Lisa pulled back her cardigan rather nervously. This was a bit close to being asked to perform for the men in the office.

Cheryl stood up. 'We've had other cases where a blouse has been torn and buttons pulled off like this. Lisa, why don't you cover up? Please tell the inspector about your book.' Lisa pulled her cardigan closed with relief.

'I've had this job for nearly a year and during that time I have kept a book of the times I have been sexually harassed in this office. It isn't Mr Barnes every time, but often he's encouraging it. I would say there are two or three entries every week.'

'Thank you.' Cheryl said and waited for the inspector.

'Sergeant, are we wasting our time or is there something to go on here? Lisa, do you mind waiting outside while we discuss this? The constable will fetch you if we have more questions.'

Cheryl

Lisa picked up her mug and left the room. The three police officers sat and thought while Cheryl continued to check her notes.

'Constable, you've called me here because you found a button on the floor. This is a one-off in an office. That doesn't make him the baddie.'

'No Guv, but he put his hand into her blouse and when he pulled away the blouse was torn. Like when the Judo woman was attacked in the park. There was also a button at the site of the first park murder. It's an odd coincidence that he should put his hand in the blouse like that and pull a button off.'

'What do you think sergeant?'

'It looks like a solid hunch to me. We don't have to take much more time here to have a chat with Mr Barnes and see what he says.'

Sonny

The pencil stops. I want to back off. I'm worried now that the inspector will ignore the insight that the button has given to Cheryl. Then, off to the side of the paper my pencil doodles Max looking furious.

He says, 'There's nothing you can do. For once in your life stop running away. Face it and let the story run.'

I have to pick up the pencil again and restart.

Cheryl

The inspector had made his mind up. As he spoke, Cheryl realised that he was going to consider her theory a bit further. Now she hoped she wasn't wasting his time.

'Fetch Lisa again.' Cheryl found Lisa sitting with Clare.

'Lisa. We need you for a little longer.' Cheryl followed Lisa into the makeshift interview room. It was crowded with four of them.

The inspector asked:

'Lisa, if I arrest this man and charge him, are you prepared to stand up in court and tell your story? Are you prepared to face a lawyer who will ask you a lot of searching questions about the case?'

Lisa paused. 'Yes sir. I have had a year of hell. The woman who had the job before me went through the same, and they sacked her when there was a risk that she would cause trouble. Someone has to do something or it'll carry on.'

221

'Thank you. Constable, have you got that? Do you have contact details for Lisa? And get contact details for the other woman while you are at it.' Cheryl noted his question. She already had Lisa's details.

'Yes sir.'

'Lisa, what are you going to do now?'

'Go home. Have you finished with me?'

'Yes, you head off home. I expect a few hours away from here will help you feel better. We'll be in touch if we need anything.'

'Thank you.'

'We'd better go and meet Mr Barnes. How do we find him?'

For Cheryl they were now approaching the moment of truth. She wondered whether the man would betray himself early on, or whether they would have to do a lot of forensic tests to prove he was the man they wanted. Lisa was talking again.

'Clare outside will take you. I need my bag from upstairs. She can fetch it for me.'

'Constable, do you know the way?'

'Yes, sir. Up one floor and into the big office,' said Cheryl.

'Clare will get Mike Penshirst for you,' said Lisa.

'Who's Mike Penshirst?'

'He's our HR Manager. He'll want to know what you're doing; he'll know where Guy Barnes is now and will arrange for anything else you need.'

The inspector thanked Lisa, who introduced them to Clare. She took the police up in the lift and then went to fetch Lisa's handbag and keys.

Lisa went to look for Rhodri.

Lisa

Lisa set off into the HR department to find Rhodri again. As before he was working with Gareth on some partitions. As she reached him, she didn't know what to say. They hadn't spoken properly since she had run away from him.

'Hello you.' Was the best she could say.

'Hello yourself,' said Rhodri. But she took comfort in his smile. She remembered his earlier hug.

'Can you give me one of those bear hugs? That's what I need right now.'

'Come here then,' he said, wrapping his arms round her and holding her tightly.

This is how it should have been last Saturday, she thought and tears ran freely from her eyes; which were this time tears of relief. He held her for a long time as she sobbed. She wanted it to last for ever, safe now from the beasts in the office above.

'Rhodri, my boy, are we going to finish this today or are you coming back tomorrow?' The voice of Gareth broke into her moment. Rhodri let her go. He turned to Gareth.

'Will it be okay to leave it till tomorrow? We've got a couple of hours left here from what we've done so far. I've got a more important job to do.'

'No problem,' said Gareth. 'Let's tidy up and call it a day.'

'Thanks. I'll see you in the morning.' Lisa watched as the two men made the area tidy without words, impressed that they understood each other.

'See you tomorrow,' said Gareth. 'You go and look after Lisa, and if I hear from her you've been a problem; you've got me to answer to.' He winked at Lisa and headed for the lift.

'Take me away from this place please Rhodri,' Lisa said. 'I'll tell you about it.'

'Of course. Anything you want.' He put his arm round her and gently steered her towards the lift.

'No, wait. Clare was getting my handbag. I have to have that. I have to tell her I'm going. She's upstairs.'

'No. She's been back at her desk for a little while. She passed us when we were …'

Rhodri held up Lisa's handbag which Gareth had left on top of Rhodri's tools.

They headed down in the lift and out to where Rhodri's van was parked. He put his tools into the back of the van.

'What do you want to do? I'll follow you,' he said.

'No. Take me back to your flat. My car can wait till tomorrow.'

'Are you sure?' Lisa saw uncertainty in Rhodri's eyes. He too was remembering pain from last Saturday.

'Quite sure. I've got to tell you some stuff and we've got some unfinished business. On a purely practical note, have you got any frozen peas in your flat?'

'What on earth for?'

'To try and get some of this swelling down. I can't see anything out of this eye.'

They both laughed as the return to the practical defused the rest of the tension between them.

Cheryl

Clare had led the three policemen up in the lift to the broking floor, where no one even gave them a glance. They were engrossed in the machines and talking into telephones.

'Wait,' said Cheryl. 'Let me show you Lisa's desk.' She had seen it before and wanted them to see as well.

She showed them how the chair had tipped over, where the bin had caught Lisa's face and where the button had landed. As she was doing it, she saw Clare pick up Lisa's handbag. 'I'll be back in a moment' she said and headed off up the room.

Clare was back in next to no time with a man who Cheryl had already met, but the inspector got to him first.

'Inspector Gregory. And you are?'

'Mike Penshirst, HR Manager. Thank you, Clare.' Mike Penshirst released Clare and turned back to the inspector. 'Now what can I do for you?'

'I understand that Lisa – whose desk this is – was attacked in your offices today, and I would like to talk to the man who did it please.'

'Are you sure that's strictly necessary? Isn't this a bit heavy for a little contretemps in an office?'

'We are here now,' said the inspector. 'And it's up to us to decide whether this is something or nothing, don't you think?'

Cheryl remembered how hard it was to argue against him when he had an idea to follow.

'If you must. He's in one of the conference rooms. We can continue this discussion away from the prying eyes.' *Mike Penshirst is on the defensive,* thought Cheryl.

They walked through the trading floor where everyone remained very busy. She wondered why.

The door into the conference room was in a passageway out of sight of the brokers. Cheryl noted that it was the same as the floor below with different partitions, so this room was a combination of the interview rooms she'd been in on the floor below.

As they got to the doorway Mike Penshirst stopped them.

'Do you have to talk to him? We could get some very bad publicity from this if the press finds out.'

'Mr Penshirst. That young lady had a serious black eye and lesions when I saw her. I wouldn't be surprised if the CPS call that ABH. We do need to talk to the perpetrator.'

'Do you? He's going to be sacked anyway, so he's going to suffer as a result of what he has done. Why make it worse?'

'That's my business to decide. The fact you intend to sack him underlines how serious the case is against him. What's his name, Carter?'

'Guy Barnes sir.'

'Mr Penshirst. Can we interview Mr Barnes in here or would you prefer we took him back to the station?'

Cheryl saw the defeat in Mike Penshirst's eyes.

'No. You can use this room for as long as you want.'

'How do we find you afterwards?'

'Any phone. Dial two, three, two, five; Clare will get me.'

'Got that Carter?'

'Yes sir.'

She saw Mike Penshirst watch them go into the room, and as he turned away his shoulders sagged. She followed the sergeant into the room where behind a table a man was sitting with some paper in front of him on which he had been writing. *He's like a cornered fox, alert and cunning,* she thought. Odd for a man who had just been sacked. His hands were under the table by the time she got into the room.

'Mr Barnes?' asked the inspector.

'Yes.'

'My name is Inspector Gregory and this is Sergeant Townsend and Constable Carter. I understand that you attacked your colleague earlier today. What have you to say?'

'She got under my skin. She blamed me for a situation where our company was exposed to huge losses. What right has she to do that? She dived off the chair onto the floor. It wasn't my fault that she got bashed. She's just a young girl. I got annoyed. Anyone would if faced with that lack of respect. You would have done the same thing if it happened to you.'

225

'I doubt it Mr Barnes. Now would you stand up please. Carter? Would you please go and stand next to Mr Barnes?'

'What's this? What's me standing up got to do with that Lisa?'

'Please do as we ask.'

Cheryl walked round the table as the inspector had asked, and before Guy Barnes had started to move she saw his bandaged left hand. In that moment her spirits lurched. She was right! She had to consciously repress her emotions.

Guy Barnes reluctantly stood up and faced Cheryl as she walked up to him. By doing so his hand was hidden from the inspector, who didn't seem interested in it. She wondered what to do. Should she speak and risk his wrath afterwards? She looked at the sergeant, willing him to understand.

'He's the right height,' said the inspector. 'What do you think, Mike?'

'Excuse me Mr Barnes, can you show us your hands?' the sergeant asked.

'Why?' said Guy Barnes.

'Please do it,' said the inspector, still conversational. 'If we don't see what we are looking for you haven't got anything to worry about, have you?'

Cheryl wanted to grab the hand and hold it up for the inspector to see the bandage. She instinctively knew Barnes had used his right hand to caress Lisa as his left hand had been injured on another blouse.

Barnes looked about as though intending to escape, but the two big policemen were between him and the door. He stared at Cheryl, as if he knew she had brought the inspector. Guy Barnes's eyes had something in them that terrified her. They bored through to her memory of that day in the park. She stepped away from him.

Reluctantly, Guy Barnes turned the palms of his two hands towards the inspector.

'There,' Barnes said. 'Satisfied?'

Cheryl knew this was the man they were after, who had caused her so many sleepless nights. She hoped that the inspector would understand that he had a major catch in his hands. Why was he so slow?

'What's your full name please?' The inspector's question surprised her. Now what was he doing?

'Guy Higham Barnes.'

'Carter, notebook please,' the inspector said. 'Guy Higham Barnes, I am arresting you for the actual bodily harm ...'

Cheryl wrote down the wording of the arrest.

'Constable, please handcuff Mr Barnes.'

She pulled the cuffs from her belt and went back to handcuff Guy Barnes. As she did it, she wondered if he realised the irony that a woman had this task after the damage he had done. *I should be feeling triumphant,* she thought. *But I don't.* She was running through in her mind all the things needed to prove that this man was the one they had been unable to find for so long. They had to be so careful to make the case unassailable.

'Mr Barnes,' said the inspector. 'We've decided that we would like to continue this discussion at the station.'

'Whatever,' said Guy Barnes. 'I want to see my lawyer.'

'You can sit down again now. Carter, can you get Mr Penshirst and tell him that we're taking Mr Barnes to the station. Ask him to make arrangements for you to get statements from everyone you need to from this place.'

Cheryl went to the phone she had seen by the window when they had first come in and dialled the number she'd been given.

'HR.'

'Is Mike Penshirst there, please?'

'It's Clare here, would you like me to send him up?'

'Yes, thanks.'

The phone call ended. Cheryl looked out of the window and breathed a sigh of relief. She had seen the eyes of this man and now knew that once the forensics people got to grips with this Mr Barnes, they would find him guilty of far more than ABH.

'Carter, what's happening?'

'Sorry sir. Mr Penshirst is coming up straight away.'

Mike Penshirst knocked and came in. The inspector explained that Mr Barnes had been arrested, and they were going to take him to the station for further questioning.

'Are you sure that's quite necessary?'

'Absolutely,' the inspector said. 'Now, if we can be on our way. Please can you let Constable Carter take statements from the members of staff here who witnessed the assault.'

'You'd better all come with me.' Mike Penshirst was visibly shaken by what he had heard.

The inspector turned to Guy Barnes. 'Come on. Sooner we get to the station, sooner we can get started. We may decide to let you off with a caution.'

Guy Barnes said nothing, but he followed the inspector and Mike Penshirst.

Later, Cheryl met her sergeant when she returned with the statements.

'How did you get on?' he asked.

'I think I've got it all. What a horrible man. Did you see his eyes? It's like they've been looking at me all morning. Have you let him go?'

'No. He's refused to say anything until he has his lawyer and the man he's chosen hasn't showed up yet.'

'What's going to happen?' said Cheryl.

'I expect he'll get a caution for now. He'll argue in court that she dived off her chair and her injury is her own fault.'

'So we haven't got anything?'

'He could argue that the judo star knocked him down and injured him, so he's got a defence there as well,' said the sergeant. 'All we've got is the contents of his wallet. He was carrying a small number of pills which we will have to have analysed, but I'm guessing they will be date rape pills. Carrying them doesn't look like much of an offence. Oh, and a single earring. No, he's going to walk out of here.'

Cheryl felt a clammy sweat wash over her as the look in Guy Barnes's eyes came back to her. She remembered the button on the carpet in the office and then the buttons in the parks. They all spoke of violence. She grabbed his arm to steady herself.

'Whoa. Are you alright?' he asked.

'Sarge. The earring. There was one missing from the woman in the park.'

'You sure?'

'I think so.'

'Would he be that stupid?'

They both stood looking at each other.

'I'd better go,' he said. 'Good one, Cheryl. Really good one. I'll talk to you later.'

That evening Cheryl was putting away her shopping when her phone rang.

'Evening Sarge. You don't normally ring me at home unless you want me to work an extra shift.'

'Cheryl. I had to ring. No, I haven't got an extra shift for you this time.' She waited.

'I had to ring to let you know. The earring matched the one in the evidence. Mr Barnes has now been arrested on suspicion of the October 2011 murder in the park. The clock's ticking to get him to court.'

'That's a relief. He really frightened me. He's better locked up.'

'He must have kept the earring as a trophy, so maybe we'll find other things when we search his flat and office. All down to you. We'll make a copper of you yet!'

They chatted some more.

'I'll see you tomorrow,' said the sergeant.

'Thanks. I'll probably be able to sleep now.'

Cheryl put down the phone. She'd never seen the earrings but they seemed to be taking the place of the buttons. She went back to putting her shopping away, but her mind was elsewhere; churning over all the things that it took to get a case to court, and she carefully put the washing up liquid in the fridge along with the milk.

Sonny

The pencil stops. I hope they get it right. I know he's the right one as I've seen him in some of my pictures. I sense that this chapter is finished and Cheryl will be able to sleep again. Lisa too is safe. I can move on to some new frames away from that hateful harassment which she bore so bravely; unaware of the real danger she was in.

I am relieved for other women in my story – Elin, Megan and Jessica. Now I hope they are safe too.

I start a new frame, feeling a bit like Cheryl; happy that the man has been caught but getting no comfort from it. In the new picture the pencil creates a building in City. This is the building where Rhodri's flat is. It's the evening and Lisa is standing on the balcony enjoying the view. Rhodri is behind her with his arms wrapped around her. They both look utterly happy. To my surprise there is a ghostly choir on the roof of the building singing '… i chwalu holl amheuon.' ('… to demolish all doubts.')

I want to leave them in peace and privacy, but the pencil carries on.

Lisa and Rhodri

'Rhodri, I simply have to make one phone call. With everything that's gone on, I had forgotten how the drama started with a foolish bet.'

'So?'

'He's my client. He's been my friend, and he helped me with the lawyer. He knows as much about what went on as you do – until today of course.'

'Then make the call.'

Lisa found her phone in her handbag and smiled at Rhodri as he stood back and looked at her. She wondered how bad her face was, as seeing out of her right eye was quite hard.

'Tony Jones?'

'Lisa here, how are you?'

'I've had a day on a roller coaster if the truth be known. I got so scared at what I had done I ran away from it for a while and went walking. It's come out okay though.'

'I'm sorry, I've had a bit of a day too. What's happened to the Footsie?'

'It's crashed. I stand to make a big gain but I'll never bet again, you can be sure of that. It was too stressful. It's down about three hundred points.'

'That much. Wow, you've made about one and a half million! At least your system worked. You can be proud of that. I can quite see why you don't want to bet again, and with that kind of money I expect you won't have to.'

'It's been a bit too much to bear, so I'm glad it will be over in the morning. Anyway, enough about me. How are you? How was your day?'

'Horrific. I don't think I can go back to work there after today. I was attacked in the office and have a massive black eye to show for it. It was odd though; the police came and were far more interested than a little office fracas would merit.'

'Have you spoken to Alistair?'

'Yes. He wants it written down – and photographs – but so does the nice Police Constable who came. Strange, at first she seemed rather bored of the whole incident. Clare in the office said she found a button on the floor and changed in a second.'

'What did Alistair say?'

'He thinks I should go at them with all guns blazing. Loss of earnings, punitive damages, lack of proper protection for people in the workplace and a whole raft of equality issues.'

'My advice is to give him what he wants and leave it to him. He should find a way to make them pay him and if he doesn't, I expect I can afford it.'

'It's not your fight. Listen. I've had enough of it today. I'll talk to you in a week or so, when things have quietened down a bit.'

'Lisa, take care. I'll see you soon.'

Lisa ended the call. She looked at Rhodri and said, 'Time for a session with the frozen peas.'

'I couldn't help hearing. How much money did he make?'

'Over a million. I shouldn't discuss my clients with you, but he was spread betting – which I would never advise you to do. He was lucky. If it had gone the other way, he would have lost millions that he did not have. We could have had difficulties too for allowing the bet.'

'Who's "we"?'

'Good question. I shall have to think that out. Now, I'm starving. What's the patient having for her evening meal? The rest of the treatment has been fine, but I have to keep my strength up.'

Rhodri made a playful grab for her, which she didn't bother to avoid. *How the events of a day have changed me,* she thought. Soon the choir would be singing on the roof again.

Chapter 12: Late May 2013

Lisa 15th May 2013

Next morning Rhodri drove Lisa back to the brokers so that she could fetch her car, and Rhodri could finish the job for Gareth. As they drove into the car park Lisa rang Jeremy.

'Hi Jeremy, Lisa here. How's it going?'

'Chaotic. First Bob Sullivan has told us that Guy Barnes is never coming back and later today there's a visit from some head office managers. He didn't know how long they intend to stay, but I reckon Bob's worrying about his future as well.'

'He should have stopped it. He knew, but for some reason he never bit the bullet.'

'Wait, there's more. The police turned up with a search warrant. They want to go through Guy Barnes's office.'

'The police seemed far more interested in him than my black eye. I wonder what he was doing.'

'I expect it'll be in the news soon. Meanwhile this place has gone mad.'

'I'll stay away. Who's handling Tony Jones?'

'Bob Sullivan has given me access to the account "While we find out what Lisa wants to do." I'll make sure he gets looked after. His bet made over one and a half million, so you should get the bonus on that into any claims you make.'

'Thanks. I spoke to him last night. He had such a rough ride. I don't think he'll be betting anymore, but he'll need some investment help.'

'What are you going to do?'

Lisa didn't know. She liked Jeremy, but he was a man working with the people who had made her life hell. She decided that she would hedge until she was certain.

'I don't know. I am certainly out for a week. I can hardly see out of one eye, so I'm taking one day at a time.'

She nearly said she would have to come in sometime to clear her desk but remembered that would be admitting that she was leaving.

'Thanks for your help Jeremy. I hope it works out for you.'

They ended the call.

Rhodri was standing patiently waiting.

'Don't go in there whatever you do. Give it at least a week. Where are you going now?'

'I'll go home and sort my clothes out a bit, and then ...' Lisa looked at the glorious May weather. 'Do you know what? I'll think I'll go and take Blister for a blast if no one else is riding him today.'

'That's a good plan. I'll come out and join you when I'm finished.'

'Don't you have other work?'

'Nothing that won't wait. You go and ride Blister. I'm sure you know how to waste time at the stables! I'll come as soon as I can.' He kissed her tenderly and they had a brief hug. She had told him why gentle touching was a mistake and that he needed to be a bit firmer; at least until she had got over the touching sensation that she had come to fear.

'Be careful,' he said, and picked up his tools, locked his van and headed into the brokers.

Later, she arrived at the stables where Beth was busy saddling a horse.

'How's it going?' said Lisa.

'Hello Lisa. A bit hectic, truth to tell. We don't have enough people anymore, and Mrs Howells has had to take a group out this morning to give us a hand.'

'I can give you today ...'

But Beth had looked at her for the first time since she'd arrived and saw the purple swelling on Lisa's face.

'Hey look at you. Who did that? That's awful. Are you alright?' The horse was forgotten for a moment – although he was tied to a ring so wasn't likely to go anywhere.

'Yes, it's a bit bad, isn't it? Don't worry, I'm told it'll die down in about a fortnight. It doesn't feel so bad now and I'm starting to see out again.'

'I hope whoever did it gets what they deserve.'

'I don't know. The police took him away and I haven't heard any more. That's why I'm not working today, so I thought I'd come and have a blast with Blister to get my spirits up. Is anyone on him?'

'You must be joking. It's holidaymakers at this time of year and we have few regulars who'll risk him. He's in the bottom field. Fetch him up, he could do with a run.' Beth looked at Lisa. 'Could you take my eleven o'clock for me? That would help.'

'Of course, what are they?'

'Reasonably experienced. You'll be okay on Blister. Here, I haven't time to gossip; I need to get on. Can you manage?'

'No problem.' Lisa headed to the tack room, fetched a halter for Blister and set off down the track to the bottom field. She couldn't see many horses in the paddocks and guessed this was because they were being ridden. She hopped over the gate and started across the field, shaking the halter and whistling. The great horse had seen her coming and came over willingly. She was relieved; catching a horse wasn't always straightforward.

She fitted the halter, talked to him for a few moments and decided that it would be safer to lead him back. In her madder days she would have ridden a horse bareback to the stables, but Blister was rather too high spirited to risk.

As Beth had said, the group were competent and she was able to take them on a good run through the woodland; where her spirits rose with the feel of the great horse beneath her. They stopped at a pond to let the horses drink a little because the day was getting rather hot. She checked each of the riders at the pond side.

'Watch you keep your heels down. Alec, you need to look where you're going.' Those of the group who had ridden with Alec before laughed.

'Make sure you all have good contact with the horse's mouth but try not to jab him. I'm glad to see you are all sitting well down into your saddles today.'

She took them back to the stables rather less quickly, and they were very grateful.

At the end of the ride she saw to the horses and made sure that everything was ready for the group that Beth said would be coming after lunch. She got herself a bottle of water and went to sit on a bench in the yard to enjoy the sun. She was sitting with her eyes closed and feeling no pressure for the first time in ages, when she felt someone sit down next to her. Without opening her eyes, she imagined Rhodri but the voice surprised her. It was Mrs Howells.

'Hello Lisa. You've been in the wars? Are you okay? Rhodri called and said you'd had a bad time.'

'Yes, I'm fine. Apart from the battle scars I haven't felt so good for ages. I'm taking the rest of the week off, but from what Beth says I could be needed here.'

'Lisa, we're going under. I haven't found another stable hand like Beth who can keep the yard together, and I'm finding I have to spend so much time down here that I haven't time to manage the business. By all means spend the rest of the week here. Truly, we need you.'

Lisa took a sip from her glass of water, leaned back and closed her eyes again. What should she say? Mrs Howells couldn't possibly know she had discovered how totally in love she was with Rhodri, nor that her job was at an end. She knew Mrs Howells did know how much she loved being out in all weathers on top of a horse.

'Are you alright?' Mrs Howells said. 'Will you able to take the group after lunch?'

Lisa sat up again. She had made her decision. 'Yesterday I was assaulted in the office. A man put his hand inside my bra while I was at my desk. I've had enough. I have to get out. What would you say if I asked you to give me a job for the rest of the year while I decide what to do with myself? I'll need some days off to sort out some of the remaining mess.'

Mrs Howells's worried face brightened into a smile, and she took Lisa's hand firmly.

'Are you winding me up?' Lisa's face told her that she was serious. 'I'll have to work out some terms and conditions and how much to pay you – although if we keep having the current numbers it won't be a problem.'

'I have to change my life. I need time but who knows, this might be right. At least I can help you until you can train up some more staff.'

'Until WE can train up some new staff. Lisa, what are you doing for lunch?'

'I haven't got that far yet. I'm sorting out the rest of my life.'

They both laughed as Mrs Howells got up and headed for the house.

'Come on, let's have some soup and a sandwich.'

During their lunch break Mrs Howells talked about what she thought her business needed, and Lisa gave her suggestions from her experience in the brokers. They were drinking coffee when Rhodri texted:

Job gone awry. Be at stables at four, or somewhere else? Love you. Rhodri. X

Come to stables. Working hard. Love you too, Lisa XXX

Lisa looked at Mrs Howells across the table and wondered what to say but in the end said nothing. Mrs Howells would find out soon enough. She thanked her for the lunch and headed back to collect the horses and group together for the afternoon ride. Some commented on her black eye, but she laughed it off. This group were a lot less experienced, so Blister was frustrated and consequently friskier. The heat was a problem too. For a brief time, she remembered her comfortable desk and chair but quickly threw out that thought. Whatever the disadvantages, this was what she wanted.

As she worked at helping the riders improve their style, she became absorbed and the time flew. In what felt like a few short minutes the hour was up and the riders were thanking her. She was back to sorting out the horses and making sure they had feed and water. She returned to Blister who was looking hot and bothered. The temptation was to get back onto him and go for a run in the woodlands where she could choose a pace more suited to the great horse.

'Sorry old thing. I think you'd prefer it back in the bottom paddock minding your own business.'

She stripped off the saddle and hosed him down. She walked him back down to the paddock, taking in the growth everywhere. The countryside was green and flourishing. Blister too was looking at the weeds by the side of the track and would occasionally jerk Lisa to a stop as he tried to grab a mouthful of something that took his fancy.

When they reached the paddock, she removed the halter and let Blister go. He gave a happy buck and cantered off. She walked back the way she had come, thinking of what she would do next. Other horses needed their saddles off and turning out, so Lisa joined Beth to get them sorted out.

'We need half a dozen for an inexperienced group at five o'clock,' said Beth.

'Is someone going to lead them?' asked Lisa.

'Yes, don't worry. Donna comes by then. You've rescued me today. Mrs Howells says you'll be here tomorrow. Is that right?'

'Yes. I'll be here all week – and all year if you'll have me. My black eye was the last straw from my previous job.'

'That'll make my life a lot easier. Don't get any more black eyes though!'

Lisa stood back. The yard was ready for the next group and she was free to go. First, she needed a shower before Rhodri arrived. When she was clean and tidy again, she discovered it was nearly five o'clock and Rhodri had expected to arrive by four. She hurried out of the yard and spotted his van by the bungalow. Annoyed she had taken so long, she rushed over to find Rhodri and Mrs Howells sat out in the conservatory drinking tea.

Rhodri called. 'Come on, the pot's new and there's plenty left. Grab a chair.'

'Rhodri has told me more about your wars. I didn't know the half. And Beth told me how you saved her life today. Thank you, you've rescued us.'

'I've had a good day. Don't thank me – Blister got bit heavy going this afternoon though. I don't think he likes some of the slower horses!'

They talked on about plans for the stables for the future, till the time came for Lisa and Rhodri to head back to City. By Rhodri's van he turned to Lisa.

'Fancy dinner tonight?' said Rhodri.

'Yes, but I'll have to spend time at home sorting out my clothing if I'm going to ride for the rest of the week. I'm only kitted out for Saturday riding.'

Rhodri looked a bit sad at this suggestion so Lisa said, 'Don't worry, I'll come and listen to the choir on your roof later.'

They agreed to meet up that evening, but Rhodri had work and wouldn't be free till Saturday afternoon for another ride with Lisa.

Lisa 17th May 2013

On Friday morning Rhodri left early and Lisa was alone in his flat when her phone rang.

'Constable Carter here. How are you?'

'Fine. My eye doesn't look too good, but I can see out now and my headache's gone.'

'Lisa, I'm glad you're okay. Guy Barnes has to be taken to court today. You'll probably see it in the news later. We're hoping to keep what gets into the press to a minimum and apply for some reporting restrictions.'

'I thought it was just ABH. Is he still in the police station?'

'No. He's someone we've been looking for in relation to other offences. We will be asking for him to be refused bail. We are unlikely to charge him with ABH – at this stage anyway. I hope that's okay with you for now.'

Lisa went through a range of emotions as she relived Tuesday morning. She was angry at her treatment. She thought Guy Barnes had it coming to him, and she was grieving the ruin of her dream job. But part of her was resistant to the idea that someone should suffer as a result of her actions. Secretly too, she thought that she had brought the black eye on herself by diving off the chair, and not because of something he had done.

'Lisa, are you still there?'

'Yes, sorry. I was just going over it again.'

'It helps if we don't charge him with ABH now. Your name won't come up. You'll be able to read about it soon enough, and then you'll see why we advise keeping your name out of the case.'

'What on earth was he doing?'

'I can't tell you, but we will take him to a magistrates' court today. We'll have to make a statement to the press, so you will see it.'

'You sound as though this is a big deal.'

'It could be, but I can't tell you anymore. Meanwhile for your own good I suggest you keep well away from the press. I'll be asking your employer to do the same.'

'Thanks. I don't think I know anyone in the press. I won't say anything.'

She rang off and sat down. What had Guy Barnes been doing? She knew he was a creep, and she knew that something had happened to Chantelle. Something else Cheryl had said had made her think. She needed to hand in her notice with the brokers. But first she would have to have a word with Alistair. Cheryl had drawn her back into the nightmare of the brokers' office; something which the riding had pushed to the back of her mind.

Sonny

When the pencil restarts a new frame, Tony is parking his car behind Elin's house.

238

Elin 18th May 2013

Elin had heard Tony park as she was sitting in the sun on the bench behind the house. She got up as he came through the back gate.

'Hello Tony. Fancy a cup of tea?'

'That would be lovely.' He came up to her and gave her a hug. That surprised Elin. He hadn't done more than peck her on the cheek before, although he appreciated her hugging him.

'Have a seat while I put the kettle on.'

She went into the kitchen and collected a tray of tea, mugs and milk. On a whim she added the packet of chocolate digestives she had been hoarding for a day when she was down.

She put the tray on the table and sat down next to Tony.

'Elin. We have things to talk about. I've had a bit of a week.' His head was down and he was looking at his hands.

'Is this good news or bad news?' She sensed that he was bursting with something and was trying to work out how to approach it.

'Good news,' he said turning to face her. 'Elin, I made a gamble on the stock market. It's complicated but when I made the bet somehow the numbers went in too big. I won over one and a half million pounds as far as I can work it out.'

'One and a half million pounds? You're joking!' Elin met his eyes and saw a sort of boyish glow that she hadn't seen in him before. He didn't answer straight away, but she could see from his expression that it must be true. One and a half million pounds. All her money troubles revolved around her head. Could she ask him?

'It's true,' he said. 'I don't know the exact amount because of a problem at the brokers the day I made the bet, so they haven't confirmed the details.'

She poured the tea, playing for time. She wanted to ask him for help while at the same time her pride and her upbringing held her back. She was driving round in Karen's car and had been trying to save enough so she could give it him back. Her mother would have told her to change the subject, but the look in Tony's face said that he had only one thing on his mind.

'What are you going to do with it?' she asked.

'What would you like me to do with it?' he said. 'I haven't a clue. The problem at the brokers means I haven't worked out with them how to invest it and how much income it could give. I'll probably give some to Jessica and Matthew. They're starting out and will be able to use it to make their lives secure. But even if I want to spend it all, I haven't got enough ideas.' He looked at her. 'You'll have to help me.'

'What do you mean?' Elin had been so constrained by her circumstances for so long that the idea of this amount of money was beyond her imagination.

'The first thing we have to do is to pay off your mortgage. I have a brother-in-law who's a lawyer. Why don't you get your papers together and we'll send them to him to sort out your house?'

'Tony, that's a bit different from lending me a car.'

'Yes, you can have that now. We can put it in your name; unless of course you want a new one?' he said, smiling.

'No. This one's fine and thank you. But the mortgage is a different problem. To sort out the mess of my life will cost over two hundred thousand pounds. I'll never be in a position to thank you or pay you back.'

'You don't have to. It will be my pleasure. That's why I rang you this morning. I was wondering how much money you need.'

Elin looked at him and in a moment of insight saw what a bizarre situation she was in. He wanted to help, and she knew in her heart that she wanted it too. Not for the money but because of him. He was focussed on the money, but she knew that if he helped her it implied a much greater commitment between them in future. His eyes told her what she needed to know.

'Tony. Anything will help to cut my mortgage down – and whatever the lawyers will cost. But it's too much to ask from you, honestly.'

'As I said. We have to pay off your mortgage. The money's there.'

'Then what?' said Elin, looking in his eyes again.

'We get the lawyers to arrange it all.'

'No. I don't mean that. I mean; then what happens? To you and me?'

Tony's eyes met hers and he gripped her hand. 'I hadn't thought,' He said. Immediately he heard Karen. *'Liar!'* was all she said. 'Okay, we take one step at a time. But you said you liked me Elin, and I like you too.'

'Let's get the money thing out the way. Then we can think what we do next,' he added.

Elin was torn in two directions. She wanted to sing. She was so happy that she had an end in sight to the burden that had stopped her being able to live ever since her parents had become ill in old age. But was it right to say yes to Tony? For some reason Kevin sprang into her head. He would have taken the money and asked for more. Poles apart from Tony; who she wanted to hug just now. She glanced at her watch. Soon she would have to set off to her job in the Railway.

'Elin, ring them. You don't have to go to work in the pub anymore.'

'I can't let them down. They've been good to me.'

'Ring them. They may have someone else who can fill in.'

'On a day like today?' she said looking up at the cloudless sky and feeling the warmth of the sun. 'Everyone will be out having barbecues if I know this weather.' She paused and then said, 'Alright. I'll see what he says.'

Elin went into the house and rang the pub.

'Bill. Elin here. Do you need me tonight? I'll be in for lunchtime tomorrow.'

'No love, we'll manage. Young Terry came home for the weekend. I'll get him to help. You enjoy the fine weather.'

'Oh, thanks Bill.'

'That's alright, love. You've filled in for me a few times at the last minute – time for you to have some of that back.'

'Thanks all the same!'

Elin walked back out and sat down on the bench. For the first time in ages she felt as though she could sit and relax. She was safe with Tony next to her, and she could see an end to her problems. She thought back to her last luxury – a bottle of olive oil – and remembered how she had prayed that a knight in shining armour would come and rescue her. She smiled. Tony didn't fit the description, arriving as he had with a broken-down car. For all that he was the knight in shining armour for her.

'Bill says he can do without me tonight.'

'Well done. Do you want to go out somewhere? Have you got any food here?'

'We've got enough to make a meal here, and frankly I want to sit here for a bit and take in your good fortune.' She sat back. 'I didn't mean I should take your fortune from you.'

They both laughed and moved a bit closer together.

'When do you finish school?' Tony asked.

'Mid-July, why?'

'We should have a holiday; you look as though you need it.'

'Oh Tony. I can't keep taking charity from you. That would be wrong.'

'No, it isn't. I can afford to have an expensive girlfriend now.'

'Cheeky.' Elin saw that a decision was being made and kissed Tony on the cheek. He was surprised, but he turned and kissed her properly. Elin felt young again, inexperienced and fumbling. She hadn't had a kiss like this for probably fifteen years. But in the context of everything that was happening with Tony, it was natural.

'Sorry, I got carried away,' said Tony.

'I hope you get carried away more often.'

'Now we have to plan a holiday. Have you got a passport?'

'No. Sorry. Neither has Megan. How long does it take to get one?'

'I've no idea. I'd forgotten about Megan. Should she come too?'

'Yes. No. I don't know. I expect she'll want to go somewhere with Owain or some of her girlfriends.'

'We'll have to ask her.'

'She'll be home soon and wonder why I'm not at work. Oh, never mind her! Where were you thinking of going?'

'I went to conferences years ago in San Francisco and Vancouver. I fancy having a better a look at those places.'

Elin had only ever been on coach tours to Paris and Amsterdam to see art galleries as part of her studies many years ago. What Tony was proposing sounded exciting beyond belief.

Tony carried on. 'I haven't had a holiday for over three years, and I don't know what I need other than some new scores for the choir, so we can expand our repertoire. That won't break the bank now will it? Let's have a holiday. I've earned it. When did you last have one?'

Elin kissed him again.

Lisa and Rhodri 18th May 2013

On Saturday, Lisa worked all morning at the stable and ate her sandwiches with Beth behind the tack room. She was settling into her new job as though she had done it for years.

'What are you doing this afternoon?' asked Beth.

'Taking Rhodri for a ride. Blister would like a hack too I expect. I didn't take him with that group this morning. He's out of their league, but he's getting used to having a run every day.'

'Busman's holiday I'd call that!' They laughed.

Later, Rhodri and Lisa rode into the woodland. Lisa's eye was purple but the swelling was going down, and to Rhodri – watching her from slightly behind – the sight of her head held high and the energy that radiated from horse and rider was one of the most wonderful sights he had ever seen.

They cantered and then let the horses drink a little at the pond before walking them home; chatting about the stables, how Rhodri's business was going and whether Lisa should move into his flat. A lot of the time they revelled in the mutual comfort of being out together in the perfect weather.

Back at the stables Rhodri hopped off his horse before they went into the yard, caught Blister's rein and looked up at the radiant Lisa in the saddle. At that moment she was more special to him than anything in the world. Even with the black eye she was beautiful.

'Lisa …'

'What?'

'Lisa, will you marry me?'

'You're not on one knee,' she said, but laughed and tossed her hair back over her shoulder, the energy in her movements making her more attractive. She threw a leg over the saddle and dropped down next to him, took both his hands and looked him straight in the eyes.

'Yes. Yes. Yes. Will you marry me?'

'Yes.'

The horses were forgotten as they hugged each other, and both horses headed into the yard to find water and food; where Beth found them. Alarmed at the appearance of riderless horses she tied them up quickly and rushed out of the yard.

Lisa and Rhodri were enclosed in their own private bubble, oblivious of the world around them.

Beth cleared her throat.

'Excuse me. Are you the riders of the two horses I found wandering in the yard?'

Rhodri and Lisa broke their hug and faced her. Lisa coloured.

'Sorry Beth, I got a bit distracted.'

'I should say so. Do I take it I have to tell the other stable girls that Rhodri is off limits?'

'Definitely,' said Lisa, and took Rhodri's arm. 'We're going to get married just as soon as I can get rid of this black eye.'

'Congratulations. I'm really happy you've had some good news for a change. You'd better go and see Mrs Howells. I'll tend to the horses,' said Beth before adding with a smile, 'Just this once mind.'

'Oh thanks. Just this once, honestly.'

'How many more proposals are you expecting?' said Beth.

Rhodri and Lisa walked up to the bungalow where Mrs Howells was busy in the kitchen making lemonade again.

'Mum. Can we talk to you?'

Mrs Howells stood with her back to the worktop and folded her arms defensively, but with a twinkle in her eye.

'I suppose so,' she said.

'Mum ...' started Rhodri. Lisa interrupted.

'Mrs Howells. Can I marry Rhodri, please?'

Mrs Howells crossed the room and somehow managed to hug them both at the same time.

'Of course you can. Have you asked him yet? Men can be a bit slow.'

'He wasn't. He asked me – very properly – except we forgot the horses and Beth had to come and tell us off.'

Rhodri asked, 'Do I have to ask your parents?'

'Of course you should,' said Mrs Howells.

'You can ask my Mam; I live with her. I'm not sure about my Dad. I've never met him.'

'How's that?' asked Mrs Howells.

'They split up. He pays Mam but she won't talk about him. Oddly, my sister sees him sometimes. She found out he lives near her so they meet sometimes. Mam has told her not to say anything about us.'

'I didn't know you had a sister,' said Rhodri.

'Yes, she hardly comes home. Our flat isn't big enough for guests.'

Sonny

Lisa has a sister. That's news to me as well. I knew the pencil was hiding bits of the story from me. I wonder what other surprises it has in store. Max appears at the side of the page.

'Keep going Sonny. Lisa's happy. Tony's life is turning around. Maybe yours is too.'

Another day, when I restart, Tony is back studying his computer. I'm inclined to stop as this is a dull scene. But Max has told me I'm not allowed to run away.

Tony 22nd May 2013

A few days later Tony was sitting at his computer googling different ways of having a holiday with Elin. The phone rang.

'Tony Jones.'

'It's Lisa here, Tony. I have to apologise for not ringing earlier, but I owe you this call to let you know what's happened.'

'That sounds rather formal.'

'Oh sorry. I didn't mean to be.'

'What's up?'

'I've been speaking to Alistair and have decided to give up my job after last week. It was horrible. I haven't been back. Your account has been moved to someone called Jeremy Dudley who is one of the few people in that office who isn't a raving misogynist. You should be alright with him.'

'Will he know how much money the bet made?'

'Haven't they told you already? I know it was chaotic, but you should know that. Isn't it on your account screen?'

'I haven't looked. I was so shocked I'm not sure I dare even open it.'

'It's quite safe, as long as you don't go to the spread betting page.' They laughed.

'What are you going to do with your life?'

'I've taken a job at a riding stables for the rest of the year, to try to forget it all. Actually, it's a bit more complicated than that ... I've got engaged to the son of the owner.'

'Congratulations. That's wonderful. And I'm sure you will find life outdoors much less stressful. Was that rather sudden?'

'No. I've fancied Rhodri for ages but he was being a bit slow. He's been quick now though and has booked it for the 6th July.'

'Golly, that is quick! Is there anything I can do?'

'No. I don't think so. My Mam says that if we've decided, we're as well getting on with it.'

'Where's the reception? I can play piano for you if the venue suits it.'

'The Valley Lodge. What sort of music do you play?'

'I can play most things. You have to decide what you want or give me an idea and I'll work something out. I know the Valley Lodge; it's not far from where I live.'

'I'll have to ask Rhodri. He's more into music than I am.'

'The offer stands. I'm quite good at it, I've played all my life and I play for the choir here every week. And in the pub afterwards for that matter.'

'You mean you play without music?'

'Yes, I can. But I try to learn the pieces from the score as otherwise they all sound the same.'

'Oh, thank you. People have been so nice since last week. It was awful at the time and now it's like a big cloud has lifted.'

'What's happened to the man who attacked you?'

'He got sacked on the spot, but Jeremy told me he was taken out in handcuffs by the police. Somehow they worked out that he's the man who's been doing the murders in the parks.'

'That man? I saw him on the news. It sounds as though you were lucky. I'm really sorry it happened to you. And you'll never go back there?'

'No. I've got loads to do anyway with the horses and planning the wedding.'

'Don't forget, if you need a pianist I'm here.'

'Thanks. I call you soon.'

Tony went back to his holiday planning but remembered what Lisa had said and opened his account at the brokers.

Together with what had been in the account – and now the new bet – the sum was over two million pounds. He shook his head. He wasn't used to being rich. He'd been comfortable with Karen, but this was way over anything he had ever dreamed of. The money brought him a new set of problems.

The Final Chapter: June/July 2013

Sonny

I'm watching the story appear under the pencil again. It's drawing Lisa and she's heading off to the shops.

She keeps checking her watch and looking around while standing outside the main door of a big department store. The shop isn't far from here when I think about it. I wonder what has brought her into London.

Now she's met someone else. In the first frame I can't see this woman very well, but she hasn't been in my novel before. She says, 'Are you ready for this? Have you got a list?'

'Yes,' says Lisa, 'I have a book called "Planning a Wedding" from Mam, and I've been through it.'

They turn and go into the store, and now I can see the second woman.

My pencil comes to an abrupt halt, and I step back in shock. It's Jen. How can she be in my novel? She's in my real life.

I move back to the drawing board to look at her more closely. It is Jen. I let the pencil doodle in the margin and Max appears looking like a know-all.

'It's your story.' Max says.

'I know,' I say. 'I hold the pencil.' *It's obvious isn't it?* I think.

'No,' repeats Max. 'This is your story.'

I step back again, put down the pencil and decide that I'd better make myself a cup of tea and try to understand this development. Before the kettle even boils, I have to go back and let the pencil carry on so I can watch.

When my pencil restarts, I can tell Jen and Lisa have been shopping for a while as they have bags to carry.

'Let's go for coffee and see what we've still got to get,' says Lisa.

They head out of the shop and into a coffee shop quite close to my flat. Are they really here? Max pops up in the margin again.

'There's only one way you are going to find out. Go and join them.'

The suggestion gives me a chill as it challenges my whole world of fiction. The idea that it might not be fiction is unsettling. However I look at it, I have to go.

I rush out to the coffee shop but as I get closer, I slow down. Do I want to know the truth of what is in the picture? Do I want to get involved?

I go into the coffee shop and initially I don't see Jen. She is further back into the shop with the other woman, who has her back to me. I dither. Should I make myself known to them or run away?

But I'm too late. Jen has seen me. She gets up and walks towards me.

'Hello Dad,' she says. 'What brings you here?'

I don't know what to say. She can see I'm in a bit of a state.

'Come on, let's get you a cup of tea. There's someone I'd like you to meet here. It's lucky you came today; she doesn't come to London often.'

Jen knows I drink tea. There isn't much of a queue, and she gets me a cup while I dither, unsure where to stand. Should I go to the table or stay with Jen?

'Come on. I've got a surprise for you. Come and meet Lisa.'

She has the right name. Am I in a dream or is this reality? Jen carries the tea as I would have spilt it with my shaking hands.

At the table Lisa stands up when we come.

'Lisa. This is Dad. By chance he walked in here at the same time you are here, but we were going to have arranged it sometime. Dad, are you all right? I've told Lisa all about you.'

Lisa turns to face me and she is the beautiful girl from my novel. I don't know what to say. I don't understand what Jen is saying. Why does she want me to meet Lisa? She doesn't know that Lisa is in my novel and otherwise nothing to do with me. Come to that how does she know Lisa?

'Hello Dad,' Lisa says, seeing my discomfort. 'You'd better sit down.'

She said 'Dad'. What does she mean? I turn back to Jen.

'Is there a big secret here you're hiding from me?'

'Dad. You really didn't know? Lisa's my sister. She's your daughter.'

My whole world is making a seismic shift. This is going to take some getting used to.

'Dad. Sit down! Are you alright?'

I sit down. These two lovely women sit down too. The merging of reality and my world of pictures scrambles my thoughts. Lisa carries on.

'You've never ever talked to me about Mam, and she wouldn't hear anyone talk about you. I didn't dare say anything as she said whatever she did, you didn't want to come back. Lisa was born after you left. Mam was pregnant, which she said was why she was tired and irritable at the time you left. Stop looking like you've seen a ghost and say hello to Lisa.'

I turn back to Lisa, and now I see the beauty that her mother has. She has the distinct yellow of the fading black eye. This is unreal. When will I wake up?

'Lisa. I feel I know you.' I stop. What can I say that won't sound creepy, like I've been stalking her? 'You look like your mother.'

She laughs. 'So people say. I'm getting married. Jen and I want to give you an invitation. You're the father of the bride.'

Jen breaks in. 'There's a step before that. You'll have to meet Mam.'

There it is, the elephant in the room. I have to meet Gabby again. I don't know what to say. After all these years of staying away.

'Yes,' says Lisa. 'You should. The wedding day can't be the first time you meet again after all this time. I want a happy wedding without any unexpected shocks. I've had enough unpleasantness to last a lifetime.'

'But she won't want to meet me. I ran away. Why should she?'

Lisa and Jen look at each other. What does that mean? I need time before they land any more bombshells on me. I look at these two beautiful young women in front of me and think of my sad little flat. I do have a family; I don't have to live alone.

Jen takes my hand. 'Dad, she'd like to meet you. We don't understand all of it, but Mam thinks it's her fault you left. Granny spent a lot of time with us after you left, but now she's dead. Mam'll be lonely when Lisa moves out, and she's never given up on you.'

'How do you know?'

'She reads Max every day.' Lisa says. 'Every day. She used to say that lady friend of Max's looks like her, but now she says she looks like me.'

'We've talked about it,' says Jen. 'Elsa looks more like Lisa than me.'

The tea and coffee cups are empty and the people sitting near us have changed. It's time to move. And I need some time to process our discussions.

'I shall have to think. I've had a lot of shocks today. I need time.' I don't want to say what Max told me but should I tell them? I'm not sure. I need time to myself now. I'm not used to having people discussing my life. I have to try and understand it myself before I can explain it. How do Max and the pencil know the story as they do?

I turn to Lisa. 'How long are you up here? Can I take you both to lunch tomorrow? I need to get my head round everything.'

'Good idea,' says Jen. 'I'll book a table for Sunday lunch at the George for twelve-thirty.' We'd eaten there a few times in the past; it wasn't so much special as reliable and without fuss.

We get up and go out into the street where Jen gives me the usual peck on the cheek, and Lisa copies her.

'Thank you for coming, I didn't know how I was going to start this conversation with you.' Jen says, 'We'll see you tomorrow at the George. Now we have to finish our shopping.'

I watch them for a while as they walk away down the street. My two daughters. Who'd have thought that?

I walk slowly back to the flat. At first I want to give Max a chance to tell me about what's going on, but when I reach the flat it dawns on me that I have to work this out myself. I decide that I will be better keeping away from Max for a while, so set off again in the direction of the park to walk some more and try to work out my future.

My choice is between Max and Gabby. That's what she told me. That's why I ran away. Somehow that choice hasn't changed. Jen and Lisa have obviously talked about it and given me the idea that Gabby would consider having me back, but I guess I have to make the first move. How confusing it is.

Added to those questions, I'm struggling to understand how my pencil has told this story that is now turning into real life. My novel has no future set out within it either, and Max is coming to an end as well. In a single cup of tea my life has been turned on its head, my certainties changed and my future thrown up in the air. I want to run away and hide from the world; under my duvet as I did when I was in my deepest depression.

It churns round in my mind – unresolved – as I walk, and when I finally get back to the flat and close my front door, I'm hungry. The day is nearly gone and I've not had lunch yet. What am I going to do?

I didn't sleep much last night as I turned over in my mind what I should be doing. I can imagine what Max would say. 'Whatever you do, keep me alive.' But Max has to come to an end if I retire. Then I will no longer have contact with the editorial office and become a recluse, unless … unless I build a new life with my family. Come to think of it, Jen will be one of the people who I will have in my life. Lisa is getting married – maybe she'll have children and I could illustrate some books for them … I don't know.

I spend the morning avoiding my drawing board and pencil in case Max has a go at me. At lunchtime I walk to the George to meet Jen and Lisa.

At the George, Jen is first as usual. She finds me and leads me to a nice secluded table in a bit of an alcove, where Lisa's sitting.

'Hello Dad,' Lisa says. 'It sounds odd that. I never expected to say it. But it sounds nice too.'

'Hello Lisa. You're right, Dad sounds nice to me as well.' I wonder if I sound sincere after my night of tossing and turning.

Ever practical, Jen asks me what I want to drink, goes to the bar and fetches drinks for the three of us. I don't as a rule drink at lunchtime but decide today is different. I hang my jacket on the back of the chair and sit down. I haven't a clue what to ask her as I feel as though I know lots about her already – and worse than that I feel as though I've been prying.

'How long are you up in London?' I ask.

'Another couple of days. I've given up my job and am working at a local riding stables. I had a rather bad experience in a firm of brokers which ended up with me getting this black eye, so I've left them.'

'Isn't Jen working tomorrow?'

'Yes, but she's taken it off. She has some plan or other to do with sorting out the wedding.'

'Do you have a date for that yet?'

'Yes we do, Saturday 6th July.'

'That's barely a month away. Golly, how long have you known that?'

'Rhodri – my fiancé – arranged it. We were lucky. There was a cancellation at a hotel quite close to the stables where Rhodri's mother lives, and Rhodri happened to ring them first.'

I have to meet Gabby within the next month if I am going to come to the wedding. Lisa said that yesterday. If I had a sleepless night last night, I am going to have sleepless nights until the wedding is over. Gabby will want to kill me after what I've put her through. I am trying to be happy for Lisa, but my worries of yesterday resurface. Jen comes back with drinks and menus, so I have time to avoid more discussion while I digest this latest information.

We decide what to eat and this time I go to the bar to order and make sure I am the one who pays. I should pay; they are my daughters. I join them back at the table, having decided that the rush to sort things out with Gabby might be for the best. At least it forces me to make the decisions which – being honest – I've been putting off ever since I left her.

Lisa and Jen talk about the plans for the wedding, and Lisa tells me that I have to make a speech if I come. I've never done public speaking. Even when Max won awards, I avoided doing more than thanking. What on earth will I say about a daughter I hardly know?

'That's not my thing. I'm just a cartoonist. I'm not even an artist anymore.'

'Come on, every Dad has to make a speech for his daughter's wedding.'

'I'll have to make peace with your mother first.' I stop and look at them but neither offer to fill the void. 'I deserted her. That was bad. Now I find I deserted her when she was expecting. That's worse. How is she going to react?'

'One day you turned up at my door,' says Jen. 'I didn't hold you to account for going, did I? I talked to Mam. She's agreed to meet you – if you will. Life hasn't been so bad for her. You did pay for everything, didn't you?'

'Yes, I suppose I did.'

'I talked to her too,' says Lisa. 'She thinks you left because she was so miserable and it was her fault being depressed, not realising that she was pregnant. She wanted Max to be a success as she saw it meant so much to you. She didn't want to wreck that for you.'

'But she never told me about you.'

'No. There are some things you'll have to talk to her about. We don't understand either.' I can tell that Lisa and Jen agree and have talked about this before.

Jen goes on. 'It was pure luck that you walked in on us in the coffee shop yesterday. The truth is we were wondering how to spring Lisa on you, and how we'd get you to talk to Mam.'

A waiter arrives with our food and I am able to take another break from this conversation.

'Dad,' says Lisa. She's facing me full on across the table, and I'm struck by how even with the yellowing black eye she is really beautiful. She reminds me of Gabby too. I haven't quite got to grips with the idea that she's my daughter. 'Can you come and meet Mam? She won't travel here. She says this is where Max lives.'

'Max.' I say. 'The truth is I have been trying to retire Max for a while now. I know that your Mam won't want to live in the same house as him. I'm sixty-eight now and the newspaper has been dropping hints that I can retire any time I want. The agency won't want me to. They see me as a source of regular income.'

'Retire. Go back to Mam. She'll be lonely when I move out completely.' Lisa's eyes plead with me.

'Have you talked about this with your mother? Have you made a plan?'

Lisa's smiling. 'Of course we have, in amongst the chat about my wedding. I live with her. She told me the flat will be lonely when I leave. Ask her. I think she'll let you come back.'

'What have you decided?'

'We haven't. But you could come back with me on Wednesday if you want?'

Wednesday. That's three more sleepless nights. I understand now that this has to be, and it might as well be sooner rather than later. Two days will be enough to do some Max strips to give me the time. My life has changed too. I am no longer drawing my 'novel'. I take a deep breath.

'Yes, that would be for the best. What train were you planning to catch?'

Lisa and Jen laugh.

'I've got a car!' says Lisa. 'Don't tell me you are another member of the family who doesn't drive? I'll pick you up.'

'I have got a licence from years ago, but I haven't driven since I left your Mam.'

We carry on with our meal and I see these two beautiful women – my daughters – relax now that I have agreed to go with Lisa to meet Gabby. I think I'm relieved enough too to have a dig at Lisa.

I turn to Jen. 'What's this Rhodri like? Have you met him? Should we have him in the family?

As we sit in the car heading along the motorway, I can watch Lisa. My daughter. I'm getting a bit more used to it now. She asks me questions about Max and my life as a cartoonist. She's easy to talk to. After all, I've known her for a while now.

She stops talking while traffic struggles past some slower lorries.

'There's something else you have to do while you are here. You have to meet Rhodri. Knowing him he will want to formally ask you if he can marry me.'

'Is he the one for you? Does he make you happy?'

'Yes. I knew from the beginning, although I was a bit slow getting to meet him.'

'And what right do I have to refuse him? I hardly know you.'

'You seem to know me quite well.'

I'm not sure I will ever explain that.

'I would like to meet him of course, but I'm not qualified to give approval as an absentee father.'

We chatter on. I am so comfortable sat in this car with Lisa. Content. But I'm angry too. Why did I allow these years to pass when I could have known her growing up? How stupid and stubborn I've been. Am I still? I think of how Max has spent the last few months telling me home truths.

'Dad. Are you alright?'

'Yes, I'm fine.' What can I say? I want to hide again but that would be to carry on as before. 'I have to change from the boring old recluse with a pencil into a proper father. I'm having trouble taking it in.'

'I suppose it's a bit the same for me. Getting used to having a father. Mind you Jen talked about you, so I've known about you for a while.'

I want to change the subject.

'Lisa, who's paying for the wedding?'

'I've got enough. Mam offered. I set some by for a deposit on somewhere to live, but Rhodri has a flat already. Apart from that I have a lawyer who thinks my black eye is worth a lot of money from my ex-employers. So I was avoiding asking Mam.'

'I'll pay. No point in having a father who can't.'

Lisa was quiet for a while. There was something on her mind, and she was looking for the words to say something.

'Dad, you don't have to pay. I see it now; what Mam says. She said I'd never meet anyone as generous as you. When you helped Jen in college and afterwards with her flat, it was as though you sent Mam a message. I think she wants you back.'

We sat in silence for several miles, but I insisted I would pay for the wedding. We spend the rest of the journey talking about what has to be paid for and how much it would cost. By the time we arrive I am thinking my offer is a bit generous. I didn't know weddings were so expensive!

Lisa parks the car under a block of flats which I recognise.

'We'll leave the stuff in the car for now. Come on up and meet Rhodri. He should be home by now.'

I meet Rhodri – who I know already – and he asks me if he can marry my daughter, so I shake his hand and say yes. But what right do I have to say anything?

We drink a cup of tea and chat about the wedding. While Lisa had been in London, Rhodri and his mother had discussed their ideas about the wedding, and Lisa and he chat more about the costs; which to my relief are coming down a bit.

My mug is empty and I am a bit out of the conversation as Lisa and Rhodri carry on talking. They are so relaxed with each other. I wonder what it will be like to meet Gabby. The time is coming and I can feel myself wanting to run away again. I can imagine Max telling me to keep going.

'We need to go over and see Mam. Are you ready?'

Would I ever be ready?

'No. But needs must.'

'What do you want to do?'

'You had better drop me off and disappear. To be honest I have no plan. I'm terrified.'

'Don't be. She's waiting for you.'

As we drive to her flat, I remember that she liked having fresh flowers. Lisa stops at a supermarket and I buy some.

We arrive. Lisa and Jen talked about the flat but it's not a flat, it's a shop. There are six in a block, probably built sometime in the sixties. A newsagent's, a post office, a bakery with chairs and tables outside and a hair salon. I don't notice the others now I've seen the salon.

Gabby talked about starting her own salon once Jen was older. Here it is and the light is on.

The pencil must have known that if it had drawn this scene in my story, I could have guessed that Lisa was something to do with me. Lisa had said what Gabby said; Max's Elsa does look like Lisa. I'd never even noticed that Elsa had looked like Gabby.

'Dad, this is it. You have to get out.'

'Sorry Lisa. There's a lot going on.'

'Mam will be in the salon, closing up and waiting for you. She knows we are coming. I'll leave your bag in the flat, and I'll probably see you tomorrow sometime.'

I get out but stand looking. The confusion of running away comes back to me but avoiding a problem doesn't make it go away.

'Dad …'

I close the car door and clutch the flowers. It's now.

I walk across the pavement. The Salon door says 'closed', but I can see her watching me from inside. I have to go in. This is not something to do with her neighbours watching.

I go through the door and let it close.

'Hello Sonny.'

'Hello Gabby. I brought you some flowers.'

She takes them from me and holds them. She's close to me.

'Thank you. It's been a long time since you gave me flowers.' It was probably before we were married.

'I remembered you like them fresh. I thought they were a good way to say sorry …'

'Sonny, it's lovely of you to think that. I'm sorry too.'

The flowers are between us. She holds them with one hand. The other takes mine and leads me to the back of the salon to a tiny kitchen, scarcely more than a sink and enough work surface for a kettle and microwave. She puts the flowers into the sink and runs some water for them while still managing to hold my hand.

'They'll be okay for now.'

She turns back to face me. I'm trapped in this tiny kitchen, very close to her. I don't know what she thinks of me.

'Let me look at you.' Still dressed as the beautician, she checks me over like a car salesman with a potential trade in. 'You don't look too bad. Keeping fit anyway.' She squeezes my hand. To me she doesn't look a day older than the Gabby I ran away from.

'Sonny, I have to lock up. Someone may come in.'

She lets my hand go and I follow her back to the front door. Nearby there's a low sofa and coffee table for waiting customers. On the table is the paper. My paper, where Max is hiding between the pages. He must not come between us again. She turns back to me.

'Come upstairs and have a drink. Do you still drink?'

'Not much. I haven't stopped though. I occasionally have a pint.'

I follow her to the back of the shop again and up into the flat above, past dustbins and parked cars and up slightly rusty stairs to a walkway where the doors to the flats are lined up, one above each shop. Into her lounge – which has a big window covered by a net curtain – presumably above the front of the salon. At one end is a three-piece suite, some shelves and a TV. At the other end of the room is a small dining table with four chairs. Among the pictures on the walls are some I remember.

She turns to face me. This is the moment I've avoided all these years.

'Sonny, thank you for coming back. Jen has been keeping me up to date with how you were doing. There's a place for you here if you want.'

'Jen told me on Saturday. She said you were here waiting.'

As I stand looking at her, I am taken back to good times we had together. I see the life in her eyes and see this is the life that emanates from Lisa. This is the vitality that I loved before. I take her two hands and look her straight in the eye. No more running away. It's time for my speech.

'Gabby, I'm truly sorry for what I've done. It was me that ran away. It's all my fault. I've spent my life running away. The longer it went on the harder it got. I have to stop. Jen and Lisa told me I had to come and see you if I'm to come to the wedding, so here I am. Somehow our past should not affect their future. I'm just sorry.'

I look down. I've made an attempt at a confession and am surprised as Gabby grips my hands and pulls them towards her. I look up again. There are tears in her eyes, but light as well.

'Oh Sonny, Sonny. I thought it was my fault. I didn't know Lisa was coming. I was struggling to keep going. Jen was so busy and I felt as though the whole world was against me, including you. You disappeared into the world of Max, and I thought how unfair that was. I was tired out. I didn't mean to make an ultimatum. I wanted more of you and it went wrong. Then when you resisted my attempts to get you back, I thought that you were still angry with me.'

'No. I didn't think I deserved to come home. I've never been angry with you. I thought it was my fault. I still do. I'm sorry.'

'We should have talked more,' she says to the room.

'I don't know what to say,' I say.

Her hand grips mine.

'Sonny … Come home … Please.'

257

Elin 29th June 2013

Elin and Megan were sitting at the kitchen table on Saturday morning.

'What are you doing today?' Elin asked.

'Owain and I are going to walk up to the trig point if the weather stays good.'

'Aren't you helping in the Railway?'

'Only lunch time. He's picking me up at the end of my shift. What are you doing?'

'Shopping. Probably walking with Tony. He vaguely suggested I should meet members of his family, but that won't be today.'

'Is he going to make an honest woman of you?'

Elin looked at her. She had no answer. Tony was a bit older than her, and she had been so affected by Kevin's behaviour that she had closed her mind to the possibility of another man. But Tony lifted her heart every time she saw him.

'I don't know. Is Owain going to make an honest woman of you?'

'No way. At least not for a few years. Who knows what could happen?'

'Exactly. Who knows what could happen?'

The phone rang in the front room.

'It'll be lover boy,' said Megan, and Elin went to take the call – hoping it was. She needed to plan her day with Tony.

'Elin Paterson.'

'Bill here, Elin.' Elin's heart sank. This could wreck her day.

'Hello Bill. What can I do for you?'

'Elin. I know you've given up waitressing, but Steven Campbell from the Valley Lodge called me. He's had a bit of a staffing difficulty with illness and people on holiday.'

'Yes …' said Elin.

'He says he can cope, except that he has a wedding next Saturday when he's going to be in trouble. Could you and Megan help him out?'

'I expect so, if you can spare Megan.' After finishing her exams Megan had taken on Elin's job.

'We should manage. There's a few days to sort things.'

'Okay, hang on. I'll ask Megan.'

Elin went back into the kitchen and asked Megan, then returned to the phone.

'Yes, we can do that.'

'Oh, thanks Elin. You'd better ring him.'

'Give me his number, then.'

Elin wrote down the number, rang off and called Steven. He explained what he wanted and thanked her. She went back to the kitchen.

'I thought you'd given up being a waitress now you have a rich boyfriend,' said Megan.

'So did I, but I don't like letting people down and things must have been bad if Bill rang us here.'

Elin rang Tony to ask him what he was up to.

'Hi Elin. The weather's good – why don't we head for the coast? I have a lunch venue I like and there's a chance Matthew will join us. Jessica's busy today and says we can come next weekend, but I can't.'

'No, I can't either. Next Saturday Megs and I are doing a favour for Bill from the Railway and are going to be waitresses at a wedding.'

'Where?'

'The Valley Lodge. You know, up past you.'

'Yes, I know. I know the bride. She looked after my money at the brokers. She's asked me to play the piano. We can enjoy the wedding together.'

Elin remembered Tony playing piano for her in the pub at Christmas.

'Has she heard you playing before?'

'No. She's taking a big risk, isn't she? Mind you, not as much as the risk she took with that manager.'

'I remember. What happened to him?'

'Lisa told me that they connected him to the parks murders and denied him bail. He's in jail waiting for the case to come to the crown court. She got away with a black eye, so she was lucky.'

Elin agreed to pick up Tony later and they ended the call.

Megan had been listening.

'Is he coming to the Valley Lodge too?'

'Yes. He's coming to play the piano. Have you ever heard him play? He can be romantic.'

Elin stopped. She hadn't meant to say that.

'Is there something you aren't telling me?' said Megan.

So Elin had to explain how Tony had played in the pub at Christmas.

'Megan fach, you'll have to judge for yourself next Saturday. Maybe something will happen to you!'

Sonny
The wedding 6th July 2013

Between the planning of Lisa, Gabby and Mrs Howells, the wedding is beautiful. The whole thing takes place at the hotel which fits cleverly into the shape of the hillside and is designed with many small details to make weddings run smoothly. Outside, places for photography have been designed into the gardens and among the trees and the decorations are out of this world. There are flowers everywhere and everything runs like clockwork. The registrar runs the ceremony sensitively, speaking well and with plenty of humour. The pianist plays in the background which adds to the romance of the occasion.

Lisa is utterly radiant. I can't believe that there has ever been a more beautiful bride – no longer showing any hint of a black eye. Jen as the bridesmaid is a close second in my eyes. When they see me holding hands with Gabby, they both clap and have a little hug together. You get the idea. It's idyllic.

As father of the bride I have asked that we do the speeches before the food and the party starts so that I can relax. As part of my penchant for running away I avoided public speaking, but my three beautiful ladies have told me in no uncertain terms that I have to do it today. I look forward to my moment with dread. Gabby has helped, thank goodness.

Eventually the ceremonies and the photography are over, and the guests have found their seats in the dining hall. The best man takes the microphone and tentatively calls for silence.

'Please be upstanding for the bride and groom, Mr and Mrs Howells – Lisa and Rhodri.'

To a huge round of applause Lisa and Rhodri walk hand-in-hand to the high table. She is simply gorgeous, and I have to admit that he complements her admirably. Not long ago these two were just pictures in my book. How my life has changed.

But now the best man calls for quiet again. Some guests near him bang spoons to help and the room calms. He reads some cards and texts from absent friends and stops for a moment.

'Ladies and Gentlemen, the father of the bride has asked me to let him speak early, and to put him out of his misery I have agreed. So here he is – Sonny, father of the bride, Mr James Jones.'

260

Standing by a sideboard with Elin and Megan at the back of the room, Tony jerked alert. Sonny's real name was James Jones. Tony swayed. He studied Sonny as he fumbled with his notes at the microphone. Was that a tall copy of his father standing there?

'What?' whispered Elin.

'I don't know.' said Tony, to himself, ignoring Elin.

Elin turned to Megan. 'Who's Sonny?'

'You know, Mama. He draws Max in the newspaper.'

Elin pulled a napkin towards her and found her biro. Quickly she sketched a picture of Max.

'Here, that's Max.'

'Thanks. I remember now.' She looked at Tony who was staring at Sonny standing at the microphone.

Sonny was working his way down his list of thanks – which was the best man's job – but he wanted to do it to settle himself for the real meat of what he had to say.

'... and finally, I'd like to thank the pianist who has ...' he stopped and turned away from the microphone to Lisa.

'Lisa, what's his name?'

'Tony. Tony Jones.'

Sonny's hand went to his mouth, and he dropped his papers and stepped back.

'What? Dad, are you alright?'

'Tony the Tinkler. It's Antony.'

At the other end of the room, now Tony knew as well.

'Sonny ... Jones, James ... Sonny Jim.' he said.

'What?' said Elin, confused.

'He's my brother.' Tony was dithering.

'Your brother? Wow. You never told me. Tony, go to him. Go now! Look at him. He knows too.'

Elin pushed Tony forward. But Tony turned to her with an expression of pure love and affection. Somehow in the moment of discovery that Sonny was his brother, he heard Elin's voice where Karen had been for so long, and he felt a great weight lifting. Karen had found a way to release him. Silently he thanked her. He kissed Elin and set off though the chairs towards Sonny.

At the top table Lisa was picking up Sonny's notes as he watched Tony crossing the room. She stood up. Jen slipped onto the stage to check Lisa's dress was okay and to find out what had spooked their father.

'Dad, what is it? What's wrong? Who is he?' said Jen.

Sonny looked at the two sisters together.

'Nothing's wrong. It's Antony. He's my brother. I suppose that makes him your uncle.' They watched the approaching Tony.

'Uncle Antony,' said Lisa. 'Since when did we have an Uncle Tony? What a day.'

The rest of the room was in confusion about what was going on. Lisa went to the microphone and made the announcement.

'Ladies and Gentlemen. Some of you are already confused that I have a father who is moving back in with my mother. Now my dad's just realised that the pianist is his brother who he hasn't seen for, like, fifty years. Amazing. Jen and me now have an uncle!' She clapped, turned to Rhodri and waved her fingers to him. 'And I've got a husband. I'm so happy.'

Sonny and Tony hugged each other and stood looking at one another. Slowly the room calmed down.

'You'd better finish your job,' said Tony. 'We can talk later.'

'Right.' Sonny took his papers back from Lisa and went back to the microphone.

Megan looks back to the napkin and lets the pen start again. To her surprise Max speaks to her.

'Go to him. Go to him now! Show him this!'

She wants to say 'Why?' But how do you say that to a napkin?

'Go now!' says Max again. 'He's going to kill me off in his speech and only you can save me.'